The Story of Her Redemption

J.A. SMITH

Copyright © 2022 J.A. Smith All rights reserved

The characters and events portrayed in this book are fictitious. Any similarity to real persons, living or dead, is coincidental and not intended by the author.

No part of this book may be reproduced, or stored in a retrieval system, or transmitted in any form or by any means, electronic, mechanical, photocopying, recording, or otherwise, without express written permission of the publisher.

ISBN-13: 979-8-218-00558-0

To Tina.

You've been my biggest fan, my favorite cheerleader, and my greatest motivator. You've brought a vast amount of color to my life, and I thank God every day for being able to call you my family.

I love you to the moon and back.

Always.

Contents

Chapter 1 1
Chapter 2 14
Chapter 3 28
Chapter 4 40
Chapter 5 55
Chapter 6 70
Chapter 7 81
Chapter 8 93
Chapter 9 104
Chapter 10 114
Chapter 11 121
Chapter 12 130
Chapter 13 144
Chapter 14 156
Chapter 15 167
Chapter 16 176
Chapter 17 189
Chapter 18 200
Chapter 19 208
Chapter 20 218
Chapter 21 226
Chapter 22 238
Chapter 23 245

Chapter 24	256
Chapter 25	261
Chapter 26	268
Chapter 27	275
Chapter 28	286
Chapter 29	295
Chapter 30	306
Epilogue	316
Dear reader	i
Acknowledgements	ii
About The Author	iv

Chapter 1

Cypress

Removing the last rubber band from the tie-dyed picnic blanket, I lift the corners and turn toward the selfie light where my phone is mounted. "Alright, wanderers." I pause and smile to myself as I watch the bright, brilliant colors unfurl in front of me. I've been creating colorful tie-dyed items for years now and it never ceases to amaze me as each new item takes on a life of its own. This blanket was made using a spiral tie technique that I hadn't tried on such a large object before, and I couldn't be more pleased with the outcome.

"Mmm." I continue, turning my gaze back to the phone. "So beautiful. I hope you were able to add some color and clarity to your own lives today. Stay wild and free." After a few seconds of smiling, I walk over to the phone and remove it from the mount, turning off the recording with the touch of a finger. There won't be much editing to do before I'm able to post the video online.

Tossing the blanket down on the table, I take my phone off do not disturb and gaze out the window at the empty sidewalk. My boutique, Poppy Petals, has been surprisingly slow today, which I blame on the weather. The sky is overcast with pregnant clouds just waiting for an opportunity to dump their tears on innocent shoppers leaving my normally busy Friday afternoon quiet. At only one in the afternoon, it might not be a bad idea to close up for the day. Save on utilities at least, this place is already costing me a fortune.

I almost feel guilty as I lock the door and turn off the open sign. Growing up on the road, I spent majority of my time working festivals with my mother. We traveled the country in an Airstream camper and set up a tent anywhere that we could rent a space to sell our wares. There were days we had no choice but to break down our tent and pack up our merchandise, missing out on a few days at a time waiting for the weather to clear. Changes in the weather would make the difference of whether or not we would eat the following day.

I have no regrets from my childhood, not many women my age can say they'd visited nearly every state in the nation before reaching puberty. If anything, I may regret not spending more time in a few places. New Orleans, for instance, was definitely the most memorable. We spent nearly a week there when I was twelve with a booth in a street festival. Of all the places we visited while I was growing up, New Orleans is one of the only places that made the list of cities I'd like to go back to. Sadly, though, I haven't been able to take the time to go back yet. Maybe this'll be the year.

My phone rings in my left hand while I'm locking the door, interrupting me from my thoughts of travelling. Seeing the word 'Mom' on the screen brings a smile to my face. I haven't spoken to her for a few days, so I wonder where she's calling me from. "Hi, Mom," I answer in greeting as I walk back to the counter to empty out the cash register.

"Hey, Baby. Happy birthday!" She exclaims.

"Thank you." I close my eyes, willing away the tears threatening to break free. This will be the first birthday I've ever spent alone. I left my nomadic lifestyle behind years ago when I decided to attend college in Arizona, but I've at least had friends surrounding me on my birthday, even when I couldn't spend it with my mother. Part of me had hoped that I could have seen her today, but I know that's not always possible. She'd be travelling of course to wherever the festivals take her. "Where are you today?"

"We're in St. Louis. There's a river festival here close to the arch. I was thinking of riding the elevator to the top. Can you imagine the view from up there?"

I giggle silently knowing that she'll never actually go to the top of the arch. I tried to get her to go up with me years ago, the first time we were there for a river festival. I've never had a fear of heights, I was always fascinated by them actually. My mother on the other hand, she's happy with both feet planted firmly on the ground. We had walked around the visitor's center at the base of the arch for several hours, looking at all the photographs of the arch being built. She stared at the elevator for a long time trying to convince herself to take it up to the top with me but eventually succumbed to her fear. I never did take that ride to the top, I was only ten at the time and there was no way she would let me go up by myself.

"David says he'll take pictures for both of us if I can't bring myself to go up with him," she says. A shudder goes down my spine at the mention of my stepfather's name. My mother married him when I was thirteen, moving both him and his fifteen-year-old son into our little Airstream with us. My own father had left before I was born so I never knew him.

"Maybe today will be your day," I tell her.

"I doubt it," she sighs heavily. "Speaking of which, David and Jase say happy birthday."

"Jase is still travelling with you?" I shake my head while putting the bank pouch into my hobo bag. Jase is two years older than me, and I figured he would have moved on by now. He never wanted to do any work at the festivals we visited. He hated them as far as I knew. He used to tell me the only reason he kept going to them with his father was for the 'scenery'. It wasn't until later that I realized the 'scenery' that he was referring to was of the female variety. He had a thing for the ladies.

"Oh, yes. He's still with us. He's become quite helpful actually and he's handy with a wrench. If it weren't for him, we would have been forced to park ages ago. I still believe he's the only reason our old truck is still running."

"You're still driving that old truck?" I ask, trying to change the subject away from David and Jase. I don't want to talk about either one of them. I don't have fond memories of them since they blasted into our lives thirteen years ago. They were both living in a run-down motel in Des Moines when my mother met David. She fell for his charms almost instantly making Des Moines the longest tour we had together. My mother found a flea market close to the motel and set up a booth outside for almost three months just to keep us in the area.

When we finally left Des Moines, she had moved David and Jase into the Airstream with us. She swore she was in love, and married David only a few months later during a trip through Las Vegas. I knew right away there was something *not right* with both of them. But my mother wouldn't hear of it. She was in love, there was nothing I could do to convince her otherwise.

"Yes," she answers. "But I don't know how much longer Jase will be able to keep it running. It might be time to start looking for a replacement."

"You could always find a place to settle down. Stop travelling all together." I've been trying to get her to stop travelling for years, ever since I gave it up myself and realized how much more rewarding it was to plant my roots in one place.

"You know I'll never stop travelling. It's all I've ever known, I couldn't possibly give it up yet. One day, maybe, when my body can't do it anymore."

I shudder just thinking about her body not being able to tolerate the travel anymore. I can only hope when she does get to that point that she settles somewhere close enough to me that I can help take care of her.

"I miss you, Mom." I whisper into the phone.

"I know, Baby. I miss you too."

"Thank you for calling me." A tear escapes despite my best efforts to keep it contained. "I gotta go. I'm closing up the shop early today because of the weather and it looks like it's going to start raining any minute. I need to get to the bus stop before the bottom falls out."

"Okay. I love you, Cypress. I'll talk to you again soon."

"Bye mama. I love you too." Hanging up the phone, I grab my bag and sling it over my shoulder. I turn off the lights and lock the door on my way out before turning my gaze to the heavy rain clouds overhead. The bus stop is two blocks away and I hope I can get on the bus before the rain starts. At least there's a nice breeze today, the temperature's not too warm considering it's the beginning of January. Of all the places I visited growing up, I'm glad to be in a location that doesn't have harsh winter weather. You don't realize how cold some places get in the winter until you're living in a tin can and trying to warm up under a mass of blankets and second-hand sweaters.

Thankfully, I don't have to wait long for the bus to arrive and I make it into my apartment building only seconds before the sky falls down on the empty sidewalk behind me. Literally. It starts pouring right as the door closes behind me.

"Hello, Cypress. You're back early today." I'm greeted by a sweet voice as soon as I enter the building.

"Hello, Mrs. Abernathy," I answer. "There wasn't any reason to stay open with this weather moving in." Mrs. Abernathy is the apartment manager that lives on the first floor. She's a tiny little grey-haired widow who likes to think she's everyone's grandmother, at least everyone that lives in this building. She never had any children of her own and lost her husband of forty years only a few years ago. The two of them lived in the apartment that she's currently standing in until he passed away. I look at her over my shoulder as I open my mailbox. Mrs. Abernathy is sipping her tea in her doorway as she watches me with a smile on her face.

"Oh yes. I've been watching the clouds moving in all day. It's about time too, it hasn't rained here in almost three years. It's a good thing I didn't have to go out anywhere today though, I just had my hair done."

"It looks lovely." I smile down at her as I walk toward the elevator.

"Thank you, dear."

"Have a nice day, Mrs. Abernathy." I call out as the elevator opens. This is a small building, only five floors with two units on each floor. I live on the top floor in a small one bedroom facing the street. It's cheap and conveniently located close to the yoga studio, Celestial Beings, where I teach a yoga class two days each week. I started teaching there a few months ago when the regular instructor got injured and had to take some time off. Since she's returned full time, I only fill in as needed. Thankfully, since opening my boutique in Echo Park, I haven't needed to pick up as many yoga classes to make ends meet.

Once inside my apartment, I lock the door and set the chain before sliding the curtain to cover it. I installed a thick curtain to the door the day I moved in, one that covers it from top to bottom sealing off any light around the edges. I flip the switch next to the door to turn on the overhead lights in the living space and hallway. There's only one window in the living room which is covered with a thick curtain keeping it dark and private in my apartment. The bedroom similarly has only one window which is also covered with a thick curtain blocking out all outside light.

The apartment I rent is small and private. I selected the apartment on the top floor without the balcony so there is no access from the outside at all. The windows have bars installed on them just for additional safety even though you'd have to be Spider-Man to gain access to either of my windows, but one can never be too safe.

I don't share any walls with my neighbors since there are only two apartments on this floor. My closest neighbor is across the hallway from me leaving at least three feet of space between the two of us at all times. I've never met my neighbor across the hall, despite Mrs. Abernathy's matchmaking attempts. She means well, I'm sure, but I just haven't wanted to take that step. I'm not good at meeting people and often give the wrong first impression. I've been known to be awkward when it comes to flirting.

Once I'm sure the curtain is in place and the door completely covered, I move to the bedroom. Placing my bag on top of the dresser, I close the bedroom door and repeat the same actions as before, securing the lock before pulling another curtain closed over the bedroom door. I move to the window and double check the curtain covering the window to make sure it hasn't shifted during the day to allow any light to enter from outside before moving to my closet to change my clothes.

I remove my ankle length hemp skirt and toss it into the hamper in the corner of the room before pulling a pair of yoga pants from the closet. Slipping my sweater over my head, I replace it with a loose-fitting t-shirt before opening the curtain and bedroom door to walk out to the kitchen.

I decide to grab the small pint of pistachio ice cream out of the freezer before moving to the couch with my kindle. I splurged this morning on a book by Lauren Landish for my birthday. Just because I have to spend my birthday alone, doesn't mean that I can't spend some time with my new book boyfriend, Connor. "Happy birthday to me." I exclaim as I curl my legs up on the couch beneath me.

One thing to be said about being single at twenty-six is not having to feel guilty about spending the afternoon on the couch with a good book. I don't have anyone to cook for, no one to wait on hand and foot. Not that I don't want that, eventually. But I'm just not in a place to have it yet. To be honest, I'm not sure if I will be any time soon. It's hard to meet someone when you don't trust people.

I don't have long to be able to read before I need to leave for the yoga studio to teach a late class. The normal instructor, Cindy, had gotten sick a few days ago and I agreed to take her class tonight.

I finish a few chapters of my book before I check the time and notice it's after six. I'll have to rush if I want to catch the next bus downtown. I could walk, but that would put me at the studio only fifteen minutes before the next class starts and wouldn't give me enough time to warm up before all the ladies start coming in.

Setting my kindle down on the coffee table, I take the empty ice cream pint to the kitchen and toss my spoon in the sink. Stopping by the hall closet, I grab my cardigan and leave, locking the door before pulling it shut. It's not until I'm on the sidewalk outside that I realize I left my purse upstairs on my dresser. There isn't enough to time to run back up and grab it without missing the bus, thankfully my bus pass is on my phone.

I realize once I'm on the bus headed downtown that I don't have my apartment key either. I'm not sure why I should be surprised at my forgetfulness, it isn't anything new for me. Some days I'm sure I would leave my head at home if it weren't already attached to my shoulders. I can only hope that Mrs. Abernathy is still awake when I get back tonight so she can let me into my apartment. I'll just have to rush after the class is over to get back home before she falls asleep.

Class goes smoothly at least. The rain finally passed through a few hours ago so it didn't stop anyone from being able to show up tonight. It's always nice to see some familiar faces in the crowd, as well as some new ones. I do recognize one familiar face though that I'm glad to see. She always stood out to me before thanks to her cotton candy pink hair. I believe her name is Marie. I remember a few months ago seeing her in one of my classes and she had looked like she wasn't sleeping well. I'm glad to see that she's looking more rested these days, so I hope these classes are at least helping her to relax.

On the way out of the studio, I stop by Marie in the hall as she's putting her mat away. "Good to see you," I say, laying a hand softly on her shoulder. "It's been a while. How have you been?"

"Great, thank you for asking." She smiles at me as she stands up straight and steps away from the mat rack. "I want you to meet my friend, Julie." She holds her hand out to her left toward an auburn-haired woman with adorable tortoise shell glasses.

"Nice to meet you. I'm Cypress," I say holding my hand out toward her.

She places her hand in mine and squeezes lightly. "You too. I had a great time tonight. Sorry I didn't know most of the moves, I'm still a beginner."

"Doesn't matter." I assure her with a smile. I knew right away that she was a beginner, something about her off balance poses and the way her cheeks would turn the slightest shade of pink when she would catch herself before hitting the floor. "Yoga isn't about being perfect. It's about letting go and relaxing. Besides, your friend is pretty good at it. She can probably help you improve your balance."

"Not to mention flexibility." She says with a giggle. "I've realized I'm not as flexible as I thought I was after doing some of these poses tonight. My muscles are barking at me."

"A warm bath is perfect for that," I tell her. "Anyway, nice to see you ladies." Before either of them can respond, I back away and turn to the exit. I didn't bring anything with me besides my phone and my cardigan, so I don't have to stop by the locker room before rushing to the bus stop. "Good night, Stephanie." I yell over my shoulder as I walk out the studio door onto the sidewalk.

Taking a deep breath, I walk toward the bus stop two blocks away. The sidewalk is crowded tonight being that it's Friday so I'm not able to walk as fast as I would like to. Unfortunately, that means the last bus is pulling away as the bench comes into sight. Stopping in the middle of the sidewalk, I release a heavy sigh and hang my head. No sense in rushing now, looks like I'm walking.

Getting jolted by someone bumping my shoulder gets me moving again, blending into the foot traffic as best I can. The sidewalks are filled with people in typical Friday night fashion. This neighborhood has several high-end clubs that have lines of waiting patrons sometimes as long as two city blocks. I have no desire to be part of the waiting crowd, I just want to get home before Mrs. Abernathy falls asleep and I have to spend the night out in the hallway of my apartment building.

I make it only a few blocks before I feel the rain drops on my forehead. It's about that time that people start to walk faster, pushing each other to get through the crowd and to a safe dry place before getting drenched by the oncoming rain.

My knees hit the pavement hard as I'm pushed out of the way by someone causing me to trip. Trying to stand up, I'm shoved again by another person rushing to get to their destination quickly. I shouldn't be surprised by the carelessness of people in their blind rush to outrun the rain. Each time I attempt to get to my feet, I'm pushed back down against the unforgiving sidewalk and my knees are protesting harshly.

Hoping to preserve the skin on my knees, I stay down in my current position and curl into a protective ball. Both of my hands are pulled into my chest, my phone fisted in one hand protectively, as I wait for the crowd to thin out enough for me to stand. The rain picks up at that point, soaking the cardigan against my back and sending a chill through my body.

"Hey! Watch it!" I hear a deep voice bellow from nearby, but I don't lift my head to see where it's coming from. The rain stops suddenly when I feel a hand press softly against my back. Lifting my head, I'm instantly lost in the most brilliant green eyes I've ever seen. "Are you okay?" He asks me in a deep timber, low enough to be mistaken for a growl.

"Y-yes," I say, my voice shaky as a shiver runs down my spine.

He wraps his hand around my bicep and pulls softly, helping me to my feet. It's then that I notice the umbrella that he's holding over my head, stopping the rain from soaking me further than it has already. He notices when I wince while standing and he stops moving. "Are you hurt?" He asks, his concerned expression unmistakable as he looks me over from head to toe and back up again.

"My knees." I reach down and put a palm against one of my knees and clench my teeth against the pain. "Ouch."

"Come on." He says, removing his hand from my arm and placing it against the small of my back. "I'll give you a ride."

"No." I protest. "I'm okay, I was just going to walk." Taking a step away from him, I nearly go down again when the pain shoots up my leg. I guess I hit the sidewalk harder than I thought.

He watches me for a moment, one eyebrow raised, and his head cocked to one side. "How far do you have to go?"

Pulling my bottom lip between my teeth, I debate how much to disclose to him. I don't know this man even though he's the only person out here that was nice enough to even help me up. But getting a ride from him? That's a line that I should definitely not cross. How can I trust him? "I usually take the bus," I admit reluctantly.

"Well, unfortunately there aren't any more of those tonight. Come on, I'll take you home." I watch as he moves his blazer out of the way and puts his hand into his pocket presumably for his keys. When his blazer moves, I see the shield clipped to his belt and relief washes over me.

"You're a cop?"

"Detective." He answers proudly. He looks a little young to be a detective. Don't they have to be older or something? Still, I should feel safer about the fact that he's in law enforcement at least.

Truth be told, the only reason that I'm agreeing to this gorgeous man giving me a ride home is because my knees hurt too bad to walk all the way home. My normal forty-five-minute walk would end up being more like two hours in this rain with my newly formed limp. "Fine." I relent.

He smiles as he steps closer, moving the umbrella to ensure that it's still blocking the rain from soaking me further and placing his hand on the small of my back. Thankfully, we don't have to go far. He has an SUV parked on the street just a few feet away. We stop next to the passenger door, and he removes his hand long enough to unlock and open the door for me. "Here you go." He says as he helps me into the car. Only when I'm situated in the front passenger seat with my seatbelt on does he finally close the door and walk around to the driver's side.

"Thank you for helping me out." I say as he closes his door and puts the key into the ignition.

"No problem." He smiles at me as he buckles his seatbelt. "So, where to?" I rattle off the address and he lowers his brows as he looks back at me. "Seriously?"

"Yeah. Why?" He just laughs as he turns his gaze out the front windshield and pulls out into traffic.

Chapter 2

Chris

"Wendy," I say, starting to lose my patience. "Come on. We've known each other for years. You can be honest with me."

Wendy and I have been friends for almost five years, since my first case as a detective. I was young and worked my ass off to become more than just a beat cop having known that I wanted to be a detective when I signed up for the force right out of high school. My father was a cop until he was killed in the line of duty when I was thirteen. My mother was left with two teenagers, my sister Amy being only two years older than me. She did the best she could while suffering with depression after my father had died.

Not even two months after graduating, my sister Amy ran off with her boyfriend to Vegas and got married. Mom and I hated Brad. We knew he was bad news, but Amy was in love and refused to listen to either of us. It wasn't until she disappeared a year later that I'd wished I'd pushed harder for her to listen to me. All the clues were right there but I was too blind to see it. I wasn't able to step in and protect my own sister before something bad happened.

The cops and detectives working the case of my missing sister were amazing. They let me sit with them while they discussed their findings with my mother, which was perfect since she was too beside herself to have paid any attention. I was fascinated with how they worked the case. Unfortunately, though, her case didn't end the way we wanted it to.

Brad had beaten Amy. I always knew he had a temper, and I was afraid of what he would do to Amy behind closed doors. I knew it would get bad and tried to talk her into dumping him so many times over the years. He'd convinced her to run away with him to Vegas after they graduated from high school. They stayed with us for a few months when they came back married, having nowhere else to go. Amy got a job and saved up enough money for them to get a cheap apartment on the other side of town.

When Amy moved out of our house with her husband, I thought I'd never see her again. It was just me and Mom, and even then, I was basically on my own. My mother had checked out mentally years before when my father died. I'll never know what they argued about or what her last thoughts were before she ended up dead. Brad had beaten her so badly that she passed out and he left her. When he got back, he had apparently found her dead. In a fit of panic, he dumped her body in the desert in Nevada.

The coroner's report said she had died from an intracranial hemorrhage. Basically, she was hit hard enough in the head that it caused her brain to bleed which is what caused her to pass out. The pressure on her brain was too much without medical attention and she died from her injuries. She had already been dead for three days before her body was found.

Brad was arrested and confessed to everything. He hung himself in the jail cell while awaiting his trial.

My mother was diagnosed with lung cancer a month before I turned seventeen. She refused to do any treatment saying she was ready to be reunited with my father and she died a month after I graduated.

I had effectively lost my entire family in the first eighteen years of my life. I never knew my grandparents. Both of my parents were only children, so I had no aunts or uncles. I was officially alone.

I sold our family home, moved into an apartment in the city and joined the police academy the following month. I knew right away that I wanted to be a detective and would do whatever it took to get there. After what my family went through with my sister, I knew I didn't want any other family to have to go through something similar. I wanted other families to have closure or to find their missing loved ones.

I primarily work on cases with abused or battered women in honor of my sister. I've been able to recover abducted women before they were sold into slavery. I've located missing women and arrested their captors. I've even rescued women that were being held captive by their own husbands. That's how I met Wendy so many years ago.

My first case as a detective, I was teamed up with narcotics. We went undercover trying to get an 'in' on a local kingpin of a drug ring that was getting out of control. Someone was pushing a bad drug and it was getting people killed. LA has enough problems as it is without adding to it with drugs making their way through schools and killing kids. What we didn't expect when we got to one of the dealer's houses, was a proposition to partake in some 'new' goods.

Brian Evans had been identified as the main supplier to the local high school. As it turned out, what he was offering was an hour with his wife who happened to be chained up in the basement. This motherfucker had been charging people $50 to spend an hour raping his wife while she was chained to a wall in the basement of his run-down house in Echo Park.

What we found when we entered the basement was an emaciated woman wearing a blood and body fluid-stained t-shirt with chains cutting into her wrists and ankles while she was bolted to the cinderblock wall. She was covered in infected cuts, bruises covered whatever exposed skin you could see behind the grit and grime covering the rest of her body.

Circumstances changed in that instant, and we blew our cover to get her out before it was too late to save her. We saved Brian's wife, Wendy, and arrested Brian on multiple charges of torture and endangerment on top of all the drug charges we were initially after.

Wendy spent months in the hospital recovering from the injuries she sustained while being chained up and repeatedly abused for almost a year. When she was released, she went to an inpatient psychiatric facility for post-traumatic stress. Brian still remains locked up to this day having been sentenced to life in prison just for charges involved with the torture of his wife. Not to mention the drug charges on top of that. I don't expect to see him getting out in my lifetime.

I got to know Wendy very well while visiting her in the hospital. The only family she has in the area is her Uncle Travis, who owns a local newspaper. She moved in with him for a while when she was finally released from the hospital, staying with him until she purchased an old building in downtown LA. She had the building renovated putting luxury apartments in the upper four floors and her gentlemen's club, The Penthouse, on the main floor. The Penthouse is an exclusive members only club that requires a substantial membership fee and background checks on all its members.

Three years after she was freed from her abusive marriage, she started an outreach for other abuse survivors who are looking for a way to get back on their own feet. Not only does she set them up with employment at her club, but she provides them with a safe place to live until they're able to go out on their own. She even provides them with legal services while they press charges against their spouses or file for divorce.

I initially helped her get it started, offering to run background checks on all her security and staff. When I come across victims that I think will benefit from her outreach program, I give them her contact information. Some people may not agree with what she does with her outreach, but I see it as a safety net for the abuse victims. Dancing isn't prostitution. What Wendy is able to do with her club keeps these women off the streets and gives them a new life.

Tonight, Wendy and I are having dinner at a bistro not far from her club. She called me as I was walking to my car after work and asked me to meet her here saying she needed advice. Wendy, for all intents and purposes, is my best friend. Being only ten years older than me, she's the closest thing I have to family anymore. She's more like an aunt to me honestly.

"I am being honest, Chris." She finally replies. "I don't know if I'm ready yet."

"Wendy." Reaching out I place my hand over top of hers on the table between us. "It's been almost five years. You deserve to be happy." I can't even imagine the war that is probably waging within her own mind. She went through hell with her ex-husband, unfathomable hell. I know she's reluctant to trust anyone else and I don't know if she will ever get to that point. But she'd be hurting herself more if she didn't at least try. She won't know if she shuts herself down completely from the possibility of being happy with someone again.

"I am happy. I have my club and my girls. They're all like the children that I was never able to have of my own. They're my family."

"I know. But you don't see the way Braiden looks at you." Braiden Parker is Wendy's personal bodyguard and driver. He's been watching over Wendy for the last two years and I know he cares about her.

"I'll think about it." She relents. "I just don't know if it's a good idea. What if it doesn't work out? He's great at his job and I'd hate to lose him."

"I don't think that's going to be a problem, Wendy." Turning my head, I see that it's starting to rain. "Do you need a lift back to the club, it's starting to rain."

"No. Braiden is over by the bar."

"Of course, he is." I laugh while removing my wallet and throwing some cash on the table to cover our meals and a tip. We both stand at the same time and Wendy wraps her arms around my waist for a close hug. It took her a lot of years to get to the point of allowing herself to be touched by another man. We've come a long way for her to allow me to hug her back. I run my hand over her back and kiss the top of her head before she finally releases me and backs away a few steps.

"Thank you for meeting with me."

"Anytime. Just promise me that you really will think about it."

"I will, Chris. I promise." She doesn't say anything else before walking over to the bar. Braiden sees her coming and stands up as she approaches. He helps her put on her jacket and nods his head once in my direction before leading her to the door. I don't miss the fact that he places a hand possessively against the small of her back.

Shaking my head slowly, I grab my blazer from the back of the chair and my umbrella which is leaning against the chair next to mine and walk out of the restaurant. Opening my umbrella before stepping out from under the awning, I watch as the crowd starts to move faster hoping to get to their destinations before getting soaked.

Blending into the crowd, I start to walk the block to where I parked my SUV. The rain is picking up and people are starting to run past me, pausing long enough to move around someone that appears to have been pushed to the ground. When I look closer, she's balled up into herself protectively to keep from being trampled.

"Hey! Watch it!" I yell as I start to push people out of the way and get closer to the woman crouched down in the middle of the sidewalk. Kneeling next to her small frame, I place a hand in the center of her back. "Are you okay?"

"Yes." She practically whispers so quietly I could barely hear it over the rain hitting the umbrella. I move it more so she's covered from the cold rain, I can see she's already soaked through and shivering.

With my free hand, I grab her arm and help her to stand slowly. She flinches as her legs straighten and nearly goes down again before I grip her a little tighter. "Are you hurt?"

"My knees." She says, reaching down to touch one of them through a hole in her stretchy pants. "Ouch." Fuck, she's adorable.

"Come on. I'll give you a ride." Letting go of her arm now that she's standing, I place my hand on the small of her back and attempt to turn her toward my car.

She freezes immediately, her eyes opening wide and locking with mine. It gives me a minute to look over her features. She's a tiny thing, the top of her head barely reaching my chest. She has her dark brown hair pulled into a tight bun on the back of her head and I wonder just how long her dark locks really are. But her eyes are so expressive. I can clearly see the shock in her hazel eyes. "No," she says quickly. "I'm okay, I was just going to walk." She moves a few steps before nearly falling again and I know her knees are hurting her.

Lifting one brow and cocking my head to the side, I watch as she attempts to take another step. "How far do you have to go?"

"I usually take the bus." She says pulling her lower lip between her teeth and it's all I can do not to reach up and pull it free.

"Well, unfortunately there aren't any more of those tonight. Come on, I'll take you home." I offer again. Switching hands holding the umbrella, I move my blazer aside to reach into my pocket for my keys. I watch her closely as her eyes follow my movements, and I can see the moment she notices my shield.

"You're a cop?"

"Detective." I answer, my chest bowing out proudly.

She nods her head a few times before asking, "What's your name?"

"Chris."

"Cypress." She holds her hand out to me sideways as if waiting to shake, and I reluctantly place my hand in hers. "Fine." She finally agrees. "Since we're no longer strangers." She giggles softly and takes a step toward me.

Smiling, I move closer and place my hand back against the small of her back. Luckily, my SUV is right here so we don't have to go far. I help her inside and make sure she's secure before closing the door and walking around to the other side.

"Thank you for helping me out." She says as I climb into the driver's seat and place the key in the ignition.

"No problem. So, where to?" She tells me the address and I have to laugh at the irony of where we're going. "Seriously?"

"Yeah. Why?" She asks, her fists twisting in her lap. I can only laugh as I pull out into traffic. "Really. Why is that so funny?"

Shaking my head slowly, I turn to look at her as I stop at a red light. "How long have you rented from Mrs. Abernathy?"

"Oh, do you know her? I've been there for three years."

"Yeah, I know her. I knew her husband too before he passed away." I don't tell her that I've been renting an apartment from Mrs. Abernathy for the last seven years. I hold that piece of information for a while longer, figuring I'll tell her before the night is over but not wanting to scare her away yet.

The rest of the drive is quiet, I watch her out the corner of my eye. She rubs one of her knees as she gazes out the passenger window. I wonder if she'll let me help her clean them when I get her back to her apartment.

Pulling up to the brick apartment complex, I find an empty spot at the curb not far from the front door. I hear Cypress release a sigh before she reaches over to unbuckle her seatbelt and open her door. "Wait there, I'll come around and help you out." Removing my own seatbelt quickly, I rush out of the car and around the front before she has a chance to step out and hurt herself further.

"Thank you." She looks up at me as I push her door closed behind her. "I hope Mrs. Abernathy is still awake." She begins walking quickly, limping rather, toward the door and I follow her closely, putting my hands into my pockets to keep from reaching out for her again.

Following her into the building, she goes directly to the apartment on the first floor and knocks quietly. It only takes a few minutes for the door to open, Mrs. Abernathy stands inside the doorway with a sweet smile on her face. "Cypress? Are you okay?" She asks, genuine concern showing brightly in her eyes.

"Yes, ma'am. I just locked myself out of my apartment. I was hoping you had a spare key?" Cypress asks timidly.

"Of course, dear." Mrs. Abernathy walks away, leaving the door open. She returns a few seconds later with a key, her hand reaching out to Cypress. She looks over Cypress' shoulder and her smile widens as she notices me standing behind her. I shake my head slowly side to side and wink at her, hoping beyond hope that she doesn't say anything. Thankfully, she has learned over the years how to read minds and keeps her thoughts to herself. "You can just bring it back in the morning."

"Thank you, Mrs. Abernathy." Cypress says as she takes the key and closes her fist around it. I tip my head at the old woman before she closes the door then follow Cypress toward the elevator. Cypress looks at me over her shoulder and stops walking before she turns to face me fully. "You don't have to follow me. I'm sure you're ready to go home yourself."

"Now what kind of a man would I be if I didn't see you to your door?" I ask while offering her an innocent smile. Not to mention, I'd be lying to myself if I wasn't curious as to which apartment was hers.

"Suit yourself then." She giggles before turning back toward the elevator. We both enter the empty car when the doors open, and I laugh quietly to myself when I see her push the five on the control panel. I can hardly overlook the irony of our situation. "This is me." She says as we reach her apartment door, and she places the key into the deadbolt. "Thank you for walking me home." She turns back to me once the door is open and looks up at me bashfully.

Maybe I'm a bastard. Maybe I just want to spend a little more time in her company. I'm not sure which one is more accurate before I open my mouth. "I'd really like to take a look at your knees. Help you clean them up."

"You a doctor now?" She asks. She giggles when I lower my brows at her, my confusion obviously humorous to her. "I'm kidding. I could at least offer you a drink for all your trouble. Come on in."

I wait as she walks into her apartment and holds the door open for me. Once I'm inside, I turn and watch curiously as she closes the door and pulls a full-length curtain over it, blocking out any outside light from the hallway. I find it odd, but I refuse to question her on it right now. Turning away from the door and facing me, she notices me watching her and her cheeks turn the most adorable shade of pink. She limps past me into the main living area of her apartment and motions for me to have a seat on the sofa.

"Water okay? I don't have much else to offer unless you want coffee, but I think it's a little late for that."

"Water is fine. Thank you." I walk the few steps it takes to reach the sofa and sit on the end. "Do you have a first aid kit?"

"I do." She ambles over and hands me a glass of water. "I'll be right back." I watch her as she disappears through the hallway we entered from. Taking a sip of my water, I look around the space. She has a single small window in the living room that is covered completely with thick curtains. The apartment is small, almost the same size as my own only the layout is different. Her kitchen and living area are attached as one big room where mine is a separate galley kitchen. And of course, my apartment doesn't face the street, so I have a balcony.

I'm lost in thoughts of having her in my own apartment when she comes back into the room. Looking up, I notice that she's changed into a pair of shorts, so her knees are exposed. From a distance, they look worse than I expected, and I cringe at the thought of her being in pain. Standing, I move to allow her space to sit before I reach to take the first aid kit from her small hands. She sits on the end of the sofa I just vacated, and I move to sit next to her on the middle cushion.

"Here." I start as I reach for her legs to pull them across my own lap. "Let me take a look at your knees." She doesn't flinch at my touch, something I'm grateful for since she was so hesitant to allow me to bring her home in the first place.

Opening the kit, I remove several large bandages and cleaning supplies before setting to work on her wounds. She hisses through her teeth when I touch the first knee with the cleaning cloth. My hand pulls back immediately, hating the thought of being the cause of her pain. "It's okay," She whispers, her eyes pinched shut.

"I'm sorry," I tell her honestly. My jaw clamps tight as I finish cleaning both of her knees. I softly cover each one with ointment before placing a bandage over them. "What were you doing out there in the rain?"

"Missing the bus, apparently." She answers, her eyes still closed and her head leaning against the back of the sofa. A laugh escapes my chest, and her head shoots up, her eyes open wide and locked on mine. "Sorry."

"For what?"

"Being awkward. That was a bad attempt at humor. I was coming back from a yoga class. I teach occasionally at Celestial Beings. They had called me earlier tonight and asked me to fill in and I rushed out of here without my purse or keys. I was rushing to get to the bus stop before missing the bus but obviously failed. Then it started to rain, and I got knocked down."

"Well, you're lucky the damage wasn't worse. Your knees are going to be sore for a few days but I'm sure you'll be fine."

"Thank you. For everything."

We both sit awkwardly for a few minutes staring at each other. This is the part that I'm not good at. Do I stay? Do I go? Do I ask to see her again?

I'm no stranger when it comes to hooking up with a woman. I've had my fair share of one-night stands over the last seven years.

This is different though. Cypress isn't the type of woman that I would want just one night with. I can already tell, just after the events of tonight, that one night wouldn't be enough with her. I would want more.

"Give me your phone." I say to her, my hand still splayed across her thigh just above one of her knees.

"My phone?" She asks. I can see the confusion in her eyes.

"I want to give you my number. I have a feeling that we're going to be seeing more of each other." Not to mention that we'll probably run into each other a time or two since we live in the same building.

"Oh." She leans over and grabs her phone from the coffee table, unlocking it before handing it to me.

I take my time entering my number into her phone, then send a text message to myself. A smile spreads across my face the instant I hear the text notification go off in my inside jacket pocket. "There. Now you have my number, and I have yours. What are you doing this weekend?"

She looks down at the phone in her hand, her expression almost blank before she looks back up at me. "I have to work. My shop is open tomorrow and I missed out on a lot of sales today because of the weather."

Lifting a brow in question as I ask, "Your shop?"

"Yeah." She looks so innocent as she looks back down at her phone. I'm starting to think she just doesn't want to make eye contact with me, and I wonder why she would be so shy. "I have a boutique in Echo Park."

"Okay." My thumb absently rubs against the inside of her thigh. "I'd love to see you again sometime if that's okay. Maybe take you out for dinner."

"Um." She hesitates. "Okay."

"Thank you." I whisper before moving her legs away from my lap. I immediately miss the warm feeling of her legs against my own. "I'll show myself out." Standing, I step around her legs before bending down to kiss her cheek. "Have a good night, Cypress."

She doesn't say anything as I walk out of the room, moving the curtain away from the door so I can open it. I lock the doorknob on my way out of her apartment but I know she'll be off the couch soon so she can lock the deadbolt and the chain as well. The curtain alone lets me know there's a story there and I want to know what it is. But I'll be patient. She'll tell me about it when she's ready.

If I have my way, we'll get to know each other well enough that she'll be comfortable telling me the story. I want her to be able to tell me all the stories. I want to know everything about her.

Shaking my head slowly, I remove my keys from my pocket and unlock my own door. Opening the door to my apartment and stepping inside, I look back toward her door across the hall and wonder how it is that she's lived across the hall from me for three years and I've never seen her before. That's definitely something that I'm going to have to remedy. I'll do anything in my power to be able to see her again.

Chapter 3

Cypress

What the hell was that? I think to myself. He swooped in like my knight in shining armor and helped me home. I don't know what confuses me more; the fact that I let him bring me home, or that I allowed him into my apartment. But his touch was gentle, and his kiss was soft. Three years I've lived in this apartment and he's the first person I've ever allowed to come in. This is my sanctuary, my safe place.

I waited, my teeth practically clenched the entire time.

I waited for the unease to start. For the fear to set in. For the insecurity to take over.

I waited for him to make a move, proving that he couldn't be trusted. That he was no different than the men I'd met in the past.

But it didn't come. I felt myself gradually relaxing in his presence. There was nothing to fear, nothing to worry about. He was a complete gentleman the entire time he was in my apartment. He cleaned the wounds on my knees and made sure I was comfortable before leaving.

But my cheek is still tingling from where he kissed me before he left.

Shaking my head to clear my thoughts, I stand and limp my way to the door to make sure it's locked. Pulling the curtain aside, I see that he locked the doorknob on his way out. Butterflies take flight deep in my stomach at the thought of him realizing my obsessions but not questioning it. He didn't question me about the curtain when we entered the apartment, even though I know he saw me pull it over the door.

Willing myself not to overthink the events of earlier, I lock the deadbolt and place the chain on the door before securing the curtain back in place.

It's been a long day and I need sleep. I can already feel the exhaustion settling in and I'm ready to put today behind me.

Tomorrow is a new day.

After locking the bedroom door and spreading the curtain to cover it, I fall on the bed laying on top of the blanket. I'm so tired, I don't even bother pulling the sheet back. My sleep is fitful and filled with angry dreams.

My alarm wakes me with enough time to grab a cup of coffee before heading out the door for the bus stop. Opening the door to my shop, I'm greeted with the familiar jingle of the bell hanging overhead. I immediately flip the open sign to the on position before moving throughout the shop making sure it's ready to open. It's Saturday and I'm anxious for a busy day to make up for the lack of sales yesterday.

It's still early, not even eight yet, and the foot traffic outside is barely moving as the sun begins to peak over the tops of the buildings across the street.

Walking into the storage room in the back of the shop, I grab the picnic blanket I left sitting on the table. It turned out perfectly with the mandala pattern created by the spiral tied technique I chose to use. Walking back out to the shop, I set the blanket on the counter next to the register and pull out my laptop to begin editing the video hoping to post it online today.

Several minutes later, I stand and stretch my arms over my head. The bell chimes over the door signaling someone entering the shop and I look up to see Marie and her friend Julie from my yoga class. Lowering my arms, I smile in their direction. "Good morning, ladies." I greet as I walk around the counter.

"Cypress?" Marie looks stunned to see me standing in the shop. "I didn't expect to see you here."

"This is my shop." I smile in return. "Welcome to Poppy Petals."

"Wow!" She exclaims. "I didn't know this was your place. I've seen it a few times while cruising through the neighborhood with Matt and have been wanting to stop in. You remember my friend, Julie? From last night."

"Of course. How are you, Julie?"

"I'm good. It's great to see you again." Julie says.

"How are you feeling today? I know last night was your first time at yoga."

"Oh yeah." He looks down bashfully. "Devan ran me a bath when I got home to help me relax." Her cheeks turn a light shade of pink at the admission, and I can't help but wonder if she actually got any relaxation from her bath. Not that it's any of my business. Maybe I'm a little jealous if I'm being honest.

"This place is amazing." I look toward Marie to see her perusing the shelves of hand-crafted incense burners, completely unfazed by her friend's blushing. "These burners are beautiful."

I don't make the incense burners, I have no talent for something like that. My talent is limited to tie dying fabrics. "Thank you. I have a friend in Tucson that makes them." I smile at the memory of my roommate Amanda and all the art supplies she used to leave laying around our tiny apartment. She took over the entire dining room and turned it into her make-shift studio. Our apartment was a tiny two bedroom so she didn't have much space to work on her hobby, but we made do the best we could.

I had met Amanda while attending college in Arizona. We actually met through a Facebook ad she had posted looking for a roommate, but we hit it off right away. We shared the tiny apartment for three years until we both graduated. She married her high school sweetheart right after graduating from college and started her online boutique selling her hand-crafted items. I left Arizona and ended up here in Los Angeles. I haven't seen her in a few years, but we still keep in touch via social media.

"Julie." Marie calls from across the store. "Come over here and take a look at these shirts."

"Sorry." Julie apologizes to me. "She's really excited to be here, as you can see."

"No problem. Let me know if I can help you with anything." I move back behind the counter to finish up my video so I can get it posted. Once that's done, I find a hanger for the blanket and add it with the other tie-dyed items are the front of the shop. I'm just reaching the register once more when the bell rings over the door again.

"Delivery for Cypress Harris." I hear someone announce as I turn toward the door. There's a young man standing in the doorway with headphones on his head, wearing a light brown jacket, and a lovely bouquet of flowers in his hand.

"Um." I hesitate, wondering to myself why anyone would be sending flowers to my shop. "That's me." I step out from behind the counter as the delivery man walks toward me, his arm outstretched with the beautiful flowers which I now realize is a small arrangement of poppies and daisies. "Is there a card?"

"Yes, ma'am. Have a nice day." He turns and walks out of the shop without another word.

Looking around, I see that Marie and Julie have both turned their attention to me. Ignoring their stares and smiles, I search through the fragrant flowers and find the card.

Wanted to give you something to make you smile since I've been smiling since I left you last night.
Chris

Wow.

I've never received flowers from anyone before. They're beautiful too with the bright orange poppies and delicate white daisy petals. The arrangement is placed delicately into a small glass mason jar making the entire bouquet as unique as the man that sent them to me. A smile spreads across my face at the memory of the kiss he placed on my cheek before leaving last night and I catch myself bringing my fingers up to the spot where his lips pressed softly.

"I know that look." Marie interrupts my thoughts.

"Those are really pretty." Julie says, her and Marie both approaching the counter to get a closer look at the flowers.

"They really are." I say, my gaze focused on the flowers sitting on the counter while the card remains pinched tightly between my fingers.

"What's that look for?" Marie asks and I realize that I'm shaking my head slowly side to side while staring blankly at the orange and white bouquet.

Looking up at her, I finally stop shaking my head. "I just don't understand. Why would he send me flowers?"

Marie narrows her eyes at me before responding to my question. "What do you mean? Obviously, you did something to impress him if he's sending you flowers."

"But I just met him. He helped me home after I missed my bus last night. Why would he send me flowers?"

"I take it you're not used to getting flowers then."

"No. To be honest, I'm not sure what I did to deserve them. I was a mess last night."

"What do you mean?" Julie asks.

"It started to rain, and I got knocked down on the sidewalk. People were shoving each other and running to get out of the rain. He helped me up and gave me a ride home. I figured he was safe since he was a detective and all. Otherwise, I would have ignored him and walked myself home, but my knees were hurt from hitting the sidewalk so hard and he felt sorry for me. It certainly wasn't something deserving of flowers."

"A detective?" Marie asks, her and Julie looking at each other with similar expressions on their faces.

"Yeah." I agree, remembering the shield I saw clipped to his belt. I feel the smile fall when I think about how he found my shop. I didn't tell him what the name of my shop was.

"What's that face for?" Julie asks me, stepping closer to the counter.

"I didn't tell him the name of my shop. Or my last name. How'd he know where to send flowers?"

"Umm, hello?" Marie starts. "Detective." She says the last word as if it were a question.

"So," Julie starts. "What's this detective's name?"

"Chris." I answer her as I reach my hand out to run over the petals of one of the poppies. I can feel the heat rushing to my face as I remember how sweet he was last night cleaning the abrasions on my knees. Looking up, I see both of them looking at each other somewhat suspiciously. "What?" I ask, pulling my hand back from the flowers as if they suddenly sprouted thorns.

"Are you going to see him again?" Marie asks.

"No." I say. "He was just being nice and gave me a ride home."

"You're kidding right?" Julie says, lowering her eyebrows as she looks at me skeptically.

"Why would I see him again? He was just a nice guy, and he gave me a ride home." I don't tell them about him taking care of me after getting me to my apartment. Or the fact that he kissed my cheek before leaving. Or that he made me feel safer than any man has made me feel in my entire life.

"Hmm." I look up to see Marie squinting her eyes at me and realize that my hand is pressed against my cheek where I can still feel the tingling from the kiss Chris left there last night. "So, it's completely normal for a guy to help you by giving you a ride home in the rain, send you flowers the following day, and make you look like *that* when you think about him?"

"I don't…" I begin but don't know how to finish that sentence without making myself seem pathetic. Even though I am. I have no experience with nice guys. I don't know what a nice guy would do in this situation. "I guess I don't really know."

"Did he give you his number?" Julie asks.

"Yeah. He put it in my phone before he left last night."

"Good. Then what you're going to do is send him a text and thank him for the flowers. Then let it blossom from there, no pun intended."

"The sooner the better." Marie interjects.

My head shakes slowly side to side, my eyes opening wider with each passing second. "I wouldn't even know what to say."

"That's easy. Just say thank you for the flowers."

"Just like that?"

"Just like that."

I feel so stupid. I've never had to send a message to anyone thanking them for anything like this before. I shouldn't be as nervous about it as I am, but I can't help it. Nice gestures from guys aren't something that I'm used to getting. Flowers or otherwise. "Okay." I concede. "I'll text him." Pulling my phone out of my purse below the register, I take a final glance at the flowers and open my messaging app.

Me: Thank you for the flowers. They're beautiful.

I watch as the three dots appear right away and realize that he's already typing out his response. My heart is beating so fast against my ribs as I watch for his message to appear that I'm afraid it's going to jump out of my chest.

Chris: You're welcome. Did they work?
Me: What do you mean?
Chris: Did they make you smile?
Me: They did. I haven't stopped since they were delivered.
Chris: Good. Neither have I.

"See how easy that was?" Julie asks. I look up at her and realize that I'm still smiling stupidly but I can't make myself stop. Julie and Marie both smile at me in return.

"Should I say something else?" I ask, not sure what the proper etiquette is for text communication between two single adults of the opposite sex.

"Nope." Marie answers as she walks back to the shelf with the incense burners. "You've opened up that communication, let him make the next move." She walks back to the register with three of the burners in her arms. "Do you have incense too?"

"I do." I point to the corner of the counter where the incense sticks and cones are on display.

"This is perfect!" She exclaims as she moves to the side and starts picking out incense cones for her new burners.

"Since when do you burn incense?" Julie asks her, moving over to stand behind Marie and peer over her shoulder.

"Hush." Marie elbows her in the ribs and they both start laughing. "This is a new me. I can finally relax for the first time in my entire life."

I watch from a distance as they giggle at each other as if this is just a typical day for them. A part of me burns with jealousy at them and the relationship they have. I've never had any friends like that. Yeah, I had my roommate Amanda, but we weren't even as close as these two appear to be.

I swallow around the lump forming in my throat as I grab some tissue paper from beneath the counter to wrap the burners, place them each in their own boxes, then bag her purchases up for her. When I look up, I see Marie approaching the register with several selections of incense cones, a sucker sticker sticking out between her lips.

"Your shop is amazing, Cypress. I'll definitely be back." She proclaims as she pays for her purchases.

"Thank you." I say sincerely, handing her the bag. "I'm here every day except Sunday."

"Good luck with Chris." Julie calls out as they walk out the front door, the bell ringing overhead.

It's only a few minutes of silence before the bell rings again, signaling someone else entering my shop. Looking up from the shirts I'm unpacking from a shipment that came in yesterday, I see a beautiful blond-haired woman wearing an ankle length hemp skirt similar to my own and several bangle bracelets adorning her wrist. She is accompanied by a handsome man appearing to be in his mid-thirties with his arm wrapped tightly around her shoulders. He's several inches taller than her, her head barely meeting his shoulder. They're an adorable couple I realize as they move slowly through the shop.

He stays with her while she peruses the tie-dyed shirts and hemp skirts lining the wall. Walking around the counter, I approach them cautiously so as not to startle her. "Welcome to Poppy Petals. Can I help you find anything?"

"No, thank you. We're visiting from out of town and were just walking past, and I wanted to come in. Your shop is so inviting from outside." She answers without taking her eyes away from the shirts.

"No problem." I take a few steps back. "I'll just be over here if you need anything." Before I turn to walk back behind the register, the man turns his gaze toward me and winks once. I'm confused by his action considering he has his arm wrapped so tightly around the woman shopping with him. Right as I open my mouth to question his actions, he winks again. *What the hell?* I think to myself.

Feeling more uncomfortable by his winking, I decide to engage conversation with her. "Visiting from out of town? What brings you to Echo Park?"

"We're spending the weekend at the beach." She turns her bright smile toward me. This doesn't help me feel any more comfortable, that's for sure. If they're together, why would he be winking at another woman? I can feel the hairs on the back on my neck standing up, a shiver running down my spine as he smiles and winks at me yet again.

My eyes narrow at him angrily and the smile fades quickly from his face. But do you think that stops him from winking again? Not at all. He winks, yet a fourth time at me while making direct eye contact with me. There's no mistaking that the wink was directed at me, and he has yet to look away. She must notice my expression because she turns her attention to him and places a hand on the middle of his chest.

Ohmygod. They're not swingers, are they? I've heard of things like this. Open marriages I think they're called. I could never be a part of that. How do I ask politely for them to leave my shop before this gets any weirder? I don't want to be caught up in something like this. And… OH MY GOD he just winked at me again.

"Are you okay?" I ask him, not knowing what else to do at this point. My hands are fisted at my sides trying to keep them from shaking.

"I'm sorry?" He asks even as he, you guessed it, winks at me again.

"Is there something in your eye?"

"Oh." The woman says, swinging around to look at me sympathetically. "I'm so sorry." Why is she apologizing for his actions? My brows furrow at her apology as I swing my gaze to her. "He has Tourette's."

"What?" I shake my head slowly trying to comprehend what that means. "I don't know what that is." I admit. Of course, as soon as I look back to him, he winks at me again.

"He has these uncontrollable tics. Winking is just one of them." She explains with a soft smile on her face. She places her hand on his shoulder to soothe him.

"I'm really sorry." He winks again. "It gets worse when I'm around new people or nervous." Another wink.

"Well." I take a breath and turn my eyes to the floor. "No need to be nervous here." I turn and walk back toward the counter and the box I left sitting on the floor. "Let me know if I can help you with anything." They both turn their attention back to the rack of shirts, forgetting about me entirely and I can't say that I mind. I've never encountered anyone with Tourette's before, but I make a mental note to research it when I get home.

It has never ceased to amaze me in the time I've been in Los Angeles the variety of people that I meet from one day to another. Some are really sweet like Marie and her friend Julie. Some are rude like the people that knocked me down on the sidewalk last night or the ones that just walked around me rather than help me up. Some are even heroic like Chris and the help he gave me last night, or the flowers he had sent to me today.

I can't stop my thoughts from trailing back to him. Do I want to see him again? Would I be willing to go out with him if he texted me again? It's been a long time since I've been able to trust a man, but I can genuinely see myself trusting Chris. I mean, how bad could he be? He is a detective after all.

Chapter 4

Chris

My lips tingled – literally tingled – when I kissed her cheek before leaving her apartment last night. It took everything in me to release my hold on her legs, to stand from the couch and ready myself to walk away from her. I had to touch her one last time before leaving though.

I can still feel the velvety softness of her skin against my lips. I can feel the tingle still just thinking about it, my fingers brushing lightly over my bottom lip at the sensation of her lingering there. The taste of her still there.

What are the odds? That the only woman that I've ever had such a visceral reaction to be the one that's lived right across the hall from me for the last three years. How is it possible that we haven't run into each other at least once in that time?

Mrs. Abernathy has been trying for at least the last two years to set me up with someone living in this building, I can't help but wonder if it was her all this time. Especially judging by the look that she gave me over Cypress' shoulder last night when we stopped by her apartment for a key.

I woke up this morning feeling restless, unsettled. I'm sure it's my overprotectiveness kicking in, but my mind keeps going back to the curtain over her door. I've devoted my entire career to protecting women from abuse and violent crimes. I've trained myself to recognize the signs of someone that's been through something horrible or is hiding from things in her past. I know Cypress has a story to tell but I can't ask her about it. It's killing me not to, but she has to be able to share it with me on her own terms. She has to trust me to be able to tell me her story.

I have to – no, I want to – earn her trust.

After a quick shower, I grab a cup of coffee before going downstairs to check the mail. It's been a busy week at work, so I know my mailbox is probably over filled with junk and bills. I step into the elevator, coffee in hand, and press the button for the first floor.

I take a few extra seconds after emptying my mailbox, placing most of it into the recycling bin in the corner of the lobby, before gazing at the box next to mine. There are only two apartments on each floor, so it's easy to guess which box belongs to my lovely neighbor.

Harris the label reads on the front of the box. *Cypress Harris*. At least now I know her name.

Tucking the rest of my mail beneath my arm, I turn back toward the elevator before I'm pulled from my thoughts. "Good morning, Chris."

Stopping in my tracks, I turn and offer an innocent smile. "Good morning, Mrs. Abernathy." Stepping closer, I notice that she's still wearing her slippers and housecoat and I wonder if she's feeling alright. She's usually so put together first thing in the morning. "How are you today?"

"Oh, I'm okay. I sat up too late last night reading and just haven't gotten around to doing my hair yet this morning."

"Oh. I know how that is." I tell her. "I tend to always try to get just one more chapter in myself."

"Oh, yes. That never seems to work out very well does it." She laughs lightly, placing a hand on her chest. I smile in agreement before she continues. "I saw you met our dear Cypress. She's a darling little thing, isn't she?"

I smile at her description of Cypress. "She certainly is."

"I'm surprised you haven't bumped into each other before. Of course, she does spend a lot of time at her shop. Poppy Petals, I think it's called." I make a note of the name she gives me. Cypress mentioned last night that she was working at her shop in Echo Park today. At least now I know what it's called. "It's all she has after all. That and her yoga classes. Such a sweet girl to be here all alone. And at such a young age too."

"All alone? What do you mean? She has no family here?" I take a few steps closer to her, my head tilting to the side as I digest what she's telling me.

"Oh no, dear. She doesn't have any family here. She's not originally from Los Angeles. I'm not exactly sure where she's from. But she's on her own."

"I see. Well, you have a nice day Mrs. Abernathy." I tell her before turning back toward the elevator. I don't hear anything else she says as I walk away, my head already spinning with this new information.

Cypress is alone here. She has no family here. So, what is she hiding from?

Well, she doesn't have to be alone anymore. At least, not if she doesn't want to be. She certainly doesn't need to be hiding anymore either. I vow silently to myself to make it my personal mission to slay her demons. I've never wanted to be anyone's knight in shining armor before, but for her I'd be willing to take on that role.

Opening my apartment door, I hear my phone ringing from the coffee table where I left it. Picking it up, I see Wendy's name flashing across the screen before I answer with a smile on my face. "Good morning, Wendy."

"Good morning, Chris. I wanted to thank you again for our little chat last night. I think you might be right after all."

"Of course, I am. When am I not?"

"Don't let your ego get in the way, Chris. All I'm saying is that I don't know how I didn't see it before. But after we left last night, I watched him. It was like I was seeing him for the first time; the way he checks on me in the rearview mirror or reaches his hand out for mine when he opens my door. Not to mention, he's the only one of the guys that makes eye contact with me. But I finally see it and I wanted to let you know you were right."

I don't know why, but it feels like a weight is lifted when she admits that what I told her about Braiden was right. I know she's been through hell, but she deserves a second chance at happiness. My heart swells several sizes for my friend knowing that she might be getting that second chance after all. She just needed to get out of her own way. "I'm glad to hear it."

"I won't keep you, Chris. I just wanted to let you know that you were right. And to thank you."

"Thank me? For what?"

"Opening my eyes. I don't know if I'm really ready for a relationship with anyone. It's hard for me to feel like I can trust anyone like that again. But I might be ready to take it slow with him. See where it goes."

"You deserve it, Wendy."

"I know. So, what are you up to today?"

"Well," I start, wondering how much of a shock this is going to be to her. I've known Wendy for years and I don't think I've ever mentioned a woman to her before. "I think I met someone."

"What? When?"

I laugh lightly at the shock in her voice. There I was last night trying to give her relationship advice, and now I'm fixing to ask her for some in return. "Last night. After you left."

"Well, that was fast." She giggles into the phone. "Tell me about her."

"There isn't much to tell. I helped her up after she was knocked down on the sidewalk right next to my car. She had missed the bus, so I gave her a ride home. Turns out, she's my neighbor."

"You're kidding." She actually starts laughing now and I join her. It is rather ironic after all.

"Not at all. I helped her home and made sure she was okay before I left. She banged her knees up pretty bad on the sidewalk. But I can't stop thinking about her, Wendy. She's adorable and mysterious. She has a shop in Echo Park that she's working at today, but I really want to see her again. I just don't want it to seem like I'm stalking her apartment all day waiting for her to get home. I'm in uncharted territory here and I don't know what to do."

"Hmm. Sounds like you were really taken by her."

"You have no idea."

"You should send her flowers. Let her know that you're still thinking about her. Put the ball in her court, see if she responds to the gesture."

"Flowers." Standing from the sofa, I walk over to the table on the other side of the room and open up my laptop to Google florists in Echo Park. "That's a good idea. I never would have thought about that. Thank you."

"No problem. Good luck with the girl. Let me know how it goes."

"Thank you, Wendy." She disconnects the call before saying anything else. Setting my phone down, I check the listings for a florist and pick one that offers quick delivery. Mrs. Abernathy says her shop is called Poppy Petals, so I pick a small arrangement with orange poppies and white daisies. There's even a spot where I can put a message for the card on the order. It takes me several minutes to decide what to put on the card. I finally go with *"Wanted to give you something to make you smile since I've been smiling since I left you last night."*

As soon as the order is placed, I stand and go into my kitchen to fix something for breakfast. Taking my plate of bacon, toast, and eggs out to the balcony table, I eat while soaking up the California sun. This is my favorite spot to sit in my apartment. The balcony overlooks the courtyard behind the building. It's a peaceful oasis of lush greenery, palm trees, and a fountain in the middle that's shared with the surrounding buildings.

My phone chimes with a message indicating that the flowers have been delivered and I smile to myself, sitting back in my chair and lacing my fingers together behind my head. *Now we wait* I think to myself. For what, I don't know yet. But I try not to dwell on it, or my nerves will get the better of me. I've never had to try to woo a woman before and I don't know if I'll do it right. I've never cared enough to try.

I'd do better to keep myself busy rather than sit here all day waiting to hear from Cypress. After cleaning up my breakfast dishes and changing into a faded pair of jeans and long-sleeved grey t-shirt, I gather my laundry for the week and take the elevator down to the basement. I'm just switching my clothes over to the dryer when my phone dings with an incoming text. Smiling, I see the text is from Cypress thanking me for the flowers.

Not wasting any time, I reply back to her, and we spend a few minutes texting back and forth. I can't remember when the last time was that my cheeks hurt from smiling this much. Not to mention, I haven't sent this many text messages to anyone in a long time. At least not since high school. Even Wendy prefers casual phone conversation over text messaging.

Deciding not to seem too eager, I finish my laundry and take it back upstairs to put away before texting her back.

Me: What time does your shop close?
Cypress: 5
Me: Any plans tonight?
Cypress: Frozen pizza and a good book.

I laugh at her reply, she can do so much better than frozen pizza. Looking at the clock, I see that it's already after four. I didn't realize that my laundry would take so long. I'm beginning to think it's time for Mrs. Abernathy to get a new dryer.

Once the laundry is put away and the basket placed back in the bathroom closet, I grab my leather jacket and keys and leave the apartment. As soon as I'm in my car, I send another text to Cypress.

Me: Change of plans.

Putting the phone in my inside jacket pocket, I start the car and pull out of the parking lot. I don't bother looking to see what her reply is, she won't be able to talk me out of it anyway. If she wants pizza, I can give her pizza but it for damn sure won't be a frozen pizza.

Fifteen minutes later, I find a parking space right in front of Poppy Petals. The outside of the shop is brightly colored and immediately makes me think of her. The sign hanging above the door and display window is bright pink with white writing. The door and window are both framed with an aqua blue that stands out against the pink while the rest of the building is red brick. Her shop is the brightest thing on the block making it impossible for anyone to miss.

The display in the window features bright colored shirts and long flowing skirts with random trinkets and items set neatly around them. It's not hard to imagine what the inside of the shop looks like if the display is anything to go by.

Pulling the key from the ignition, I debate for a few minutes whether or not to go inside or wait for her to come out. I make the decision that it would be best to step inside the shop rather than scare her on her way out. She seemed jumpy enough last night, and I don't want to give her any reason to be frightened by me.

As soon as I step inside the shop, I'm greeted by the jingle of a bell over the door and the scent of vanilla and sandalwood. Looking around, I realize that the fragrance is coming from an incense burner sitting on the counter beside the cash register.

"I'll be right with you." I hear her call out from somewhere near the back of the store, smiling to myself at the sound of her voice. "Sorry about that."

Turning toward her voice, I see her walking out of a doorway in the back corner. Several empty clothes hangers in each hand. She stops moving when she looks up and her eyes meet mine, hers opening wider when she notices me standing in the middle of the shop. I don't move, waiting to see what her reaction will be to seeing me standing here.

"Chris." She breathes my name, and a chill goes down my spine at the sound of it on her lips.

"Cypress." I say back in a low tone and her eyes close at the sound. I watch as she opens her eyes and steps around the counter, closer to me, before stopping a few feet away.

"What are you doing here?"

"I thought we could have dinner together."

"You want to have dinner with me?" She asks before moving her hands. She looks down as if she just realized she was still holding the clothes hangers before turning to set them down on the counter. When she turns back toward me, she's wringing her hands together nervously. "W-why?" She asks me, her voice low and somewhat shaky.

"I told you I wanted to see you again." I take a step in her direction, and she looks up at me. The look in her eyes is enough to make me stop dead in my tracks. She looks so innocent and shy. As if someone wanting to have dinner with her is something new.

"Oh." She says quietly, lowering her head to look at her feet.

"Hey." I say, stepping closer to her, suddenly feeling guilty for the insecurity that's written all over her face. Reaching out, I place my index finger beneath her chin and tilt her head back so I can see her eyes. "What's wrong?"

"Nothing." She continues to wring her hands together in front of her chest but doesn't take her eyes away from mine. "I just…" She inhales a shaky breath. "It's nothing."

"It's not nothing. What's going on in that gorgeous head of yours?"

"I just met you. You're really sweet, and you sent me flowers." She turns her gaze to the flowers on the counter next to where she's standing. "They're really pretty by the way. No one's ever sent me flowers before. I mean, I didn't even get a card in the mail yesterday for my birthday. And now here you are." She turns back to look at me. "I didn't think you meant it."

"Wait." I place my palm against her cheek. "Yesterday was your birthday?"

"Yeah." She backs away from me causing me to lower my arm back down to my side, and I somehow manage not to rub at the pain it causes in my chest at her rejection.

"Well, that settles it then."

Her eyebrows lift as her eyes widen and I chuckle at her expression. "Settles what?"

"We're definitely having dinner. And cake. Definitely cake."

"Cake?" She lowers her brows and tilts her head to the side. She really is adorable.

"Yep. You can't have a birthday without cake."

"Umm." She finally lowers her arms down to her side. "Okay?" She draws out the last word and I chuckle again at how innocent she truly is.

Lifting my wrist, I check the time on my smart watch. It's after five so I know it's time to close the shop. "You ready to go?"

"Now?" Her brows lift again. She so expressive I can't help but smile down at her.

"Yes. Now."

"Yeah. Just let me grab my things and lock up." She spins around to leave me, her braid whipping over her shoulder and her long, flowing skirt billowing out around her legs from the movement.

I stand in place and wait for several minutes before she comes back through the doorway in the back of the shop wearing a baggy sweater with a brightly colored bag slung over her shoulder, keys in hand. She walks toward the door, and I step around her to hold it open for her. As soon as she finishes setting the alarm, she walks out and waits for me to close the door so she can lock it.

"It's a nice evening out." I say as she finishes locking the door. "Would you like to walk?"

"Umm." She places her keys in her bag before looking at me. "Yes. I think I would."

"Here." I hit the key fob in my pocket to unlock my car door. "You can leave your bag locked up in my car if you want to. I'll take you home after dinner."

"Okay." She hands me her bag and I open the car, placing her bag on the floor behind the passenger seat then lock the door again before reaching out for her hand.

We walk together at a steady pace, her small hand engulfed in mine, our fingers laced together. My thumb strokes softly over her knuckles and I can feel the tension releasing from her posture as she walks. She's getting more comfortable with me, and my heart swells several sizes at the realization. "I was thinking we could get pizza."

She giggles softly. "Pizza sounds great."

"There's a great little place just right up the road here. How do you feel about pineapple on pizza?"

"Oh, the great pineapple debate. I don't see anything wrong with pineapple on pizza depending on the other toppings."

"Great." I smile down at her before turning my gaze ahead. "They have a pineapple, prosciutto and jalapeno pizza that I've been wanting to try."

"That sounds amazing actually."

I hold the door for her again when we get to the restaurant. We both order an unsweetened tea and sip on it slowly while waiting for our pizza to arrive. The restaurant is quite a bit warmer inside, a drastic change from the cooler evening air outside. I watch as Cypress slips off her cardigan to set in the booth next to her and I do the same with my jacket. That's when I get a good look at her wrist and notice the bright orange and blue butterfly she has tattooed on her right wrist.

"May I?" I ask as I point toward her wrist while she sets down her glass of tea. She looks where I'm pointing and holds her arm out for me to get a better look. "This is lovely."

"Thank you."

I know that butterflies are sometimes meant as a way of memorializing the loss of a loved one and I'm curious to know if that's what this one symbolizes to her. "Why a butterfly?"

"Butterflies are beautiful." She pulls her wrist back and traces the wings of the butterfly with the thumb on her left hand. She's quiet for several seconds as if lost in her own thoughts. "They're mystical creatures that represent spiritual rebirth, hope and change. For me, they symbolize my ability to move on from my past, to learn from my mistakes, and have hope for a better future."

I wonder, not for the first time, what she's running away from. "Is that what you want?" I ask, reaching out to take her hand in mine. "To forget about your past?"

"Parts of it." My finger rubs absently along the ink on her wrist. "Everyone has something in their past they're not proud of. I'm no different than anyone else."

I pull my hand back from hers when the waitress appears with our pizza. She sets a plate down in front of each of us and the pizza in the middle of the table.

"This looks amazing." Cypress says as she reaches out to grab a square slice from the pan. She doesn't wait before taking a huge bite of it, gooey cheese stretching in a long string between her mouth and the pizza as she pulls it away. I watch in awe as she enjoys the first bite. Finally, the cheese string breaks, and she sets the slice down on her plate with one hand, grabbing the cheese dangling from her mouth with the other to slip between her lips without missing a single beat.

"Good?" I ask, my eyes still fixated on her lips which are currently glistening from the grease left from the pizza.

"Mm-hmm." She hums while chewing, her eyes closed while she savors the gooey morsel. Opening her eyes, she catches me staring and immediately grabs her napkin to wipe her mouth. "I'm sorry." She says almost breathlessly. "I have a secret love affair with pizza."

"Don't apologize." I reach out and grab a slice for myself. "It's comforting to have dinner with a woman that isn't afraid to enjoy her dinner. However, it seems I may have some competition." She giggles before picking the pizza up from her plate for another bite.

We finish our dinner in silence. "I can't believe I've never eaten here before." She picks up her glass and drinks down the rest of her tea before wiping her hands and mouth with another napkin. "That was really good. So much better than the frozen pizzas I have in my freezer at home."

"It was. I've been wanting to try this place for a while. Thank you for coming with me."

"Thank you for bringing me."

Placing enough cash on the table to cover our meal and a tip, I grab my jacket from the bench next to me and stand. Reaching my hand out, I help Cypress stand and put her sweater back on before grabbing her hand again. "Now, to find some cake."

"You really don't have to do that." She says, her gaze turning down to the sidewalk as we exit the restaurant.

"I know." Thankfully there is a bakery between here and my car that's still open and I'm able to go inside and get one of the last cupcakes in the display case. I have it placed in a small box so Cypress can take it home with her if she doesn't want to eat it now.

"Thank you." She says, taking the box from me as I walk back out of the bakery.

"Happy Birthday." I tell her before grabbing her free hand again and walking back toward the car.

On the drive back to the apartment building, I figure I should come clean with her. She's going to figure it out sooner or later, and I'd much prefer if I just told her rather than have her jump to conclusions later on. "I have to tell you something."

"Uh oh. I don't know if I like the sound of that." She turns to face me as I stop at a red-light. "Are you married?"

"No. I'm not married." I turn to face forward right as the light turns green. "You might think this is funny. Or ironic. But we're actually neighbors."

"What?"

"Remember when I told you that I knew Mrs. Abernathy?"

"Yeah." She says it almost like a question.

"I've lived in the same building as you for the last seven years. We're neighbors."

"You're kidding."

"Nope. And it gets even better."

"Don't tell me…"

"I live on the fifth floor." I interrupt her.

"Wow." Well, that's a better reaction that I thought she'd have. "I mean, what are the odds?"

"I know."

"I guess we were destined to meet. Maybe it was fate."

I park in the lot next to the building and we walk hand in hand inside. Stepping into the elevator, I press the number five and we ride in silence to the top floor. Once we're standing outside her apartment door, I wait while she gets her keys out of her bag.

As soon as she opens the apartment door, I place my palm against her cheek and stop her from walking inside. She turns toward me, her eyes locking with mine. "Thank you for tonight, Cypress."

"Thank you for everything. Dinner. The flowers. The cupcake. I had a really great day today."

"What are you doing tomorrow?" I ask her, not ready for this night to end yet.

"I don't have anything planned. Sundays are my lazy day since it's the only day the shop is closed."

"Spend it with me."

"Are you sure?" She asks, her insecurities coming out again.

"Of course, I'm sure. We can do whatever you want. Go for a walk. Watch a movie. Sit in silence and read books. I don't care what we do, I just want you to spend it with me."

"I think I'd like that."

Bending down, I kiss her softly on the cheek. "Good night, Cypress."

"Good night," she says. I watch her as she walks inside and closes the door, a slight smile on her face. I listen as she locks the door before turning and walking across the hall to my own apartment. Seven years I've been in this apartment. She's been here for the last three years, and I didn't even know she existed before finding her on that sidewalk last night in the rain. Three years. I can't imagine anyone else I'd rather have living across the hall from me.

I can't wait to get to know her better and unlock her secrets.

Chapter 5

Cypress

During the bus ride to Echo Park, I take the time to check on my social media postings. I haven't done another video since my birthday almost a month ago. It's not that I haven't wanted to, but I've been spending so much time getting to know Chris that I just haven't had the extra time to plan the videos. Business at the boutique has been steady, making it impossible to work on a video during store hours.

I've taken time over the last few weeks to feature some of the hand-crafted items in my shop. Especially the incense burners that my friend, Amanda, makes. She texted me last night saying the visits to her online store had increased since I started the feature on my page. It gives me a warm, fluttery feeling knowing that I was able to help her, even in a small way.

Opening my calendar and scheduling app, I decide to make a list of other items in the shop that I want to feature. It worked out so well with Amanda that I'm thinking of spending a week on each area of my boutique over the next few months. That's one of my favorite parts of Poppy Petals – more than half of my inventory is sold on consignment from other local artists and vendors. Yes, I have several items that I stock on my own, as well as my tie-dyed items, but I know what it's like to be a vendor and run a small crafting business. I like to have the ability to help others in the same business bring in a little extra money.

Looking up from my phone, I see that the bus is approaching my stop. Putting my phone in my purse, I grab my keys and brace myself for the bus to stop moving. I hate taking the bus every day, but I've never owned my own car. I don't even have a driver's license, I've never had a reason to get one. Chris has met me at the shop several times to give me a ride home when his schedule allows it.

We've been seeing each other almost a month now and it's been amazing. I still can't believe that he's lived right across the hall from me for the last three years and we never met before now.

Standing up as the bus comes to a full stop, I grab my bag from the seat next to me and throw it over my shoulder with my purse. One hand on the straps securing my bags tightly, my other hand gathers the fabric of my skirt to keep it from being stepped on by anyone while I descend the steps to the sidewalk. Stepping a few feet from the bus, I lift my face to the sky, close my eyes, and soak in the sunshine. It's a bright, beautiful February morning and the sunshine feels wonderful on my face. That's one thing I'll never tire of here in Southern California, the endless sun.

Growing up on the road, we saw all sorts of weather from snow to rain to sunshine, but mainly snow and rain. Do I miss being in a place with four distinct seasons? Maybe, but I'll never miss the sunshine. I could stay here forever and never grow tired of the weather.

My boutique is only a block from my bus stop, so it doesn't take me long to get to the storefront to find Marie waiting patiently for me to open up for the day. I know it's her as soon as I see her standing there, her long cotton candy pink tresses are a dead giveaway. "Good morning, Marie." I greet her as I walk up to the door, ready to invite her inside.

"Good morning. Sorry, I'm here so early. I was in the neighborhood and wanted to stop in for some more incense." She smiles brightly as I hold the door open and gesture for her to come inside.

"No problem. I just got some new cones in the other day that I think you'll like." Flipping on the lights and turning the sign to open, I lead Marie to the counter where the incense sticks and cones are on display and show her all the new fragrances that I got in the mail the other day. I needed to restock them after running a few features on Amanda's burners.

"I want something nice smelling, not too strong. Valentine's Day is coming up and I have plans with Matt." I smile at Marie at the mention of Valentine's Day. I've never had a Valentine before so I'm excited that this year might be different. Marie has her bright pink hair pulled back in two French braids, one on each side of her head. She's wearing a bright purple sweater and black yoga pants with pink tennis shoes that match her hair. I've never seen anyone that can pull off such bright colors as well as she does, but it works with her.

"I have the perfect one for you. This one is called Romance." I pick up a cone and hand it to her to smell. "It's the perfect blend of vanilla and citrus. Not too strong or overpowering. Perfect to use in any room of the house." I wink at her hoping she'll get my meaning. She giggles in response.

"Mmm." She closes her eyes as she holds the cone beneath her nose to smell. "This is perfect." I watch as she places the cone back on the display and grabs a box from beneath them. "So, I've been meaning to ask," she starts as she hands me the box to ring up for her. "How are things with you and Chris? I haven't seen you in a few weeks, so I haven't been able to ask."

"He's a great guy actually. We've been seeing each other almost a month now. And you'll never believe this, but it turns out he's my neighbor." I smile as I place her purchase in a small bag and hand to her.

"You're kidding!" She exclaims.

"Nope. He's lived across the hall from me for the last three years and I didn't even know it."

"Wow. That's amazing."

"I know." I look up as the bell rings over the door and take a minute to greet the group of ladies that walk into the shop. They immediately head to the clothing rack on the far wall, and I turn back to Marie. "It was like fate or something that we even met. We've gone out to dinner several times. He always walks me to my door and kisses my cheek before leaving."

Marie lowers her brows slightly before speaking again. "That's sweet." She stops and I'm confused about the expression on her face.

"What?" I ask.

"Nothing. It just sounds like he's being really sweet."

My smile fades and I lower my gaze to the counter as what she's saying finally sinks in. He hasn't actually kissed me yet, only a few quick kisses on my cheek at the end of a date. "Do you think there's something wrong with me?"

"What? No," she says quickly. "Look, I'm all for taking it slow and all but how many dates have you guys been on?"

"I don't know. It's been almost a month so probably five or six. Do you think that's weird?"

"No. I don't think it's weird. Like I said, I think it's sweet. But I'm still surprised, I mean, a kiss on the cheek is really sweet but."

She stops and purses her lips together tightly like she's afraid of saying something wrong.

"You can say it, Marie. It's weird. I know it's weird."

"It's not that. I'm just wondering if he's trying to take it slow for you. Maybe he doesn't want to be the one to make the first move."

"Why wouldn't he want to make the first move?"

"I don't know," she says as she tilts her head to the side and bites her lower lip. "Chivalry maybe? There's no explaining what men do sometimes. All I'm saying is, maybe you should make the first move. I mean, you do want to kiss him, don't you?"

"Well, yeah. I really do."

"There you go." She says excitedly as if encouraging me. "When are you seeing him again?"

"He's meeting me here at five."

"Okay. So, here's what I want you do to." She leans her elbows on the counter, getting closer to me so she can lower her voice. "Go have a great time with him tonight. Wherever he's taking you, whatever you end up doing. When he takes you home and goes to kiss your cheek, I want you to grab him and kiss him on the mouth."

"Oh, I don't know if I can do that." I back away, shaking my head slowly side to side.

"Why not? Girl, sometimes you gotta take control."

"I would never do that."

"I think you could do it. You might be surprised." She says honestly but I just don't feel comfortable taking that kind of control. I don't have that much experience with guys, and I've never been the one to initiate anything. "I've never done anything like that before. I don't know if I can do it."

Her brows lift at my confession as if she's surprised. "Just think about it. Okay? If you're still not sure after your date with him tonight, then forget I said anything."

"I'll think about it." I concede.

I watch as Marie grabs a pen next to the register and one of my business cards. She writes on the back of it before holding it out to me. "This is my cell. Text me anytime, Cypress. Really. And have fun on your date tonight."

"Thank you." I take the card from her and look down at the number written on the back. When I look up again, Marie is walking toward the door and tossing a wave over her shoulder on the way out. I notice the group of ladies are still looking through the clothing racks on the far wall and begin to move around the counter to see if they need any help when I hear the message notification on my phone.

Chris: *Good morning, Butterfly.*

He started calling me Butterfly a few weeks ago after our third date. It was sweet and makes me blush every time he does it. I can still feel the tingling sensation in my wrist, from when he first touched my tattoo, every time I hear his tenor voice breathe out the word. Just thinking about it now; a tightness builds in my chest, and I can feel my nipples straining against the lace of my bra.

Me: *Good morning.*
Chris: *I can't wait to see you later. It's been too long.*
Me: *It's only been a few days.*
Chris: *A few days too long.*

I can't ignore my customers any longer, so I place the phone on the shelf below the register and walk across the store. I hear my phone going off again indicating another text message but I choose to ignore it so I can help my customers.

These ladies are excited about the colors and patterns from the tie-dyed shirts on the wall. We talk for several minutes about tie-dye techniques and where to get supplies and I give them my card with my social media information so they can look up my how-to videos. They buy several different blouses and t-shirts before leaving the store and I smile to myself as I picture some of the designs they'll be able to come up with on their own.

Now that the store is empty for a few minutes, I walk to the back room to get a bottle of water from the refrigerator I keep stocked in there. Walking back out to the counter so I can keep an eye on the store, I sip my water and remove my lunch from my bag beneath the register. Grabbing my phone, I check the notifications and see that I've missed four messages on my Instagram, six text messages, and a missed call from my mother. I decide to listen to my mom's voicemail first.

Hi, honey. I just wanted to call and let you know that we're in Vegas this weekend. We're not doing any shows or anything. We were just close by, and David wanted to hit the casinos. It's been a while since we've been here. Jase is with us too. I thought maybe you'd want to get together while we're this close. Let me know.

No, I really don't want to get together with any of them. If she were by herself then I might think about it. But not with David and Jase with her. I've been free of their controlling ways for far too long to fall back into them.

Taking a bite of my peanut butter and jelly sandwich, I pull up my Instagram app and read through my messages. Nothing new in there, just a few likes and offers to help me promote my page. Those are mostly scams so I keep skipping over them and deleting them as they come up. Opening my text messages, I have six unread messages all from an unknown number.

Unknown: Saw you on Instagram. You look gorgeous.
Unknown: I'd love to get together. When are you available?
Unknown: Wish you'd message me back. I'd love to see you in person.
Unknown: That's alright. I know where you are. I'll see you soon.
Unknown: Mmm. You look even better than I remembered.
Unknown: Don't worry darlin'. I'll leave you alone. For now.

Swiping my shaky finger across the screen, I delete all six of the text messages. I lean over and toss the remainder of my sandwich in the trash, having officially lost my appetite. I have a suspicion that Jase is the one messaging me. Especially after hearing from my mother that they are only a few hours away from me. He's the last person that I want to see.

I keep myself busy for the next few hours with putting away new incense burners and shirts. My entire body relaxes when I look out the window and see Chris' SUV parked at the curb in front of the boutique. I don't even care what time it is, there's no one here so I'm closing up. As soon as I have my bags from behind the counter, I flip the lights off and set the alarm, then make my way across the sidewalk.

Chris stands leaning against the passenger door of his SUV with both arms outstretched in invitation. He looks sexy as hell in his faded blue jeans, dark blue t-shirt, and leather jacket. His dirty blonde hair is slightly messy and itching to have my fingers running through it. He immediately wraps his arms around me and pulls me into his chest, my arms going around his waist as I breathe in the heavenly scent of his cologne. He always smells so good, like worn leather and musk.

"Hey." He says before kissing the top of my head and rubbing his hand up and down on my back. "What's wrong? You're shaking."

"Nothing. It was just a long day. I'm glad you're here." I unwrap myself from his body and step back to look up at his handsome face.

He bends down to kiss me on the cheek before stepping aside and opening the door for me. I don't waste any time getting into the seat, I don't want to be here any longer for in case Jase is still creeping around watching me. I crane my neck in all directions to see if I can see him anywhere while Chris walks around the SUV to the driver's side. "Where are we going tonight?" I ask him as he takes his seat behind the wheel and turns the key in the ignition.

"I was thinking we could go to the park." He smiles at me before putting the car in gear and pulling into traffic.

"The park?" That's different. We've gone out for pizza, burgers, tacos. Name a small restaurant in Echo Park and we've probably eaten there already over the last month. But what could possibly be at the park?

"Yep." He says, keeping his eyes aimed straight ahead. He isn't going to give me any hints it seems.

"Okay." I say it almost as a question even though my pulse increases at the possibilities. What could he have planned for this evening? I realize, as I relax against the back of my seat, that it doesn't matter. I'm happy doing anything with this man. I've never felt safer than I do when I'm with him.

Several minutes later, thanks to the weekend traffic, we're pulling into the park. What I see is nothing like I had imagined it to be. When he said park, I was picturing families with small children playing on swings and slides. But this is the opposite. There are several raised platforms lining the far end of the park with lights shining on each one in multiple colors. I see a drum set on one and I imagine that a band will be playing there shortly.

Between where we're parked, and the stages set up on the far end of the park, are numerous tents with vendors selling various merchandise. It looks very familiar and reminds me of something that my mother and I would have set up at when I was growing up. "A street fair!" I exclaim excitedly from my seat while attempting to unbuckle my seatbelt. "I had no idea there was anything like this going on today."

"A good surprise then?" He asks me while reaching over and helping me with the seatbelt. I peer up at him and see his smile lighting up his entire face, even his eyes are twinkling with delight. He's really outdone himself today.

"Absolutely." Finally free of my seatbelt, I reach impatiently for the door handle and jump out of the SUV before the door has completely opened. Chris rushes around the front of the car to meet me and grab my hand, our fingers lacing together tightly as he leans down and brushes another kiss to my cheek. A warm fire blooms deep in my belly every time he does that; I don't care what Marie says, it's sweet and I love it.

We take our time walking from tent to tent, enjoying the local craft vendors. Thankfully, I have business cards in my purse, and I hand them out to several of the vendors hoping they'll be interested in placing some of their items in my boutique. A few were skeptical, but most of them were open to the opportunity.

Especially when I explained my new features on social media and how they'd driven business to my friend Amanda's online store.

Chris doesn't interrupt a single pitch to these crafters. He stands back and watches, his eyes burning into my back the entire time. I'm honestly surprised that I was able to focus on the conversations with these ladies knowing that he was watching me so closely. I purchase several small trinkets from a few of the vendors, promising positive feedback with their information on my Instagram account. We leave the craft tents hand in hand with a collection of business cards sitting neatly in my purse. I'll follow up with each of them in the weeks to come and go over details about moving some of their wares into my store.

"You're amazing." He says, leaning down to brush a soft kiss against the top of my head and squeezing my hand tightly in admiration. Looking up at him, I smile sweetly and watch as his gaze moves down to my mouth. I turn my gaze quickly away, not ready yet for the public display if this is the moment of our lips finally becoming acquainted. My stomach twists unexpectedly at the disappointment, even though I was the one rejecting his advance.

"The band is setting up." I nod my head toward the center stage where several people are mounting microphones to stands. "I wonder what kind of music they play."

"I don't know." He turns his gaze to follow my own. "I don't know the band. Should we move closer so we can listen."

"Definitely." I smile at him again and pull his hand in the direction of the stage. I don't get the opportunity to listen to music very often. With a limited data plan on my phone and no television in my apartment, I'm not attuned with any local music. I try to save the data on my phone for my social media postings. My favorite part of growing up in traveling festivals was the live music though.

I didn't get to watch them perform while I was working our booth, but I always enjoyed listening to them in the background. This time, though, I get to have a front row seat.

We pick a spot on the grass not far from the center of the stage. I watch, amazed, as the band walks out. They all have long hair, past their shoulders, and are covered in tattoos. There are five of them, each with a similar appearance, and I wonder if they're related.

Chris sits behind me, his legs caging me in on either side of my hips, his arms wrapped around my waist pulling me into his chest. I relax against him as the guitar music serenades us. Laying my head back against his shoulder, I place one of my hands against his forearm and trace circles and swirls against his arm softly.

The singer starts, his voice gravelly and deep, and shivers run down my spine. The song is soulful and intense, the lyrics spinning a tale about a lost love and finding the strength to carry on. "Wow." I whisper when the song ends.

"They're pretty good." Chris admits, tightening his hold around my waist and kissing me softly on the top of my head. We sit and listen for several more songs, a few more upbeat than the first. When one of the men moves to sit on a stool rather than stand, he begins playing a slower tune. Chris releases his hold on me and begins to stand, pulling me up with him. He turns me to face him before pulling me back into his chest. "Dance with me." He whispers into my ear.

Looking around, I see several people dancing to the music now playing, and I can feel my cheeks begin to burn with fire. A fire that runs deep and hot through my body as my arms raise to wrap around Chris' neck. He holds me tight around the waist and together we begin to sway to the music.

"Darling, just hold my hand." Chris begins to sing along with the band, his voice low enough for only me to hear. "Be my girl, I'll be your man. I see my future in your eyes."

Closing my eyes, I lean my cheek against his chest and soak in the words of the most beautiful song I've ever heard. The way Chris sang those words in my ear, the gentle touch of his hands on my hips, and the feel of his heart beating against my cheek. How could I not fall for this man?

When the music stops, we stand there still wrapped in each other for several seconds while people around us cheer and clap for the band. "Come on." Chris releases his hold on me and steps back. "It's getting chilly out. Let's get you home." He reaches for my hand, wrapping my tiny hand in his, and pulls me along with him.

The drive home is quiet, the only sound in the car is our breathing along with my heart beating loudly in my ears. The energy from the music and dancing wrapped in his arms is still running through my veins. He helps me out of the car when we arrive back at the apartment building and walks me to my door when we reach the top floor. I fumble with my keys and unlock the door before he leans down and kisses my cheek.

"I had a great time tonight. Thank you for that." I suck in a quick breath and swallow a few times to moisten my mouth. I don't know why I'm so nervous all of a sudden. "Can I ask you a question?" I whisper, not even looking at him for fear of seeing his rejection.

"Anything," He whispers back as he lifts his palm to caress my cheek softly.

"Is there something wrong with me?"

"Something wrong with you?" He parrots my question back and I can hear the confusion in his voice.

"I love seeing you Chris, spending time with you. I've loved every minute that we've been together over the last month. But…" I pause and take a deep, shaky breath. Marie says I should just do it, take the lead. But I can't muster up the courage to reach out to him. Closing my eyes, I force myself to mouth the words. "Why haven't you kissed me?"

"I'm trying to be a gentleman here." He growls as he pushes my back against the door, pressing the full hardness of his body against mine, both hands cradling my face softly while his thumbs trace my cheekbones. "Don't think I don't want you, Cypress." He rocks his hips against me, and I can feel the hard length of him pressed against my belly. "I do want you." He kisses me again, dragging his lips across mine. "To taste you." He traces my lips with his tongue, and I open up for him, my hands fisting the front of his shirt. One of his hands leaves my cheek as he deepens the kiss, tracing his fingers down my neck, along my shoulder, then down my back until his palm rests flat and hard against my lower back, pulling me tightly against him.

Breaking the kiss, he rests his forehead against mine and closes his eyes. "Oh." Is the only thing that I can say, words have completely escaped me and my brain is lost in that foggy half-awake place.

He chuckles lightly, his breath ghosting against my lips. "Yeah. Oh." He steps away, moving both hands to my shoulders as he looks at me from one eye to the other as if searching my soul for unspoken truths. "Open the door, Butterfly."

My heart quickens at the sound of his name for me. My eyes locked on his, I reach behind myself and turn the doorknob, pushing the door open all the way. I stand for several seconds just watching him to see what he'll do. His eyes narrow on mine before lowering to my lips when suddenly, he reaches both hands up and cups my face between his palms, his mouth crashing into mine, and he pushes me backwards into my apartment.

Chapter 6

Chris

Having Cypress in my arms, sitting on the grass while listening to the band play, was heaven. There was a tightness in my chest, a lump stuck in my throat, fluttering deep in my bones. It was something I had never felt with any other woman before. The dance, holding her in my arms, pressed tightly into my chest. Nothing compares to that feeling. And the song was perfect. Literally. I've never heard Ed Sheeran's "Perfect" performed quite like that band that performed it tonight.

In that moment, everything changed. Cypress was no longer the woman I was trying to woo, she became the woman I was falling for. She truly is perfect, in every way. Watching her interact with the vendors at the park was stunning, just to watch her in her element. The way she fluttered around those craft tents like a graceful butterfly, her skirt blowing in the breeze around her as she moved from one tent to the next.

I've been good, a perfect gentleman, every time we've been together. My control and protective tendencies are on full alert with her at all times. Cypress is guarded, I can see it in her eyes when we're out in public, the way she watches everyone around her as if expecting the worst. I've watched as she checks and double checks the locks on the door to her apartment before moving the full-length curtain to cover it completely. I've seen her hesitation at using public restrooms and refusal to try on clothing at stores when we've gone shopping together. I don't know what she's been through that's made her that way, I have no idea what she's hiding from. But I'll do everything in my power to make sure she's safe going forward. She'll never have to hide from anything when I'm around.

But the look on her face now, the look of insecurity and doubt. I never want to be the reason that she feels so insecure. She thinks there's something wrong with her, when the truth is that I've been holding myself back for fear of scaring her away. I'm terrified of losing her so early on in our relationship when I can see so much of a future with her. But that look on her face has broken me, causing my control to crumble to my feet.

Pressing her back against her apartment door, I lower my mouth to hers, finally taking that first coveted taste of her. It's everything I imagined it would be and more. It causes something in me to snap into place, my pulse beating in time with hers and nearly pounding a hole in my chest. It takes all the strength I possess to break that kiss and pull back from her. I will not take her for the first time in this hallway. She deserves so much better than that. She deserves to be worshiped like a queen.

"Open the door, Butterfly." As soon as she does, my mouth is on hers again, her face cradled in my palms as I back her into the apartment. I break away from her long enough to close and lock the door behind me, my eyes never leaving hers. I watch as her breathing quickens, and I can practically smell her arousal. I know she wants me as much as I want her in this moment.

Wrapping my hands around her small waist, I lift her off the floor and her legs wrap around my waist. Her fingers thread through my hair as she brings her mouth to mine, our tongues instantly dancing and tangling with each other. Lowering my hands, I gently squeeze the rounded globes of her ass as I start moving toward what I assume is her bedroom. Her apartment is almost a mirror image of my own.

I'm shocked momentarily upon entering her dark bedroom and seeing the thick curtain over her window, similar to the one in the living room. When I break away from her, she slides seductively down the front of my body, the look in her eyes completely mesmerizing. I turn my attention to the doorway we entered and notice a curtain similar to the one donning her front door and decide to file that away for another day as I walk over and turn the lock on the bedroom door. I want her to feel comfortable with me in her space. She smiles almost bashfully as I turn and begin walking back toward where I left her at the foot of her bed.

A low growl rumbles through my chest as I trail my gaze over her, starting at her feet and working my way back up to her eyes. My hands go to her shoulders, pushing her cardigan off to slide down her arms to the floor. Grabbing her waist, I pull her against me and lower my mouth to hers, trailing my lips across her mouth before kissing her cheek, her jaw, below her ear. I trail open mouth kisses down her neck and along her shoulder and collar bone and I can feel her tremble beneath my lips, her hands squeezing my shoulders. I run my tongue from one shoulder, across her exposed chest, to the other shoulder memorizing her flavor; she tastes sweet with a hint of vanilla.

I don't think I'll ever get enough of her, the way she closes her eyes and sucks in a quick breath when my hands graze her waist. Pulling her shirt higher, I trail my fingertips along her lower abdomen and watch as she throws her head back slightly. I watch her closely, ready to pull back instantly if she begins to get uncomfortable, as I raise her shirt higher and higher until I can see the purple lace of her bra. She releases my shoulders to lift her arms in the air, allowing me to remove the shirt and toss it on the floor.

God, she's perfect.

I drag my fingertips down her arms and cup a breast in each hand, testing their weight and feeling her nipples harden beneath my thumbs through the lace of her bra. Gently squeezing and caressing her breasts, I move my mouth back to hers and she opens for me immediately. Deepening the kiss, I release her breasts and move my hands down her ribs and over her hips. Hooking my fingers beneath the waist band of her skirt, I push it down to the floor leaving her standing before me in her matching purple lace bra and panties.

"Fuck, you're gorgeous!" I exclaim. Her ivory complexion is practically glowing in the dark, the only light in the room from a small salt lamp in the corner by the window. She has a slight hourglass shape, with toned abs and shapely thighs. Definitely the body of a yoga instructor, I can tell she takes care of herself.

She lowers her gaze to the floor. Her shoulders slump with apprehension and I know that she's not used to receiving compliments. Pinching her chin between my thumb and index finger, I raise her face so I can look into her eyes. I want her to see the sincerity of my words. "You're beautiful, Butterfly." I watch her smile widen, even with her lower lip pinched between her teeth. Moving my thumb, I pull her lower lip away from her teeth before bending down and sucking that lip between my teeth. "Get on the bed." My voice is deeper, gravellier than I expect.

Her eyes widen for a fraction of a second before she sits slowly on the foot of the bed. Pulling her feet up to the mattress, she pushes herself to the middle of the bed and I crawl over top of her still fully clothed. I tell myself that I'm not taking her too far tonight, I'm not fucking her. I do, however, plan to worship her fully.

Grabbing both of her arms, I raise them above her head and wrap a hand around both of her wrists. My other hand begins to caress her body slowly, lightly running my fingertips from the underside of her arm to her waist and back again. I bring my hand to her breast while taking her mouth with mine. Grabbing the lace shielding her from my ministrations, I pull the cup down and expose one of her breasts, pinching her nipple between my fingers softly.

Moving my mouth to her jaw and running my lips down her neck to her collar bone, I pinch her nipple a little harder and give it a slight tug. The soft mewl that escapes from her throat lets me know it wasn't too hard. I twist her nipple one more time before moving my hand to her waist and pulling her nipple into my mouth, wrapping my lips around it tightly and biting down just enough to graze my teeth against it while flicking lightly with my tongue. She undulates beneath me, fueling the fire burning deep in my belly and causing me to press my hips harder into her.

Lifting my head to look up at her, I remove my other hand from her wrists. "Don't move." I demand as I move my hand down to her other breast. My mouth returns to her nipple, while I lower the other cup of her bra and show the same attention to her other breast. I only stop when I feel her fingers threading through my hair. Grabbing her wrists, I move them above her head again. "I said don't move." She smiles at me but doesn't argue, her eyes glimmering with lust and desire.

Lowering my mouth to hers, I gently suck on her tongue before trailing my lips to her chest, between her breasts, and down her belly. I trace the waistband of her lace panties with my tongue before hooking my fingers in the elastic and pulling them down her legs. Lifting my eyes to her face, I see her watching me, her eyes alight with hunger for what she knows I'm about to do, and it encourages me to continue. Thankfully, I see that her arms haven't moved, her hands still fisted above her head tight enough that I'm sure her fingernails are cutting into her palms.

She lifts her feet so I can remove the thin scrap of lace and toss it across the room. Kissing her mound, I smile against her flesh, loving that she's natural and only slightly trimmed at the sides, but fully woman. That's something that's so hard to find these days. Women take their personal grooming to the extreme when removing enough hair to leave them with the appearance of a pre-pubescent teenager. My eagerness overwhelms me at the mature woman beneath me now, my control writhing beneath the surface as I tell myself again and again that I'm not going too far tonight.

God, this woman is going to be the death of me. Using the palms of my hands, I push her legs apart, opening her up for me like a flower. Breathing deeply, I inhale the scent of her, closing my eyes and reveling in the honey and vanilla scented moment. Using my thumbs, I open her further and run the tip of my tongue up her slit from bottom to top.

Her hips thrust against me momentarily before settling against the mattress. Lifting my gaze, I see her eyes closed and her mouth partially open, but her arms are still above her head. *Good*, I think to myself.

Flattening my tongue, I run the length of her again to taste her sweetness before narrowing in on her clit and pulling it into my mouth. She moans sweetly above me, only fueling my desire to hear her screaming my name. I continue torturing her clit until she begins to roll her hips against my mouth, inserting first one then two fingers into her and curling my fingers up until her moans get louder, her screams becoming more incoherent.

She breaks apart beautifully before finally starting to settle and relax against the mattress. Only when her movements still do I finally pull away, taking one final taste of her before kissing my way across her thigh down to her knee then repeating on the other leg. I kiss my way across her belly and between her breasts before kneeling over her, my arms caging her in on either side of her shoulders. "You are magnificent."

She smiles, her eyes still closed as her body trembles with the aftershocks of her release. Reaching up, she wraps her arms around my neck and pulls me down to her. My mouth crashes into hers with a frenzy as I struggle to maintain my control. I allow her to deepen the kiss before pulling away from her and brushing the hair from her forehead that escaped her braid as she reaches for the waist of my jeans.

I catch her hands before she can reach her destination, pulling them both to my mouth and kissing each of her knuckles. "No, Butterfly." I kiss the palm of each of her hands before cradling them to my chest. "Not tonight. You need sleep." I lean down and kiss her forehead softly and watch as she closes her eyes.

I wait for her breathing to even out, knowing that she's fallen asleep, before I stand and walk across the room. Pulling the curtain over the bedroom door, I pull the door closed as I walk out. Making sure the curtain is closed over the apartment door, I do the same, locking the door on my way out into the hallway.

I walk absently through my own apartment, her taste still lingering on my lips, and crawl into my own bed for the night. As much as I wanted to stay with Cypress curled up in my arms, I wouldn't have been able to keep my control reigned in with her so close to me. The time will come for that.

Monday morning, I'm met by my sergeant as soon as I get off the elevator. *This can't be good,* I think to myself as I stop in front of him. He's standing with a stern expression and his arms crossed over his chest. "We need to talk." He says in greeting as I stop in front of him. He turns on his heel and walks toward his office, I follow obediently.

"What's up, Sarge?" I take a seat in one of the uncomfortable armchairs facing his desk. The vinyl of the seat creaks with age as I sit on the edge, my elbows resting on my knees.

"There was a festival in the park over the weekend. In Echo Park." He tells me as he opens a drawer on his desk and begins pulling out folders. He sets the folders on the desk in front of him and flattens his palms over top of them, looking up at me at the same time.

"I'm aware. I was there Saturday evening with my girlfriend." I pause and lower my head, hopefully hiding the smile that spreads over my face at the term. It's the first time I've actually referred to Cypress as my girlfriend to anyone and I really like the way it feels to admit it out loud. "The band was really great."

"Right." He says nonchalantly, pushing the folders across the desk before removing his hands. "Well, we've had a few missing persons reports from the weekend. Three women, to be exact, all went missing during the festival. There are no leads, no suspects, no witnesses. Each of the women were there working as craft vendors, but they weren't there alone. Each of them was reported to have walked away from their tents to either go get food or go to the restroom but never returned."

"I see." I take the folders from the desk and begin flipping through the information included in each one. "And why are you handing this to me? My cases are generally trafficking or abuse victims. I don't work in missing persons." Looking through the files, I notice these women are all young, ranging from seventeen to twenty-five.

"I've been looking over these files all morning, Chris." Sarge sits back in his chair, running his fingers through his hair. "There've been several missing persons reports over the last several weeks in surrounding areas. All young women ranging from fifteen to thirty, all reported missing after craft fairs or street festivals. Each of them leaving no witness or clues. They walk away for what's supposed to only be a few minutes and never come back. It's too suspicious."

"I see." Leaning forward, I place the file folders back on the desk in front of me.

"I think there's more going on than just a few missing women," Sarge states.

"Trafficking?"

He doesn't answer right away, just nods his head slowly while looking past me, not focused on anything. "Chris, you're the best we have at this." He moves a hand to the back of his neck and closes his eyes. "You've had more luck at finding victims recently than any of my other detectives."

My head nods once before I turn my gaze to the floor, my hands fisted together in my lap. I know he's referring to my most recent cases with Julie Harrington and Marie Tolson, both having been taken against their will and held captive. They weren't trafficking situations though. Julie was taken by a group of men that were involved in a string of burglaries around the city. They were just looking to shut her up and keep her from printing the story. Marie was taken by an ex that thought he owned her.

This is different. These women are basically alone, aside from whoever they were working their craft tents with. No husbands, boyfriends, or close family. The people they were with weren't related to them, just friends or co-workers. Julie and Marie had their boyfriends actively searching for them as well. These women aren't even from around here, they have no one out searching for them at all.

"I've got a list for you." He reaches into the drawer of his desk again and pulls out a slip of paper. "This is a list of women that have gone missing over the last week in surrounding areas. I've got the contact information of the detectives that are working their cases. I figured you might want to compare information, see if anything clicks."

"Thanks, Sarge." Reaching out, I take the list from him and place it on top of the stack of files.

"Keep me informed."

"I will." I grab the folders and contact information before standing to leave the office. Once I'm at my desk, I grab a notepad and begin to compile similarities between the missing women before reaching out to the other detectives to get information on their missing victims.

As always, searching for missing victims wears me down. My entire week is filled with phone calls and house visits, as well as trips to surrounding towns to talk in person with the other detectives. Every case involves women that were taken from craft fairs and trades shows, every woman with no family in the area. None of them left any evidence, suspects, or witnesses. They just disappeared. The hard truth of these types of cases is that these victims are rarely found.

This case is hitting too close to home for me at the moment. I keep thinking about Cypress and her telling me about growing up on the road. She lived in a small Airstream camper with her mother, travelling around the country for festivals and craft fairs. I'm plagued by nightmares at night about her being taken from one of those fairs. Just dragged away by a faceless person, never to be seen again.

The long hours this week, working this case, has kept me from being able to see Cypress. All I want is to hold her tight and never let her go, just the thought of her being one of these victims is enough to make me lose sleep at night. I couldn't bear the thought of anything happening to her.

Valentine's Day is this weekend and I intend to make it special for her. I've never wanted to do for another woman the things I would do for this one. For the first time since Cypress and I met, she's coming to my apartment for dinner. I'm cooking, yes, I can cook believe it or not. I'll serve her dinner with candlelight and flowers. We'll cuddle on the couch and watch a romantic movie together. We'll fall asleep curled up in each other's arms. I'm desperately falling in love with this woman, and I just want to keep her safe.

Chapter 7

Chris

"How was your week, Wendy?" Reaching out to pick my glass up from the table, I take a sip of my tea. Wendy and I are having lunch today at a small sandwich shop in Hollywood. It's her turn to pick, so I'm slightly surprised at her choice. She normally chooses some swanky place with a bar in it. This is peaceful, however, and quiet.

"I'm still single, if that's what you want to know." She smiles at me from across the table. I watch as she picks the pickles out of her sandwich, pinching them carefully with her fingernails, and placing them to the side of her plate.

My eyes focus on a pickle as she sets it down next to her sandwich. "You know, you could have just ordered your sandwich without pickles."

"I know." She smiles up at me before removing another pickle slice. "I don't eat the pickles, but I like the flavor they leave behind on the sandwich."

Shaking my head slowly, I take a bite of my potato wedge. "So, nothing new going on with you this week?"

"No." She finishes removing her pickles before placing the top slice of bread back on her sandwich and picking it up for a bite. She moans lightly as she chews which makes me smile. It's always nice to see her get so much pleasure out of the simple things in life.

Things that she was neglected of for so long. Setting her sandwich down, she wipes her hands on her napkin, tilting her head to the side as she watches me. "What about you? You look tired, Chris. Are you okay?"

"Yeah." I take another sip of my tea, my appetite nonexistent. "I'm good. Just had a long week and haven't been getting much sleep."

"Everything okay?"

"It will be. It's just this case that I've been working on. It's a coordinated effort with divisions across Southern California. Looks like a trafficking expedition."

"Oh no." She stops with her sandwich only inches from her mouth. Setting it back down on her plate, she reaches across the table and places her hand over top of mine. "How many?" She knows exactly what this means, more girls that are going to need help. More traumatized victims.

"I've got three. Altogether, it looks like at least ten just from this area alone. There's no telling how many more that we don't even know about." Closing my eyes, I push the thoughts of Cypress aside. The thoughts that have haunted me all week about her being one of the victims.

"What's wrong?" She knows me so well, it's like she can read my thoughts even when I try to keep them from her. She doesn't need to get inside my head, not after everything she's already dealt with in her past.

"It's nothing. Really."

"Chris?" She pauses and takes a sip of her drink. "Don't lie to me. I can tell you've got things going on in that head of yours. Sometimes it helps to talk it out."

I release a sigh in frustration knowing that she won't let me get away without telling her what's going on in my head. She's right though, it will help to talk it out with someone. I haven't mentioned any of it to Cypress yet because I don't want her to worry or be frightened. "It's the girls." I take a sip of my tea to wet my suddenly dry mouth. "They were all taken from craft fairs and festivals. There are no suspects. There were no witnesses. They just disappeared."

"I see." She looks at me quizzically while taking another bite out of her sandwich. "Let me guess." She takes a sip of her drink before wiping her hands again on her napkin. "You're thinking about Cypress. The fact that she used to do travelling festivals with her mother. And you're thinking about how easily she could have been one of these girls. You don't have to worry about her, you know. She doesn't do festivals anymore. She has a nice boutique safely located in Echo Park."

"How do you do that?"

"Do what?" She asks, lifting a single brow and smiling.

"How do you always know so much?"

"It comes with the territory. Looking after those that I care about requires knowing about who they care about also. You're not mad, are you?"

"No. I would have expected nothing less."

"Relax, Chris. Enjoy your weekend with Cypress. Don't stress over this case. You deserve to be happy."

"So do you." I tell her. Lifting my eyebrows, I turn my head to the table closest to the door and nod my head toward Braiden.

"I'm trying. I just haven't gotten there yet." She giggles as she picks up her glass. "Maybe this weekend will be the right time. Tomorrow is Valentine's Day after all."

"Yes, it is." I smile, thinking about the plans I have for tomorrow. I'll be spending the entire day with my Butterfly.

"Do you have plans tomorrow with Cypress?"

"Yes. I'm spending the day with her tomorrow. Then I'm cooking her dinner at my place."

"Are you?" She pushes her plate away and sits back in her seat. "What's on the menu then?"

"Cocoa rubbed steaks and twice baked potatoes." Her brows lift in question, and I chuckle. "I might have Googled the recipe."

"Well, it sounds wonderful. I hope you have a good time." I watch as she grabs her purse and jacket from the bench next to her and drapes the jacket over her arm. She places her palm flat on the table before standing. "I have to go. Thank you for having lunch with me, Chris. Let me know if you need anything."

Standing, I pull Wendy in for a quick hug. "I will." Wendy has a team of security guards that help with her club, and she's helped out before on cases. She has a tech guy that's very good at tracking people down, finding people that don't want to be found. He hasn't been with her long, but from what I've heard from her he's really good at what he does. Her old guy, Will, landed himself in some trouble when he offered his assistance to his cousin a few months ago. That was another case I had the pleasure of working on, with Marie Tolson and Matthew Peterson. Marie's ex was an abuser and thought he still owned her. Will helped him track her down and abducted her, killing another one of Wendy's guards in the process.

Standing in place, I watch as Braiden stands and helps Wendy with her jacket. He walks out with her, his hand on the small of her back. I wait until I see their car pull away from the curb before grabbing my own jacket and walking out of the restaurant.

Checking the time on my watch as I step out onto the sidewalk, I decide to make a stop at the grocery store before going to pick Cypress up from her shop. I still need to get the ingredients for tomorrow's dinner, not to mention desert and flowers. Come to think of it, I don't think I have any candles either. I make a mental list in my head as I drive across town.

Dropping the groceries off at my apartment, I check my mail and say a quick hello to Mrs. Abernathy before leaving for Echo Park. I plucked a single daisy from the flowers I picked for tomorrow and have it sitting on the passenger seat next to me.

It's late enough in the afternoon when I arrive at Poppy Petals that I don't have to search for a parking spot for long. There's an opening right in front of the shop. Cypress will be closing the store in a few minutes, so I decide to stand outside and wait for her.

I'm leaning against the passenger door with the single daisy in my hand when she comes out of the shop, closing and locking the door behind her. Turning toward the street, she finally notices me and my heart swells ten times when I see the smile bloom across her lovely face. She skips over to me, heedless of the other people walking down the street. My arms open for her just in time to catch her as she throws herself at me, crushing herself against my chest as I bury my face in her vanilla scented hair.

"Damn, Butterfly. I missed you so much this week." My arms wrap around her tight enough to turn her into a part of my own body, squeezing tight enough that I fear I may break her. Five whole days of not being able to see this little woman has been absolute hell. I make a silent promise to myself not to go so long in the future, it's not like I have to travel far to get to her being that she lives right across the hall from me. Sure, we've sent text messages to each other over the last few days, but it isn't the same as hearing her sweet voice.

"I missed you too." She says quietly, her voice muffled against my chest. I reluctantly unwrap my arms from her and hold the flower up so she can see it. She grabs the daisy from me before throwing her arms around my neck and pulling me down to her.

My lips angle over hers perfectly and she doesn't hesitate to open for me, deepening the kiss immediately while my hands grab her waist and pull her close.

"What do you want to do tonight?" I ask her, pulling away and resting my forehead against hers, my eyes closed as I breathe her in.

"Umm." She pulls back and I can see that she's nervous. "I just want to be with you. I don't care what we do."

"How about we pick up dinner and just hang out at my place. Or yours. We can watch a movie."

She lowers her gaze and I wonder if she's embarrassed about something. "I don't have a TV."

"Oh." Placing a gentle kiss on her forehead, I move to the side and open the passenger door for her. "We'll watch a movie at my place then." I wait until she's seated before closing her door and walking around to the other side. "What are you in the mood to eat?"

"Pizza." She answers, her hands fidgeting in her lap.

"You really like pizza, don't you?" I chuckle as I turn the key in the ignition.

"I do. It was always the most convenient thing to get when I was growing up. I mean, even the gas stations make pizza."

"Okay." Reaching over the console, I grab her hand and lace our fingers together. "Pizza it is then."

Forty-five minutes later, we're walking into my apartment hand in hand with a large pizza loaded with meat and jalapenos. I lead her into my living room, skipping the dining table all together and setting the pizza down on the coffee table. I leave her sitting on the couch while I wander to the kitchen for two bottles of water and napkins. I'm saving the wine for dinner tomorrow.

"This is a nice apartment," she says as I walk back toward her, my arm outstretched to hand her a bottle.

Reaching out for a slice of pizza, I sit on the couch next to Cypress. "Thank you," I say, taking my first bite. Pulling the pizza away, I reach up with my other hand to break the string of cheese that's connecting my mouth to the gooey dough. I watch out of the corner of my eye as she looks around nervously. I don't miss how her eyes continue to focus on the sliding patio door. "I like it here, been here seven years already. It's small but it's enough for me."

Cypress leans forward and grabs her own slice of pizza before sitting back on the couch. "So, what should we watch?"

Tossing the rest of my slice back into the box, I grab the remote and turn on the TV, navigating to the guide to find movie listings. We select a romantic comedy that I haven't seen before.

"I don't get to watch movies very often. I don't like going to the theater and I don't have a TV. I prefer to read books to be honest."

"Ah." Grabbing my water bottle, I take a long sip before putting it back on the table. "I don't have much time to read. Most days, I'm too tired to even watch TV when I get home from work."

"Oh no. I have to make time to read, it's my escape from my real life."

Tilting my head slightly, I turn to look at her and wonder what she needs to escape from. I don't ask her though, she'll open up to me when she's ready. "What do you like to read?"

"Anything really. But mostly romance." My eyes focus on the way her cheeks turn the slightest shade of pink at the admission. I don't know why she would be embarrassed if that's truly what she wants to read. There's nothing to be ashamed of.

"I see." Holding my arm out, I trail the back of my knuckles down the pink of her cheek, loving the warm feel. She leans slightly into my touch, not enough to have noticed it with the naked eye, but enough that I could feel the added pressure against my fingers. "I don't remember seeing any bookshelves in your apartment."

"Oh, no. As much as I love books, I don't have space to be storing them. I read far too many to try to find shelf space for them all. I use my phone mostly, or my Kindle."

We eat in silence for several minutes while watching the movie. Or try to anyway. I'm much too aware of the distance between us as we sit side by side on the couch, our legs touching. She keeps her hands folded in her lap as if she's afraid of touching me, but her outer thigh keeps pressing harder and harder into my own.

I can't take it anymore, my control is already stretched so thin that it's starting to fray at the edges. The more I try to focus on the movie, the more I remember the taste of her from last weekend. The more I want more of that taste on my tongue, my lips. With a shaky finger, I sweep a fallen strand of her hair away from her face, tucking it gently behind her ear. She turns her eyes to mine, pure innocence gazing back at me. I can practically feel the waves of desire rolling off her.

My palm rests softly against her warm cheek, my thumb caressing her cheekbone as she closes her eyes and presses back against my hand. Her lips part slightly on a sigh before she pulls her bottom lip between her teeth and bites hard enough that I can see the skin whitening around the bite. With a growl rumbling low in my throat, I lean down and kiss the corner of her mouth. She releases her bottom lip and I immediately suck it between my lips, causing her to moan softly. That sound alone sends a shiver down my spine that I can't refuse.

Grabbing Cypress by the waist, I position her with quick movements so she's straddling my lap, facing me completely. Her eyes open wide in shock from being moved so easily but she quickly relaxes against me, her hands resting on my shoulders. Keeping one hand on her waist and the other going to the nape of her neck, I pull her down for another kiss and crash my mouth against hers. I immediately deepen the kiss, releasing my own animalistic sounds as her taste explodes on my tongue.

Cypress presses down against me as she slowly begins to rock her hips back and forth and I know she can feel my desire pressing against her, only separated by a few layers of clothing. Her hands move to the buttons on my shirt as I break away from her mouth and trail open mouth kisses across her jaw and down her neck. She throws her head back to give me more access to her throat and I scrape my teeth against the sensitive skin, feeling her pulse beating wildly against my lips.

With trembling fingers, she releases several of my buttons exposing my chest before thrusting her fingers beneath the fabric. The warmth coming from her palms as they ghost across my flesh entices another growl to form in my throat and I want more.

Leaning forward enough to pull my back away from the couch, I grab my shirt on either side of the buttons running down the front and yank. Buttons fly in every direction, I can hear them pinging off the wall and the floor like spilled ice chips, but I don't care. She helps me to push my shirt off my shoulders and down my arms as I lift my hands back to her face, angling her just right to taste her lips again.

Her palms rub over my pecs and down my abdomen before circling around the sides and running back up my ribcage. Her rocking gets harder and more demanding against me and I'm afraid if she keeps it up, I'll end up embarrassing myself. I move my hands to her hips to slow her movements and she moans in protest but stills for several seconds. Moving my hands to her waist, I pull her shirt out of the waistband of her skirt and lift slowly, trailing my fingers up her sides and delighting in the tremors I can feel moving through her body.

She lifts her arms as I break our kiss long enough to raise her shirt over her head, tossing it toward the TV without a care as to where it lands. I cup her breasts, one in each hand, and marvel at the fullness of them. The way they perfectly fit the size of my hands without spilling over. The way her nipples harden against my palms as I squeeze and massage the rounded globes. My lips trail down her neck to her collar bone as I pinch the front clasp of her bra between two fingers, releasing her breasts from their confinement. My mouth homes in on one of her rosy, pink nipples, pulling it into my mouth with a steady, pulling suction. She nearly screams in response to my actions, and it spurs me forward.

Her hands leave my sides to fist her fingers into my hair, holding me against her breast as I suckle each one in turn as if devouring my last meal. My hands trail up her legs, lifting her long skirt in the process until it's bunched at her hips. Cupping one hand against her pussy, I can feel her wetness soaking through her panties and nearly lose it like an adolescent teenager. She rocks in earnest, pressing harder against my hand and her fingers tighten in my hair, pulling at the root. The pain urges me on, anxious to see where this all ends.

I coax one finger under the elastic of her panties, sinking into her tightness with a groan. Eagerly, I pump first one, then two fingers into her while circling her clit with my thumb. All the while I'm still pulling and sucking on her nipple, grazing my teeth against it occasionally, encouraging her to nearly squeal in pleasure. Her hands release from my hair, and she trails her fingertips down my body again, stopping at the button fastening my jeans. I don't stop her this time as she releases the button and begins to lower the zipper.

Lifting my hips slightly, she pushes my jeans below my hips, and I hear her gasp when she realizes that I've gone commando beneath the denim. The way she wraps her hand around my cock, rubbing her thumb over the slit to spread the wetness that's beaded there, has me speeding my efforts and thrusting my fingers into her harder, faster. I release her nipple with a pop and pull my head back to look at her. She's beautiful, with her head thrown back, her eyes closed and her mouth hanging open.

"Like this." I wrap my hand around hers, tightening her hold on my cock and moving her in slow, steady movements. Showing her exactly how I like it. There's no stopping it now, the beast crawling below the surface is prowling now, nearly out of control. "Cypress..." Her name is a prayer on my lips, my desperation for her evident.

"Oh, God!" She nearly screams when she breaks apart in my arms. It's nearly my undoing. Without thinking, I grab her by the waist and lift her up before slamming her down on my cock, sheathing myself in her to the hilt in a single thrust. We both moan in unison at the force of our connection, the feeling of greatness between us. She doesn't hesitate to move against me, rocking her hips back and forth, riding out her pleasure against me.

My hips thrust with her, our movements fluid and perfectly choreographed as if we've been doing this for thousands of years. Her body presses against mine, her breasts crushed against my chest as our mouths collide in a tangle of teeth and tongue. Wrapping my arms around her waist, I pull her tight against me and continue my movements, rocking into her roughly in a daze. My brain is clouded with lust and desire as the sensations overwhelm me completely. She cries out my name, her voice ringing loudly through the room and bouncing off the sliding door of the patio and for once I'm thankful that we don't have more neighbors on this floor.

The feeling of her pulsing against me is my undoing and I break down, unable to contain it anymore. Pulse after pulse, I empty myself deep inside her. I come so hard I don't think I'll ever be able to stop, I've never felt this way with anyone before in my life. The euphoria that sweeps through my entire body, not just a pleasant sensation in my cock like what I'm used to, but a deep, soul searing pleasure that etches itself deep in the marrow of my bones. We sit with our arms wrapped tight around each other, our foreheads pressed against each other, as we struggle to catch our breaths and slow our heartrates.

It's only when I feel the wetness rolling down my balls that it occurs to me that this was probably the best sex I've had in my entire life. Probably made more so for the fact that…

"Shit. We forgot a condom."

Chapter 8

Cypress

"Shit. We forgot a condom," Chris says, his breath fanning across my mouth.

Opening my eyes, still panting for breath, I pull away from him and look into his eyes. "It's okay." I place my palm against his cheek. "I'm on the pill."

"I'm so sorry." He kisses my cheek. "I wasn't thinking." He kisses me again, this time on the tip of my nose. "I swear, I've never done that before. I've always used a condom. I would never endanger you like that."

"It's okay. I trust you." Leaning in, I kiss him on the mouth softly. His arms tighten around my waist, and I melt into him. I never want to move from this position, just to feel his arms caging me in and keeping my demons at bay. I've never felt safer in my entire life than I do at this moment.

"Come on." He pushes me from his lap, helping me to stand on steady legs. Standing, he grabs my hand and pulls me behind him. "Let's get you cleaned up."

My heart speeds up, beating against the inside of my ribcage. I don't say anything as I allow him to lead me down the hallway and around the corner to his bathroom. He leans in and starts the shower to heating while helping me out of my skirt and panties, my ballet flats already having been kicked off somewhere in the living room.

He holds me under the hot shower spray as he kisses me thoroughly, dragging his mouth across my jaw and down my neck. Pulling back, he lathers the shampoo into my long hair, my entire body relaxing under his touch. Shivers run down my spine as he massages my scalp, taking extra care to run his fingers through my hair. After rinsing, he lathers soap all over my body, massaging my breasts with his soapy hands. He cleans me everywhere, my entire body down to my feet. When he's done, I repeat the gesture on him.

Working my hands over his body, I take time to trace his muscular frame and run my fingers over each of his tattoos. He has a lot of them, covering one entire arm, half his torso, and down one leg. It's almost as if he was dipped in ink the way the line cuts down the center of his chest and abdomen, leaving one entire side of his body untouched. I've never seen anything like it. The tattoos stop at his wrist, the base of his neck, and his ankle on one side of him. There's no real theme to it, it's a collage of different scenes and designs. But at the same time, it's the most beautiful thing I've ever seen.

Some of the lines on his chest look almost like swirling smoke, others like flames. There are no colors to the tattoos, everything is done in various shades of black ink, but it's amazing. Turning him around to wash his back, I see the ink was continued there as well. Again, the ink stops at the middle, a straight line running down the length of his spine. He's even covered on one hip, one rounded cheek of his ass, and down the back side of that leg. He's completely covered on the entire left side of his body.

How did I not notice this when I tore his shirt off of him earlier? There's so much to look at here, I don't think I will ever be tired of seeing it. I could look at him every day for the rest of my life and see something different on his body that I hadn't seen before. I want to ask him about it, I want to know if there's a story behind all this artwork, but I know he'll tell me about it when he's ready.

Still kneeling on my knees when he turns back to face me, I look up at him through my lashes and wrap my fist around his already hard cock. My other hand comes up to cup his balls and he throws his head back with a growl. I massage his balls, lightly squeezing and pulling them as I stroke my hand up and down his shaft, running my thumb over the bead of moisture gathered there. Licking my lips, I wonder what he tastes like. I've given head before, not because I wanted to but because it was expected of me. This is different though, for the first time, I want to do it because I want to make him feel good.

My tongue runs around the broad head of him before I pull him into my mouth. He's long and thick, and I know there's no way I can fit all of him in, so I keep my hand wrapped around his base and take him as deep as I can. Swallowing around him, I try to ignore my gag reflex. It's almost impossible the first time he bumps the back of my throat and I gag a little before pulling back.

His hand comes to the back of my head, fisting my hair in his hand. But he doesn't push me, he isn't trying to move me in any way. He's just supporting me, almost holding me so he doesn't fall over. Peeking up at him, I see he's watching me, and it turns me on like I've never been turned on before. I moan around him and watch as his stomach muscles tighten before I start moving on him again. His abdomen and thighs are practically shivering as I bob my head back and forth, all the while stroking him and rolling his balls in my other hand.

I listen as his breathing quickens and watch his abdomen tighten up, but I don't pull back. His other hand comes to the back of my head, holding me still but not pushing against me at all. He isn't using any force with me, he isn't moving against me in a rough way like I've known men to do in my past. With a deep grunt, he releases into my throat, and I take the time to swallow him down. As soon as he finishes pulsing against my tongue, I release him with a pop and stand up facing him.

He wraps his arms around my waist and pulls me into him, crashing his mouth against mine. I gasp in shock of the sudden movement, and he pushes his tongue into my mouth. I return the kiss eagerly, sure he can taste himself on my tongue.

"Fuck, you're amazing," he says, breaking the kiss and leaning his forehead against mine. He's still practically panting for breath, and I smile, excited at the fact that I did that to him. "Stay with me tonight."

"Okay." I almost hesitate to answer him because I've never been in this apartment before. He has a patio and no bars on his windows so I'm not sure if anyone would be able to get in while we're sleeping. But I feel so safe with him, I know he'll keep me protected.

Stepping out of the shower, Chris wraps me in a towel and turns me away from him. He pulls my hair to my back and begins brushing it softly, being careful to release the tangles without causing me pain. One of the downsides to having my thick wavy hair is that it's always tangled. And it's only made worse from being wet.

After he gets the tangles out of my wet hair, he leads me to his bedroom and grabs a t-shirt from the top drawer of his dresser. Tossing it to me, I catch the shirt in the air and slip it over my head, all the while watching him as he pulls on a pair of tight, black boxer briefs. He walks to the bed and turns down the sheet, holding it out for me to crawl in before he settles himself behind me.

Wrapping me in his arms, he pulls me into his chest and kisses the top of my head. We don't say anything, the only sound in the room is our breathing. I take a final look around the room before closing my eyes and relaxing into his hold.

When I wake in the morning, I'm disoriented and struggling to focus on my surroundings. It takes me several minutes to remember that I'm not in my own apartment. It's only when I feel the soft kisses on my shoulder that I remember falling asleep in Chris' arms. Closing my eyes, I lean my head further into the pillow to give him more room to caress my neck. He kisses me softly before dragging his teeth down the side of my neck and biting softly were my neck and shoulder meet, sending shivers down my spine and causing goosebumps to break out all over my body.

Feeling his hardness pressing into my backside, I reach my hand back and stroke him lightly over his boxers. He groans low in his throat as his teeth clamp onto my earlobe. "Good morning, Butterfly," he whispers seductively in my ear. Raising my hand enough to reach his waistband, I slip my hand down his boxers and wrap my fist around the hard length of him, grabbing him hard enough to make him moan, just like he showed me last night on the couch.

"Good morning," I whisper back.

He doesn't say anything else, just lifts his hips from the mattress and kicks off his boxers. Grabbing my leg, he raises it up and pulls it over his, entering me slowly from behind. This angle is different than the one I felt last night, even though I was sitting on his lap at the time. This angle has him hitting a different spot inside me that has me moaning and begging for more right away.

I arch my back slightly to give him a better angle, allowing him to push even deeper, and he doesn't disappoint. He takes his time, stroking in and out of me in long, steady movements. One of his hands is pinching and pulling on a nipple through the cotton of the t-shirt I'm still wearing, the other palm flat against my belly and pulling me into him. He begins to lower the hand on my belly and presses on my clit with one finger, moving it in slow circles and driving me wild. It doesn't take more than a few minutes and I'm practically screaming his name.

He follows me quickly, groaning my name before biting down on my earlobe and pulling it into his mouth. I turn my head enough to meet his lips and he kisses me deeply, passionately, before pulling away and walking out to the bathroom. He comes back a few minutes later wearing a pair of faded denim jeans with holes in the knees and carrying a damp washcloth. I lay on my back, stunned by the action, as he cleans me up. Again, this is something that I'm not used to with a man taking so much care of me.

"What are you doing today?" He asks as he tosses the washcloth toward the hamper in the corner of the bedroom.

"I don't have any plans." I pull myself into a seated position, flinching lightly at the delectable soreness between my thighs.

"Spend it here. With me." He looks almost vulnerable when he says it, as if he's afraid I'll reject him and run away.

"Okay." Because I'm so great at coming up with words in awkward situations. "I just need to run across the hall and change my clothes."

"Okay. I'll leave the door unlocked for you. Just come back in when you're done."

He smiles at me as he reaches his hand out to help me off the bed. He kisses me on the cheek before leading me out of the bedroom to find my clothes from last night. Grabbing my discarded clothes, I walk out of his apartment and unlock my door. Turning back, I see he's standing in his doorway watching me and I smile at him over my shoulder as I walk inside and close the door.

I rush through my morning routine – brushing my teeth, pulling my hair up into a ponytail, and changing into a pair of yoga pants and a tank top. I grab a cardigan before going back to Chris' apartment for just in case he has plans on going anywhere else today. I don't know what he has planned, but I want to be prepared at least.

When I get back to Chris' apartment several minutes later, he's standing in his small, galley kitchen making breakfast. "I wasn't sure what you wanted to eat, but I have scrambled eggs and toast."

"That sounds wonderful." I help him grab the plates and silverware, and the coffee that he made while I was gone. He leads me out through the living room and onto the patio.

"I hope you don't mind, but I like to sit out here in the mornings. The view is amazing, and I think you'll like it."

I follow him out and set my plate and coffee down on the patio table before sitting across from him. "Oh, wow. This is amazing." The back side of the apartment building is like a garden oasis. There's even a fountain in the middle of it. "I never knew this was here."

"Yeah." He says before taking a sip of his coffee. "It's like a secret garden. It's just hidden by these buildings. Only people that live here know about it."

"I've been here for three years, and I didn't know about it."

"That's because you're on the wrong side of the building."

"That's true, but I like it on my side of the building."

"But you don't have this wonderful view, you don't have as many windows on that side to even look out of."

My breath catches in my throat, my hands instinctively move below the table to fist together in my lap. He doesn't know. He couldn't possibly understand.

"Hey." He reaches out and places his palm against my cheek. "What is it?"

"Nothing. I'm sorry."

"Cypress. Please don't shut me out. You can tell me anything, you know."

"It's just…" I hesitate. The look in his eyes is so sincere, so caring. I don't want to shut him out but how will he ever understand? "I like my apartment. I like not having many windows and no balcony. It's safe… safer." I watch as his brows furrow, causing a wrinkle on the skin between them. Like he's trying to understand what I'm saying but not quite getting it.

The wrinkle smooths itself out and he stands, walking around the patio table and kneeling in front of me. Placing a palm against my cheek he says, "I understand. Just know that you're safe when you're here, with me. Nothing is going to get into this apartment, Cypress. No one will see you through these windows."

I release a breath that I hadn't realized I was holding and my eyes close of their own accord. Like a weight lifted off my shoulders. "Thank you," I whisper as he presses his lips against my forehead.

He looks in my eyes and chews on his lip for several minutes as if he has something else that he wants to say but he doesn't. I'm sure he wants to know more but I appreciate that he's not pushing the issue. I appreciate that he's giving me that time, letting me wait until I'm ready to tell him my story. But will I ever be ready, will I get to the point that I'll be able to tell him my truths? I don't even know if I'm ready to know my own truths yet.

I watch him later in the afternoon while he's cooking dinner. He looks comfortable in the kitchen, something that I've never been very good at. I mean, yeah, I can cook frozen dinners in a microwave. But when it comes to actually cooking, I'm at a loss. Growing up in a camper, I didn't really have a chance to use a kitchen or a real stove. I never really learned how to cook anything.

Watching Chris move around his kitchen, me standing with my hip leaning against the doorway, I could get used to this. When he finishes, I watch him set the table with flowers and candles. We have red wine with our dinner which he says is cocoa rubbed steak. Cocoa, can you believe it? I never would have thought of using cocoa on steak but it's delicious. "Mmm," I moan around a bite of my steak. "This is amazing."

Opening my eyes, I see Chris watching me closely, his eyes open wide and focused on my mouth. He's barely touched his own food and when I see him watching me so closely, I can feel the blush heating my face. "If you keep moaning like that, I'm not going to be able to let you finish eating."

Turning my gaze back to my own plate, I try my hardest to eat without making any more noise. I decide to start conversation instead. "So, let's talk then."

"Okay." He takes a bite of his steak and closes his eyes. "Wow," he says around a bite of his own steak. "You were right, this is good." He finishes his bite and washes it down with a sip of his wine. "So, what did you want to talk about?"

"Well, you know what I do during the week. But what about you? What kept you so busy this last week." He looks up at me and chews the inside of his cheek for a minute.

"Do you really want to know?"

"Of course. I want to know everything about you." I realize as soon as I say it that I mean it.

"Okay." He takes another sip of wine and starts cutting another piece of his steak before talking again. "You know I'm a detective." I nod my head in response while taking another bite. "I mostly work with cases involving women." I tilt my head and lower my brows, looking up at him. I didn't know that. "Abuse victims, abductions, things like that." He takes another bite and takes the time to chew before continuing. "I got a new case on Monday that's been a little rough and it kept me pretty busy all week."

"Is it a big case?"

"I wouldn't say a big case, just a lot going on. Do you remember the fair at the park last weekend?"

"Yeah. The craft fair."

"There were a few women that disappeared from it."

"What?" I ask breathlessly, the shock evident in my voice.

"Yeah. Apparently, they disappeared without a trace. There were no witnesses, no leads. Turns out there have been several that disappeared under similar circumstances all across Southern California, so I've been working with other divisions. We're thinking some sort of trafficking is involved."

"Oh my God." I push my plate away, suddenly losing my appetite. The timing of this is all wrong. I started getting texts from Jase a couple weeks ago and I've been ignoring them. Now this, it's too much of a coincidence. I don't know what to do.

"Hey." He reaches across the table and places his hand over mine. I grip his fingers tightly, still not looking up from my plate. I don't want him to see the guilt written in my face. "It's okay. I know it's probably too much for you to take in but it's going to be okay." He's completely misreading my emotions and I don't have the heart to tell him. "Don't worry about it. Okay?"

I just nod my head a few times but don't say anything else. He doesn't push me to say anything. After cleaning up the dinner dishes, we curl up on his couch together and watch movies for a while.

"I have to leave early for work in the morning. Do you want to stay again tonight?"

"I think I'll go back to my apartment."

"Okay." He kisses my forehead before standing and helping me to my feet. "I'll walk you home."

I giggle as I stand from the couch. "How chivalrous of you." He holds my hand, our fingers laced together, as we walk across the hall. He stands with me and waits for me to unlock my door.

"Thank you for spending the weekend with me." He bends down and kisses me sweetly. I open for him and wrap my hands around his neck, deepening the kiss. When he pulls away, I see everything in his eyes. Love. Concern. Desire. I'm falling for this man so fast my head is spinning and I'm sure he can see it in my eyes too. "Happy Valentine's Day." He whispers with a slight smile.

"Thank you, Chris. I had a great weekend." Before either of us can say anything else, I back into my apartment. He stands and watches as I close the door. I don't hear his door close until after I've locked my own.

After a shower, I lay in my bed wondering if I can help him at all with his case without giving up too much of my own past. I can't help but wonder if Jase is involved at all. I'm worried what Chris will think of me if he is.

Chapter 9

Chris

Every night, for the past week, I've been haunted by the look on Cypress' face when I told her about the case I'm working on. I can't help but wonder if she feels the same way I do, that it hits a little too close to home for her. Couple that with her reaction to the windows and patio comment I made.

Hanging my head in my hands, I keep seeing the look on her face. She admitted that her apartment was safer because of her windows.

I haven't missed the fact that her apartment is the only one in the entire building with bars on the windows. I wonder if she had them installed when she moved in three years ago. I try to think back to when I first moved into the building, but I can't remember if there were any bars on the windows then.

What happened to her to make her so scared of her windows? Why is she so afraid of someone seeing her that she has to keep her doors covered with curtains?

I want to know more about my Butterfly. I need to know her past in order to understand who she is today. I just don't want to push. I don't want to overstep my bounds.

I haven't gotten any further on my case in the last week then I did the week before. We still have no leads, no suspects in the disappearance of these girls. The only plus is that there haven't been any more disappearances. With no additional leads, that doesn't help with where to go from here. These are the cases that I dread working on, I don't like having nowhere to go. It rarely leads to a positive outcome for the victims.

It's been another five days since I've been able to see Cypress and I hate it. I hate that I live right across the hall from her, and I can't even make the time to see her in passing. My hours have been crazy since I've been handed this case to work on. That has to change. I really like this girl, I want to spend as much time with her as possible.

Walking her back to her apartment Sunday night was torture. We had a perfect weekend together that when it was over, it felt like the end of the world. I want to be a part of her world more and more every day that we're apart.

Checking the time, it's after four. I'm not getting any further on this case today than I have all week so there's no reason for me to stay here staring at the information on my computer for a minute longer.

Thirty minutes later, I'm pulling up to the curb a block away from Poppy Petals. I smile to myself as I step out of my SUV and wonder if she'll be surprised to see me.

Opening the door to the boutique, I hear the ring of the bell above my head, and I smile to myself. Closing my eyes, I breathe in the fragrance of vanilla and sandalwood, the familiar scent that surrounds Cypress every time I see her. I see the incense burner sitting on the counter next to the register and realize the fragrance is coming from there.

"I'll be right there," I hear her say from somewhere in the back of the shop. I walk to the counter and wait.

"Oh!" She exclaims as she walks out of the doorway in the back corner of the shop. I look up to see a huge smile spread across her face, my own smile widening in response. "What are you doing here?" She practically skips toward me, and I hold my arms out for her as she approaches.

"I wanted to surprise you." I catch her as she throws herself against me, pulling her tightly into my chest and burying my face in her vanilla scented hair. "We gotta stop doing this."

"Doing what?" She pulls away and looks up into my eyes, a look of concern in her own.

"Spending so much time away from each other. I can't do it. I miss you too much during the week."

"I know." She stands on her tiptoes, and I bend down to meet her in the middle for a quick kiss. Cupping her cheeks, I kiss her again, deeper this time. "I miss you too."

"I don't want to be away from you a single minute this weekend." I kiss her cheek, her temple, then her forehead.

"You know I have to be here tomorrow. I have to open the shop."

"I know. I'm coming with you."

"You're going to come with me tomorrow? You're going to spend the day in my boutique?"

"Yep." I kiss her again and run my hand down the long braid hanging down her back, fisting my hand around the end of it and pulling lightly to angle her head back for me. I bend down and nibble lightly on her neck where it meets her shoulder, and she mewls sweetly. She fists my shirt at my chest, holding me in place. I release a chuckle against her skin before standing upright.

"I'm glad you're here," She whispers against my chest when I pull her close.

"Me too." She wraps her arms around my waist, and I kiss the top of her head, wrapping my own arms around her shoulders and holding her for several minutes, not ready to let her go.

"Will you take me home?"

"Do you want to get something for dinner first?"

"No. I just want you to take me home." Pulling back to look at her, I see a sadness in her eyes that wasn't there before, and I wonder what caused it.

"Okay, Butterfly. Are you ready to go?"

"Yeah. Let me just grab my bag and I'll lock up." I watch as she walks away from me, going into the back room and disappearing from view for several minutes. She comes back with her bag slung over her shoulder and wearing her cardigan.

When she looks up at me, she smiles, but it doesn't reach her eyes. I want to ask her what happened today, but I'll wait until we're in the car on the way home.

I don't get an opportunity to talk to her during the ride, it just didn't seem like the right time to ask her. She keeps to herself the entire ride, her gaze turned out the passenger window. I keep hold of her hand on the center console while driving and she occasionally squeezes my fingers. Right now, she seems just content to be close to me, so I let it go. She doesn't even pull away from me when her phone buzzes in her purse several times during the trip across town even though I can see her get tense every time it does.

When we get to the apartment, I walk her to her door. "Do you want to watch movies tonight? Or order something for dinner?"

"I just want to sit for a bit and relax. It's been a long week."

"Oh." The smile fades from my face and I wonder if something happened.

"Don't leave though. I'd like it if you came in with me."

"Okay." I watch as she opens the apartment door and follow her inside. She covers the door with the curtain after locking it and turns to grab my hand, leading me through the hallway to her living room. We both sit on the couch, and I pull her into my side. She relaxes against me as I rub circles across her back.

Her phone buzzes in her purse on the coffee table a few minutes later and she tenses against me. I watch silently as she grabs her phone and presses the power button without reading the text. She tosses it back on the table when she's done turning it off and curls back into my side.

"Are you okay?" I kiss the top of her head.

"Yeah." She doesn't offer any more information than that and I can't help but wonder what's going on in that head of hers.

"You didn't want to read your messages?"

"No." Still tense, she leans her head against my shoulder and pulls her knees up beneath her on the couch.

My hands run absently up and down her back, dragging my fingers down her braid every few passes. After several minutes, her breathing begins to even out and I know she's fallen asleep. Pressing back against the couch, I put my feet up on the coffee table and hold Cypress tight against my chest. This is not a bad way to spend a Friday night after a long week of work.

I wake later to the sound of muffled crying. Rubbing my palms over my face, I wipe away the last traces of sleep and take a look around the dark living room. Cypress is no longer sitting on the couch next to me, there are no lights on in the room and the curtain over the window is thick enough that I can't tell if it's dark outside yet or not. Standing, I stretch my back and legs slowly to allow the blood to start flowing again through my body, I must have slept longer than I thought since my entire body feels like it's asleep.

The sounds of crying reach me again and I realize they are coming from the bedroom. Slowly, I walk over and try the doorknob, only to find it locked. Knocking softly, I try to get her attention. "Cypress?" Laying my palm against the door I wait for a response and get nothing. "Cypress? Are you okay?" Tapping again, I wait for several seconds, holding my breath at the same time and hoping to hear something other than crying from the other side of the door. Finally, after several long seconds, I hear her footsteps on the other side of the door.

The door opens, and Cypress stands just inside the room staring at her feet. Her hair is wet, and she's changed into yoga pants and a purple tank top with no shoes. She doesn't look at me, but I can tell by her ragged breathing and sniffling that she's been crying. Lifting her chin with my index finger, I angle her face so I can see her eyes. They're puffy and red and she's chewing on her bottom lip. Pulling her lip away from her teeth with my thumb, my other hand moves to wipe away her tears.

She practically launches herself at me at the same time as I pull my hand away from her cheek, instantly wrapping her arms around my waist. She shudders against me for several long seconds as her tears soak my shirt. My heart shatters at the sounds of her sobbing and I scoop her tiny body up into my arms and carry her toward the bed. Refusing to let go of her, I turn and sit on the edge of the mattress and cradle her against my chest. I don't say anything at first, just let her cry while offering my silent support.

"Do you want to talk about it?" She shrugs at my question, her arms tightening against me. "I'm a good listener." She still doesn't move away from me, but I can tell she isn't crying anymore so I take it as a win. Whatever it is, whatever is troubling her, I just want to take it from her. I want to protect her from whatever it is that has her this upset. "It's okay," I whisper against her ear, pulling her tighter into my chest. "You can just cry if you need to cry. It doesn't bother me." I feel her tense beneath my arms. "Crying is just your eyes telling me something is wrong, even if you can't find the words to explain it. And I'll be here to help you pick up the pieces when it passes. I'll listen when you're ready to talk. But for now, I'll just hold you." She nods her head against my chest, and I bend down to kiss the top of her head.

"Thank you," she says, quiet enough that I almost don't hear her.

"For what?"

"Being here.

"Hey." She finally looks up at me then. "There's nowhere else I'd rather be." Holding her chin between my thumb and index finger, I kiss her softly on the lips and marvel at how sweet she tastes even through the salt of her tears. "Are you hungry?"

We both laugh when her stomach growls loudly in response.

"Come on." Standing, I help her to her feet before taking her hand in mine. "I have all the fixings for spaghetti in my apartment. Unless you have something here that you'd rather cook."

"Oh no." She follows me out of the bedroom. "I can't cook. I mean, I can heat a frozen meal in the microwave or cook a frozen pizza but that's about it."

"Well, surely you can boil water, right?" I smile down at her as I pull her out into the hallway.

As it turns out, which I find out thirty minutes later, the answer to my question is no. She can't even boil water. Shaking my head slowly side to side, I pour the lightly toasted spaghetti noodles into a bowl and sort through them to remove the darker colored ones. We only end up losing about a third of the noodles.

"I think we're still good." Moving toward the stove, I pour the remaining pasta into the pan of sauce and mix it all together.

"Thank you."

"What is it with you constantly thanking me?" Moving to set the bowl in the sink, I bump her hip and she jumps out of the way with a giggle.

"I don't know. Just seems like you're always doing something for me to thank you for."

"Hmm," I start before grabbing the plates and forks from the counter and serving us each some spaghetti. She follows me to the small table set along the edge of my living room, against the wall separating the living room from the kitchen.

"Not eating outside tonight?" She takes the seat across from me.

"No." Walking back into the kitchen, I grab two glasses of tea and walk back out with my arm extended, handing her one of the glasses. "I figured we could stay inside tonight. The view is much better in the morning anyway. Not as much to see at night."

"Okay." She takes a sip of her tea and sets the glass down on the table. I watch her for a few minutes as she twirls the spaghetti around her fork, getting the perfect mouthful before taking a bite. She even makes eating spaghetti look attractive.

Smiling to myself, I twirl my own spaghetti and take a bite, struggling to keep the noodle from dragging along my chin and making a mess. Of course, I fail miserably, and the spaghetti noodle breaks before making it to my mouth then lands in the center of my chest, on my white shirt. Shrugging my shoulders, I take another bite while Cypress giggles at me. "Are you laughing at me?" I look up at her, my eyebrow raised in question and my fork halfway to my mouth.

"Nope." She shakes her head while twirling her fork, gathering another bite of her own. She looks up at me, her lips pursed tightly leaving her adorable dimples on full display. Narrowing my eyes at her in mock agitation, I place the forkful in my mouth and chew slowly.

Her eyes lower slowly from my eyes to my mouth then to my chest where the spaghetti sauce has soaked into the fabric of my shirt. She blinks once and looks me in the eye as she raises the fork to her mouth. I watch as she pauses, the fork only inches from her lips, her eyes still locked on mine. She lowers the fork to her chin and drags the spaghetti down her neck, leaving a trail of red sauce all the way down into her cleavage. "Oops," she whispers before raising the fork and placing it into her mouth.

My head shakes slowly, my tongue sweeping over my bottom lip as I imagine the taste of the spaghetti sauce combined with the sweetness of her skin. Setting my fork on my plate, I push my chair away from the table and stand. Walking around to the other side of the table, I grab her chair and spin it toward me, careful to cage her into the seat with my hands on either side of her legs. Bending at the waist, I lick the sauce from her skin starting at her chest and slowly working my way up to her chin.

"You seem to have made a mess," I whisper against her mouth before nipping at her bottom lip. "Let me help you." Releasing her chair with one hand, I grab her fork and drag the tines through the sauce on her plate. Bringing the fork to her cheek, I leave a trail of sauce from her ear to her mouth, dragging it slowly over her lips with my eyes locked on hers the entire time. Then I follow the trail with my tongue, crashing my mouth into hers and licking across her lips until she opens for me.

Her arms go around my neck as I deepen the kiss, tasting her sweetness with the tang of spaghetti sauce and moaning against her. Dragging her out of her chair, I lift her off the floor by her waist and she immediately wraps her legs around me. Her hands fist in my hair as I carry her through my apartment, our mouths constantly tangled in a mash of teeth and tongue. Releasing my hold on her as I step into the bathroom, she slides slowly down my body and steps away from me a few inches as I grab her shirt and rip it over her head, my breath catching in my throat when I see she isn't wearing a bra.

Reaching into the shower, I turn the water on to heat before wrapping my arms around her to loosen her braid. My fingers run freely through her long locks, and she closes her eyes, her palms lying flat against my chest to keep her grounded. She fists my shirt with both hands and pulls it free of my waistband, I reach one hand behind my head and pull the shirt off the rest of the way. Our eyes stay locked on each other as we kick our shoes and pants off before I grab her and lift her back off the floor.

As soon as she wraps around me, clinging to me like a koala bear, I step into the shower where she squeals at the hot spray against her back. Turning her away from the hot water, I press her back against the cool tile and drag my teeth down the side of her neck, biting lightly where her neck and shoulder meet. One hand kneading the rounded flesh of her ass, my other moves down her abdomen and lower to part her slick folds. Finding her already dripping, I plunge into her silky warmth and we both moan in unison.

Chapter 10

Cypress

I'm excited at the prospect of seeing more of Chris. This past weekend, he promised that I would see more of him, and he made true on his promise to spend the day with me at the boutique last Saturday. He spent the entire day here with me stocking shelves and helping me with product photos around the store. He was adorably out of his element but did it with a smile on his face the entire time.

The two of us did a video for my Instagram site where I taught him how to properly tie a t-shirt for tie-dye. It was adorable how determined he was to get it perfect the first time. I haven't posted the video online yet because I can't stop laughing at him antics long enough to get it edited properly. The way he chews on his bottom lip, or the tip of his tongue peaks out the corner of his mouth, when he's concentrating on the intricate ties. He made a huge mess when it was time to rinse out the dye. He turned the faucet on all the way and water shot out in all directions, soaking us both in the process. Of course, I got it all on video.

I honestly don't know what turned out better, the crazy design of his shirt, or the mess he made of both of us when he opened the dye powder packet with too much gusto. Powder went everywhere; in our hair, on our clothes, all over the workbench. I had to close the store early because of the mess. It took us too long to get everything cleaned up and I wasn't paying attention to the door. We didn't have anyone coming in anyway, it was a surprisingly dead Saturday. But at least it ended with pizza and a movie once we got back to Chris' apartment.

I admit, I didn't get any work done while he was here at the store. This weekend, I'm almost grateful to be here alone. Even though he wanted to come in with me, he got a call this morning from one of the other detectives working a similar case to his in San Diego. After dropping me off at the boutique, he left to drive south to meet with the detective. I haven't heard anything from him all day and I'm starting to wonder how his meeting has been going.

I've texted him a few times already and gotten nothing in return. I'm starting to get worried that either he hasn't made it there, or the meeting isn't going as expected.

Deciding it best to keep my mind from drifting to the absolute worst-case scenario, I've taken to rearranging my window display. Spring is in the air and it's time to incorporate some color to attract some of the foot traffic walking by during the day. I tie-dyed another picnic blanket in spring pastel colors and have it draped loosely along the bottom of the window. Several displays of brightly colored incense burners sit on the blanket with silk flower petals tossed throughout.

"Welcome to Poppy Petals." I greet as a customer walks into the store, the echoing metallic ding of the bell drawing my attention from my work. There haven't been many patrons to the boutique yet today, so I'm excited at the prospect of new business.

"Hello, sister." A deep, husky voice from my past sends a shiver down my spine. My eyes close of their own accord, my teeth clamping together tight enough to cause a pain in my jaw.

"I'm not your sister," I force out between my teeth. I refuse to turn around, I don't want to look at the man standing in the doorway. I don't want to see his face, his eyes already haunt my dreams. I see them in the shadows even when I know he isn't there. They follow me from a distance even though I know he's halfway across the country.

But he isn't, is he?

He's here. In my shop.

"Now is that any way to greet your brother?"

My eyes are still closed, but I can hear his footsteps as he moves freely around the inside of my shop. "What are you doing here?"

"You've been ignoring my messages," he answers back, his voice completely devoid of emotion.

"I have nothing to say to you." Opening my eyes, I focus my gaze out the store window, willing someone, anyone, to come into the shop. My eyes land on a familiar face sitting at an outdoor café table across the street and I pause in my searching, willing her to make eye contact with me. I don't know why her face is so familiar to me, but I want her to look at me and see the desperation in my gaze. See that I need help.

She looks directly at me, her eyes locking with mine and I try with everything in me to convey a silent message to her with my eyes. Asking, begging her for help. But instead, she looks away. I watch as she grabs her belonging and stands to walk away, all my hope walking away with her.

"You're wrong," he breathes into my ear, and I shudder realizing how close he is to me now. His chest moves against my back as he inhales slowly. "Your mother was disappointed you didn't call her back." I flinch away slightly when he runs his fingertips down the side of my neck. He tsks me as he pulls away from me and I hear the click of the door lock and see him flip the sign to closed out the corner of my eye.

"What are you doing?" I ask, my wavering voice betraying my nerves as my hands fist at my sides tight enough that I can feel the bite of my fingernails as they dig into my palms.

"I think it's time we caught up. Have ourselves a little chat."

"I told you, I have nothing to say to you."

"Perhaps. But I think you should at least listen to what I have to say to you." He steps closer and reaches out to grab my hand. I pull it away from him before he can make contact and realize too late that it was the wrong move. All I manage to do in fuel his hatred and anger toward me.

I don't have time to step away before he wraps his fingers tightly, with bruising force, around my bicep and pulls me roughly out of the window. I stumble backwards before falling hard on my butt, his hand still fisted around my bicep. He jerks me off the floor, pulling hard enough that I wonder if my arm will become detached at the shoulder.

"Chris will be back any minute to take me home. I think you should leave." I try to plead with him, hoping that I'm not telling him a lie.

"Yeah, I don't think so." He keeps walking around the counter, grabbing a chair with his free hand and dragging it, and me, into the back room. He pulls me around to face him and shoves me into the chair before kneeling in front of me, both of his hands resting on my knees. The unwanted intimacy of his touch causes my stomach to lurch. "It's so good to see you."

Keeping my eyes locked on his face, I wrap my arms tightly around my torso in a feeble attempt to hide from his gaze. "What do you want, Jase?"

"I told you." He looks me over from my feet up to my hair. Reaching out with one hand, he grabs the braid that's draped over my shoulder and runs his fingers down the length of it, wrapping the end around his index finger. "We need to have a little chat."

"Well get on with it already." My arms still folded over my chest, I tuck my hands beneath my armpits hoping that he doesn't see how they're shaking. I don't want him to see how his presence affects me. I don't like looking vulnerable in front of him.

"Come on," he starts. "We haven't spoken to each other in a long time." Releasing my braid, he cups my cheek in his hand, his thumb tracing my cheekbone. His hand is large enough that his fingertips reach behind my ear, tickling the baby hairs at the back of my neck. I bite my lip to keep from trembling at his touch.

There's a fire burning in his gaze as his eyes lock with my own. It isn't affection, or even adoration. It almost resembles contempt. I can clearly see it in his eyes, his desire to control me. To scare me into submission. I refuse to look away from him even as the burning hatred in his eyes eats away at my strength.

I should have known today was going to be rough. My horoscope this morning warned me that it would be a challenging day and to keep my loved ones close. Little did I know as I watched Chris drive away from my shop that I would be facing fear head on, alone.

Jase moves closer, his nose running down the length of my own, and it's all I can do not to pull away from him. I hold my breath but keep my eyes open the entire time. I refuse to close him out, keeping an eye on him so he doesn't have any chance to surprise me. He's already done that once today, wandering into my shop without me seeing him coming. There's no telling how long he'd been watching me already, how long he'd been hanging around the shop waiting for me to be here alone. "What do you want, Jase?"

"You," he answers without hesitation. His voice is strong and unwavering, laced with want and desire.

"You're disgusting." I actually do flinch away from him then, finally closing my eyes tightly to block out his sinister smile.

"You said yourself that I'm not your brother." His hand lowers back to my leg, gripping my thigh. His thumb moves back and forth, dragging the fabric of my skirt against the delicate skin at the bend of my knee.

"Please, just leave." Placing my hands against Jase's chest, I try to push him away, but he doesn't move. He stays in place like a stone sentinel. Jase is not a well-built man, but he is a solid man. He's the type of man that could put muscle on like a suit of armor, but he's always been too lazy to bother working out. It's never stopped him from picking fights though. He's always been good at throwing his weight around, using his size to his advantage. He's always been intimidating considering he's basically a six-foot solid brick wall.

"You think I don't know? You think I don't see you?" I wince at his choice of words. "I've always seen you, Cypress." He stands finally, removing his hands from my legs and stepping away from me. "This is a nice place." He spins around, his hands going into his pants pockets. "You seem to be doing pretty well on your own." I watch him as he turns back to face me. "It'd be a shame to see anything happen to it. Watch your back, sis." He winks at me once before turning and walking away.

Still sitting in the chair in my back room, I attempt to control the shivers wracking my entire body. I listen as he walks through the shop and out the front door. It takes me several more minutes to control my breathing before I stand and run to the front door to make sure it's locked.

With wobbly legs, I walk back to the register counter and grab my cell phone. I see a missed call and text from Chris, but I don't return either one. Instead, I clutch the phone tightly to my chest and sink to the floor.

Drawing my knees up to my chest, I lower my head and allow the tears to come. I knew it was only a matter of time. I've always known that Jase was still watching, keeping an eye on me even from a distance. It doesn't matter where I go or how much I try to survive on my own, he'll never stop. There's nothing I'll ever be able to do to get away from him.

The truth of my situation hits me like a punch to the gut and I can feel the splinters starting in my heart. I'll never be free of my stepbrother. No matter how hard I try to block him out of my life. To keep him from seeing me. I'll never be free of him.

Chapter 11

Chris

This has been a colossal waste of time. What I wouldn't give to be spending the day at Poppy Petals with Cypress. But instead, I'm standing here, in the middle of San Diego with a bunch of detectives that have no more evidence in the missing women's case than I do. "Why am I here?" I grit out between my teeth, tossing the folder of worthless information to the center of the conference table.

I already looked through the folder, the information similar to what I have in my own folder back in my office. No witnesses. No connection from one woman to another besides their weekend activities in rented booth space. A shudder runs down my spine as I think about my Butterfly and how she grew up. How easily she could have been one of these victims at one of the street fairs she worked at with her mother while growing up.

"I was wondering the same thing," Jackson, a detective from Beaumont, says as he leans back in his chair and crosses his arms over his chest. Everyone in this room can see his frustration clearly in his narrowed eyes as he looks at each of them one by one.

"Evidence suggests," begins Noah, a detective from here in San Diego, "that the girls have been taken across the border." He reaches to the middle of the table and pulls the folder closer to him before sitting at the head of the table.

"How do you figure?" Ethan asks as he paces anxiously across the small conference room. Ethan is a seasoned detective from San Bernadino. He's also the only one here that I've worked with in the past. He's good at what he does and has a big heart for his victims and their families. I sometimes wonder if his past is similar to my own. That perhaps there was someone close to him that was a victim.

"Lucas?" Noah calls out as he sits back and places his hands in his lap.

"Right." Lucas stands and walks around to the front of the conference room, smoothing the front of his shirt as he goes. Lucas and Noah are from the same agency and have obviously worked together before. "If everyone will have a seat, please, I'll be happy to explain."

Ethan stops pacing and moves to a seat across the table from where I'm standing. He and I both sit at the same time. He tips his chin in my direction before clasping his hands together on top of the table.

"Gentlemen," Lucas grabs a tablet off the table and turns his gaze to the large screen on the back wall. Immediately, the lights in the room dim and the screen glows white before loading a map of Southern California. I watch as brightly colored pins appear on the map while he talks. "Street festivals. Craft shows. Farmer's markets."

"What about them?" Jackson interrupts, clearly not seeing the relationship between each pin on the map.

"These are where the women were last seen," Noah answers before Lucas gets the chance. "Pay attention to the timeline." He nods his head toward the screen and each of us turn to watch the map again.

"Best we can tell," Lucas starts again. "The first one was taken from a craft show taking place in Palmdale. Two more disappeared the following day from a street festival in Pasadena, then three more the next weekend in Echo Park. From there, another was taken from Riverside, then two more from Temecula."

"They were headed south to the border," Ethan points out.

"Exactly," Lucas agrees. "The last three disappeared from a farmer's market in San Diego. That's a total of twelve girls taken over the course of a few weeks. Then it stopped. Judging by the direction they were headed and the timeline before stopping, I'm guessing they crossed the border. We need to look in Mexico."

"How the fuck do you suggest we do that?" Jackson jumps up from his chair, throwing up his hands in exasperation. "We have no jurisdiction there."

"I've been in touch with the Chief Investigator of the Federal Ministerial Police in Mexico City." Noah states. "The PFM is fully cooperating with us and has agents in the field currently. They'll keep us apprised of their findings."

"Right," I sigh. "And again, I ask. Why are we here?" I place my hands palms down on the conference table, my thumbs tapping out an unknown beat as the only display of my own frustration. "You couldn't tell us all this over the phone?"

Noah gives a half shrug as he leans forward and rests his elbows on the table, his fingers steepling together in front of his face. "We could have. But I thought you'd all want to be here yourselves to speak to Investigator Martinez."

"Who the fuck is that?" Ethan asks.

"He's the Chief Investigator leading the joint effort on the Mexico side of this investigation. And he's due for a call in about…" He pauses and looks down at his wrist. "Five minutes." The cocky bastard grins, actually grins, as he sits back in his chair and crosses his arms over his chest.

Just over two hours later, I'm finally pulling up in front of Poppy Petals. I'm so anxious to see my Butterfly that my skin is tingling, shivers running up and down my spine. Before I can get out of my SUV, I notice the closed sign displayed in the door and all the lights are off inside the shop. It's early afternoon and Cypress usually keeps the shop open until at least five on Saturdays.

Pulling my phone from my inner pocket, I check to see if I've missed any calls or texts from her telling me that she was going home early. Maybe she got sick and didn't want to hang out all day waiting for me to come pick her up.

Nothing.

I call her number and wait. She doesn't pick up after three rings and the call goes to voicemail. "Hi, Butterfly. It's me. I just pulled in front of your shop and see that you closed early today. Are you okay? Call me."

Chewing the inside of my lip, I place the phone back into my inner pocket and put the truck in gear. Pulling away slowly from the curb, I decide to head back to the apartment and see if she is home already.

My skin is still crawling when I step off the elevator and walk toward Cypress' door. I know before I even raise my fist to knock that she isn't home yet either. There's just enough light in her apartment to brighten up the peephole; it would be completely blacked out if the curtain were pulled over the door on the other side. She would never be in her apartment alone without the security of that curtain.

I knock anyway and wait for several seconds, leaning closer to the door to listen for any movement from the other side. My hands are fisted so tightly at my sides as I stand up straight and back away from the door that my knuckles are turning white. *Maybe I just missed her,* I think to myself. *Maybe she stopped at the store before coming home.* Pulling my keys from my pocket, I walk across the hall to my own apartment door.

I toss the keys on the side table next to the door while pulling my phone out of my inside jacket pocket. Leaving the door unlocked for just in case Cypress decides to stop by when she gets home, I move into the living room and lower myself into the sofa.

Me: *Hey Butterfly. Just got home. Wanted to make sure you were okay.*

Tossing my phone onto the coffee table, I rest my elbows on my knees and lower my head into my hands. The entire day was wasted today, no new information was revealed by talking to the other detectives. Nothing new after talking to Investigator Martinez either.

My day would have so much better spent being with Cypress at her boutique. That had been the original plan to begin with, spend the day with her and watch her make a video for her social media followers on a new tie-dye technique that she had seen on YouTube this week. She was anxious to try it but insisted on waiting until she was at the shop because she has more room to work there than in her tiny apartment. I've never had a creative bone in my body and have certainly not tie-died anything before, so I was looking forward to it.

After several minutes, and a short trip to the bathroom, I decide I should probably get some lunch. I didn't stop for anything in San Diego or before coming back home because I really wanted to catch Cypress still at her shop. I had hoped that maybe we could go out to dinner together after the shop closed.

I'm just putting the final touches on my cold cut when I hear a noise in the hallway outside my apartment. Moving silently through the hallway, I lean closer to the door and peer through the peephole. I watch for several seconds as Cypress fumbles with her keys, attempting to unlock her door before dropping them on the floor at her feet. *Something's wrong.* I think to myself.

My door is open and I'm practically launching across the hall before I have a chance to think about what I'm doing. Cypress jumps away from me, closing her eyes and holding her bag in front of her as if using it as a shield. I wince in response to her movement while internally chastising myself for scaring the shit out of her. *What the fuck happened today?*

"Hey," I start, my hands held up in capitulation and my voice soft and soothing. I know the signs of someone in shock and I don't want to scare her any more than I already have. I should have known better than to storm toward her after seeing how she was shaking so hard she couldn't even unlock her door. "It's me." I take a step closer, my hands still raised. "You're okay. Cypress, it's me."

No longer moving, my arms still raised slightly, I wait. I watch as she takes several deep breaths before cracking her eyes open one at a time. "Chris," she whispers, and time slows down.

My eyes widen and I have just enough time to convince my feet to move and my arms to reach for her as she starts to collapse like a Jenga tower that just lost one of its final foundation pieces. Her arms drop to her sides limply, the bag falling to the floor that she had only moments ago been holding up as a shield. Her knees buckle and her head falls back as if she can no longer support its weight on her shoulders.

My knees hit the carpet, my right shoulder slamming into the door of her apartment that remains locked because her keys are still on the floor and are now digging into my shin painfully. I manage to reach out with one hand to grab one of her arms and pull her toward me, using my other arm to catch her falling body behind her shoulders and keeping her from hitting the floor. Only one of us should be bruised from this encounter and I'll be damned if it's going to be her.

Pulling her in close, her head falls against my shoulder, and I lean my cheek against the top of her head. I have no idea what happened today to put her in this state, but there's no way in hell I'm going to let her stay by herself in her apartment to deal with it on her own. Lifting my right leg, I grab her keys that have carved an impression into my shin and put them in my pocket. Grabbing her bag next, I lay it across her stomach as I support her and stand slowly, stifling a moan at the pain in my knees where they hit the unforgiving floor. Thankfully, my door is still open so I'm able to walk into my apartment while supporting my Butterfly with both arms, kicking the door shut behind me as I move through the apartment.

I don't want to be far from her while she's unconscious – she shouldn't have to wake frightened and alone – but I'm still hungry and have a sandwich sitting on the counter in the small galley kitchen waiting for me. Laying Cypress on my sofa, I place a throw pillow beneath her head and brush her hair away from her face, kissing her softly on the forehead before I stand and step away from her.

Ironically, I wouldn't even have those throw pillows if it weren't for the Butterfly laying her sweet head against one. She surprised me one day not long ago when I came home and found the small pop of color on my tan sofa. She accused me of being boring with my decorating choices, or lack thereof. I guess they're useful after all for something other than creating an eyesore of brightness in my dully colored life.

Fine, they're not that bad. It isn't like she threw some fluffy hot-pink pillows around my living room. They're still somewhat manly in a dark blue and green plaid print.

Standing in the doorway separating my galley kitchen from the living room, I lean against the wall and cross my right ankle over the left. I keep an eye on Cypress as I take a bite of my sandwich. Something spooked her today and I wish I knew what it was. I've already eaten half of my sandwich before she starts to move in her sleep. She's shivering as if the air is too cold in the room. I guess it is getting cooler as the sun starts to set outside the patio windows.

Setting the rest of my sandwich down on the kitchen counter, I go to the hall closet to grab a blanket. Covering her up, I notice a slight bruise around her left bicep that I hadn't seen before. Wracking my brain, I try to remember if I had grabbed that arm when she was collapsing in the hall. A mental fist is bashing against my chest while I'm trying to figure out if I hurt her without meaning to. I'll never forgive myself for causing her pain.

The scene plays through my head like a video on slow motion – a benefit of a photographic memory that has helped me several times over the years. I realize after several minutes of replaying the events of earlier that I didn't even touch her left arm. There's no way I could have caused that bruise on her bicep. Looking closer, I can see the shape wrapping around her arm in the perfect impression of a hand. Someone grabbed her hard enough to leave a bruise.

My pulse skyrockets, my heart beating hard against the inside of my ribcage and my breath begins to quicken.

I'm pretty pissed off.

I want to know who did this.

Covering Cypress up gently with the blanket, I back away before I do something stupid like wake her up and demand answers from her. Instead, I grab my laptop and set it up at the table on the other end of the living room where I can keep an eye on my Butterfly. It's time to order a security system for that little shop of hers.

Chapter 12

Cypress

I wake slowly and know right away that I'm not in my apartment. The lights are off in the room when my eyes finally open, and there is no sun shining through the patio windows. I have no recollection of the time, whether it is late at night or early in the morning. The faint light on the other end of the living room illuminating Chris' face brings me peace and clears my mind of everything that happened earlier at the shop.

I remember the visit with Jase clearly. I remember wishing that he would just leave me alone and let me live my life in peace, without worrying about him lurking around a corner or in the shadows like I have for most of my life. I was still shaking when I got back to my apartment and remember not being able to get my key in the door to unlock it when someone came up behind me.

No. Not someone. It was Chris.

Ohmygod, I think to myself. I freaked out on Chris and now I'm waking up on his couch.

I completely blew off his call and text and he still came to my aid when I passed out in the hallway. And from the looks of it, he hasn't slept since I've been here.

How long have I been here?

Is it still Saturday?

Sitting up slowly, I watch as Chris lifts his gaze from the screen on his laptop. He watches me closely, not making a sound. As I stand and walk slowly toward him, he pushes his chair away from the table and I stop mere inches away from him.

God, he looks delicious in his t-shirt and stressed jeans. He isn't wearing shoes, his bare toes curling slightly into the lush carpet. He moves his hands to the seat of the chair and wraps his fingers around it as if fighting to keep from reaching for me. I can see the muscles in his biceps bulging and flexing against the sleeves of his shirt, his lips pursed together tightly but never breaking eye contact with me.

Damn, I could climb this man like a tree. Right now, I just want to get close to him. To show him how grateful I am for him being there when I got home. For picking up my shattered pieces when I fell apart like the weak girl that I've always been.

Reaching down to just above my knees, I gather my skirt and lift as I take another tentative step toward where Chris is still sitting and watching me. His eyes lower to my legs as the fabric raises, exposing the bare skin of my legs, and I see the muscles in his jaw clench as he presses his lips together in a hard line.

Damn, this skirt has so much fabric. Maybe it would have been better to just remove it, letting it drop to the floor. I've never been good at these seductive approaches. I'm learning as I go. But, God, do I want to learn.

I take a slow breath as I continue my approach, Chris' gaze lifting back to mine. I watch as his pupils dilate and his nostrils flare. He hasn't moved, aside from tilting his head slightly back to look up at me standing over him. His hands are still fisted against the seat of the chair tight enough that his knuckles are turning white.

I stop moving, close enough that the fabric of my skirt is touching his knees, and he still isn't moving. Obviously, he's letting me lead this show. Waiting to see how far I'm willing to go. Considering the day I've had, his patience is making me fall more in love with him.

Wait. What?

Well, I guess it was inevitable. I've been falling for this gorgeous tank of a man since he brought me home that first night nearly two months ago.

Shaking the thought away, I watch as Chris tilts his head slightly to one side and lifts a single brow in question. For some reason, that look makes me blush and one corner of my mouth lifts in a shy half-smile.

I'm close enough now, I straddle his lap and lower slowly to sit on his thighs. His hands immediately move to my waist to hold me in place and my fingers thread through his hair as I lower my mouth to his. The kiss is soft, tentative, my last bit of insecurity bleeding out. This will never do. He doesn't move as I break away and look at his mouth. I run my tongue over my bottom lip before pulling it between my teeth.

I can do this.

I crash my mouth back into his, more forceful and surer this time, and he opens for me immediately. Without hesitation, I deepen the kiss, claiming every inch of his mouth before sucking his bottom lip. A deep growl rumbles through his chest as his hands move from my waist to my back, pulling me tighter against him.

Seems like I've broken this man already as he begins to take over. His mouth is pressed tightly against mine in a desperate kiss. Almost a claiming or reaffirmation that I'm okay. I moan as he pulls my bottom lip between his teeth, and I can feel his arousal pressing against me.

Damn, I didn't think this through very well. There are still too many layers separating us.

He deepens the kiss again, pulling me tighter into his chest with both of his palms pressed flat against my back. Moaning again, I press my center harder against his lap. That awards me with another deep growl as he thrusts his hips upward. Even through the fabric separating us, I can feel his desire pressing against me in just the right spot.

Without warning, Chris moves to stand. My arms tighten around his neck and his hands move down to support my legs as they wrap around his waist. As well as possible given the amount of fabric bunched up from my skirt. Keeping his eyes locked on mine, he carries me through his apartment.

Placing a knee on his mattress, he lowers me softly to the bed before kissing me deeply. His hands trail up my sides, my arms lifting automatically when he breaks the kiss and lifts my shirt over my head. His mouth is back on mine as he reaches around me to unfasten my bra before sliding it off my shoulders and down my arms.

Trailing soft, open-mouthed kisses along my jaw and down my neck, Chris runs his fingertips over my breasts and down my ribs. He hooks his fingers into the waistband of my skirt and begins pushing it down my legs as he greedily pulls one of my nipples into his mouth before flicking it roughly with the tip of his tongue. After releasing with a pop, he continues his decent, trailing wet kisses across my abdomen and nipping lightly on my hipbone.

Settling on the mattress between my legs, Chris places his palms against my inner thighs and pushes them open. My head falls back against the bed, my breath releasing in a rush when I feel his mouth make contact with my most intimate area. He doesn't waste any time working into anything, just devours me like I'm his last meal.

Within seconds I'm writhing beneath him, my hands fisted in the sheets in a feeble attempt to keep me grounded. If eating pussy were an Olympic sport, he would definitely take a gold medal. He just keeps going and going. Continuously licking and sucking and nibbling his way through my sensitive folds, relentlessly bringing me back to the edge without giving me a chance to descend from my last blast into orbit.

Finally, he breaks away and places soft kisses on my mound. My breaths are still coming in short gasps as he works his way back up my body, leaving open-mouthed kisses along my belly and between my breasts. My hands finally peel away from the bedding and wrap around his shoulders as his mouth presses against my own. *When did he take off his shirt?*

Chris places one palm against my cheek, his thumb gently tracing my cheek bone and wiping away a tear that I didn't realize had fallen. Breaking his kiss, he pulls back enough to gaze into my eyes as he slowly pushes into me. He takes his time, moving back and forth through my wetness. His hips tilting in just the right angle to hit that sensitive spot deep inside, making me moan with each of his thrusts.

He continues to move, slowly in and out, as he angles his mouth over mine again. His tongue tangles with mine, the same rhythm as his hips as he continues to stroke us both closer and closer to climax. This is different than any other time we've been together. There's no urgency, no rush to the finish. This is unlike anything I've ever experienced. Not just the slowness of his movements. He's holding back like he's afraid of shattering my fragile existence.

He's making love to me.

My heart practically bursts as I'm overcome with emotion. He needs this as much as I do. He needs to not only know that I'm okay after the day I've had and the condition he found me in this afternoon. But he needs to show me that he is okay, too. I didn't even think earlier about what I had put him through by not reaching out to him. By not responding to him before coming home.

My hands smooth up his back and over his shoulders before cupping his face. His jaw is lined in stubble from at least a day's growth, and it tickles my palms. Our eyes lock, his brows soften and the line between them disappears, and I know he sees what I'm still too afraid to put into words.

I am without a doubt in love with this man. I never expected it to happen. I never thought I was worthy of anyone like him.

I can't change my past, but I can take control of my future. I still need to determine what direction my future is going to go. But I know that I want it to include him.

Chris is my fortress. My protector. My other half. I've been living a half-life for too long. I never realized what I was missing before now. But now I know that with Chris, my life is complete. My soul is intact. That only means there's one more thing I have to do.

I have to tell him about my past.

The sun is shining through the windows in the bedroom as I come fully awake again. I'm not alone on the couch this time. Chris is pressed against my back, his slow breaths matching my own. His arm is still wrapped around my waist, pulling me tightly against him. I can feel his erection pressing against my ass when I squirm, and he moans softly in my ear.

"Mmm," he moans when I try to move again. "Good morning, Butterfly." The sleepy rasp of his voice sends a chill down my spine and my arms break out in gooseflesh.

"Morning," I respond when I can find my voice. Mine isn't near as sexy as his first thing in the morning. I'm sure I sound more like a whimpering puppy. But as much as I would love to lay here and have him continue rasping in my ear, I have to get up. "I have to pee," I announce unceremoniously, and he immediately releases his hold on my waist.

Rolling away from him before sitting and throwing my legs over the edge of the bed, I rush to my feet so fast my head spins. Standing still long enough to right myself before I fall on my face, my feet shuffle along the carpet toward the bathroom.

After doing my business and washing my hands, I return to the bedroom to find it empty. My heart sinks immediately and I regret having to break the intimacy of the morning. I really wanted to repay him for his gentleness last night.

Damn bladder.

Stepping softly across the floor, a shudder runs through me at being naked and alone in the room. There are no blackout curtains on Chris' windows like there are on my own. Anyone could see me through the sheer fabric covering his windows and I can't stop my mind from imagining someone sitting across the oasis in his back yard with a pair of binoculars. I want nothing more than to cover myself and protect my dignity without knowing for sure if there is anyone out there or not. The chance of it being real alone are enough to force movement into my limbs.

Rushing over to Chris' dresser, I pull the top drawer open to find his t-shirts folded neatly inside. I grab the first one my eye stops on and throw it over my head before bending to grab my panties from the floor where he tossed them last night.

The smell of coffee and bacon pull me from the bedroom and toward the galley kitchen where Chris is standing over the stove in nothing but a tight black pair of boxer briefs. My gaze zeros in on his tight ass, accentuated by his movements when he turns the bacon in the pan with a pair of silicone tongs.

I don't realize a moan escapes my lips until he looks over his shoulder and catches me ogling his ass. *Oops.*

"I hope you're hungry." He interrupts my thoughts.

"Starving."

He places the tongs on a paper towel lined plate before turning fully to face me. I don't even move as he saunters over and places a soft kiss against my mouth. Stepping back, he runs his gaze down my body before chuckling softly. "Nice shirt."

Finally tearing my gaze away from him, I look down at the front of my shirt. "Detective. Cop-A-Feel." Well, it isn't wrong.

"A friend of mine gave me that. I mean, I guess he's a friend. I found his girlfriend after she'd been abducted, and we've been kind of close ever since."

"Really?" I ask as he turns back to the stove and starts cracking eggs into a pan.

"Yeah. Well, I guess she's actually his fiancé now. They're getting married next weekend. I was thinking of asking you to go with me to their wedding."

"Okay," I say breathlessly. I've never been to a real wedding before, but I've always wanted to. There's just something about the decorating and dresses that has always fascinated me. When my mom married David, she didn't have a wedding. I don't even know what I should wear to someone's wedding.

I watch for a few more minutes as Chris takes the bacon out of the pan and places it on the paper towel. "I made coffee." He says without turning around. "There's a cup on the counter for you if you want some. Go sit on the patio and I'll bring breakfast out in a minute."

Walking over to the counter, I grab a cup from in front of the coffee pot and doctor it up with sugar and cream. I like a little coffee with my sugar. I snag a small piece of bacon before turning to walk out.

"I saw that." Chris chuckles as I walk across the living room toward the closed patio doors. Without meaning to, I pause and look out the doors before making the decision to open them. I check every window and patio across the way for anyone that may be looking in this direction. I even check the courtyard below for possible voyeurs before finally opening the door and sitting at the table outside. Finishing off my bacon, I curl both hands around the steaming mug of coffee before taking a sip.

Chris saunters out with two plates – one in his hand and the other balanced precariously on his forearm – and a cup of coffee. Setting the coffee down on the table first, he grabs the plate on his arm and sets it in front of me. I smile at the bacon, eggs, and toast that he's laid down in front of me before picking up the fork laid across the toast.

"Thank you," I tell him before taking a bite of my egg. "This looks delicious."

"You're welcome." He takes the seat across from me and immediately picks up his own fork in one hand and a piece of toast in the other. I watch as he presses a corner of the toast into the yolk of his egg, coating it in the pasty yellow goo before taking a bite.

Looking down at my plate, I marvel at the perfection of his cooking. He made perfect eggs, the yolks still intact. I've never been able to make a perfect egg before. My yolks always break when I flip them, so I end up with scrambled every time whether I wanted them that way or not. I've never tried dipping toast in a yolk before since I've never had one to dip it in. Taking his lead, I pick up a slice of my toast and dip a corner into the yolk before taking a bite. My eyes close of their own accord, a moan rumbling deep in my chest in response to the flavor of the creamy yolk and crunchy, buttery toast. A culinary masterpiece.

"This has got to be my new favorite way to eat eggs." I say after finally chewing and swallowing my bite. Opening my eyes, I see Chris' eyes locked on my mouth from his seat across from me.

"You've never had over-medium eggs before?" He asks after blinking several times.

"Nope." I take another bite of yolk covered toast. "I can't make eggs like this. My yolks break every time."

"Hmm." He takes another bite before setting his toast down and grabbing a piece of bacon. "Maybe I'll teach you sometime."

"I'd like that." Neither of us say anything else as we finish our breakfast and coffee. We sit in peaceful silence for several minutes, looking out over the oasis below us and soaking up the warmth of the Southern California sun.

The tightness in my chest returns, similar to the feelings overwhelming me last night. I know we need to have a conversation about what happened yesterday, but I don't know if I can bring myself to start it. Rather than start talking, I grab the dishes from the bistro table and carry them into the apartment. Chris made breakfast, the least I can do is clean up.

Rinsing the plates and coffee cups in the sink, I'm placing them into the dishwasher when I hear the patio door close. Minutes later, I hear the shower starting in the bathroom. I finish cleaning up and wipe the splattered bacon grease from the stovetop before turning off the kitchen light and wandering into the bedroom.

The bathroom door is open and it's a temptation that I can't stop myself from giving in to. I walk slowly into the bathroom, pulling Chris' t-shirt over my head and stepping out of my panties. I pull the curtain back just enough to step in and watch as Chris soaps up his hair. His eyes lock on mine and a smile spreads slowly across his face.

He rinses the shampoo from his hair before trading me places and running his fingers through my hair as it gets wet under the spray of water. I stand, my hands on his shoulders, as he soaps up my hair. He gently kneads his fingers against my scalp, making sure he gets the ends of my hair clean as well, before helping me to rinse the suds away.

We take turns soaping each other up, cleaning each of our bodies in their entirety. He pays extra close attention to my breasts and the small patch of hair between my legs. I do the same for him, cleaning his balls carefully before running a soapy hand along the length of his shaft. A groan rumbles up from his chest as my thumb rubs soap around the ridge of his cock and over the thick head. I gasp as his cock gets impossibly thicker and harder in my hand.

Chris wraps his hands around my waist and lifts, pressing me against the cold tile of the shower, pressing his hips into me to hold me in place. Both of my hands come up and brace against his shoulders. He lowers one hand to grab his cock around the base and drags the tip along my slit before lining up with my opening. We both moan in unison when he presses into me, filling me completely.

His mouth trails along my jaw, nipping me with his teeth below my ear before latching to my pulse point on the side of my neck.

He sucks lightly as he continues to thrust into me. This is nothing like last night, there is no soft slow strokes in and out.

This is a claiming.

I love it when he loses control.

Don't get me wrong, I loved what he did to me last night. The feeling of safety and completeness. But that isn't what I need right now.

We need to have a conversation today that I don't know that I'm ready for. What I need right now is this. His control.

My ankles lock together behind his hips as he continues to pound into me, my back bouncing against the tile wall with each thrust. His mouth angles over mine, invading me with his tongue. We're a clash of tongue and teeth as his hands move around to cup my breasts, his thumbs rubbing circles around my stiff nipples.

It's too much. I feel him everywhere at once. His teeth dragging along my jaw, his hands caressing my breasts, his cock dragging along my inner walls while his pelvis brushes against my clit. I can't take it and I burst apart at the seams. Tiny pieces shattering along the floor of the shower, washing down the drain with the water and soap bubbles.

I think I scream his name at least once along with several other unrecognizable phrases. The scratchy feeling in my throat giving away the overflow of emotions. If he wasn't still pressing me against the wall, I would be a puddle at his feet.

His movements become erratic, his forehead pressed lightly against mine. He grunts along with his last few deep thrusts, and I know he's spent. Feeling him pulse against my inner walls nearly sets me off yet again.

Unwrapping my legs from his waist, I slide slowly down his body until my feet hit the shower floor. He kisses the top of my head before turning me to the spray of water and cleaning me up gently. After taking care of himself, he reaches around me to shut off the water.

Stepping out, I grab a towel and wrap it around my body, he does the same and wraps a towel around his waist. "Give me a few minutes and I'll go across the hall with you so you can grab some clean clothes."

"Okay." I stay standing in the doorway to the bathroom while he gets dressed. I watch as he slips a t-shirt over his head that's almost long enough to meet the waistband of his sweatpants. When he finishes getting dressed, I tear my eyes away from his gorgeous body and move away from the doorway. Gliding across the carpet, I bend to grab my discarded clothes from last night and clutch them to my chest. He places his hand at the small of my back as we walk toward the front door and out into the hall.

Having grabbed my apartment key before walking out the door, he unlocks my apartment for me. I walk in and continue down the hallway toward my bedroom while he locks my door and moves the curtain to block any light peaking in around the edges. My heart skips a beat at this selfless act that he does for me every time he comes over. Never once has he asked me about the curtains on my doors.

I take my time running a brush through my wet hair, after spraying it down with a leave-in conditioner. After pulling it up into a loose bun, I dress in an oversized t-shirt and black yoga pants. Slipping my feet into sandals, I saunter out into the living room to find Chris sitting on my sofa with his hands fisted together in his lap. He watches me as I walk closer and sit on the cushion to his left.

"We should talk," he begins. His voice is soft and soothing as if he were talking to a scared child. I feel bad thinking that he's afraid of bringing it up but at the same time I feel like I owe it to him. He deserves to know the truth.

Most of it anyway.

"Yeah." I stay on the edge of the sofa, my own hands folding together and resting on my knees. I can't look at him right now, my gaze remaining focused on my hands.

He reaches across my lap and traces a faint bruise on my left bicep. I hadn't realized it was there until just now and I suck in a quick breath. "Does it hurt?" He asks as his thumb continues to trace the bruise.

"No."

"Do you want to tell me what happened yesterday?"

"Yes," I whisper. Closing my eyes, I lower my head, so my chin is practically against my chest. Digging deep within myself, I try to locate my courage. I've never told anyone about my past. Yeah, he knows about my upbringing. He knows about me growing up on the road with my mother. But I've never told him all of it. I haven't told him about my stepdad, David, or my stepbrother, Jase.

Chapter 13

Chris

I watch as my Butterfly withdraws into herself. She's wilting before my eyes, and I want nothing more than to pull her against me and tell her it'll be alright. But I don't know if that will help. I know there is something that she needs to talk to me about and I don't believe that it's just about what happened to her yesterday.

All I can do for her right now is be there for her. Show her that she's not alone. Support her while she fights her demons. I don't want her to have to fight them alone. I want to slay her dragons for her, show her that the world can be a beautiful place. That no matter how harsh the terrain is, we can get through it together. We can get through anything. I want her to lean on me and know that I'll be there to carry her through it all.

Swallowing over the lump building in my throat as I watch her fight with her thoughts, I realize something. I'm not just falling for this petite woman.

I've already fallen.

Hard.

I crash landed at the bottom and survived the entire way down.

I am completely in love with her.

I want to shout it from the highest rooftops. Boast it all over the Southern California coastline. But this isn't the time to reveal my feelings. Not yet. We'll have plenty of time for that later. Right now, my Butterfly needs me.

Wrapping my arms around her, I pull her closer and let her rest her head against my shoulder. I lay my cheek against her head and wait for her to find her words. "Take your time, baby." She nods her head against my chest.

"I don't know where to start," she whispers.

"You don't have to tell me any more than what you're ready to talk about." I kiss the top of her head and rub my hand up and down her back.

"Thank you." She lifts her left hand and rests it against my chest. I place my hand over top of it and rub my thumb over her knuckles softly. "It's almost Spring." She begins but takes a few breaths before continuing. "I was resetting the display window at the shop yesterday. Switching things around to add more color to bring in the season. I remember daydreaming about you and wishing that you were there with me."

"I'm sorry that I wasn't able to be there yesterday," I interrupt before thinking better of it.

"No." She lifts her head and looks me in the eyes. "I don't blame you for not being there. I understand that you had to go to San Diego. I was just daydreaming and wasn't paying attention to who was walking into my shop."

I nod my head in understanding and wait as she lowers her head back to my shoulder.

"Jase came in and I didn't realize it was him." She pauses again and I wonder to myself who Jase is. Is he an ex? Someone that hurt her in the past. I make a mental note to find out more about him. "He locked the shop door and flipped the sign to closed before I had a chance to get him to leave. He yanked me out of the window and took me to the back room. He wasn't happy that I didn't want him there and he made that clear. I didn't even realize that he knew where my shop was, but I guess I shouldn't be surprised. He said he always saw me. He always watches me. He always has."

My brows furrow and I can feel my pulse quickening as the anger rages through my veins. What does she mean by that? Is he the reason why she keeps everything covered in her apartment? She doesn't want him looking in on her while she's here alone. My arms tighten around her, and I can feel her tremble against me. She's scared. I don't know who this person is but she's afraid of him.

"No matter how far I go, he will always find me. I thought I got away from him when I stopped traveling with my mom in her camper. I thought that part of my life was over." She takes a few shallow breaths before continuing. "I always knew he would find me. I got complacent with my shop thinking that I was safe there. It only has the one window and door. There are no other windows in the shop that I have to keep an eye on. Nothing else that I have to keep covered. I was in the window when he came in, I should have seen him coming."

"Shh." I move my hand up and down her back in a soothing gesture.

"He said he just wanted to talk."

"Baby." I place my finger beneath her chin and tilt her face up to mine. "Did he do anything yesterday while he was there?" Holding my breath, I wait for her to answer me.

"No."

I release my breath in a rush of air through her hair.

"He just wanted to talk. He said I should have called my mother back. He said she was disappointed that I haven't called her back. But I didn't want to talk to her. I knew she wasn't far away, and I didn't want to see them."

"I'm confused. What does this Jase person have to do with your mother?"

"Jase is my stepbrother."

"Your stepbrother?"

"Yeah." She sits up and pushes away from me.

I let her go knowing that she needs a little space to gather her thoughts. I can see her trying to shut it all out, but I know she needs to get this out. Rage is boiling beneath my skin and I'm trying not to let her see it. I'm still upset about the mark he left on her arm yesterday, but I don't want to scare her. She needs to know that she can talk to me without me losing my temper or doing anything rash.

"Oh, God. I'm messing this up." She turns away from me and fidgets with the hem of her shirt. "I'm trying to tell you everything but I'm messing it up."

"No." I reach up and move a stray hair behind her ear. "You're not messing anything up. Take your time, Butterfly. There's no rush. I'm not going anywhere." I have a bad feeling about where this is going but I need to know the history, so I know how to help her heal. This isn't the first time I've heard something like this. Granted, it's the first time I've had a leg in the race, but this is a race I intend to win.

I sit back against the sofa as Cypress stands and begins to pace around the room. I watch as she moves to the window and adjusts the edges of the curtain, shutting out any light peaking in around the edges. "Would you like a drink?" She asks as she wanders into her attached kitchen.

"Sure."

She grabs two bottles out of the refrigerator and walks back to the living room, placing them both on the coffee table. "It's kombucha. It's a little fruity and a little strong if you've never had it before."

"It's fine. Thank you." I grab a bottle and twist off the top, taking a tentative sip while watching her starting to pace again. It's not bad but not something that I would drink on a regular basis. Replacing the cap, I place the bottle back on the table and sit back with my hands fisted in my lap.

"My mom met my stepdad, David, when I was thirteen years old. We were in Des Moines for a street fair, and she met him there. He had a son, Jase, who's two years older than me. We ended up staying in Des Moines longer than we had anywhere else just so she could spend more time with David. When we left there, he and Jace loaded up with us in our little Airstream camper and went with us. They married shortly after on a trip we took through Vegas, and I had ended up with both a new stepdad and stepbrother."

She stops talking and leans against the wall across the room from me, her arms crossed over her chest. "It was great at first," she starts again. "Yeah, the camper was small, but it was nice having someone around besides just me and my mom. We were able to get more inventory moved in and out of the fairs we frequented. The extra hands setting up our tents made it easier moving in and out of our venues. It had just been me and mom for thirteen years, so it was nice to have someone else to spend time with and Jase and I were quickly becoming friends. We were both homeschooled on the road so it wasn't like I had any other friends anyway and you can't really meet people at fairs when you aren't going to be there long enough to get to know them."

Cypress pushes away from the wall and wanders to the armchair. I watch as she sits and curls her arms around a throw pillow she places in her lap. I swallow down the disappointment at her not sitting close enough for me to touch her, to reassure her as she continues with her story.

"Things started to get weird after a while. Mom and I would be in our tent working our booth during a fair. David and Jase would be sitting nearby but not in our tent. It was like they didn't want to be part of our business or something, they would be off doing their own thing. But they didn't have anything to sell most of the time. To be honest, I didn't even know why they were there half the time. David said he liked to stay close to make sure me and mom were safe. I knew it was something else though. It wasn't always busy at the fairs, so I was able to watch them more often than mom was. I noticed when they would get distracted by the scenery."

She makes finger quotes of the last word and I cock my head at her in silent question.

"The scenery was the other women at the fair. Both David and Jase liked to watch the women. I didn't miss it when they would wander away and start talking to them either."

I can feel my hackles rise as I picture the women that have disappeared recently. The case that I've been working on. I wonder how similar her story is to that of the missing girls. Were they approached by someone at the fair that showed interest in them?

"Jase had just turned sixteen and he was interested in the ladies. He was basically a player, and his dad encouraged his behavior. It was weird honestly. Like his dad would scope out the available girls and point to the ones that he thought Jase should go talk to. I told my mom about it, and she said I was just imagining it. So, I started ignoring them. I started spending more time working on my own thing. I had a love of old clothes and would gather clothing that other people didn't want and would make it into something different. Something pretty."

"Is that when you learned tie-dye?"

"No." She smiles at me before turning her gaze back to her lap. "I learned that much later. My roommate in college actually taught me how to tie-dye fabric. This was more like something to keep me busy. To keep me occupied so I wouldn't spend as much time with David and Jase. When the fairs would close at night, rather than sit inside the camper with my family, I would sit outside and tear apart old shirts. Save the buttons to use on something else. Rip off pockets to place on pants or make purses with old jeans. David didn't like me spending so much time with myself. He said it wasn't safe for me to be outside at night even though I was right next to our camper, and they could hear me yell if something happened or if I had hurt myself with the scissors or seam ripper. I argued with him and said I was fine. I was fourteen at this point and figured I was old enough to take care of myself. He insisted that Jase keep an eye on me to make sure I was safe. That it was his duty as the older brother to watch over me." She uses the finger quotes again on the last part.

"It wasn't a big deal at first. He kept his distance and stayed out of my way when I was haggling the older ladies for some of their unsold second-hand clothes. I guess I got used to the fact that he was keeping an eye on me so to speak. But then, after a while, it started to change.

"Not long after I turned fifteen, I started to change physically. My clothes started to get too tight in the chest and my hips were starting to fill out. I wasn't able to wear the same clothes that I had been wearing before. I had to start adding new things to my wardrobe in order to make sure I was covered and supported in areas that I never had to worry about before. Part of getting older I suppose. My mother was too busy working the craft booth to take me shopping so David volunteered to take me to the store for new clothing. Of course, Jase came along with us."

She stops talking for several minutes and I wonder if she's trying to gather her words before continuing. I'm already starting to get nervous for where I think this conversation is going only, I'm afraid to ask her.

I don't want to push.

"David was a gentlemen, he stayed outside the dressing rooms while I tried on clothes. He would pick up garments throughout the store that he thought I might like and hold them for me while we walked around. Jase, on the other hand, was insanely curious at how they all fit. He followed me into the dressing room and stood on the other side of the curtain the entire time. He insisted that I show him literally everything that I tried on. It was like I was his own personal Barbie doll, and he was playing dress-up. After a while it started to creep me out and I refused to continue trying on clothes. I knew what sizes I needed already based on what I'd already tried on so I grabbed several outfits that I liked and took them back to David so we could pay and leave.

"Over the next several months, I knew I was being watched more closely than before. It was like the hairs on the back of my neck would stand on end when I would go to the bathroom or take a shower. Any time I got dressed, I felt like someone was watching me even when I couldn't see them."

She stands on shaky legs and I watch as she walks back over to the wall across from where I'm still sitting on the couch. She stops and faces the wall, wrapping her arms around her waist. "Did you tell your mom?" I ask in hopes that she continues her story.

Turning to face me, she drops her arms to her side. "Yes." She nods her head quickly a few times. "I told her that I thought I was being watched. She said I was being paranoid and to ignore the feeling. She said there was no way that anyone could see me through the walls separating us. I don't know if you know anything about old campers, but the walls are really thin. The bathroom in our little Airstream was between the bunk that Jase slept in and the dinette. The shower in a camper is really small and sometimes it takes some creative acrobatics to make sure you get everything clean or shaved. I was bending over one day to shave my lower leg and happened to look up and I saw it. There was a perfect little hole behind the faucet. It wasn't very big, maybe the size of a pencil eraser. I don't know why I never noticed it before. But I moved close enough to it when I saw it that I was able to see through it clearly. Jase's bunk was through that hole, and he was laying on his bed with his face right next to it. I didn't see him looking through it at the time, but I'm sure that he had been until I had noticed it was there."

"Fuck," I whisper between clenched teeth.

"Things started to escalate from there. I plugged the hole in the shower, but I started to inspect the walls every time I walked into the bathroom to use it. Always looking for any new holes or gaps in the paneling where someone could see in. I would wake up sometimes in the middle of the night and I could hear someone breathing heavily near my bunk. I never looked to see who it was because I was afraid of who or what I might see. Even when I moved away from my family to attend college in Arizona, I continued to check for holes in every room I entered whether it was my bedroom or the bathroom. I was always afraid that someone was watching me."

"Did he ever…" Closing my eyes tight, I swallow several times to clear the lump in my throat. "Did he ever touch you?"

"No. It never got that far. I don't know if it would have if I hadn't moved away and went out on my own, but I wasn't going to give him that chance."

I can't take it anymore. I stand from the couch and walk over to her. I don't give her an option at this point, and she doesn't fight me. Grabbing her shoulders, I pull her into my chest and wrap my arms around her tightly. She returns the gesture, wrapping her arms around my waist and resting her cheek against my chest. I can feel the tension in her entire embrace. "I'm so sorry that you had to deal with that."

"Don't." She whispers against my chest.

"Don't what?"

She pushes away from me, and I step back and watch her. "I don't need you feeling sorry for me. I don't want your pity. My life ended years ago, and I've slowly come to accept it. It isn't your fault that I am the way I am. That I can't go into a room without looking closely for hidden access points, knowing where all the exits are. That I can't take my clothes off before checking the room for holes, anywhere that someone could see in without my knowledge. I can't take a shower for fear of someone walking in on me and watching me before I even realize they're there."

"Hey," I interrupt her and place my palm lightly against her cheek, cradling her face softly. Using my thumb, I wipe a tear away from under her eye. "It's not pity that I feel right now." I have to choose my words wisely. She's in a delicate state after telling me that story. I know it had to have been hard for her to get out. "There are so many feelings running through me right now, but I can promise you that pity isn't one of them. Anger maybe at Jase for what he did to you. Not only while you were growing up but also for yesterday. For sure at that bruise I can still see around your left bicep. Maybe even anger at your mother for allowing it to continue when you tried to confide in her. She should have protected you. But I don't feel pity for you. I feel protective of you though."

"You don't think I'm crazy?"

"For what? Because you've developed some eccentricities over the years? You're not crazy."

She finally smiles for the first time all afternoon and my heart bursts with joy at the sight of it. "I'm not eccentric."

"Hmm." I kiss her softly on the corner of her mouth. "Maybe just a little. But I don't blame you one bit. But you don't have to fight this on your own anymore. You're mine little Butterfly. I won't let anything happen to you."

"You can't be with me all hours of the day and night. I still have a shop to run."

"True. But I did order you some security cameras." I watch as her brows lift to her hairline. "Don't start. I won't be watching you all day while you work. But it will make me feel better to know that you're being looked after in case anything was to happen. Is that okay?"

"Yeah," she whispers in response before stepping into my arms again. She finally relaxes against my chest, and I feel like I can finally breathe again. "When will you be able to get them installed?"

"They'll be here on Wednesday, and I'll have a couple guys help me get them set up."

"Okay. I think I'll leave the shop closed until you have them installed."

"I think that would be a good idea." I kiss the top of her head again and chuckle when I hear a soft grumble in her stomach. "What do you say we go out for dinner? I think it's time that I feed you."

"Can we get pizza?"

This crazy, beautiful woman. I throw my head back and laugh. "Yeah, Butterfly. We can get pizza."

Chapter 14

Cypress

It feels weird to be opening the boutique in the middle of the week after being closed for two extra days. Chris ordered me a security camera setup that he's having installed today. He came with me this morning to open the shop at the normal time and has been busy with someone named Pete installing the cameras around the shop for the last hour.

I spent most of the morning finishing my window display that I had started on Saturday. Now that it's finished, I grab my phone from beneath the register and walk outside to get some pictures for my Instagram page.

I shoot a couple of close-up pics, careful not to catch my reflection in the window. Then wander across the street for a front view of the entire shop. I've never changed the color of the shop itself, having fallen in love with the wild appearance of it. The trim around the window itself is a faded teal green while the door is aqua blue. The contrast alone is enough to make it stand out but add to that the bright pink Poppy Petals sign above the shop and it really catches your attention.

Now that the window display is finished, there's just enough pop of spring color to accent the rest of the building and hopefully catch the eye of potential shoppers walking by. My mind is already spinning with ideas on products in the shop to get photos of to fill my social media calendar for the season.

I step up to the curb and stop to wait for traffic before crossing when the fine hairs on the back of my neck stand on end. It's the uncomfortable feeling of being watched, a feeling I'm all too familiar with. Spinning around, I look for any possible location where Jase might be hiding out and keeping an eye on me, but I don't see him anywhere. I look along the shop entrances lining this side of the street before turning to the opposite side and checking again and still don't see him. A quick glance at the cars parked along the street doesn't reveal anyone sitting inside any of them watching me.

Conceding that it may just be my imagination after all, I turn back to the street and ready myself to cross. One last glance over my shoulder toward the outdoor seating at the café and my stomach drops. It's not Jase that I see, but a curious gentleman seated by himself is watching me intently. He looks familiar to me, but I can't think of why. I make eye contact with him, and he doesn't look away but does something even stranger…

He winks at me.

It's not a cute wink as if he were attempting to flirt with me. Not that I have much experience with being the recipient of a random flirt. It's a creepy wink but it picks at something deep in my memory as being faintly familiar. Only I can't think of where I've seen this man before.

Glaring back in his direction one last time before crossing the street, I try to think of where I've seen him before and come up blank. After making my way back to the door of my shop, I turn around for one last glance, one last chance to jog my memory of why I know the man winking at me, and he's gone. The café table completely void of any evidence of him ever having been there.

"What's wrong?" Chris walks toward me as I enter the shop, his brows furrowed in concern.

Stepping into his embrace, I shake my head. "Nothing. I just thought I saw someone familiar at the café across the street." I feel his posture stiffen and his arms tighten around me, pulling me harder into his chest. "It wasn't him if that's what you're thinking."

Placing his hands on my shoulders, he pulls away and bends down to look in my eyes before responding. "Okay," he says. Straightening, he places a hand at the small of my back and pulls me alongside him. "Come with me. Let me show you what we did."

As we walk through the shop, Chris points out the cameras in the corners. "You can see every angle," he says. "There's not a section of the shop that's hidden. The way most of your displays are against a wall helps. It means there aren't isles with blind spots." He continues to lead me past the register counter and into the back room. "We put a camera in here too." He points to the far wall. "It faces the entrance to the room."

"Who will be monitoring these cameras while I'm here?" A chill sweeps over me as I wonder if someone is going to be watching me. I understand why Chris wants the cameras to be up, but I still don't know how I feel about a random person keeping an eye on me while I'm working. It isn't much different than having to look over my shoulder everywhere I go.

Chris reads my body language in the stiffening of my posture and spins me around to face him, both hands placed gently on my shoulders. "Hey," he starts as he moves one hand up to cup my cheek. "No one is going to be watching you while you work. This is just a precaution, a way of making sure you're safe during the day. Pete, over there, works for a friend of mine as surveillance for her club. This is what he does for a living, keeps an eye on people to make sure they're safe. He won't be watching you all hours of the day if that's what you're worried about. He has other things to keep an eye on. But your video feed will be recorded so if something happens, we'll at least have it on video."

"Okay," I whisper even though every cell of my being is feeling opposite of comforted.

"Would it help if I said I had access to the video feed too?" I move my gaze to his face and see him smiling back at me, a playful twinkle in his eye. "The cameras run on a digital signal and are powered by a solar panel installed on the roof. They aren't able to be tampered with if someone were to break in and cut the power lines in your shop. There's an app I have on my phone that will show me the video feed anytime. I can download it to your phone too if you want."

"Okay," I concede. "I don't need the app, but I do feel better knowing you're keeping an eye on me."

"Always, Butterfly." He kisses me lightly on the forehead. I close my eyes as he pulls me tighter into his chest. "Your safety is my number one concern."

Wrapping my arms around his waist, I close my eyes and relax into his hold. "Thank you," I whisper against his chest.

The weather is beautiful for an outdoor wedding. Chris assures me that it will be a small gathering and that he already RSVP'd adding me as his plus one. I don't know why I'm so nervous about going. From what he told me, he became friends with both the bride and groom after he helped to find her when she was abducted. Of course, he didn't tell me the entire story – not that it was any of my business – but I just can't shake the nerves that are overtaking my body and mind about going to this wedding. It isn't like I know the people getting married.

Not that that's a good excuse. I've been in Los Angeles for three years and have a successful boutique in Echo Park. It isn't like I haven't had a chance to meet people. Between the shop and the occasional yoga instructing, I've been around people almost daily. But since Jase showed up last week, I've been extra edgy and just haven't been able to shake it.

Chris and I pull up to a charming house in the early afternoon. I wait as he walks around the car and opens the door for me before getting out. He looks handsome today dressed in a broken suit sans tie – dark slacks and a light grey suit jacket open at the waist, the top two buttons of his shirt undone. His short hair is slightly disheveled giving him a sexy windblown appearance. I dressed simple in an ankle length sleeveless wrap dress in a floral print and strappy sandals.

Walking into the house, I take in the simple decorations in the wide-open space. There are a few tables set up in what looks like a living room and twinkle lights hanging from the ceiling throughout the room. Each table is covered with a white cloth and adorned with a simple frayed burlap square and mason jar filled with more twinkle lights and white roses. "Wow." I exclaim as we walk through the room to the open patio doors on the other side.

We step into the backyard where other guests have already begun to gather. The pergola over the patio has been strung with more twinkle lights and draped with white chiffon, tied back in the corners with strips of burlap. The far side of the yard is set up with rows of folding chairs, burlap and chiffon draped along the backs of each chair. "Is that a pool?" I ask Chris as we sit.

"It is." He says as he takes my hand, twining our fingers together and resting our linked hands on his knee.

"How did they do that?" The pool has a floor built over the top of it that looks like a rustic deck.

"The groom's best friend owns a construction company and remodels houses. I'm sure he built it. Actually, now that I think of it, I think he did most of the work on this house too. He probably built the pergola over the back patio."

"That's amazing." The way the chairs are facing, where the pool used to be, there's almost a stage with a beautiful arbor in the back, also wood of course. It matches the deck covered pool perfectly as if it were supposed to be a permanent fixture for this backyard oasis. The arbor, just like the pergola, is draped in white chiffon and burlap but has beautiful arrangements of white roses throughout. Squinting my eyes for a better look, I try to make sense of what I'm looking at. "Are those feathers?"

"What?" Chris turns his gaze to follow my own and squints as well. "I think you're right. Huh." Picking my hand up, he kisses my knuckles softly before placing it back on his lap.

We sit silently, soaking up the sunshine, as more guests arrive and take their seats around us. No one is being ushered to a seat so I'm not sure if there are more guests for either the groom's or bride's side. Soft music plays from speakers placed throughout the backyard, though I haven't noticed where they are located yet. The entire ambiance is relaxing and peaceful, the total opposite of what I was expecting when I woke up this morning.

A handsome man walks up to Chris and shakes his hand. "Glad you made it, Chris." He says as Chris releases my hand to stand up and greet him. I wonder if he's the groom. He's dressed in grey slacks and vest with a white shirt, the sleeves rolled to his elbows. He has a white rose and feather pinned to the lapel.

"Devan." Chris greets him. "Nice to see you. Have you met Cypress?" He asks as he turns and extends his hand to me. Taking it, I stand and offer a gentle smile.

"I haven't." His eyes widen as he looks at me and smiles. "Nice to meet you, Cypress." He grabs my hand and lifts it to place a light kiss along my knuckle. "Welcome to my home."

"Thank you." I place my hand on Chris' arm, unsure how I should respond. I'm not normally shy, but things have been really weird lately and I'm just not sure how I'm supposed to react.

Devan walks away and begins to greet other guests before taking his place at the front of the pool deck in front of the arbor. Before we get a chance to sit back down, I notice another man approaching Chris.

"Matt." Chris says in greeting as he extends his hand to shake. This man is also dressed similarly to Devan in a pair of grey slacks and vest with a white rose and feather pinned to his lapel as well. He has longer dark hair, just past his shoulder, the top and sides tied back neatly. He must be the friend. "Good to see you, man."

"Detective." He takes Chris' hand and shakes it, a smile spreading across his face as he looks past Chris' shoulder and notices me standing closely behind him. "Who's this?" He cocks his head to the side and lifts a brow in question.

"This is Cypress." Chris pulls me closer to his side to introduce me and wraps an arm around my waist.

"Hello, beautiful. What on earth are you doing with this guy?" My brows furrow and I wonder what would possess him to ask such a question. He chuckles at my obvious confusion.

"I'm sure she's trying to figure that out herself." Chris laughs and I realize it was a joke. He kisses my temple and chucks my chin and I feel myself beginning to blush.

"Well," Matt starts before placing his hands in his pockets. "I'm glad you're both here."

"The backyard looks great. I'm guessing you had something to do with that."

"I did. It was great practice. I've never covered a pool with wood before."

"Practice for your own big day I'm guessing." Chris says.

"You know it." He smiles and I watch as it lights up his entire face. "You better be at that one too."

"Wouldn't miss it." Turning back to me, Chris places a hand on my shoulder and helps me back to my seat. He takes my hand again immediately once we've sat back down. I watch as Matt makes his rounds and greets several people in attendance before taking his place next to Matt at the arbor.

I watch Chris' profile as he eyes the men standing at the front. Smiling to myself, I realize something that I hadn't bothered to think of before. They really breed good looking men around here. I'm still staring when he turns his gaze to mine. Lifting my hand to his mouth, he kisses each of my knuckles in turn before winking and smiling at me. I feel my cheeks heat with blush after being caught staring at him.

Catching a flash of cotton-candy pink over his shoulder, I gasp. "Marie," I whisper. Chris turns to follow my gaze.

"You know her?" He asks after turning back to me.

"Yeah," I admit as I watch her walk this way. She looks amazing in a shiny silver dress that matches the men's vests. She has her hair pulled back in a loose chignon and I can see white feathers peaking over the crown of her head like a fancy headdress. It's nearly magical in appearance. "She's in my yoga class and she's come into the shop a few times."

The music changes and everyone begins to stand around us. I don't know why I'm surprised when I see Marie's friend, Julie, walking slowly toward us. She looks beautiful in her sleeveless white dress. The fitted bodice has a sweetheart neckline, and she looks amazing. Her hair is also pulled back in a chignon and adorned with white feathers and baby's breath. She's carrying a bouquet of white roses with more white feathers included throughout. The entire bouquet is wrapped in a silver cloth with a single blue ribbon. I watch in awe as she walks by herself up the aisle.

The entire ceremony goes by in a flash. Wiping a few tears away from beneath my eyes, I watch as they exchange their vows and finish with a nearly jaw-dropping kiss. The entire crowd of onlookers breaks out in applause, and they walk back down the aisle holding hands.

We wait while everyone begins to move away from the chairs before Chris leads me to the covered patio. He shakes the groom's hand, Devan I think he had said before. "Congratulations."

"Thank you, Detective."

"Please. It's just Chris today."

"Glad you were able to be here Chris. Today would have never happened if it weren't for you."

My brows shoot up at that. I know Chris had something to do with helping to find his fiancé, well wife now I suppose. But he hasn't told me the story.

"Nonsense." Chris places a hand on Devan's shoulder before stepping away. "You and I both know that we wouldn't have closed the case if it weren't for the work she did investigating."

Huh. Seems there really is a story there.

"Yeah." He wraps an arm around Julie's waist and pulls her into his side before kissing the top of her head. "She is badass."

"I'll give her that." Chris concedes before reaching a hand out to Julie. "Congratulations, Julie. You look beautiful today."

"No." She pushes his hand away and steps into his chest, wrapping her arms around his waist. "I'm so glad you're here." She steps away after he finally embraces her softly and faces me. "Hello, Cypress. I'm glad you're here too." She reaches for me, and I step close enough to give her a soft hug of my own.

"The ceremony was beautiful." Stepping away, I look up at her hair and take several seconds to look at the beautiful feathers peeking out from her chignon. "What's with all the feathers?"

"Devan calls me Angel." She giggles in reply. "I thought it would be a good touch."

"Wow. That's amazing. I've never seen so many feathers at a wedding before. Nice touch."

"Thank you. I hope you both will stay for the reception. We have cake." She announces as she steps back into Devan's embrace.

"Wouldn't miss it." Chris replies before putting his hand around my waist and pulling me closer.

We don't stay for very long. Chris and I dance to several slow songs and watch as Devan twirls his new wife around the yard a few times. Before the cake is even cut, I find myself feeling tired and Chris catches me yawning a few times.

"You okay, Butterfly?" He kisses my temple and places his arm around my shoulders.

"Yeah." I lean into him and close my eyes for a few seconds. "I don't know why I'm so tired today."

"Why don't we get out of here." He sits back far enough to look me in the eye, placing a single finger beneath my chin to tilt my face up. "You've had a long week and I know you need to relax."

"We don't have to go yet. I'll be alright."

He leans in and places a soft kiss on my lips. "No. I'm ready to get you back home. I feel the need to worship you thoroughly and I can't very well do that here with all these people around."

"Mmm." I moan against his lips as he presses his against mine again. "I like the sound of that."

Chapter 15

Chris

"What brings you here today, Ethan?" I ask the man sitting across my desk from me. Ethan strolled into my office ten minutes ago, his hands in his pockets as he paused and leaned against my doorframe and crossed his legs casually at the ankle. He waited for me to look up from the pile of notes on my desk before he sauntered in and sat quietly in the chair across from me.

"I was in the area," he says quietly, his hands folded in his lap. He cocks his head to the side as he studies me before speaking again. I've worked with Ethan a few times in the past on several cases. He's a detective from San Bernadino, one that I've gotten to know well over the years. "You look tired, Chris. You getting enough sleep at night?"

"Oh yeah." I chuckle deeply. "I've been plenty worn out before my head hits the pillow at night."

"So, what's up then? You look like shit."

"Thanks," I deadpan. "It's just this case. I've been all over the reports and I can't find anything that might point us in the right direction. I mean, don't get me wrong. I agree the girls are in Mexico and I'm all for going south of the border to get them back. I'll even be one of the first to volunteer to be on the extraction team. But I'm trying to figure out how to stop it from happening again. How do we find the people responsible?"

"I know what you mean. But," I watch as he stands up and puts his hands back in his pockets. He's a little extra fidgety today and it makes me wonder if he's nervous about something. Maybe he's the one that isn't getting enough sleep. "I've got something that might help."

"Really?" Cocking my head to the side, I chew my bottom lip and wait to see what he could have possibly found out that I haven't already come across in my notes and the reports littering my desk.

"My partner found a witness." He smiles and shuffles from one foot to another a few times before removing his hands from his pockets and sitting down again.

"No shit," I respond to his statement, shocked. His partner, Tammy, has been working with him for almost ten years. The two of them have gone undercover a few times over the years, posing as a married couple even though I know she's happily married to her high school sweetheart. She's a brilliant detective that specializes mostly in cyber crime and is a wiz on the computer. It's actually a little spooky some of the things I've heard of her doing online since I first met Ethan. I'm just happy to be on her good side.

"Yep," he grunts back, closing his eyes tightly. I wait for him to regain control of his faculties before continuing, knowing that he needs a minute sometimes to calm his nerves. "We don't have an ID on the suspect yet, but we do have a truck. I wanted to give you a heads up because it's been seen around Echo Park. That's your neck of the woods, not mine."

He tosses a folded piece of paper on the desk, and I reach out to grab it. Without saying anything, I unfold the paper and read a description of the truck in question. Eighties model chevy, square body, brown and tan two-tone, rusted, and white camper shell on the back. "Shouldn't be too hard to locate. Not many of these around here anymore."

"Nope. But the last time Tammy caught it on camera was about a month ago. Not sure if it's still in the area or not and we haven't caught it on any traffic cams lately. Just thought you'd want to keep an eye out in case it turns up again."

"Thank you." Standing, I hold my hand out toward Ethan. He doesn't hesitate to grip it and shake my hand.

Ethan releases my hand and tips his chin before turning to walk away from my desk. He stops at the door, his hand on the doorframe as he turns to peak over his shoulder. "So, you got a girl then? That the reason you're not getting any sleep at night?"

I chuckle lightly to myself thinking about just how much sleep I've been missing out on thanks to my little Butterfly. "Yeah. Something like that."

"Keep her close. Okay?"

"Plan on it."

Ethan doesn't say anything else before walking away. The entire conversation leaves an uneasy feeling in my gut. There haven't been any more disappearances lately and there aren't any street fairs or markets taking place in Echo Park. Why would Tammy have found the suspect's truck loitering around the area?

Something just doesn't add up.

Pushing my chair away from my desk, I toss my pen into the middle of the reports still cluttering the smooth surface and stand. I've had enough for today and I'm ready to see my Butterfly. I've updated the report to include the truck description but that's all I can do for now.

What I need right now is the step away from this bullshit case and wrap my arms around Cypress. My thoughts keep straying back to her as I walk out of my office and enter the elevator at the end of the hallway. Walking through the parking garage, I pull my keys out of my pocket and click the unlock button on the fob, reaching for the door handle at the same time with my other hand.

Not even twenty minutes later, I'm parked at the curb in front of Poppy Petals. I sit in the driver's seat of my SUV and watch through the window on the door to the boutique as Cypress works her magic on a group of girls. They're browsing the incense burners that Cypress' friend in Arizona makes for her to sell on consignment in her shop.

I stare in awe of my beautiful Butterfly as she speaks animatedly about each of the burners before leading the girls to the incense display on the register counter. I can't take my eyes off of her as she continues to speak in earnest to her patrons. She loves what she does, and it shows in everything that she does with her boutique. There is so much of her light and energy in every inch of that shop.

Her energy is one of the things that I love the most about her, I can't deny that. She has brought so much life into my dull existence since I first found her curled up on that sidewalk. She's everything that I never thought I would find in a person. She's honest and caring. She's excited about everything that life has to offer, I could see that when I took her to the festival at the park several weeks ago. The way she flitted around the vendor booths, her skirt billowing around her legs like a cloud as she floated gracefully from one tent to another.

She's the same way now as she walks her shoppers to the door. She continues to talk to them, probably treating them as if they are her best friends from way back. She's never seemed to know a stranger, despite how timid she is about being watched.

I'm stepping out of the SUV before she's even reached the door from the other side. I walk around the front of the car and stand on the sidewalk as she holds the door open for the girls to walk out.

I watch as she looks around outside before she starts to step back into the open doorway. She pauses as her eyes land on mine and my heart skips a beat when she smiles that award winning smile reserved only for me.

My hands are still in my jacket pockets as I watch her step closer to me. Before she can reach for me, I'm removing my hands from my pockets and reaching out for her, cupping her cheeks in my palms softly as I bend to her level and angle my mouth over hers. She opens for me immediately and I deepen the kiss, my need to possess her mind, body, and spirit bleeding out through my touch. I'm drunk on the taste and feel of her, her vanilla and sandalwood a heady fragrance lighting every nerve in my body on fire.

I break our kiss slowly, kissing each corner of her mouth one at a time but never releasing her beautiful face. Her eyes are closed when I pull back enough to look at her, her pink tongue peaking out and dragging slowly over her bottom lip.

"Hi," she whispers, her eyes still closed tightly as if afraid of waking from a dream.

"Hi," I say back, my voice gravellier than I expected.

She lifts one of her hands and places it over mine, still pressed against her cheek. "I missed you today."

"I missed you too, Butterfly."

She finally opens her eyes, her smile brightening up her face as she locks her gaze with mine.

"Are you ready to get out of here?" I ask, hopeful that she is ready to leave. I need to get her home, in my bed, so I can show her just how much I missed her today.

"Yeah." She pulls back a step and I allow my hands to fall to my sides. "Just let me grab my bag and lock the door and we can go."

I stay on the sidewalk outside her shop, my hands in my jacket pockets, as I wait for her to return. Once her boutique is closed and the door locked, I approach and take her purse from her before wrapping my arm around her waist. Pulling her against my side, I bend down to brush a soft kiss against her hair. "Are you hungry, Butterfly?"

"Um," she pauses. "Not really."

"Good." I open the passenger door for her and wait for her to be situated before closing it behind her and jogging around the front of the SUV to the other side. Not wasting any time, I turn the key in the ignition and pull into traffic. I'm anxious to get back across town to our apartment. "I'd love for you to stay with me tonight. Why don't we stop by your apartment, and you can grab a few things, then we'll go back to my place. We can order delivery if you want, or we can watch a movie." I turn and look at her profile when we stop at a traffic light.

"I'd like that," she agrees quietly. She reaches her hand across the console and rests it on my thigh and just that simple touch alone has me hard as iron and ready for her.

Clearing my throat, I adjust in my seat. She giggles softly from her side of the car, and I know she knows what she's doing to me. A growl rumbles deep in my chest as I think of how I'm going to punish her for torturing me while I'm trying to drive safely across town. The last thing I need is to get distracted by her touch and get us both injured in an accident.

Neither of us speak as we walk into the apartment building a few minutes later, my hand wrapped tightly around hers. I punch the call button for the elevator a few times impatiently knowing that it doesn't move any faster by repeated pushes of the button. She giggles again and I feel my blood heating in my veins.

I don't enter her apartment as she goes inside, leaving her door open for me. She takes her time going through her bedroom and packing a few changes of clothes. If I have my way, she'll be in my apartment all weekend. I doubt she'll end up needing any of the clothes that she packs but I don't mind her bringing extra. My cock twitches against my zipper as I think of her clothes hanging in my closet, mixed with my own long-sleeved shirts and suit jackets. Just the thought of her panties mixed into my underwear drawer is enough to make me in jeopardy of shooting off like a teenager.

Swallowing several times over the lump in my throat, I struggle to maintain my self-control. Her familiar fragrance surrounds me, and I know she's on her way out into the hallway again. Without looking at her, I turn and open my apartment door. Stepping inside my apartment, I hold the door open for her to follow me into the entryway.

She drops her bag to the floor as I push the door open and grab her around the waist. Pulling her in front of me, I press her firmly against the closed apartment door, my mouth crashing into hers. One of my hands fist in her hair. Grabbing the long braid hanging down her back, I angle her head so I can deepen the kiss. My other hand lowers to her ass as I lift her off the floor, pressing her against the door and holding her in place with my hips.

Breaking away from her sweet tasting lips, I place open mouthed kisses along her jaw and down her neck, nipping on her collar bone. She mewls softly, her hands fisting in my hair. "Chris," she moans my name sweetly.

"Cypress," I parrot back at her in a soft growl, and she giggles. Fuck, she's adorable. I could listen to that giggle for the rest of my life. Her happiness fuels my own like an aphrodisiac to my soul. "I need you, baby."

"Yes," she moans as her arms wrap around my shoulders and her legs around my hips.

Pulling away from the door, I carry her through my apartment. I don't bother picking her bag up from the entryway floor, it'll still be there later. I carry my Butterfly into my bedroom and lower us both on the mattress softly. I make quick work of removing Cypress' clothes before taking care of my own, then I'm over her again.

Kissing her deeply, I reach my hand down and trace a finger through her wetness. She's ready for me and I don't know if I have enough control left to wait. I'll take my time with her later.

Moving my lips down to her throat, I grab my cock at the base and line the tip up with her opening before pushing in fully in a single, slow thrust. Cypress moans and throws her head back against a pillow as I fill her completely. Somehow, I find enough control to move slowly inside her, circling my hips with each thrust so I drag against her inner walls and hit that spot inside that gets her to make the sweetest sounds ever.

Grinding my pelvis against her, I wrap my lips around one of her dusky pink nipples and pull it into my mouth. My tongue flicks against the peaked tip and rolls it against the back of my teeth as her hands wrap around my biceps, her nails biting into the skin on each arm.

"Oh, God!" She exclaims and I feel her beginning to pulse around my cock. Closing my eyes, I release her nipple with a pop and grit my teeth against the sensation.

"Jesus, Butterfly. You are exquisite." I don't take my eyes off her beautiful face as she breaks apart gloriously. I watch as the same flush brightening her cheeks spreads down her neck and over her breasts. Leaning closer, I latch my mouth against the side of her neck. Dragging my teeth over where her shoulder and neck meet, I feel her pulse fluttering against my lips. I continue moving inside her, feeling the moisture from her orgasm dripping down to my balls.

I thrust one, two, three more times before the pressure in the base of my spine takes hold and all my muscles seize tight. "Fuck, Cypress," I growl against her neck, holding as deep as I can inside her as my release bursts out of me.

Rolling to the side, I drop down next to Cypress and pull her into my chest. Her hair has come loose from its braid, and I brush it behind her ear with my fingertips. She sighs as she relaxes against me, her hand flattening on my stomach.

"That was amazing," she whispers contentedly.

"I aim to please." She giggles again and I swear my heart is full to bursting. "I love you, Butterfly." I close my eyes as I realize that I just blurted out something that I should probably have told her before taking her to bed. That isn't usually something that should be said in the heat of the moment. Thinking about it, I actually have never said that to any woman before. But that doesn't mean I don't mean it. I mean it with every fiber of my being. I am madly, deeply, in love with this petite woman.

She lifts her head from my chest and looks up at me, a single tear falling down her cheek. I reach my hand up and swipe the tear away with my thumbs, my brows furrowing in confusion. She smiles sweetly and places a soft kiss against my chest. "I love you too, Chris."

Wrapping my arms tightly around her small body, I pull her hard against me and rest my cheek against her head. If I thought I'd already experienced my most treasured moments with this little woman, I was wrong. Hearing her tell me that she loves me too is probably the best thing that's ever happened to me.

I'm still holding her when I realize that her breathing has evened out. She is relaxed against me, and I don't want to be anywhere other than where I am right now. I relax, my arms still wrapped around her, and follow her into her dreams.

Chapter 16

Cypress

Waking up slowly, I roll over and face the empty side of my bed. I don't know why I bother, Chris has been gone for three days. He had to go back down to San Diego to help with the investigation he's working on with the other detectives. "I'll be out of reach for a few days," he had told me. "We are working with a group with the PFM in Mexico City and might be south of the border at some point."

It's hard to get used to waking up alone when we've spent so many nights together recently. We've gotten closer since Julie and Devan's wedding. Honestly, we might as well be living together in his apartment with as much time as I've been spending there. Even though he doesn't cover his windows and doors, I still feel safe when I'm there with him. Like nothing and no one can get to me when he's around. It makes it harder to be on my own, remembering to lock and cover the doors in the apartment.

Chris offered to let me stay in his apartment while he was gone but it just doesn't feel right being there without him. It isn't the same as having him in that space with me. I feel safe in his apartment, don't get me wrong. But I'm safer when he's there at the same time.

Sitting up, I swing my legs over the side of the bed before I'm hit by a wave of dizziness. Closing my eyes, I try to orient myself so I can stand and wander into the bathroom. It takes several minutes of deep breathing before I'm steady enough on my feet to move. "Damn," I breathe as I shuffle across the soft carpet and enter the bathroom. "I must have gotten up too fast."

After taking care of my business, I reassess the curtain over the door and start the shower. The dizziness returns for several minutes while I stand under the hot spray, and I have to lay a hand against the tile to hold myself up. "Low blood sugar. Maybe that's what this is." I was tired after working on so many projects at the shop yesterday that I didn't bother eating dinner before I crawled into my bed. Making a mental note to grab something for breakfast when I reach Echo Park, I finish my shower and get dressed for the day.

Remembering what today is, I pick up my cell phone and call my mom as I walk out the door of my apartment and head toward the elevator.

"Good morning, baby," mom answers after the second ring.

"Happy birthday, mama."

"Thank you. What are you doing today?"

"Same as every other day. I'm on my way into the boutique. I just left home, so I figured I'd call while walking to the bus stop."

"Well," she starts. "I'm in the city."

"You're what?" I ask. Shock evident in my voice. I haven't actually seen my mother for a few years. I knew they had been spending some time in Vegas recently, but I thought she would have moved on by now.

"Yes. I'm in the city. I haven't been this lost in years."

"You're in LA?"

"Umm." I wait while she says something to someone else, her voice muffled enough for me to gather that she's pressed the phone against her chest. A shudder runs down my spine as I wonder who she's talking to in the background. "Echo Park actually. Jase mentioned that he saw you a few weeks back and I wanted to see your shop. He said it was really nice and he was proud of you."

Closing my eyes as I sit on the bench at the bus stop, I take several deep breaths before responding. The last thing I need or want from Jase is his pride. Swallowing several times against the nerves forming a ball in my throat, I wonder if Jase is with her in Echo Park. I don't know if I can handle seeing him again after his last visit. "Are you alone?" I ask tentatively as I stand to board the approaching bus.

"No," she answers and my heart sinks to my feet. "David's with me. We're sitting in front of your shop waiting for you to get here."

"Oh."

"I was thinking I could hang out with you for a while today. David has other things he wants to take care of while we're in the city, so he'll probably leave when you get here."

"Well," I start as I locate a place to stand. The bus is pretty full today considering it's the middle of the work week and everyone is commuting. I'm used to having to stand but with my head still spinning from the dizziness this morning, I'm not happy about having to do it today. Add my increasing anxiety over seeing my mom and David today and I just want to run back to my apartment and lock myself inside. "I just got on the bus, so I'll be there soon."

"Okay, baby. I'll see you when you get here." She hangs up before I get a chance to respond back to her and I hold my phone close to my chest while trying to remind myself how to breathe.

"Are you okay?" I jump as someone places a hand on my shoulder.

"What?" I spin around so fast I nearly fall over before the stranger grabs my arm to steady me.

"You look a little pale. Are you okay?" He asks again, a genuine look of concern in his eyes.

"Yeah." I close my eyes and inhale slowly. God, I wish my head would stop spinning. "I'm okay."

"Here." He steps aside as far as he can considering we're practically shoulder to shoulder in the bus. "Take my seat."

"Thank you." I don't even bother arguing with him for giving up his seat. I'm more than happy to sit down for the rest of the ride to Echo Park. I watch the stranger as he steps over to the bar in the center of the bus where I was standing. He doesn't look back at me or speak to me anymore and I'm somewhat grateful for that. I need to get myself together before I get to my shop and see my mom.

As soon as I'm off the bus, I pull my phone out of my hobo bag and decide to send a text to Chris. Thankfully I don't have to wait long for his reply which is surprising since I thought he'd be out of service.

Me: Missing you today.
Chris: Miss you too, Butterfly.
Me: Wow. I didn't think I'd hear back from you so fast.
Chris: Things are going pretty good here. I might even be able to come home tonight.
Me: I hope so. I really miss you.
Chris: Everything okay?
Me: Yeah. My mom is in town. She's waiting for me at the shop.

It takes him a few minutes to get back to me again and I wonder if he got busy. I see my mom and David parked in front of the shop and slow my steps a little hoping to hear the tell-tale ding of another incoming text message.

Chris: *Just your mom?*

I know what he's really asking by that text message. He wants to make sure there aren't going to be any more issues with Jase. I smile to myself thinking about the cameras that he installed around the inside of the store last week. It actually relieves some of the tension in my shoulders to know that he'll be able to keep an eye on me if I need him to. He has the app installed on his phone so he can check on me anytime during the day when I'm here.

Me: *Yeah. David is with her but he's going to leave as soon as I get there. It's her birthday so she's going to spend the day with me.*
Chris: *Okay, Butterfly. I'll check in with you later. Need to head to another meeting in a few.*
Me: *Bye for now.*

He doesn't respond again but I don't expect him to. Tossing my phone into my bag, I grab my keys and walk up to the door. I hear the truck door close behind me at the same time that I swing the shop door open.

"Cypress." I turn in time to see my mom rushing across the sidewalk. "Oh my God, Cypress. It's so great to see you." She pulls me into a hug as soon as she gets close enough, practically crushing me against her chest.

"Hi, mom," I squeak against her shoulder, and she releases her hold on me.

Placing her hands on my shoulders, she leans back enough to look at me. I can see the scrutiny in her expression as she takes in my long hair, the braid laying lazily over my left shoulder. "You haven't changed a bit."

"Nope." I don't feed into her criticism. She's always been that way about my choices in fashion. She always wanted me to dress more my own age, or what she considered to be my own age. Honestly, I think she treated me more like a Barbie doll while I was growing up. She was always putting me in frilly dresses and curling my hair. As I got older, she would try to get me to wear tight jeans and low-cut tops. I was always more comfortable in my loose-fitting shirts and long skirts to be honest. My body is a temple, a gift that should be unwrapped only by the one I love. I've always been more comfortable hiding my figure beneath my clothes. The only person that deserves to see what I have to offer is Chris. I don't need to flaunt myself around for anyone else, despite what my mother may have wished me to do.

"Still dressing the same too, I see."

"Really, mom?" I lower my brows at her, letting my feelings on the matter be conveyed through my expression.

"Never mind. You look great. It's so nice to see you. I've missed you so much."

"I've missed you too, mom." Looking over her shoulder, I see David still sitting in the truck. I guess he's waiting for us to go in before he leaves. Lifting a hand, I cast him a quick wave before turning around to the open shop door. "Would you like to come in?"

"Of course." She waves over her shoulder to David and follows me into the store.

I take a few minutes to turn on the lights and flip the sign to open before closing the door and walking to the register to open it for the day. "So how long are you in town?"

"Only today. We're going to Florida soon. It's been a long time since we've been there. I'm excited to see a warm beach again. The water here is so cold."

"You've been to the beach?" I look up at her, confused, after placing my things below the register. "When did you get to town?"

"We've been here a few days already. We parked the camper at the beach."

I don't know what bothers me more about this conversation. The fact that Jase is still so close by. Or that my mother has been in town for a few days, and this is the first time I've heard from her, much less seen her.

"Oh, baby. Don't be like that." She walks over and places her hand against my cheek. It's all I can do not to recoil from her touch. It's so motherly but out of sorts for her. She's always been a great mother and made sure my needs were met, but she's never been the lovey-dovey affectionate type. "What's wrong?"

"You've been in town for a few days already?" I tilt my head at her, my brows tightening together enough that I feel a tingle in my forehead. "And this is the first I've heard from you?"

"It's not like that," she says, finally stepping away from me. I turn away from her and brace my hands on the counter, the dizziness returning full force.

"What have you been doing for the last few days? There hasn't been a festival here. What else would you be doing that would keep you from reaching out?"

"Well, nothing mostly." She walks away and I peek at her over my shoulder to watch as she peruses the shop. "David and Jase had business here to take care of. I mostly stayed in the camper and let them do their thing. I didn't think we'd be here more than a few days, so I didn't want you to get your hopes up."

"I see." I find it suspicious that David and Jase would have anything to do here. They don't normally go anywhere that there isn't a show. Still, it doesn't add up. Jase was here over a week ago and he didn't say anything about my mom being in the area. I was under the impression that they were still in Vegas, or somewhere in Nevada. Was he here by himself? Was he here just to spy on me?

"This is a nice boutique. You've done well for yourself." She turns my way and I straighten from the counter, finally feeling the dizziness subside enough to stand on my own. "And this location is…" She tilts her head and looks at me quizzically. "Are you okay? You look a little green."

"I'm fine. I just didn't eat anything this morning."

"Well, that won't do, now will it. I'll call David and have him pick something up for us to bring back."

"No," I stop her from reaching for her phone. "That won't be necessary. I'll just get some work done around here and we'll go out for lunch."

"Okay. Tell me what you do during the day, and I'll help. I want to know what it's like to live a day in your life."

That makes me smile.

Of course, the day drags on. We get several customers in the shop during the day and both of us keep busy restocking the clothing racks. Marie comes in at one point with her boyfriend, Matt. I remember meeting him at the wedding this past weekend.

"Hi, Marie," I greet her as she comes into the boutique.

"Cypress." She rushes up and wraps her arms around my middle. "You remember Matt?" She asks as she pulls away and reaches her arm out for him.

"I do. How are you guys?"

"We're good. We were in the area today and thought we'd stop by. I wanted Matt to see where I got those amazing incense burners."

"Of course."

"Who's this?" My mother comes up behind me, a smile plastered on her face.

"Mom." I place a hand on her shoulder. "This is Marie and Matt. And this is my mom, Willow."

"Nice to meet you." Marie smiles a friendly smile at my mom. It doesn't surprise me when I see Matt out of the corner of my eye as he scrutinizes my mom from head to toe. As if she may be hiding a concealed weapon somewhere. I wonder if Chris reached out to have them stop in today but quickly dismiss the thought. Why would he have someone coming in to check up on me when he could just check the video feeds at any time.

"Ma'am." Matt nods his head in greeting to my mother. He looks so different from when I met him at the wedding. His dark hair hangs loose around his face, falling just past his shoulders. He's dressed in a tight black t-shirt, dark wash jeans, and black motorcycle boots. Marie has her cotton-candy pink hair pulled up into adorable space buns with the back falling in loose waves down her back. She's dressed in a purple tank top and loose-fitting yellow knee-length skirt. It occurs to me that these two are total opposites, but together, they are the most adorable couple I've ever seen.

I guess it's true what they say. Opposites attract. If these two aren't the greatest example of that, I don't know what is. Maybe that's a hopeful sign that Chris and I will be great together for the long run. I certainly hope so anyway.

"I just got some new incense burners in the other day that I haven't put out on the shelves yet. Come over here and I'll show you." I reach out a hand to lead her to the counter behind the register where the boxes are waiting that I got from my friend in Arizona.

"Oh my gosh." She claps excitedly while jumping in place a few times. "I can't wait."

"I want to see these too." My mom follows us to the counter and helps me cut open the boxes. We pull out the treasures awaiting inside one by one, Marie gasping at each one in turn as they are unwrapped and removed from their protective packaging.

I look over my shoulder at Matt who is still standing sentinel in the middle of the store. A location that allows him to keep an eye on every corner as well as us in case there are any dangers lurking nearby. It confirms my suspicions that he was sent here to keep an eye on me. Considering Marie said she brought him here to see the incense burners he should at least pretend to have an interest in them.

"Oh!" Marie exclaims. "Matt, look at this one." She runs over to where Matt is still standing with his hands in his pockets. "It's a fairy."

Matt's eyes light up as she approaches him and it's clear to see the love shining through. My stomach lurches with awe and it only makes me miss Chris that much more. He said he might be home tonight, and I can't wait. "That's perfect for you, Sprite." I smile to myself, my gaze staying focused on the incense burners on the counter, when I hear his term of endearment for Marie.

"I'm going to buy it." She carries the fairy burner back to the counter and carefully places it back in the box. Setting it beside the register, she continues to help unpack the rest of the burners. "Do you want some help setting them out?" She asks as she picks up a few burners in each hand.

"Sure." I grab a few myself and follow her over to the shelf where the rest of the burners are located. We carefully arrange them while my mom cleans up the packaging behind the counter. "Don't throw the boxes away, mom. I like to be able to put them back in their own box when they sell."

"Okay. I'll just set them all under the counter," mom calls from the other side of the shop.

"So, how are you?" Marie asks while she moves a few burners around the shelf, obviously trying to look busy so we don't have to move from this spot.

"I'm okay," I answer honestly. "A little tired but it's been a long day already and I haven't had a chance to take a break."

"No, I mean with your mom being here."

The truth comes out. If I had any question about the reason for Marie and Matt to be here today, she just confirmed it. "Chris asked you to come in today, didn't he?"

"He called Matt this morning." She actually looks guilty, and I feel bad for some reason. "He was worried about you. Don't be mad at him."

"I'm not." How could I be mad at him for wanting to watch over me. "He didn't need to send you in here though. I'm sure you had more important things to be doing today."

"Not really." She turns and faces me completely. "How are things going with Chris?"

I feel the heat rise to my cheeks at her question and she giggles. I've always been easy to read. My mother always says I wear my feelings on my face. "Really good, actually."

"I was really happy to see you both together at the wedding last weekend. You both look so happy together."

"We are." I turn my gaze to the floor trying not to let her see too much on my face. "I'm in love with him." I feel the tension in my cheeks at the smile spreading over my face. I haven't said those words to anyone other than Chris and it feels good to tell someone else. I want to shout it from the rooftops.

"That's wonderful, Cypress. I'm so happy for you."

"Thank you." Smiling, I set the last incense burner on the shelf and step back to look over our work. The display looks perfect. I should have brought my phone over with us so I could take a picture for Instagram. I'll just have to remember to take one later.

"I can see that he loves you more than anything." She places a hand on my shoulder reassuringly. "I saw the way he looks at you. I know he worries about you. There's something you need to know about these guys. They keep their emotions held pretty close, under lock and key. But when they love, they love hard, and they love deep. There's nothing they won't do for the ones they love."

"You think so?"

"I know so. Remind me sometime to tell you my story."

"I'd like that." And I realize that I really would like to get to know her better. I've never been good at making friends, but Marie is about as close to one as I can get.

"Me too. Now, let me pay for that incense burner so I can get out of your hair. It's almost your closing time and I'm sure you still have things to do before you leave for the day."

"I got it, Sprite." Matt places a hand on Marie's back and follows her to the counter. I meet them both at the register and take the card out of Matt's hand to pay for the incense burner. After putting the box into a bright orange boutique bag, I hand it over the counter and Marie grabs it from me, a huge smile on her face. I watch as Matt chews his lip for several seconds while looking around the shop, his eyes landing on my mother for longer than expected before turning back to me. "Don't be a stranger, kid." He takes a card out of his wallet and grabs the pen from the counter next to the register. I watch as he scribbles on the back of the card.

"Here's mine and Marie's cell numbers. Text or call either of us anytime if you need anything. I mean that."

"Thank you." I take the card out of his outstretched hand and place it in my bag beneath the counter.

"I mean it." He narrows his eyes at me.

"I know." I smile at him and watch as Marie wraps her arms through one of his. "I promise." He glares in the direction where my mom is standing again before putting an arm around Marie's shoulder and walking toward the door. Neither of them looks back in my direction before they exit the boutique, leaving me alone again with my mother.

"Well," she says as she walks over to the window and flips the sign to closed. "I don't know about you but I'm starving. What's good to eat around here?"

Chapter 17

Chris

My mind keeps drifting as I walk down the precinct corridor this morning. We have another meeting with the PFM in a few minutes and I'm ready for this to be over so I can go home to my Butterfly.

We've made a lot of headway on the investigation over the last couple of days. I had to make a trip with Jackson and Noah, a couple of the other detectives working on this case, to Mexico City yesterday to meet with Investigator Martinez in person. His field agents found evidence to support that the trafficking victims were indeed in Mexico. They are currently being held in an unknown location, awaiting auction. It sickens me to imagine all the ways that these women are being abused while waiting for their potential buyers to purchase them. There's no telling how they're being treated or what hell they're currently going through, and I'm helpless to do anything about it.

The meeting today is supposed to go over a new strategy to locate the victims and extract them safely. Hopefully, I'll be able to go home after the meeting today.

As if conjured by my thoughts, my phone dings with an incoming text message and a smile instantly spreads over my face.

Cypress: *Missing you today.*

Yep. I'm whipped. I'm not afraid to admit it. But this woman has me wrapped around her little finger.

Me: Miss you too, Butterfly.
Cypress: Wow. I didn't think I'd hear back from you so fast.
Me: Things are going fairly good here. I might even be able to come home tonight.

Hopefully, I'm telling her the truth. There isn't much more I can do here right now while waiting on the PFM to gather more information. There's only so much that we can do without going outside our jurisdiction.

Cypress: I hope so. I really miss you.
Me: Everything okay?
Cypress: Yeah. My mom is in town. She's waiting for me at the shop.

My fingers fist around my phone so tight my knuckles turn white and I'm in danger of cracking the screen. I shouldn't worry about it since it's her mother. But if her mother is in town, does that mean her piece of shit stepbrother is there too?

Me: Just your mom?

I'll drop everything here, consequences be damned, if she says her fucking stepbrother is there too. Holding my breath while waiting for her to reply, I stand outside the conference room and listen to the people inside. I know I need to get into this meeting, but I'll be damned if I'm going to go in before I know that Cypress is safe. I'd leave right now if I thought I could get there in time to keep her from having to deal with him on her own again.

Cypress: *Yeah. David is with her but he's going to leave as soon as I get there. It's her birthday so she's going to spend the day with me.*

My breath rushes out of me, and I sag against the wall. It occurs to me that I can keep an eye on her from here if I need to since I have the app installed on my phone to monitor her cameras. I don't want to invade her privacy in such a way if I don't have to. Not to mention, I need to be able to focus on this meeting if I'm going to be able to leave for home today.

Me: *Okay, Butterfly. I'll check in with you later. Need to head to another meeting in a few.*
Cypress: *Bye for now.*

Scrolling through my contacts, I decide to call in reinforcements. I can't call Devan since he's on his honeymoon, but I can reach out to Matt. I know Cypress knows Marie since she takes her yoga class and she mentioned her coming into her shop a few times.

"Hey, Chris. What's up?" Matt answers on the second ring, and I smile to myself at his casual banter.

"Matt, I need a favor."

"Of course. Everything okay?"

"Yeah, as far as I know. I'm stuck in San Diego working on a case. Cypress has a visitor at her shop today and there's a history there that I don't want to go in to. I wanted to see if you had time to maybe stop in for a few minutes and check up on her for me. Let me know if anything's amiss. I'm working on getting back there hopefully tonight but it'll make me feel a lot better if you could check on her for me."

"Sure, man. She's familiar with Marie so I'll take her in with me. I'll check back with you after."

"I appreciate it, man."

"Don't mention it. I owe you my life, man. I got no problem helping out where I can."

"Thanks again, Matt. I gotta head into this meeting so if I don't answer when you call back, just leave a message." Disconnecting the call, I place my phone in my jacket pocket and take several deep breaths to try to relax before opening the conference room door. Everyone stops talking and turns toward the door when I walk in, and I can't help but wonder if I've already missed something important. I almost feel guilty about being late. Almost.

Turns out, I didn't miss anything. Investigator Martinez is already on the video conference discussing his field agents and where they're being stationed. He has a few locations mapped out as possible auction sites that they'll be infiltrating over the next few days on a recon mission. The only thing left for us to do is twiddle our thumbs and wait for word on the victims.

"Everyone okay with that?" Lucas, one of the detectives from the La Mesa PD, asks everyone and I realize that I've missed majority of the conversation. My mind keeps wandering back to Cypress. I shouldn't be worried about her, I trust Matt with keeping an eye on her and letting me know if there's something I need to be aware of. I nod my head in affirmation along with everyone else around the table.

"Alright," Inspector Martinez announces through the video feed. "I'll get back to you in a few days. Hopefully, we'll have more information on a possible extraction by then." The screen goes dark before anyone can reply and the room falls silent for several seconds.

I'm hungry. I'm exhausted. I'm fed the fuck up with the information that we keep going over again and again with this case. I still don't understand how someone was able to get in, grab these girls, and get out of the country undetected.

Whoever is leading this operation has been doing this for a long time. It shows by how smoothly they were able to move these girls without getting caught. They've obviously done this several – or hundreds – of times before. There's no telling how many other victims there are out there that have been traded and trafficked over the years. I wonder how many of them are still out there waiting to be rescued. How many of them have given up the thought of ever going home again?

No matter how many of these cases I work over the years, they never get any easier.

It's already dark by the time I wander out of the precinct. Walking across the dark parking lot to my SUV, I pull my phone from my jacket pocket and check for messages. I don't have any more messages from my Butterfly today and I wonder how things went with her mother.

I do have a missed call from Matt though. He didn't leave a voicemail, so I don't expect any bad news, but still, I call him back as I click the unlock button my key fob.

"Chris," he answers after the second ring.

"Hey, Matt. Sorry I didn't get back to you earlier. I was stuck in meetings all day working on this fucking case."

"No worries, man. I knew you were busy and figured I'd hear back from you when you got a minute."

"So?" I begin before taking a few deep cleansing breaths. "Did you get a chance to stop in Poppy Petals today?"

"Oh yeah. Marie had a great time too. I hadn't been in there before but it's a nice place. Little dark on the inside with the lack of windows and all, but it's a colorful place. Cypress really livens up the atmosphere, ya know."

"Yeah. She has a tendency to lighten up any atmosphere. That's for sure."

"I can see that. But her mother? Man, she's a piece of work."

"What do you mean?" I hold my breath and brace myself for unwelcome news. I haven't been able to meet her mother before, but just hearing the stories about her and how Cypress grew up, I can only imagine the tension there. I don't know if I'll ever get the chance to sit in a room with her, or that I want to for that matter. But I still wish I could have been there with them today. At least to offer my silent support for Cypress while she dealt with the visit from her mother. I know she said her stepfather, David, was dropping her off and leaving, but I still worry that something happened today that I wasn't there to guard her from.

I didn't have a chance to check the video feed today, with the meeting and all the guys gathered around. I didn't want to seem like I was too distracted to work on this case. But I still spent several nerve-wracking hours, practically crawling out of my own skin, wanting to reach for my phone and check on her at least once. I held out though, knowing that Matt was able to be there for me when I couldn't. I knew he'd have my girl's back if I wasn't able to have it myself.

"It was just her." He finally says and I release my breath. "She was the only one there. I didn't see anyone else, inside, or outside."

"Yeah, she said David dropped her mom off when she got there. I don't know where he ended up, but she said he wasn't going to hang around there all day."

"Well, he wasn't there. At least not that I was able to see. There was no one hanging around outside either when I left. But her mom, man. She's got a presence about her. Like she's the darkest spot on the entire universe."

I have no idea what he means by that, but it makes me feel even worse that I wasn't able to be there.

"She just," he pauses like he's trying to formulate the proper response. I wait several agonizing seconds while he gets his thoughts together. "She just takes control of everything. Telling Cypress what to do when a customer enters the shop. Directing her how to do things that she's probably been doing on her own, successfully I might add, for however long now. When Marie stepped in and wanted to offer a hand, the woman just glared at her and it made my skin crawl. She just had that vibe. Ya know?"

"Yeah, I know what you mean." Even though I really don't. But after everything that Matt went through with Marie, I don't think he'd hold back. If he has a bad feeling about someone then it's something that I definitely need to make note of. "So, how were things otherwise? I mean, did Cypress seem like she was upset or uncomfortable at all?"

"It was hard to tell. I mean, I've only actually met her once. But Marie seemed to think that something was wrong with her."

"Shit." I don't like the sound of that. I haven't heard anything from her since this morning and I can feel my pulse increasing, my blood pressure rising, at the thought of her being upset and me not being there to comfort her after the visit with her mom.

"Not like that, man. I know where you're going in that head of yours. Believe me, if I thought it was something like where your imagination is roaming, I wouldn't have left her there alone with her mom. I would have stayed there all day and well into the night until you were able to get yourself back here if that were the case. I just mean, she didn't seem like herself to Marie. Like she wasn't feeling a hundred percent. She was a little pale too."

"She's sick?" My stomach falls to my feet, and I lean my forehead against the steering wheel. "She didn't tell me she was sick."

"Hmm." He interrupts my thoughts with his musings. "No offense, man, but Cypress doesn't strike me as the kind of girl that is going to let a little sickness or fatigue ruin anyone's day. She knew you were busy. I'm sure she didn't want to bother you with it. But if it makes you feel any better, it didn't seem like it was holding her back at all. That is one happy go lucky lady. I have a feeling that she knows how to seek out a rainbow in the gloomiest of weather. Or maybe she'd just make one of her own." He laughs and I can't help but join him.

"You're right about that." I chuckle lightly as I lift my head, tension easing from my shoulders, and put the key in the ignition. "Look, I'm finally getting ready to leave San Diego and head home. Thanks for keeping an eye on my girl for me today."

"Anytime, man. I mean that. If it weren't for you, neither Devan nor myself would have our girls. I owe you my life, you have no idea."

"I think I do, actually." Connecting the phone up to the Bluetooth, I set it in the cradle and back out of my parking spot.

"Yeah. You might be right about that. Congratulations, man."

"For what?"

"For finding your other half."

His words sink in, and I can feel a tightness building in my chest. The simple truth of that statement warms me – body and soul. "Yeah."

"Hold on to that one, Chris. It's nice to see you with someone that completes you."

"I plan on it. I'll talk to you later." Disconnecting the call, I take a few more calming breaths while waiting for a light to turn green then call Cypress to let her know I'm on my way home. It's late, well not as late as I thought it would be, but I know she's had a long day. So, I'm not surprised when my call goes to voicemail. She's probably passed out on the couch with her latest romance novel laying on her chest.

Smiling to myself, I wait for her voicemail greeting to end so I can start my message. "Hey, Butterfly. I'm on my way home. I'll be there in a couple of hours. I miss you. I'll see you soon."

In a feeble attempt to take my mind of what might be awaiting me at home, especially if Cypress is sick or had a rough day with her mom, I select a playlist on my phone and crank the music. It's a long, boring drive back to Los Angeles from San Diego. There isn't much to see after the sun goes down. During the day, the drive is quite lovely, and the scenery is awe inspiring. One of the things that I've always enjoyed about California is the scenery. My mind is too full of my Butterfly to even think about enjoying the late drive back home.

Spacing out to music is the best way to endure the distance between us right now. It's all I can do to stay below the speed limit on the drive back. Thankfully, the two plus hour drive goes by without incident and I'm walking into the apartment building just after ten o'clock. I don't expect Cypress to still be awake this late at night, but I'm anxious to see her anyway.

I debate stopping by the mailboxes before heading upstairs and think better of it. My mail will still be waiting there for me tomorrow.

Stepping off the elevator on the fifth floor, I walk slowly down the hallway toward my apartment. I pause next to Cypress' door before turning to my own. It's quiet inside her apartment and I imagine her curled up in her bed, sleeping peacefully. It's tempting to pop in and check on her before going to my own apartment, but I think better of it.

Stepping into my apartment, I toss my keys on the table next to the door and pause. There is a lamp on in the living room that I don't remember leaving on. Closing my eyes, I inhale deeply, and I'm greeted by the scent of vanilla and sandalwood. A fragrance that tickles my senses, awakening my nerve endings. I've come to recognize the scent that tells me Cypress is nearby.

Shedding my jacket and toeing off my shoes, I pad slowly across the carpet and that's when I see her. She's curled up on my sofa, her knees pulled up into her chest as if she were trying to become the smallest thing possible. Her braid is laying behind her as her cheek is pressed into the plaid pillow, her lashes fanning softly across her cheeks. She's already dressed for a comfortable sleep in a loose-fitting t-shirt – one of mine if I'm not mistaken – and leggings.

She's beautiful, even in her peaceful sleeping state. I stand and watch her breathe peacefully for several minutes before pulling my shirt over my head and kicking my jeans to the floor.

Stepping closer, I kneel beside where she sleeps curled up on the sofa and brush a light kiss across her cheek. She doesn't wake but the corners of her full lips curl up in a sweet, innocent smile. Standing, I bring her with me, curling her body against mine. I brace my arms beneath her shoulders and legs and pull her tightly into my chest as I carry her through the apartment.

I had hoped that she was comfortable enough to sleep in my apartment while I was away. Walking into the room, I see the bed is still made same as the day I left, and I know that she hasn't slept here. Maybe she let herself in knowing that I would be coming home today. Or hoping I would anyway. I don't mind. I'm grateful that she's here. I want more than anything to curl my body around her and breathe in her vanilla fragrance while I drift off to sleep and forget about the last few days without her.

She doesn't wake as I lay her softly on the bed, after using one arm to pull back the covers. Crawling in behind her, I wrap my arms around her and pull her into my body. Burying my face in her hair, I breathe deep as sleep overtakes me. I drift off peacefully, surrounded by my Butterfly and her soothing vanilla and sandalwood fragrance.

Chapter 18

Cypress

Waking up with Chris curled around me was heaven. I know instantly by his leather and musk scent that I'm in his bed, his arms wrapped tightly around me. I can feel him pressed against my back and I want to turn to face him, but his arms get even tighter when I start to wiggle against him.

"Good morning, Butterfly," he growls into my hair. His voice raspy with sleep and it makes a chill sweep down my spine.

My nipples harden, the fabric of the t-shirt chafing against them, and butterflies take flight deep in my belly. Under normal circumstances, I would think that was a good sign. Today, however, they are staging some sort of mutiny against me, and my stomach starts to churn wildly. "Oh shit." I push harder against Chris, my legs swinging over the side of the bed at the same time, and he releases me instantly.

"Cypress?" He calls after me as I run across the room to the bathroom, his voice laced with concern.

I barely make it, my knees sliding across the last several inches of the tile floor before my stomach empties itself of anything that I managed to put into it yesterday, which thankfully wasn't much. "Oh, God." Breathing heavily, I lean my forehead against the cool porcelain and will my insides to stop dancing and turning against me.

"Baby, are you okay?" Chris wanders into the bathroom behind me and I can hear him shuffling through the cabinet beneath the sink. He turns the water on for a minute before pulling my hair back and pressing a cool cloth against my forehead.

"Oh no," I moan, closing my eyes against the embarrassment burning red across my cheeks. "Don't do that. I don't want you seeing me like this."

"Are you kidding?" He sits on the floor, his back against the side of the tub, and pulls me into his lap. Brushing my hair away from my face, he takes the wet cloth and wipes my mouth before pulling my face against his chest. "I'm not keeping you around because you're perfect. Well, not just because you're perfect."

"Ugh." Pushing against his chest, I try to sit up, but he wraps his arms around me and holds me in place as he chuckles softly.

"I want all the not so perfect parts too. I'm not running away when you get sick." I push again but he doesn't release me. "Don't fight me on this, Cypress. You won't win."

"Fine." Closing my eyes, I relax against him. He sighs and loosens his hold on me before rubbing his hand up and down my back in a soothing gesture.

"Are you okay?"

"Yes. I think so anyway."

"Okay." He kisses the top of my head. "Do you want to go back to bed? There's no rule against taking it easy when you're sick. I know you had a rough day yesterday and I won't think badly of you if you decide to relax today and take it easy."

"I can't. I have a store to run." Blinking several times to clear my eyes of the unwanted tears that have started to form, I take stock of my faculties and realize that I'm already feeling better. Yes, it's a little weird, but I don't have time to dwell on that. I need to get ready to go open the shop. "Tea. And a shower. Then I should go."

"Hey," Chris places a finger below my chin and tilts my gaze up to his. "It's your store, you know. You make the rules. You can take the day off if you need to." He sweeps a loose strand of my hair behind my ear before cupping my face in his warm palm.

"No," I sigh. "I'm okay. And I have a million new items to take pictures of today. I really need to go into the boutique. Maybe I'll just work half the day today and then come home and go back to bed."

"Okay," he relents. "You get in the shower, and I'll go make you some tea. Do you think you could eat a little bit?"

"I can try. Maybe just some toast or something light."

"You got it." Leaning closer, he kisses me on the cheek. He stands and helps me to my feet, steadying me by placing his hands on my shoulders before he turns and walks out of the bathroom.

Reaching into the shower, I turn the water on to heat before stripping out of my t-shirt and leggings. Stepping into the hot spray, I close my eyes and let the water wash over my aching body. Turning my back into the spray, I roll my shoulders around and bend forward to stretch out my back. It's amazing to me how tense my body is from only a few seconds of sickness. I can't imagine dealing with this all day.

Finally turning off the shower, I grab a towel to wrap around my body before stepping out onto the plush rug. I quickly brush my teeth, twice, before running a wide tooth comb through my knotted hair. Once I've got my tresses tamed and braided tightly, I open the door and step into the bedroom. Chris is standing at the foot of the bed, already dressed in his typical dark pants and long-sleeved shirt.

I love the way he covers his entire body, saving the art for me to unwrap like a gift kept tucked away just for me. One of these days, maybe I'll ask him why he keeps his art covered the way he does.

To be honest, I don't even know if his friends know about all the ink covering his body. Well, half of it anyway.

"Hey, Butterfly." He looks up at me, one side of his mouth curled up in a grin as he looks me over from head to toe. Even from across the room, I can see the desire burning in his eyes as he watches the water droplets running over the curve of my breast, stopping at the edge of the terry cloth wrapped tightly around my body. "Feeling any better?"

"I am, actually." I step lightly across the carpet, curling my toes with every step into the lush fibers. "I don't know, I guess I didn't eat enough yesterday. It was a pretty busy day with Matt and Marie stopping in. I skipped breakfast and we got so busy, my mom and I didn't stop to eat until after we closed the store for the night."

"Okay." Stepping closer, Chris wraps a hand around the base of my neck and draws me closer to him. He kisses my forehead before pulling away enough to look into my eyes. "I made you some tea." He reaches an arm to the side and grabs a mug of hot tea from the top of his dresser. "It's ginger, for your stomach. I hope that's okay."

"That's perfect, Chris." I take a tentative sip of the hot liquid, letting it warm me down to my toes. "Thank you." Smiling, I set the mug back on the dresser and begin gathering my clothes for the day. It's convenient to have left several pieces of my clothes here over the last few weeks. I'm here so much as it is that it's nice not to have to run across the hall every day before going to work.

"I have to leave soon for work." I watch as Chris sits on the edge of the bed and begins lacing up his boots. "Do you want me to drop you off at the shop?"

Lower my brows, I look over at the nightstand and see that it's barely seven. "No." I pause as I slip my t-shirt over my head, pulling the braid out and tossing it over my shoulder so it hangs down my back. "I think I'll finish my tea and make some toast before I go in."

"Okay, Butterfly." Standing, he slips on his jacket, and I watch as he puts his phone and wallet in the inside pocket. "Let me know if you start feeling sick again. I have several meetings I have to attend today and a phone conference with the other detectives this afternoon. But I'll sneak away if I have to."

"I will."

"I don't know if I'll be done before you close if you stay all day at the shop. Are you okay getting home by yourself if I don't make it there?"

"Yeah, of course. I'm a big girl, Chris. It isn't like I haven't taken the bus every day for the last three years."

"That's not what I mean, Cypress, and you know it."

"God, Chris." Sitting on the edge of the bed, I fist the blanket at my hips and turn my gaze to the floor. "I'm sorry. I didn't mean that. I don't even know why I said it."

"Baby." Stepping closer, he kneels in front of me and cups my face in his hands. "It's okay. Hey," he starts when my gaze doesn't meet his. I finally lift my face and look into his eyes. "I love you."

"I love you too." He smiles, the same smile I get every time I tell him that I love him. It's his secret smile saved just for me, and it melts my heart into a puddle at his feet every time he gives it to me.

"Fuck, Butterfly. I really wish I could stay here with you all day, make you stay in bed so I could take care of you. I don't like that you're sick."

"I'm okay. I told you I think it's my fault for not eating yesterday. I'll be okay."

"You better let me know if you're not."

"I will."

He pulls me closer and gives me a chaste kiss on the mouth. "Text me." I watch as he stands and walks to the bedroom door. "I may not be able to answer right away but I still want to hear from you today. And if you start to feel sick again, I expect you to come back home and go to bed."

"Yes, dear," I call out in a sing-song voice, and he chuckles as he walks out the door. I listen as he grabs his keys and walks out of the apartment. The sudden growling in my stomach kicks me into gear again and I grab my shoes and the mug of tea off the dresser before retreating to the kitchen for toast. After I've finished one piece of toast, I'm feeling much better and decide it's time to face my day.

The bus ride to Echo Park goes by without any hiccups for the first time all week. It isn't as crowded this morning, so I don't have to stand at least. Which is a good thing since my head started spinning just as soon as it started to move down the street.

This is going to be a long day.

Chris has to go to Mexico. He just found out today and left work early to come to the shop to let me know. For the last three days, I've had to ride the bus both too and from Echo Park because of meetings that Chris has had to attend for work. All of them are about the trafficking case he's been working on. Hopefully, him going to Mexico means they are ready to bring the victims home.

I shouldn't be jealous, I don't even know why I feel the way I do to be honest. Chris is a detective, an exceptionally good one. He has a job to do and there are victims out there that need his help in order to be found and brought home. He can't spend every minute of every day with me.

I don't like feeling this way. I'm still queasy and have bouts of dizziness throughout the day. But now I'm being irrational and grumpy.

I think I know what it is. Chris has been putting in long hours at work, and I've been feeling terrible lately and obviously not eating enough throughout the day. By the time we get to see each other at night, we're both tired and just want to go to bed. Yeah, we spend our nights wrapped up in each other's arms, but that's as far as it goes. Lately, we haven't even taken the time to get all our clothes off before passing out.

I'm going through withdrawal. I'm addicted to the shot of happy hormones from being intimate with Chris, and I haven't gotten my fix lately. That's messed up.

"Butterfly, are you okay?" He walks up behind me and wraps his arms around my waist, pulling my back into his front. "I know this is short notice and I'm sorry that I have to go. But we're close to being able to bring those girls home. I want to be there, I volunteered to be on the extraction team. I have to see this through."

"I know you do." Closing my eyes, I relax against him letting the warmth of his arms sink into me and help to relax some of the tension plaguing my body. We've spent so much time together over the past several weeks that Chris has finally started to open up to me about his past. He told me about his sister and how he decided what he wanted to specialize in with his career. He has spent most of his time as a detective working to save women from trafficking and abuse.

He even told me about his friend, Wendy. Even though he hasn't given me the story about how he met her, I know she was one of the victims that he rescued, and they became friends after that. I know about the outreach program that she started for helping the victims to reacclimate into their new lives.

"When do you have to leave?" I ask, my voice breaking on the last word.

"Tonight." He whispers, his cheek resting against my hair. "We're flying out by helicopter and going to Mexico City. We'll meet with agents with the PFM there and organize the operation."

"How long will you be gone?"

"I don't know. There's a lot to figure out still. We may be sending a few in undercover depending on what we find out when we get there."

"Oh, God."

"Baby, stop. Fuck, I shouldn't even be telling you this."

"Will you be safe?" I don't want to know the answer to the question that slipped out before I could stop it, but I have to know.

"Baby, don't." He turns me in his arms and cups my cheeks in his warm palms, his thumb swiping away a stray tear trailing down my cheek. "Don't worry about me."

"Please tell me you'll be safe." My voice cracks with emotion as I struggle to breathe.

"There's always a risk, Butterfly. I don't want you to think about that though. I'll take the risk in going in there and bringing those girls home. But know that I'll be thinking of you while I'm there. Just the thought of you being here waiting for me will bring me back to you. I'll be careful and as safe as I can be just to make sure that I can come home to you."

"I love you," I whisper as my hands fist in Chris' shirt.

"I love you too, Butterfly. Now, let me take you home. I want your taste on my lips before I have to leave you tonight."

Chapter 19

Cypress

"Are you okay?" Marie asks me as she and Julie wander over to the register. I wasn't expecting them to come into the shop today but I'm certainly happy to see some familiar faces. Business hasn't been going very well since I haven't been keeping up with my social media as much as before. But I've been feeling so tired lately that I just haven't had the motivation to do it. I need to snap out of it, though. If I don't, I'm liable to lose the store. There's no way I can afford to keep it open when I'm not bringing in any revenue.

I haven't been teaching any yoga classes lately either because I haven't been feeling well enough to get through it. I've taken a leave of absence from the studio in hopes of improving my health by taking more time to relax at home. It hasn't helped, however. I'm even more tired now than I was a few weeks ago. At least I haven't been getting sick lately. There is at least an improvement there.

"I'm fine. It's nice to see you." I paste a plastic smile across my face, knowing that it looks forced, but I can't help it. Is it bad when you don't even have enough energy to smile properly to two people who you claim are you friends?

Marie's brows are furrowed when I make eye contact with her. She has her hair pulled up in space buns again with the back flowing in long waves down her back. I'm envious of her and her effortless hairstyles when I can't do anything more than braid mine and let it lie over my shoulder. I watch as she crosses her arms over her chest and pops a hip out to the side.

Yeah, she isn't buying it.

"Bullshit," she exclaims, and I can't help but giggle at her expression. "You have designer luggage hanging out beneath your eyes. You obviously aren't sleeping well. Is Chris keeping you up too late?"

"Marie!" Julie snaps at her and slaps her hand lightly against Marie's shoulder.

"What?" She asks, turning her attention to Julie. "I mean, come on. It's not like you and I haven't had enough of those late nights ourselves." She turns her gaze back to me and lowers her arms to her sides. "Look, I get it. Chris is hot as fuck. I totally understand if that's the reason you look so exhausted. But honestly, I'm worried about you."

"Thank you." I smile a real smile this time. It's nice to know she cares enough to worry. Maybe we really are friends. "I appreciate it. Really, I do. But no, he hasn't been keeping me up late. He isn't even in town this week. He's been in Mexico since last Friday working on a case. I'm just tired. And I just got over this weird flu thing…"

"Wait," she interrupts me, bracing her hands flat on the counter in front of me. "What flu thing?"

"I've been sick. Well, I guess I was sick. It comes and goes really. But I'm starting to feel a lot better, I just haven't been sleeping well because of it."

"How long have you been sick?" Julie questions me, moving in beside Marie and leaning against the counter.

"I don't know. A couple of weeks I guess." I fidget with the edge of my shirt sleeve.

"That's what was wrong with you when your mom was here?" Marie asks. "I knew you weren't feeling well. You were so pale."

"Yeah," I answer. "I mean, I wasn't really sick then. Just not feeling well. And my mom showing up the way she did didn't really help."

"Hmm," Marie hums to herself and nods her head several times. I watch as Julie turns toward her, her eyes opening wider than hubcaps before she smiles so big, I think she's going to burst with excitement.

"Cypress," Julie turns back to me, the smile still plastered across her face. "Are you pregnant?"

"What?" I gasp, my hand going to my chest as I step back so fast, I nearly fall. "No, I'm not pregnant." I can't be pregnant. I'm on birth control. Closing my eyes and attempting to steady my breathing, I think back, trying to do the math in my head and try to remember when my last period was.

"Look at her," Marie whispers, probably talking to Julie. "I don't think she gets it."

"Give it a minute to sink in," Julie responds and honestly, I don't understand how these two ladies can be so calm in a time like this. My heart is beating a mile a minute and I'm on the verge of passing out.

"I think I should sit down." I whisper almost to myself. My head is suddenly spinning and there's no way I can catch my breath at this rate. I'm nearly hyperventilating with the reality that has just hit me square in the chest. "What am I going to do?" I ask to no one in particular as I move over to the chair in the back corner of the shop.

"Well, have you been to the doctor?" Marie asks me as she moves over to place a hand on my shoulder.

"No." I realize I probably should have done that when I first started getting sick, but I've been so busy with the shop and trying not to fall asleep during the day. "I'm on birth control. There's no way I can be pregnant right?"

"Well," Julie starts as she takes up a position beside Marie. "Nothing is a hundred percent effective. But you should probably stop taking those and take a test. Just to be sure."

"Oh, God." I sit up straight and put my hands on my head. "I've been taking my pills this entire time. What if something's wrong? Isn't it bad to take birth control when you're pregnant?"

"There's always a risk," Julie states matter-of-factly and I gasp. "Don't be like that. I'm just saying there's always a risk no matter what. But you should probably be sure and take a test, then make an appointment with your doctor to check on everything."

"Yeah," I agree, sitting up straighter in my chair. Folding my hands on my lap, I attempt to relax by breathing deep several times. "Yeah, I can do that."

"Great," Marie says as she starts to walk back to the counter. "There's a store up the block. I can go grab you a test if you want me to."

"You don't have to do that." I tell her honestly.

"Yeah, I think I do." She walks back over and kneels in front of me, placing her hands on my knees and smiling innocently. "You need a friend right now. Chris is out of town and you're by yourself. We're here for you, you know that."

"Thank you." I watch as she stands and walks to the door of the shop. Julie stays with me and helps me put a few things on the shelves while Marie is gone at the store.

I can't stop thinking about what I'm going to do if that test comes back positive. How am I going to tell Chris? What is he going to say? Will he be happy? Will he get angry and leave? I know he loves me. He says it all the time now so there's no denying that he does. And he already told me once before that he wanted all the not perfect parts of me too. Does this count as not perfect?

"Relax, Cypress," Julie giggles from across the store. "You're so tense I can practically see those wheels turning inside your head. I can hear the gears grinding, you're wound so tight."

"I know. I'm trying."

"You're not alone you know. And Chris is a great guy. You couldn't have found anyone better than him."

"Yeah." I blow out a long breath. "But is he ready for this?"

"Is anyone ever really ready for this? Besides, you don't even know if there is a 'this' yet." I watch as she uses finger quotes and giggle lightly. "There you go. Laugh or cry, right?"

"I'm back!" Marie announces as she comes running through the shop door. She's winded and I can't help but laugh loudly when I see the frazzled state in which she has returned.

"Did you run all the way there and back?" Julie asks her, rushing over to grab the bag wrapped around Marie's wrist.

"I did, actually." She walks over with Julie and watches me as Julie sets the bag on the counter. "You have a bathroom in this place?"

"Of course. It's in the back." I point to the door in the back corner of the shop, letting her know which direction the bathroom is in.

"Not for me, silly." Marie laughs as she takes the box out of the shopping bag on the counter and tosses it toward me. I catch it just before it smacks me in the forehead and glare at her, which in turn makes her and Julie both bust out laughing wildly. "For you. Go pee on that thing so we know what we're dealing with."

"Here?"

"Well, yeah." I stare at them both as they cross their arms and lean against the counter. "We'll wait here."

"Oh." I walk slowly toward the back-room door, reading the box as I go. There are two tests in the package, so I decide while on my way to the bathroom to take them both. Just to be sure. This is definitely something that I never thought I'd find myself doing – peeing on a stick in the back of my store.

Somehow, I realize as I try to decide the best method for taking these tests, I didn't think this through very well. Do I have to pee? Fidgeting, I shuffle from one foot to another. Yeah, I do. Do I think I have enough in me to do this twice? Chewing on my bottom lip, I realize that I don't know how much I actually have to go. This is going to be interesting.

Positioning myself precariously on the toilet, I manage to hold both test sticks – one in each hand – inside the bowl. Surprisingly, I manage to get both sticks wet with what little amount I'm actually able to pee. Is this what they mean by pee anxiety? I really thought I could have gone more than that, at least until it came down to actually doing it. Suddenly, I'm lucky I was able to catch anything at all, especially with as tiny as my targets are.

Who designed these things?

After replacing the caps on both sticks, I place them in the box and wash my hands. Carrying the box back out to the main part of the store, I place it on the shelf below the register and grab my phone to set an alarm for three minutes.

"What took you so long?" Julie asks as she watches me set my phone down on the counter.

"Sorry." Stepping away from the counter, I wring my hands together in front of my abdomen. "You wouldn't believe how difficult it is to pee under pressure. It was like I had a gun to my head or something. More of my body fluid escaped through my sweat glands than it did my bladder."

Marie taps her fingers against the register and Julie paces back and forth. Me? I just stand in one place and stare at my feet, waiting for the alarm to go off on my phone like I'm waiting for a bomb to be disarmed and I'm the only one here to witness it. I feel like my life is ending but in reality, I suppose it could be just starting.

"Is it weird that I don't know if I want it to be positive or negative?" I ask to no one in particular.

"No," Julie says as she walks over and pulls me into her side. "It's not weird at all. I'm not ready to have to go through this myself but I certainly wouldn't complain if I did. I've always wanted to be a mother. But the way I see it, if you are pregnant, then I get a chance to be an aunt."

"Really?" I look up at her, a tear slipping down my cheek.

"Of course. We're friends, aren't we? Friends make the best aunts."

"True," Marie agrees as she walks around the counter and stands on my other side. The two ladies have effectively sandwiched me between them both and I couldn't be more blessed than I am at this very moment. No matter what happens in the next two minutes, I know that I'm not in this alone.

No one is saying anything, and I nearly jump out of my skin when my alarm starts to blare from the counter. "Jesus!" I exclaim as I run over to shut it off. Bracing my hands on the countertop, I close my eyes and struggle to continue breathing. "I don't think I can look."

"Okay." Julie walks up behind me and places a hand between my shoulders. "I'll do it."

"No," Marie walks up to my other side. "We'll do it together."

Without opening my eyes, I nod my head and wait.

"Okay." I feel as Marie reaches around me and grabs the box from under the counter. "Julie, grab the other one and we'll look on the count of three. Ready?" She waits for Julie to nod her understanding. "One. Two. Three." And everything goes silent, I swear no one is even breathing right now.

Opening my eyes one at a time, I look first to Julie, then Marie. I watch as they both study the sticks in their hands. Marie looks up slowly, a smile spreading across her beautiful face. Julie wraps her arms around me from behind me and I nearly fall against her. "Well?" I ask when I finally find my voice.

"Pregnant." Marie states plainly, placing the stick back in the box.

"Same." Julie confirms, also placing the other stick in the box. "Are you okay?" She still has an arm wrapped around me and I realize that I'm not standing up straight. I'm still using her as my support.

Stealing my resolve, I push away from Julie and walk across the store. I lock the door and flip the sign to closed. Yes, it's only two in the afternoon and we're usually open until five, but I'm honestly not doing anything here today but raising the electric bill anyway. Might as well close it and wallow in my own emotional drama.

Closing my eyes, I lean against the locked door and sink to the floor. Pulling my knees up to my chest, I rest my forehead against them and wrap my arms around my calves.

"I think she's in shock," I hear Julie whisper from across the room. "Cypress? Are you okay?"

"No." I mumble. "What am I going to do?"

"Well." Marie steps closer, slowly judging by the sound of her footsteps. I feel so guilty with the way I'm acting towards these ladies. They've practically dropped everything today to be here to support me and I'm closing them out. But I can't help it. I've taken care of myself my entire life, why should this be any different. "First of all, you aren't going to do this."

Lifting my head from my knees, I glance toward Marie where she's now kneeling in front of me. "What?"

"You're not going to shut us out. We're your friends, Cypress. Whether you want us to be right now or not. And you're not shutting us out. This is a shock, and certainly not what you had planned. But it isn't the end of the world."

"She's right." Julie walks up behind Marie and puts her hands on her hips. She tries too hard to look intimidating and it's almost laughable. I guess just the thought of being able to laugh right now is a good sign since I feel like my world is crumbling down around me.

"When is Chris supposed to be back?" Marie asks as she places her hand on my knee.

"I don't know." My brows furrow. "I haven't heard from him in a couple of days. He's been so busy with this case he's working on." My eyes widen and I quickly glance around the shop. "Shit."

"What's wrong?" Julie asks, tilting her head to the side.

"The cameras." I stand quickly, almost too quickly as a wave of dizziness washes over me and I nearly fall against the door. "I forgot about the cameras. This isn't how I want him to find out. We need to move around. Or leave. Leaving would probably be better."

"We can do that." Marie reaches out and grabs my elbow. "Do you want us to hang out with you for a while? We can go grab dinner. Or you can come over to my house for a while. You don't need to be alone right now."

"I don't know if I can eat anything right now. My nerves are shot, and I don't want to end up making myself sick."

"That's fine. Why don't you come over then? We can go to my house. Maybe have some tea and watch a movie or something."

I look between these two women and a sense of warmth fills me. It's been a long time since I've just hung out with friends. Not since I was in college. I didn't have many friends growing up, all my time was spent with my mom until she married David. Then I had to spend all my time with Jase as if he were my guard dog or something. Shaking my head, I clear my thoughts of Jase. That isn't where I need to go in my mind right now.

"But first," Julie starts. "You need to call your doctor and make an appointment."

"Yeah. I'll do that now." Walking back to the counter, I grab my bag from beneath the register and fish out my phone. I call and make an appointment for tomorrow morning then put it in my calendar app, so I don't forget. There should be enough time to go to the doctor before I need to be here to open the shop. I'll open a little late, but I think I can deal with that considering. "Done."

"Great," Marie claps excitedly. "Then let's go."

Chapter 20

Cypress

Two weeks. Chris was in Mexico for two weeks. Two weeks that I've been living with a secret and wanting nothing more than to be able to tell him. He surprised me Friday by coming into the boutique just before closing time. He came back, all the girls safely extracted from Mexico.

I didn't open the shop on Saturday. I couldn't pull myself out of Chris' arms to leave him to come to work. I don't even care about missing out on sales, I was simply happy to have him back and be curled up in his arms. We spent the last two days together doing absolutely nothing and it was fabulous. I didn't even want to come into the boutique this morning, but Chris had to go to work to finish his reports.

"The hardest part of being a detective is the never-ending paperwork." He had told me when we stepped out of the shower this morning.

It's another slow day at the boutique, but I've decided to make the most of it. I got a package delivered in the mail this morning that I'm super excited about. I raided Amazon with Marie and Julie and yes, we went a little crazy on baby stuff. All plain white items of course. Receiving blankets, onesies, swaddling blankets, cloth diapers.

Today, I'm sitting at the register counter tying up the items that were just delivered by the mail carrier. I've got a new set of tie dye colors in various pastel shades, and I can't wait to see how these turn out.

According to the doctor, I'm only ten weeks pregnant, so of course I don't know yet what we're having. And I still haven't jumped the last hurdle and told Chris. It's not that I'm putting it off, the timing just hasn't been right yet. I wanted to surprise him with a gift of some sort but hadn't thought of what to give him before now. But hopefully the onesie will turn out, and I can give him that.

I don't worry anymore that he'll take it bad or that he'll be angry. We love each other more now than ever. We spend every night together and might as well move in together as much time as I spend at his apartment. I hardly even go to my own apartment anymore since most of my clothes are now in his closet.

I feel better today than I have in weeks. I actually feel like I have more energy now than I did before I got pregnant. It's amazing really, that I feel so alive right now. I don't feel sick in the mornings anymore, I'm not stopped in my tracks by dizziness, and the luggage beneath my eyes is finally unpacked and put away.

Hopefully for good.

Once all the white pieces are tied, I pull my phone out from beneath the counter and take a picture. Stacking all the pieces in my arms, I carry them to the back room and place them on the dying rack before I start mixing my colors. I do a similar color pattern on each piece, knowing they will all turn out differently because of how they're all tied, then take another picture. When they've all been rinsed and dried, I'll take a picture of the final products so I can get a post together for Instagram.

For now, while the baby items are soaking in the dye, I walk back out to the shop so I can keep an eye out for potential customers. Business has been really slow for the last month or so, and I'm a little discouraged by that, but I refuse to give up. This place was always my dream and something to keep me from having to work craft fairs anymore. I had enough of those growing up on the road with my mother.

I'm sitting on the stool behind the register, both elbows resting on the counter while I scroll through Pinterest looking at baby décor. I have some ideas of things that I can upcycle for a baby, but I've never actually done it before. I'm reminiscing about the days when I used to upcycle clothing for myself from some of the unsold clothing items from neighboring vendors at fairs when I hear the bell above the door ding. Finally, a customer. This has to be the first person to step into the shop besides myself or my friends in over a week.

"Welcome to Poppy Petals," I call out before looking up from my phone. I'm not usually so rude as to forget to make eye contact with visitors to my shop but there is a post that I'm highly interested in not losing and I want to pin it before it disappears.

"Nice to see you, Cypress." I freeze with my finger still pressed against the screen of my phone as I'm greeted by a nasally voice that I never thought I'd hear again. The voice of my stepfather, David.

His voice doesn't fit his body to be honest and I've always had a tough time not laughing at him for it. To look at him, you would expect a deep timber, or a rasp caused by years of smoking and inhaling motorcycle fumes. But that isn't the case with him. He talks with a nasally tone like someone that's had his nose broken one too many times in a bar fight. Who knows, maybe he has.

"David," I greet him as he walks closer to the counter. I hold my breath as I set the phone on the counter. My hands balling into fists as I lower them to my lap in the hope that he doesn't see them shaking. "I thought you and mom went back on the road."

"We did. She's in San Jose right now at a show. I left her there with the camper and Jase and I came back to LA for a bit. We have some business to finish here still."

I look over his shoulder toward the window at the front of the shop. I can see the truck parked along the curb but there's no one sitting inside. I take a quick glance around, as much as I can see through the small shop window, and don't see Jase standing anywhere outside either.

"He's not with me right now," David admits as if he can read my mind and know that I'm looking for him. "He's…" He pauses and chews on his bottom lip for several seconds. "Working."

My brows lower in question. What kind of work could he be doing here? Jase is lazy. He doesn't do anything if he doesn't have to. Honestly, he probably doesn't even know how to change a light bulb. I've never seen him lift a finger to help fix anything that broke in our little camper when I was growing up. I don't even know if he'd know how to plunge a toilet if it stopped up.

"Don't worry. He'll be back soon. I gave him a list of things to do for me today, so he'll be here when he's done."

Shit. He's going to be here.

Looking down at my phone, I contemplate whether I'd have time to send a text to Chris before David realizes what I'm doing but I don't think I can move my hands. I'm practically frozen in place in either fear or shock. Probably a mixture of both. My lips are pinched into a tight line as I continue to stare at my phone when David starts to speak again.

"Your boyfriend is making my life difficult lately."

"My boyfriend?" First of all, how does he know about Chris? I didn't even tell my mother about him. Second of all, what does he mean by making his life difficult. "I don't know what you're talking about." I decide it best to play stupid.

"Don't be coy, Cypress. I know you've been whoring around with that detective."

I rear back as if I've been slapped, nearly falling off the stool at the term. I don't know what he thinks is going on, but I've certainly not been whoring around with anyone. "Excuse me?" My voice comes out in a timid squeak.

"Yes, I know about your boyfriend. I know about a lot of things." He steps close enough that I can smell the rot of his breath. My stomach turns on itself as the scent of cabbage and bratwurst ride his breath in waves against my nostrils. "Poor little doll. You act as if you've forgotten that I always know where you are. What you're up to. Do you honestly think that I wouldn't always keep an eye on you? Did you think I wouldn't know?"

My head shakes of its own accord against the truth of it, my brows hanging so low I can feel the tension building in my forehead. Jase and David have always kept an eye on me. That's why I've always made sure to check for entry points in any room I've been in. I've always been trying to hide from what I've known all along. "What do you want?" The words escape me before I can think better of it.

"What do I want?" He laughs. The most hideous sound I've ever heard. Chills race down my spine at the sound that has haunted my nightmares for the last several years. A sound I had hoped to never hear again. "What I want is irrelevant." He reaches across the counter, his hand extending toward my face, and I flinch away from him. He pinches his lips together in a tight line and lowers his hand back down to his side. "You act as if I would cause you harm. Have I ever hurt you?"

"No," I admit. He's never laid a hand on me. He has other ways of making me feel uncomfortable. Ways that Jase has also mastered as a perfect mirror image of his father.

"No," he parrots back to me before pulling his lower lip between his teeth. "I've always wanted the best for you little doll. And what's best for you now is not that detective." He backs away a step and puts his hands in his pockets. "I want you to break up with him."

"What?" I gasp, my hand immediately going to my lower belly in a feeble attempt to protect the treasure growing inside. I realize my mistake but it's too late. His eyes trail lower to where my hand moves quickly away from my stomach.

"What's this?" He steps closer again, his eyes focused on me as if he can see inside. See what I want more than anything to hide from him. "He's defiled you?" His voice increases in volume, and I can see the rage glowing in the bright red veins blooming across his cheeks.

The bell above the door dings again and I peer over David's shoulder and lock eyes with Jase as he walks inside. He stops just inside the door, pushing it closed behind him and turning the lock. He reaches over without looking and flips the sign to closed before sauntering across the shop floor in our direction. His eyes stay locked on my own and I know that he heard what David said as he opened the door.

Breaking eye contact with Jase, I look back to David and see that he's got his fists bawled up so tight at his sides that his knuckles are turning white. Looking down, I glance at my phone and wonder, again, if I have time to send a quick text to Chris. Let him know that something is wrong. Maybe give him enough of a clue to look at the video app and know that I need him.

David doesn't miss where my attention is drawn and lunges for the phone at the same moment that I do. Jase pounces in that instant, leaping over the counter in a move that would have made an Olympic hurdler bow down in worship at his feet. He grabs me around my waist and pulls me away from the counter at the same time that David grabs my phone in his greedy hand before stepping out of my reach.

"No," David sneers, his head shaking side to side. "He's done enough. I think your time here is done. You've overstayed your welcome in this city."

"The only one that's overstayed their welcome is you. Both of you. I think you should leave." I hiss between clenched teeth. Jase tightens his hold on me, and I can feel the pressure against my ribs as I struggle to get out of his hold. "Let go of me."

"Oh, come on, sis. Haven't I told you before? That's no way to talk to your family." Jase growls close enough I can feel his lips against the lobe of my right ear.

"Please," I beg. My vision going blurry as my eyes fill with unshed tears. I blink several times hoping to stop them from falling down my cheeks. I refuse to show that kind of weakness to these two. "Just leave me alone."

"We tried that already. And look at what's become of you." David glances again at my phone and I regret not setting a lock on it. Chris has told me over and over again that I should put a passcode on my phone for in case anyone steals it, so they don't have access to my personal information stored on its memory. I know by the movement of David's fingers across the screen that he's using my phone and I can't imagine anything good coming from it.

"What are we going to do with her now, dad?" Jase asks over my shoulder, his grip still a bruising hold across my ribs.

"Well, she isn't much use to us now, is she?" David moves his fingers across the screen a few more times before putting my phone in his back pocket. He glares at me again, his brows knitted tight enough to form a crease in the middle of his forehead.

"None of them are now," Jase starts before pulling me tighter against his body. "Thanks to her boyfriend."

"What's he talking about?" I ask, my voice strained from the continued pressure around my ribcage.

"Shut up," David says calmly, turning his attention heavenward as if seeking the right answer. "It doesn't matter anymore. He isn't going to be an issue for much longer. Our little doll here just broke up with him."

"I did no such thing!" I exclaim.

"Oh," David pulls the phone back out of his pocket and waves it around in the air. A sinister smile on his lips. "But you did." He backs away before turning toward the door. "Put her in the truck. She's coming with us."

"No!" I scream and kick my legs against Jase's shins as he lifts me off the floor. "No! You can't do this!"

"Too late," Jace whispers in my ear. "It's already done."

A cloth is pressed over my face and my stomach turns as a new, chemical smell is introduced to my senses. I inhale deeply to scream again when my vision starts to go dark around the edges, my body going limp in Jase's hold as he walks toward the door.

Chapter 21

Chris

Cypress: I'm writing this to let you know that I'm no longer interested in being in a relationship with you. Please don't try looking for me. It's over.

I read the message several more times before picking up the phone and calling Cypress. I'm sure this has to be some kind of a joke but I'm not seeing the humor in it. Things have been going great between us for the last several weeks. We've practically moved in together and I've been thinking about asking her to make the move more permanent. I was under the impression that she was feeling the same way.

Only now, I don't know what to believe. The phone goes straight to voicemail, so I know that she has either blocked me or turned the phone off. Cypress is a lot of things – quirky but in a good way, bright and funny – but she is not someone that would break up with me via text message.

Setting the phone down on my desk, I rest my elbows on the smooth surface and press my palms against my eyes. I just don't understand what could have happened since this morning. She woke me up with tender kisses down my neck, her hand massaging my balls in a desperate embrace. She's been so insatiable lately that I've had a hard time keeping up with her, which is new and probably the sexiest thing I've ever seen. She's definitely gotten more comfortable with making the first move over the last month or so, no complaints here.

We had breakfast together on the balcony, overlooking the oasis that is our backyard. I took her to work at Poppy Petals and left her there to come to my own office to finish up paperwork after we extracted the last trafficking victim from Mexico. The case starting to wrap up now that the victims have been brought home, and I'm finally at a point where I'll be able to devote more time to our relationship. I had hoped to be able to move us into the next level by having her give up her apartment across the hall.

Snatching my phone off the desk, I read the message again just to see if I missed something important. A clue of some sort to tell me why she's had the sudden change of heart. But it hasn't changed since the first five times I read through it. Scrolling up, I read her previous messages from earlier in the day. They were all cheerful and normal, the loving banter between us evident in every text. They even ended with kissing emojis and tons of hearts.

Closing the messaging app, I open the video feed to the shop. Nothing seems out of the ordinary. Nothing is out of place. But it's empty and dark. It's only one in the afternoon, she stays open until five when I would normally be picking her up. But she isn't there. Checking the feed on the back room, I find it empty as well. She's gone. She closed the store early and she left.

Standing so quick I knock my chair back against the wall, I shove my phone in my jacket pocket and walk out of my office. I don't bother letting anyone know where I'm going, I don't even know my destination at this point. I just know I need to find out what's going on with Cypress and put an end to this charade. If she's really having second thoughts, that's fine. We'll work through it. She needs security, to feel safe. I can provide that for her. I know

I can. I have been. And I will continue to do so until she convinces me otherwise. But it's going to take a lot more than a fucking text message to convince me.

Parking at the curb in front of the boutique, I step out of my SUV and walk up to the dark window to peer inside. I don't know why I came here knowing already from the video feed that it was empty. She's not here. The door is locked, and I don't have a key. I don't know why I never bothered to make a copy knowing that her brother was lurking around. He's the reason why I had the cameras installed in the first place.

Blowing out the breath that I was holding, I turn and walk back to my SUV. Twenty minutes later, I'm parking in front of the apartment complex. Mrs. Abernathy is standing in her doorway when I enter the building and I think she calls out a greeting as I walk toward the elevator. I don't even bother to wave or acknowledge her standing there as I punch the button to call the elevator three times in rapid succession.

Stepping out onto the fifth floor, I feel the emptiness inside my chest. It's a growing chasm, a dark void that tells me what I already know. She's not here either.

I walk into my apartment first, taking the time to walk through each room in search of my Butterfly. Walking across the hallway, I open the door to Cypress' apartment and find it empty as well. The apartment is dark, thanks to her blackout curtains and closed doors. But she hasn't been inside this apartment in over a week and her scent is gone. Instead, it's invaded every part of my own apartment, her honey and vanilla fragrance seeped into the fabric of my furniture and bedsheets. Her apartment, however, smells empty. Like there is no life here whatsoever.

Skipping the elevator, I take the stairs back down to the first floor and walk over to Mrs. Abernathy's apartment door where she's still standing in her pink bathrobe. Her hair is up in rollers as if it were early in the morning, not midafternoon. "Have you seen Cypress?" I ask, desperation clouding my emotions and I can hear the tremble in my own voice.

"No, dear. I haven't seen her since you left with her this morning. Is something wrong?" She asks, her brows knit with concern.

"I don't know. I'm sure it's fine. She's probably just out shopping or something. Maybe she's with her friends."

"Oh, I'm sure she is. She's been spending a lot of time with those two lovely ladies lately."

"You're right. Have a nice day Mrs. Abernathy." I walk out the door to the parking lot, tossing a friendly wave over my shoulder as I go. She's probably right, Cypress is probably with Marie or Julie. I hesitate to call either of them because I don't want them to be alarmed if she isn't there. But I have to know that she's okay at least.

Sitting in my SUV, I rest my head against the steering wheel while I attempt to reason with myself of whether or not to call the ladies. I opt to call Matt instead. "Matt," I don't give him a chance to even answer the call, speaking the second that I hear him pick up. "Do you know if Marie is hanging out with Cypress today?"

"Well, hello to you too. No, Marie is working at the newspaper today. She'll be there 'til four, then I'm picking her up and we're going out for dinner."

"Shit." I take several deep breaths. "What about Julie. Do you think she's with Julie?"

"Dude. You're starting to worry me. Is everything okay?"

"No!" I yell and immediately feel guilty for yelling at Matt. He's done nothing wrong. "Sorry. No everything is not okay. I'm freaking out and I don't freak out. I'm usually the calm one. But I can't find Cypress and I got this weird fucking text from her breaking up with me and it doesn't make any sense. I don't know where else she could be if she isn't with the girls."

"Shit. Dude, you need to calm down."

"How the fuck am I supposed to calm down?" My voice gets louder, and I realize there's someone standing at the car next to me, obviously thinking I'm losing my mind as they stare at me with their hand on the door handle of their car. Forcing a smile on my face, I lift my hand and wave at them then watch as they get in their car and drive away. "Dammit, Matt. I'm sorry. I don't mean to keep yelling at you."

"No." He chuckles into the phone, and I clench my free hand into a tight fist. "I totally get it. I'm pretty sure I did the same thing when Marie went missing."

"I didn't say she was missing."

"I know. But you did say you didn't know where she was. And to answer your previous question, I'm pretty sure she's not with Julie either. She's on a deadline with this book she's trying to write so she's working at home today."

"Shit." Julie is actually how I became friends with Matt and Devan. She went missing after working on a story in her attempt at becoming an investigative reporter. She didn't publish the story, but the information she was able to gather was enough to help me close the case and prosecute everyone that was involved. She never went back to reporting, but as it turns out she's got a knack for writing fiction instead.

She writes suspense but all of her stories are based on true events or unsolved crimes. It's creepy actually the detail that she's able to go into in her stories. She hasn't published anything yet, but Devan likes to brag so he sends me emails every now and then with blurbs from her writing. She's been working on a manuscript recently that she hopes to release as her first full length novel. She even managed to get an agent after the news broke of her abduction and how her investigating helped to break the case against a string of robberies around the city.

"I'll tell you what." I wait as I hear Matt moving around before a car door slams. "It's almost three now. I'll call Marie and tell her I'm picking her up early and we'll have to reschedule our dinner date. How about you meet us over at Devan's and we all put our heads together and see if we can figure out what's going on."

"Okay." I relent, closing my eyes, and leaning back against the headrest. "I'll be there in twenty minutes." Disconnecting the call, I shove my phone back in my jacket pocket and turn the key in the ignition. I leave the radio off as I drive across town to Devan's house. There's no amount of music that can clear the thoughts running through my head.

"I'm guessing Matt called you?" I ask Devan as he holds his door open for me to walk in.

"Yeah," he agrees, patting my shoulder as I walk past him.

Julie is standing in the doorway to the kitchen, her arms crossed over her chest as she leans her hip against the doorway. My heart skips and nearly shatters into a million tiny shards as I force a smile in her direction. It's like déjà vu being back in this house when there's so much at stake somewhere outside of it.

"Julie." I greet her as I pause a mere foot away from her.

"I haven't seen Cypress today. I haven't heard from her." She steps closer, closing the space between us and grabs my hands in hers. She squeezes my fingers tightly before speaking again. "We'll find her."

"So, I'm guessing Matt told you most of what's going on?" I release Julie's hands and turn my attention back to Devan.

"Yep." He says as he walks past where Julie and I are still standing in the entryway. "You want a beer?"

"No. But I'll take a water." Devan steps back out of the kitchen holding two beers and a bottle of water in his hands and jerks his head toward the patio door.

"Let's sit outside and wait for the others. They'll be here in a few minutes. Then you can tell us what's going on." I nod my head silently and follow the two of them to the back patio.

It was only a couple months ago since I was last here, in this exact spot on the patio. Devan and Julie had just gotten married on a deck that Matt had built to cover their pool. The fabric draped from the pergola is still there and I notice the fairy lights are still strung through the boards overhead.

Julie notices me as I gaze up at the lights and giggle lightly. "I liked them too much to take them down after the wedding."

"Do I lose my man-card if I agree that they should stay up?" Devan chuckles from his seat across the table from me. He uses the edge of the table to knock the cap off his beer bottle and I stifle a laugh myself. He definitely still has his man-card intact.

"Not at all." I admit, twisting the cap off my bottle of water before taking a long sip.

I listen as the front door opens on the other side of the house and I know that Matt and Marie have just gotten here. Marie comes straight out to the patio and sits next to Julie. Matt comes out a few minutes later with a bottle of beer in one hand and a water in the other which he hands to Marie before sitting across from her.

"Okay," Matt begins. "Start from the beginning. Why do you think Cypress is missing?"

My brows furrow at his direct line of questioning. "You would make a good detective starting like that." I attempt to drown out my thoughts with humor, but all it does is make my chest squeeze hard enough to hurt. My heart is literally breaking and there's nothing I can do about it yet.

I'm a great detective. I'm good at my job because I can separate my feelings from the cases that I'm working on. I don't lose my cool in a crisis. The ladies sitting at this table with me are proof of that and I'm proud to be able to call them friends. But I haven't felt this desperate since my sister went missing so many years ago and I can't stop my thoughts from drifting to that outcome.

"Hey, Devan rests a hand on my shoulder, and I look over at him. "Don't go there, man. I know what you're thinking."

"You don't understand." I wrap my hands around my water bottle and my gaze drops to my lap. "I feel like I'm suffocating. It's killing me."

"Oh, I think we do." Matt places his hand on my other shoulder but I don't lift my gaze. "We've been there. And if it weren't for you, we wouldn't be where we are today. We'll get through this."

"Thanks guys." Releasing my breath, I sit back in my chair and tell them about the last few weeks with Cypress. I tell them about our morning together before I dropped her off at the boutique. Then I tell them about the text I received and the video footage showing the empty store. I tell them about her not being at the apartment and finish with us sitting where we are now. "Her phone is turned off. Or she blocked me, I don't know yet. But I can't reach her, and I don't know where she is."

"She wouldn't break up with you," Marie says quietly. "I know she wouldn't."

"I agree," Julie states. "Especially now."

"Why especially now?" I ask.

"You know," Julie starts but I don't miss the blush spreading across her cheeks. "You said yourself that you were practically living together. She loves you, Chris."

Blowing out my cheeks, I pinch the bridge of my nose and close my eyes. "I know she does. Or she did. Until a couple of hours ago anyway."

"No," Marie's voice pulls me from my thoughts. "You don't understand. She wouldn't break up with you. There has to be something that we're missing."

"Are you able to view anything else on that video?" Devan asks.

"Not from the app. The feed is live. But." I begin then pause. "Shit. Why didn't I call him before?"

"Who?" Matt asks.

"Pete." I stand quickly and pull my phone out at the same time. "He works for Wendy." I glance up at Marie. "He helped me install the cameras in Cypress' shop. He should be able to pull the video from earlier today." Scrolling through my contacts, I press on Pete's name and wait while the phone rings.

"Pete here," he answers after four rings.

"Pete. It's Chris."

"Hello, Detective. What can I do for you?" I like that he's so to the point. It makes my next request so much easier.

"I don't know what you've got going on today, but I need a favor. Are you able to pull video from earlier today in Poppy Petals? I need to know what went on there today."

"Yep. Can do. I'll send it to you in a few."

"Thanks, man." I disconnect the call and sit back down, setting my phone on the table. No one says anything while we wait for what seems like forever for my phone to ding with an incoming message. I click on the attachment and wait for it to download, but the file is big, and it just keeps spinning.

Julie must see my frustration because she stands and walks into the house. She comes back a few minutes later with her laptop and sets it on the table in front of her. "Send it to me. I can pull it up faster here."

I forward the message to her email and wait for her to bring up the video. She angles the laptop on the table where we can all see the playback. There is no sound, we didn't install microphones, so we aren't able to hear if Cypress says anything to herself while she's the only one in the shop. Maybe something that might indicate that she was thinking of leaving me.

"She looks happy," Devan points out. I nod my head in agreement even though no one is looking at me. All of us have our attention on the video playing. "What's she doing?"

"Tying something for a tie dye project of some sort." I smile to myself. It's been a while since she's created anything as colorful as her tie dye projects but I know it's something she loves to do. "I can't tell what it is though." I notice from the corner of my eye as Marie and Julie share a knowing look with each other before turning back to the video.

We continue to watch as Cypress walks into the back room, carrying the items that she's finished tying. I move my gaze to one of the other five camera angles and watch as she mixes the dye and applies several colors to each item on the dying rack. She returns to the main shop several minutes later and sits behind the register with her phone.

"She's smiling," Julie points out. "That is not the face of someone fixing to breakup with the love of her life." Noting the time on the playback, I realize that this is not when the message was sent to me, and I relax a little more. "Look." Julie points at one of the other camera angles and I see someone walk into the shop. "Who's that?"

"Probably a customer," I answer but my skin begins to crawl when I see the man walking slowly toward the counter. He doesn't look like the type of man to patron a bohemian boutique. He's tall and thin with a bushy beard and straggly hair that he has slicked back. There's so much oil or product holding his hair back from his face that you can see the light gleam against it on the black and white video feed. "Fuck, I wish we could hear what's being said."

"He doesn't look happy." Julie positions herself closer to the laptop screen as if she might be able to read their lips. I know she can't do that, but at this point I wish it were possible. "Is that her stepbrother?"

"I don't know," I reluctantly admit. "I've never seen a picture of him." I watch as Cypress flinches at something that he says. "Shit." One of the other camera angles shows another man walking into the shop. He has a similar appearance of the man still talking to Cypress, only younger. "I think it's Jase and David."

"Her stepbrother and stepfather?" Marie asks and my brows knit even tighter together.

"Fuck," Matt spits out. "He got her phone."

"Did you see that?" Devan asks and I put a hand over my own mouth to keep from shouting obscenities at the computer screen as I watch all hell break loose in Cypress' shop. "She didn't send you that text."

"No, she didn't." I struggle with my emotions as I'm conflicted on whether I should be relieved or pissed off. Relieved that she didn't break up for me, and pissed off because her stepbrother has manhandled her so much that I want to bash his face in.

"Oh, my God." Julie gasps, her fingers fisting her hair tightly. "Chloroform." We watch silently as Cypress' body goes limp against Jase and he carries her out the shop door. The camera angle facing the door is too far away to get a good look at the truck that we watch him put her in before climbing in behind her.

Then it pulls away. And my entire life drives away with it.

Chapter 22

Cypress

I blink my eyes repeatedly in an attempt to acclimate them to the darkness around me. It doesn't help, each blink only brings a burst of light behind my lids. My eyes burn with dryness and the pounding in my head only gets worse with every blink.

My whole body hurts as if I've competed in a marathon of epic proportions and my muscles are rioting in protest. I try in vain to lift my hand to my head but realize I can't move. Struggling against my restraints, a cold panic wraps its dead fingers around my soul. I hiss at the pain as I feel the bite of something digging into my wrists. My fingers curl around the edge of a solid surface, it feels like wood. I try to kick but my legs don't move either.

I realize that I'm tied to a chair, my ankles strapped to the legs leaving my feet flat on the floor.

Curling my toes, I realize that I've lost my shoes as my bare feet press into a rough texture beneath them. It's too dark in whatever room I'm in and I can't tell who or what else might be in here with me.

Opening my mouth to scream, I bite back a groan as the pain in my head increases. Okay, I'll stay quiet. For now, at least.

I swallow the lump threating to clog my throat as the memories from earlier in the day come back to me. At least, I think it was earlier today. I don't even know how long I've been out.

Oh, God. The baby. Please let the baby be okay. I haven't even had a chance to tell Chris about this little miracle yet.

A wave of dizziness washes over me and I'm thankful I'm not gagged as my stomach empties its contents down the front of my shirt. "Shit," I whisper as I attempt to spit on the floor in front of me. My mouth is so dry I don't even have enough saliva to clear the sour taste from my tongue. I continue heaving hopelessly even though there's nothing left in me to purge, and it makes my headache intensify. My vision gets fuzzy around the edges, and I can feel the darkness creeping in.

When I wake again, there's a dim light creeping in around a window that I hadn't realized was there before. Sunrise. It's a new day and with the light it brings I can see that I'm in a room consisting of only the chair I'm strapped to. Looking down, I see that my wrists and ankles are fastened tightly to the chair by plastic straps.

My headache has finally subsided and with it my vision is clearer than it was in the dark last night. There is a layer of dust on the floor that makes this room look like it hasn't seen a broom in ages. Pulling against the straps around my wrists, I attempt to free myself from my restraint only to be met with pain. The straps are so tight they are practically cutting into my delicate flesh. This skin on either side of the plastic is red and puffy, raw from my struggle.

"Don't bother trying to break free," the familiar voice of my stepbrother calls from behind me. "They're pretty tight, you'll only hurt yourself." I listen as his footsteps sound along the floor. He steps in front of me and kneels, placing his hands on my knees and kneading them slightly. His touch similar to the day he visited my shop. The difference then was that I could flinch away from him. This time, I'm not so lucky. "Such a shame that you've allowed yourself to be defiled in such a way. We haven't decided yet what we're going to do with you."

"W-where are we?" I manage to whisper through the dryness of my throat.

"An abandoned cottage in the middle of the desert. It's perfect really because it technically doesn't belong to anyone. No one will be looking for you here."

My heart sinks to the floor at the reality of my situation. I know Chris will be looking for me. The only problem is, how will he know where to look? If what Jase says is true, there's nothing to link him or David to this cottage. No one will know to look for me here. My lips pinch tightly together, and Jase cocks his head to the side as he watches me.

"I know what you're thinking." He lifts a hand and cradles my cheek in his palm. I fight the desire to pull away from him, unsure of what he'll do to me if I try to fight. "He's not going to look for you. Dad sent him a text before we left your little store. You broke up with him."

"No." My eyes begin to burn as if unable to produce any tears as my heart shatters into a million pieces.

"Yeah." His thumb caresses my cheek in what should be a caring gesture. I don't honestly think this man, or his father know the first thing about actually caring about anyone. Why else would they have spent the last thirteen years haunting me? "It's okay though. We don't need him." Pushing away from me, Jase stands and walks across the room toward the open door. "I'll be back with some breakfast. Gotta keep you healthy until we figure out what to do with that little brat inside of you."

He's not looking for me. He probably doesn't even realize I'm missing. How long will it be before Mrs. Abernathy says something about me not being around? Or maybe Julie and Marie will stop by the shop sometime and realize I haven't been there. How long will it take for someone to realize there's something wrong?

Shit. That's stupid. He'll probably think I ran away. He thinks I broke up with him, after all. He'll think I dumped him and left so I wouldn't have to see him anymore.

I can feel my life slipping away from me. Little by little. Breath by breath. Everything I've worked to build for myself over the last three years in Echo Park. The life I've started to make with Chris. The future I was just starting to look forward to with our little family, the three of us happy together.

Is it too soon to ask for a do-over?

I can't do this anymore. I knew I shouldn't have stayed long in one place. I knew deep down that I'd never be free of the watchful eye that both Jase and David have kept on me over the years. I was complacent in thinking that it had been long enough. That I was safe. I knew I'd never be able to settle down in one place but there I was, playing house with the greatest man of all time.

The love of my life.

And I'm never going to see him again.

There's no telling what's going to happen now. I have to find a way out of this. I have to protect this baby with all that I am because it's the only part of Chris that I have left. God, I don't know what I'm going to do.

The door squeaks open pulling me from my thoughts and David walks into the room carrying a tray. Kneeling in front of me, he places the tray on my thighs and grabs the bottle of water. Holding it to my lips, he offers me a sip which I graciously accept. My eyes stay glued to his as he sets the bottle down and grabs a forkful of fluffy eggs.

"Good girl," he praises me after feeding me the last bite of food on the plate. He offers me another sip of water before grabbing the tray and standing but he doesn't turn to leave. "Are you going to behave?"

"Yes," I whisper, accepting the fact that I have to cooperate until I can find a way to escape.

Three days. I've been kept in this room for three agonizing days. Jase cut the plastic ties off my wrists and ankles on my second day here. He kept me fastened to that chair for a full day, making me sleep sitting up, my neck tilted uncomfortably to the side only increasing the pain in my head.

He laughed at me when I screamed for him to let me out of my restraints. He had been bringing me water throughout the first day he was holding me here. While I was grateful to have a bit of hydration, my bladder was screaming only a few hours later. He continued to laugh and taunt me but continued to refuse to cut the ties so I could move.

I tried and tried to hold back. Hoping beyond hope that he would have pity on me and remove my restraints. But he didn't. He stood across the room from me and watched as I cried, what few tears my body was able to create considering how little water he had been giving me. He laughed even harder as the sounds of drops hitting the floor around my chair echoed through the empty room.

What little bit of dignity and strength I still held in my possession leaked out of me, with Jase watching and laughing at me from across the room. And there was nothing I could do to stop it. He was still laughing when he walked out of the room, locking the door behind him even though I was helpless to get to it.

He removed my straps the next morning, telling me that he couldn't stomach getting too close to someone that smelled like piss. He's opened the door every few hours and reached an arm in with a bottle of water, placing it on the floor just inside the door before retreating and locking the door again. Every now and then he'll return and toss in a paper plate with a small amount of food on it. But he hasn't come back into the room.

I supposed I should be grateful for that at least. I don't want him in here with me.

Three days. I've been here so far for three days. Half of which I've been pacing around the small room looking for gaps in the wall, holes in the floor, loose boards on the window. I haven't found any way out of this room yet.

When I'm not pacing around the room, inspecting the floor closely for loose boards, I'm curling up in the corner, my back against the wall.

I keep thinking about Chris. I wonder what he's doing now that I'm no longer a part of his life. Did his heart break when he got the message from David? Did he break something in anger?

I've been here three days. So that means it's been what, four days since I unknowingly broke up with Chris. Oh, if he could see me now. While he probably thinks I'm on my way to some unknown, we'll say tropical, location I am anywhere but there. This is definitely not a tropical paradise. This is a dusty, filthy, smelly, old room with no electricity, no moving air, and only a bucket in the corner to relieve myself in. I'm wearing the same thing I wore to my shop four days ago, even though the skirt is now stiff and scratchy against my legs and wreaks of dried urine. My hair is knotted and hanging heavy down my back, loose strands sticking to my cheeks and forehead as I'm covered in sweat and dirt that gets thicker and thicker every day.

Oh, I would give anything to actually be in some tropical paradise right now. Even if I did have to be there by myself because Chris thinks our life together ended four days ago. I would much prefer that paradise over the absolute hell that I'm living right now.

Chapter 23

Chris

"Wendy," I greet my friend as I sit at the table across from her. She agreed to meet up today for lunch, something that we haven't been able to do in months. The trafficking case has kept me busy, not to mention all my spare time was spent with Cypress. Until recently that is.

"You look like shit." Wendy tilts her head to the side, taking in my appearance. I haven't been sleeping more than a few hours a night since Cypress disappeared over a week ago. I'm hardly eating, I haven't shaved for several days so I'm scruffy. My hair is disheveled and greasy. "You need to take better care of yourself."

"Why?" I ask honestly. I don't feel like I have anything to live for at the moment and taking care of myself is the last thing on my mind. Every waking thought I have is for finding Cypress. Those fuckers have her somewhere and I have no idea where.

"Because you're of no use to Cypress if you aren't strong enough to help her."

"How can I help her if I don't know where she is?" Yeah, okay. I sound like a fucking pussy. This isn't normal behavior for someone that specializes in finding abducted women.

"This isn't like you." Wendy suggests as if reading my mind. Something I've learned over the years that she excels at. "You make a living finding lost souls and returning them to their loved ones. What makes this so different?"

"She's not lost. She was taken from me?"

"I ask again, what makes this so different?" I watch as she rests her forearms on the table and folds her hands together in front of her. She narrows her eyes at me as if expecting an answer, but I don't know what she wants to hear. "Chris." She pauses and sits back in her seat, placing her hands on her lap beneath the table. "Step back and look at this from my point of view."

I have no idea what she's asking of me. How can I separate myself from this? "I feel helpless, Wendy."

"I know. But look at it like a detective working a case. Not as a heartsick lover."

"I don't know how to do that." I admit reluctantly. "I'm not usually at such a loss, Wendy. I don't like feeling this way. But my heart is broken, and it physically hurts. It hurts worse than anything I've ever experienced in my life. I don't know how to function with this kind of pain."

"Why is your heart broken, Chris? You should be angry. Vengeful even. But not hurt. She didn't leave you on purpose."

"That's the problem. My heart shattered when I read that text sent to me from her phone. At first, I believed that it was her sending it to me. That she really did want to break up with me. When I couldn't find her, I believed for an instant that she actually left me of her own volition. That she really wanted to get away from me. I believed it and when I realized the truth, I had already lost part of my heart. The shattered pieces fell to the floor, and I wasn't able to put them all back together again. There's a piece still missing, and I don't know how to find that missing piece."

"Sometimes," she pauses and reaches her hand across the table to place it on my own. She rubs her thumb against the back of my hand in a reassuring gesture. "Sometimes the pieces are so small that when they fall to the floor, they get lost in the fibers of the carpet. Sometimes, those missing pieces are closer than you realize. You just need to look a little deeper."

My brows furrow in confusion. "I'm not sure I understand what you're saying."

"I'm saying you need to look closer to home." She smiles as she removes her hand from mine and sits back again.

"Do you know something that I don't?" I wonder if there's something that I've missed in my apartment.

"You already know who took her."

"Yeah. I do. But I have no idea how to find them."

"Have you talked to her mother?"

"Fuck." I rest my forehead in my hands, my elbows bouncing against the firm surface of the table. I hear rustling and look up to see Wendy digging through her purse. She places a piece of paper on the table, her hand covering it completely as she waits for me to look back up at her. "What's this?"

"Cypress' mother called her on her birthday. Did you know that? She was the only one that called her on her birthday. Pete is amazing at his job, just so you know. He's been such an asset to me since we lost Will. He was able to pull the records from Cypress' phone, that's how I know she talked to her mother. Cypress' mother is currently in Reno for a street fair. She's got her camper parked at the Shamrock RV Park. She'll be there until the end of the weekend with her vendor booth."

"Holy shit." I take the paper from the table the instant Wendy removes her hand from it. "Why didn't I think of that?"

"It's different when you're this close to the case. Sometimes you just need someone to remind you to step back and look at it from a different angle."

"Thank you, Wendy."

"You can thank me by bringing your girl home. For what it's worth, I believe she loves you very much. She's waiting for you to find her. Clean yourself up before you go to Reno. And might I suggest, you stop by Poppy Petals before you go? Take a look at what she was doing before her stepfather came in."

"She was on her phone before he came in." I cock my head trying to remember if there was anything else that I'm missing.

"What about before that?"

"She was working on a project in the back room. She didn't get to finish it though."

"Hmm." Wendy grabs her purse and stands up. "Why don't you go finish it for her. I'm sure you'll be interested in what you find there."

I watch as Wendy walks out of the restaurant, leaving me sitting at the empty table trying to decipher everything she just said to me. What could I possibly learn from one of Cypress' tie dye projects? She loves tie dying fabrics to sell in her shop. I'm sure she was working on a social media post before she was interrupted.

Pulling my phone from my jacket pocket, I decide to call in reinforcements. "What's up?" Matt answers after the second ring.

"How do you feel about breaking and entering?" I ask without giving him any more information.

"Depends. Are you going to arrest me for it?" He chuckles softly.

"Nope. I need your help." Yes, I'm a detective. I'm good at getting into places when a case warrants it. But I have a team with me and one of my team members is a lock picker. I'm not using my team though and I know that Matt has a history.

"Name it."

"Meet me at Cypress' shop in twenty? Bring Marie with you if you want. She might have a better idea of what I'm looking for."

"What are you looking for?"

"I have no idea." I admit. "I was told to check out the shop before leaving town. But I'll explain it to you when I see you."

"You got it. We'll be there in a bit." He hangs up before I can respond, and I put my phone back in my pocket before standing and walking out to my SUV.

I pull up to the shop before Matt since I was already in the area. I sit patiently in my car while waiting for him to show up. He pulls in behind me and I watch in the rear-view mirror as he walks around to the passenger side and helps Marie out with his hands around her waist. He kisses the top of her head before turning to the shop and I decide to join them on the sidewalk.

"Hey guys. Thanks for meeting me here." I greet them both as we walk up to the door of the boutique.

"Hey. So, full disclaimer, I haven't done this in a while." Matt reaches in his pocket and pulls out a small case of picks. "Actually, that's not true. I haven't done this to anything that doesn't belong to me in a while. I flip properties for a living after all and sometimes when I buy a house it doesn't come with any keys."

"No judgement here. I just didn't want to have to bust out a window to get inside."

"What are we looking for anyway?" Marie asks as she follows Matt into the shop. It only took him thirty seconds to have the door open.

My brows are still raised when I walk inside. "Nice." I pat Matt on the shoulder as I walk past him toward the back room. "Wendy said to check what she was working on before her stepfather showed up. At first, I thought she meant what she was doing on her phone but then she reminded me that Cypress was tie dying something in the back room that she never got to finish. I figure it's a longshot. She was probably just making something else for the shop or her Instagram account. But Wendy insisted that I needed to see it."

"I've never tie dyed anything before," Marie steps into the back room behind me. "Do you think it's okay since it's been in here for over a week now?"

"I don't see why not." Grabbing the dye racks, I place them in the industrial sink and turn on the water. I take the time to spray everything down until the water runs clear, just like Cypress showed me once before. Wringing the water from each item, I hand one to Marie, one to Matt, and keep the final item for myself. We move over to the worktable, and each grab a pair of scissors to start removing the ties.

Marie gets her item open first and it's a blanket. A small one that's done in swirls of light green, yellow, and blue. Matt is the next one to get into his which appears to be a slightly larger blanket but this one is done in the same colors but different pattern. Instead of swirls, his blanket is done in stripes. The item I'm attempting to unwrap is twisted several times, so it takes me several minutes to get all the ties removed. It's an explosion of the same pastel colors. This one looks like some sort of small outfit. A one piece with buttons at the shoulders and crotch.

A gasp escapes from Marie and I look up at her in confusion. She has tears trailing down her cheeks and her hand is covering her mouth. "What am I missing?" I ask.

"Does Cypress sell baby stuff in this shop?" Matt asks, clearly just as confused as I am. We both look at Marie as she shakes her head slowly from side to side.

"Baby stuff?" I look over each item again and it hits me. Baby blankets. A baby shirt. My eyes widen in horror as I begin to put the pieces of the puzzle together. My gaze snaps back to Marie and she begins sobbing into Matt's chest, his arm wrapped tightly around her shoulders. His eyes are focused on the items laying on the table and his mouth hangs open in surprise.

"Shit," Matt whispers.

"I'm so sorry." Marie whimpers against Matt's chest. Her sobs growing stronger by the minute. "I didn't say anything before because I thought she'd be home by now. I knew she hadn't told you yet because she wanted to surprise you. Then I got busy at work, and I completely forgot to bring it up. I'm so sorry, Chris." She hiccups, tears still rolling down her cheeks. "I'm sorry."

I stumble backward against the sink, my hand covering my mouth, my eyes still locked on the baby items laying on the table. "Cypress is pregnant?" Wendy knew. She knew I needed to know how important it was for me to get my shit together and bring my girl home. "I'm gonna be a father."

The reality hits me and I do something that I haven't done in years, since my sister was found dead in a ditch in Nevada. Sinking to the floor, I bury my face in my hands and I cry.

"Please don't be angry with Cypress." Marie pleads through her tears. "She was so scared when she found out." She sniffles and wipes her hands across her cheeks. "She was afraid something would be wrong since she had been faithfully taking her birth control. She didn't do this on purpose."

"I would never accuse her of that." I admit through my own tears.

"Julie and I came in the shop several weeks ago and noticed that Cypress wasn't feeling well. We convinced her to take a test and I ran up the road to purchase it for her. She took it here. Julie and I were both with her, supporting her through it."

"That's how she knew." I whisper, wiping the tears away from my cheeks. "Wendy knew I needed to find out. She told me to come check on this project so I would know." I look up and see the confusion on Marie's face. "The cameras."

"Shit. I forgot about those. We didn't even bother trying to hide it."

"What are you going to do?" Matt asks, pulling Marie tighter into his chest.

"I'm going to get my family back." I announce proudly. Standing, I place my hand on the little outfit laying on the table. "That's what I'm going to do." Without looking at either Matt or Marie, I walk out of the store and put the Shamrock RV Park in Reno in my GPS. I see Matt and Marie exit the shop in my rearview mirror as I pull away, taking the time to lock the door behind them.

Have I mentioned how much I hate Reno? It's a tourist trap from hell, even worse than Los Angeles. It's late by the time I arrive at the RV Park, so I decide to get a hotel room nearby and wait for the morning before approaching Cypress' mother. I pull into the hotel up the road from the Shamrock RV Park and grab my go bag from the trunk. Once I'm in my room, I decide to send a text to Matt and let him know I arrived.

> *Me:* *Made it to my destination. Thank you for your help earlier.*
> *Matt:* *No worries. I'm here for you anytime.*
> *Me:* *Appreciate it*
> *Matt:* *Congratulations BTW. I didn't get to tell you that earlier.*

I don't bother responding to the last text. I'm still in a bit of shock at the news of Cypress' pregnancy. I wasn't expecting to be a father anytime soon. Actually, if I'm being honest, I didn't think it was something that I would ever want to do. I've been devoted to my career since my sister's death. I didn't see myself ever settling down.

Cypress changed that for me. She brought so much life and color into my dark existence. She's opened my eyes to the possibilities of a future that includes something other than my work. Things moved quickly with her, I'll admit that. A baby was the last thing I thought would be on our radar. But I won't complain at all.

The more I think about it, the happier I am with the news. I only wish she were able to have told me herself. I wish she were here for me to wrap my arms around and celebrate the life we created together. That'll have to wait until we're able to be together again. I'm not giving up on her. Wendy was right, I need to be strong if I'm going to bring my girl home. My family, I suppose. Her and the baby.

Setting my bag on the bed, I grab a few toiletry items and head to the bathroom. After stripping down to my boxer briefs, I stare at my reflection in the mirror. My eyes follow the lines of ink trailing down the left side of my body. The ink started as a way to remember my sister and how she was taken from me. Over the years, I've added to it in a way that told the story of my life. Every picture, every design whether a flame or a swirl, has a meaning behind it. Turning to the right, I look at the part on my left shoulder blade that was inked in remembrance of my father who was killed in the line of duty when I was thirteen. The one directly below him is for my mother and the grief that she suffered until she died years later of cancer.

The Story of Her Redemption

There are so many stories inked on my body and I've haven't told all of them to Cypress. I don't know why other than they just never came up. She notices it though. She takes the time to trace my designs every time we lie in bed together. She's never asked if there was a story before, but I want to have the chance to tell her all of it.

Yes, she knows about my past. I've told her about my family and what happened to my sister. I've even told her part of how I met Wendy and how we became friends over the years. She knows about the outreach that Wendy runs with victims that I've had a hand in rescuing over the years.

But I haven't told her about the ink. I never told her that the pain of having my story inked into my skin was able to drown out my guilt over what happened to my sister. I haven't told her that every swirl etched and inked into my skin caused pain that drowned out my guilt for every victim it represents. The victims that I didn't get to in time and wasn't able to save. The pain from having those stories inked into my skin helps to cover the guilt.

Cypress is the only other person besides myself and my tattoo artist that has ever seen any of my work. It's usually hidden beneath my long pants and long sleeve shirts. I'm not ashamed of it, that isn't why I keep it hidden. It's more for professional reasons that I don't show it off. I'm proud of every single line, flame, and swirl inked along my body.

There isn't much room left on my left side that isn't already covered in ink. I've done everything solely on that side because it's closest to my heart. Everything permanently etched into my skin has meaning to me as something that I wanted to keep close. But it's all in black work. There is nothing inked on me with any color other than shades of black. Turning back to the mirror, I look at the space directly over my heart and decide that it might be time to add some color to my body after all. I make a mental note to make an appointment with my artist when I get back to the city.

For now, it's time to take Wendy's advice. I need to get myself cleaned up so I can play the part of detective tomorrow when I meet Cypress' mother for the first time.

Chapter 24

Cypress

Three weeks I've been kept in this cottage in the desert. For three weeks I've been slaving for them, cleaning this filthy cottage for them, and taking care of the other women they have stowed away in the other rooms.

I spent my first week here in that locked room by myself. Jase continued to come in every few hours and offer a bottle of water or piece of bread, but he still never entered the room. He would continue to lock it on his way back out every time, leaving me behind with nothing more than my bucket and the filthy floor to sit on.

After that first week, the door opens and someone else is pushed into the room with me. Her hands are tied behind her back, and she is blind folded and terrified. She stumbles and falls to her knees, a cry releasing from her throat as she falls forward and barely turns her head in time to keep from crushing her nose against the hard floor. Standing in shock, I wait for Jase to leave through the door from which he came, locking it behind him again as he retreats back to the other part of the cottage. Whatever other part that may be.

Rushing over, I help the stranger to sit up and frantically try to remove the restraints from around her wrists. Thankfully, they aren't restrained with the same plastic tie that was used on me, and I'm able to break it free with some effort. She immediately reaches up to remove the blind fold from around her head before rubbing her wrists to relieve the pain caused by the restraint.

She looks so young. She's smaller than me, about three inches shorter if I had to guess, with long blond hair and the brightest blue eyes I've ever seen. She looks terrified and I wish there was something I could say to alleviate her fear. Unfortunately, I can't. There's nothing I can say to her that won't be a lie.

"Where are we?" She asks me, her voice breaking with the trembling of her body.

"I don't know. Somewhere in the desert, that's all I know." I watch as she wrinkles her nose and embarrassment washes over me instantly. I back away, standing quickly and crossing to the opposite side of the room. I know I stink, there's nothing I can do about it. "What's your name?" I ask in hopes of shifting her attention to something other than the urine dried into my clothing.

"Beth." She whispers. I watch as she pushes herself across the floor, leaning her back against the wall across from where I stand. She doesn't trust me yet, not that I blame her. I listen as she cries silently, her knees pulled up to her chest as she rests her forehead against them. My heart breaks for her thinking about the family she may have out there somewhere missing her.

Over the next several days, Jase continues to push more women into the room with Beth and me. Somehow, I end up being the one that reaches out to each of the women. I help them up when they're pushed onto the floor. I remove their restraints and help to reassure them that everything is going to be okay. Even though, I don't believe that myself. I try to calm these women who are frantic and terrified. Pushing down my own fear and heartbreak, I manage to keep these women as calm as possible while continue to search for a way out of this place.

Jase never leaves. He stays all day and night keeping watch over me and the other women to make sure we don't try to leave. David comes and goes, whispering to Jase when he thinks none of us can hear him.

There are so many of us crammed into this small room right now that we barely have room to move around. We all sleep curled up on the filthy floor, shuffling around to get close enough to share each other's warmth. The days are stifling and hot in this boarded up room, but the nights are chilly. We're all so drenched with sweat by the time the air cools that we're nearly freezing at night as we try to fall asleep. We don't have anything to cover up with to contain body heat.

Including me, there are a total of thirteen women in this little cottage. I know that Jase has taken advantage of a few of them because I can hear the screams during the night when I'm pretending to sleep. David doesn't stay here during the night so he doesn't witness any of it but I'm not sure that he would do anything about it even if he did.

I've been left untouched since I got here, thankfully. Not that Jase has ever physically done anything to me. But I wouldn't have put it past him to have tried if I hadn't left for college when I did. He always had that look in his eye when he watched me, and I knew it was only a matter of time.

I tried to fight Jase off one of the women once, only once. Jase grabbed me, wrapping his hands around both of my biceps, and picked me up off the floor. Screaming at me for getting in his way, he tossed me across the room. I hit the wall and fell to the floor, landing hard enough on my side that I'm sure I bruised, if not broke, at least one rib. It still hurts to take a deep breath and I'm terrified that if I fight him again, he'll hurt me bad enough to harm my baby. That's a chance I'm not willing to take. I may never see Chris again, but I'll be damned if I'm not going to meet his child.

I still don't understand what the reasoning is behind holding all of us here. We're overcrowded and there isn't enough room to add anyone else. And the smell is becoming unbearable with all of us being filthy. There is no running water in this cottage, so we aren't able to clean up. We have a single bucket between all thirteen of us, which Jase is nice enough to allow me to carry outside to empty once a day. I don't get to carry it far, he stands and watches me from the open doorway each time as if I'm going to run off into the wide-open desert with no sense of direction. I wouldn't even know how far I'd have to go in order to find help. Not to mention, he barely gives us enough water to stay conscious, much less hydrated. There's no way I'd survive on my own in the desert.

I keep thinking back to what Chris told me about the case he had worked on recently in Mexico. He said there were twelve women taken from street fairs and farmer's markets around the area from Los Angeles down to San Diego. He worked with several other detectives from surrounding precinct to bring them all home. Several of the women that he was able to help bring back didn't have any family or anywhere to return to when they were rescued, and he set them up with his friend Wendy. I wonder if she would be interested in taking on some of the women that are here with me if I'm able to take any with me when I find a way out.

And I will find a way out.

It's only a matter of time before I figure out a way to leave this hellhole behind.

It's been three weeks though and I'm no closer now to finding a way out of here than I was when I was first taken from my shop. I've all but given up on the idea of Chris finding me, certain that he's getting on with his life since the breakup. It kills me to think that he may be spending time with someone else, but I can't blame him. He's a wonderful man and he deserves to be happy. I'll just have to find a way to live with that.

I just don't know if I'll be able to return to my life in Los Angeles or my shop in Echo Park. I don't know if I'll be able to be that close to Chris every day and watch as he moves on without me. I haven't decided yet what to tell him about the baby. If he's moved on with his life, I don't know if I'll be able to do that to him. Don't get me wrong, I don't want to keep his child from him. I could never do that to him. I just don't know how we'll be able to do this if we're not together.

For the first time since I found out I was pregnant, I actually start to wonder what would happen if I were to give the baby up for adoption. I'll be hiding from Jase and David for the rest of my life if I'm able to escape from here and that's no way to raise a child. This baby deserves a bright future, to be raised without fear. I know what it's like to grow up on the road. I couldn't do that to this baby.

Sniffling, I wipe a stray tear away from my cheek and listen for footsteps to make sure no one catches me crying. I'm trying to be the strong one for all of these women, I don't want to seem vulnerable to them.

Chapter 25

Chris

"So, here's the information we've been able to put together based on my conversation with Cypress' mother." I explain to Devan and Matt as we sit on Devan's patio. It's been a week since I got back from Reno and meeting with Willow, Cypress' mother. "She was one hell of an egg to crack, that's for sure. She didn't want to tell me anything at first. But her stories weren't lining up."

"What did she say?" Devan asks.

"At first, she said she hadn't seen her husband or stepson for several months. That they had taken off to work some construction job together in Utah and hadn't returned. But if that were true, how was she moving her camper from one festival to another? They have her truck."

"Good point." Matt agrees.

"I called her on it, and she said they were going to be back in a few days to move her to the next location. Then she said that Jase wouldn't be back with David because he was working on a special assignment. She realized at that point that she had said too much and started pacing around in front of her tent, mumbling a bunch of shit about telling them to let it go and leave the area. She said they were getting cocky and should have stopped after their last job got busted."

"Holy shit." Devan spits out, nearly choking on his beer. "Are they the ones you've been looking for?"

Devan and Matt know about the case that I'd been working on recently with the PFM in Mexico City. They know about the trafficking ring we've been trying to shut down since we were able to rescue all the victims. "The timeline adds up. So, they're pretty high on the suspect list at the moment. Not to mention the truck. It fits the description of the one that a witness was able to describe. One of my associates in San Bernadino was able to get some information on it and share with me a few weeks ago."

"Fuck," Matt sputters.

"Pretty much. I've been in contact with the group of detectives that helped out with this last case, and they know the details. Willow's been picked up as an accessory and is being detained in San Bernadino for now. She hasn't given up any information yet to pinpoint their location though. What we do know is that Willow is great with making friends at these festivals. Has been for years. She vets the women at the festival that are by themselves or don't have family back home and shares the information with David. Then Jase steps in and does his thing."

"That's fucked up," Devan states and Matt just shakes his head in agreement.

"Yep," I agree. "What's even more fucked up, though, is that Cypress was on their radar from an early age. They had hoped to make some money off of her when she got a little older by selling her to the highest bidder. David had enforced the no touching rule with Jase, despite his wishes, because he wanted her to be untouched so they could get more for her. But she went away to college before they got the chance and spoiled their plans."

"Jesus!" Matt exclaims. "What kind of a mother allows something like that to happen to her daughter?"

"So, what happens now?" Devan asks.

"Now, we try to get the location out of Willow and go get Cypress."

"And if she won't give it up?"

"That's where Pete comes in."

"Wendy's guy Pete?" I hear Marie ask from inside the house. I turn and see Julie and Marie walking out onto the patio in workout clothes and my brows furrow.

"Where did you two come from?" I ask, gesturing to their outfits.

"Yoga," Marie offers as she walks over and places herself in Matt's lap. He wraps his arms around her waist and kisses the back of her head. "Julie still sucks at it but it's good for stress relief."

"I do not suck at it!" Julie admonishes and Marie laughs.

"Yes," she giggles again. "You do actually. You fell over today and caused a domino effect when you bumped into the girl next to you. She then fell into the girl next to her who fell into the wall."

"Go ahead. Laugh it up."

"You are getting better though," Marie states, still stifling a laugh.

"Thank you."

"You fall much more gracefully now than you did when you first started." Julie throws the cap to her water bottle at Marie and Matt swats it away before we all start laughing together. It feels good to laugh. Even if it is short lived. "So, Wendy's Pete?"

"One of Wendy's guys. Yes." I answer, and she nods her head in understanding. "If we can't get a location out of Cypress' mom, Pete's going to hack her phone. See if he can get anything out of it."

"Okay," Julie starts. "So, let's talk about the other bit of information." At first, I wonder what she's referring to. But then I remember that I haven't seen her or Devan since I found out that Cypress was pregnant. I now Julie knows because Marie admitted that they were both with Cypress when she took a test.

"Yep." I grab my beer and hold it up in the air. "I'm going to be a father." I announce and cheers erupt around the table.

"Congrats, man!" Devan practically yells over all the excitement. "You're going to be a kick ass father."

"Thank you." Taking a sip of my beer, I realize that I have a great support system here. These men took me into their lives when I helped to save their women. We've grown so much closer over the last year that I'm proud to claim each and every one of these people as my friends. I know they all have my back and will bend over backward to help me get Cypress and my baby home where they belong. I'm grateful to each of them and am suddenly overcome with emotion. I take another swig of my beer to hide it.

"Well," I start after finishing the last of my beer. "It's getting late. I should get out of here."

"Keep us posted on what you find out." Marie stands and wraps her arms around me in a tight hug. I run my hand up and down her back a few times before releasing her, and Julie jumps up to do the same.

"Let me know if we can do anything." Matt offers his hand for a shake, gripping mine tightly.

"I'll walk you out." Devan stands and grabs the empty beer bottles from the table, following me into the house. He tosses them into the trashcan in the kitchen before opening the front door to follow me out. We get to my SUV before he speaks again. "Keep your chin up man. I know this is hard for you but stay strong. We got your back no matter what."

"I know. Thank you." I reach out to shake his hand and he grabs me in a side hug instead.

"We're here for Cypress too. Whatever she needs when she comes home, we'll be here for her. She's a great lady. I couldn't be happier that the two of you ended up together."

"I appreciate that and I'm sure she will too. She sure loves those ladies in there. She couldn't have any greater friends."

"Agreed." He steps back as I open the car door and sit in the driver's seat.

"You want the good news or the bad news?" Ethan, from San Bernadino PD asks. He called early this morning as I was walking into my office.

"Good news first."

"The good news is Willow Harris-Weiss is being charged with accessory to human trafficking. She's not going anywhere."

"That is good news. Do we have any information on where her husband is currently?"

"That's part of the bad news. We know he's in Nevada, but she doesn't know the exact location. She says he never shared that information with her. I don't know, maybe he didn't trust her as much as she thought he did."

"Well, that doesn't help us much."

"Nope. But that's not all of the bad news yet."

"Shit," I mumble into the phone and Ethan chuckles on the other end.

"You sitting down?" He asks me as I step around my desk.

Slumping into my desk chair, I rest my elbows on my desk and pinch the bridge of my nose. "I am now. What have you got?"

"This spans across forty states. Not to mention into Mexico, as you well know, if this is the same ring we just shut down."

"I'm sure it is."

"Me too. But, because of the enormity of it, Feds are stepping in to take over."

"Fuck!" I exclaim, slamming my fist against the desktop and bouncing my computer monitor to the point of almost knocking it over.

"My sentiments exactly. We're holding them off as long as possible. I know this is personal for you, but you know how they like to take their time. If you have any more suggestions, I'm open to them. But I suggest we move as soon as possible."

"Yeah. I got a guy ready to jump in."

"Great. Let me know what I can do."

"I'll be in touch." Disconnecting the call, I toss my phone onto the desk and rest my forehead against the smooth surface.

With no time to waste, I reach out and pick my phone back up to punch in Pete's number. "Chris." He answers on the first ring.

"Pete."

"I was hoping you'd call. Did you hear the Feds are fixing to take over your case?"

"How the fuck do you know that? I literally just got off the phone with Ethan."

"I can't answer that." Of course, he can't. I should know better than to ask.

"You're right. So, I'm assuming you have something for me then."

"Almost," he admits, and my hope begins to crumble. "These guys are smart but not smart enough. They aren't using burner phones."

"No shit?" Inhaling a deep breath, I lean back in my chair. "So, they're traceable?"

"Yep. As soon as we figure out which number is David's or Jase's, we'll be able to narrow down their location. This Willow lady makes a lot of phone calls though. There's quite a few to go through."

"Keep at it, man. I'm not ready to hand my life over to the Feds yet."

"I'll get back to you." He disconnects the call and I slump against my chair, my energy quickly drained. Thankfully, it's Friday and I don't have much to work on today before I can scoot out of here. Mostly paperwork.

Chapter 26

Cypress

"Cypress," Emily, one of the women being held in this cottage, walks up behind me, and places a hand on my shoulder. "You need to sit down."

"I will in a few minutes." Blowing out a long breath, I gather more towels into my arms and walk toward the room at the back of the cottage. Two of the ladies put up a fight last night with Jase and got beat up pretty bad. I'm trying to help keep them calm and clean up their battered bodies.

Jase has done a lot of things over the years that has frightened me, but I've never seen the amount of rage that was rolling off of him last night. He was obviously drunk when he sauntered into the back room and grabbed two of the women and tried to drag them out of the room. They fought back, scratching at his arms in an attempt to get out of his grasp. But they were weak after having been held for so long with little to no food or water. They were no match for him, even in his inebriated state.

What scared me the most about the altercation wasn't what he was doing to the women. That was horrible, don't get me wrong. But he glared at me the entire time he was battering and using those women. The pure hatred in his eyes made my skin crawl.

"This is your fault," He growled at me. "This is all your fault."

I still don't understand why he would accuse me of being the reason for his actions. His actions are all his own because of the monster I've always known him to be. He and his father both are the biggest monsters to have ever walked the face of this earth. I've known that for thirteen years.

Holding the towels tightly against my chest, I open the door to the back room. Monique and Ashley lay side by side on the floor in the corner. Jodi is kneeling next to them, brushing their hair away from their battered and bruised faces. She looks up at me as I walk closer, tears leaving white streaks against her cheeks having washed away the dirt and dust caked on her face from the weeks of being held in this cottage.

"How are they?" I ask tentatively as I kneel close to Jodi.

"They haven't woken up yet." She whispers her response, her hand still stroking over their hair. Jodi is the oldest of all the women here, me included. She just turned thirty a month before she was taken.

I've been locked in this house with these twelve women long enough to get to know each of them. Jodi is the only one with a different story than the rest. Where eleven of the women here were vendors at street fairs and farmer's markets, Jodi was a shopper. She has nothing to do with the other merchants other than her interest in their wares. She's also the calmest one here and has been called a mother hen by the other ladies more than once.

What I've learned about Jodi in the month that I've known her, is that she was alone. Her parents died when she was in high school in a house fire. She stayed with her grandmother until she was eighteen when she moved out to attend University. Her grandmother passed away from a heart attack a few years later.

Jodi married her high school sweetheart when she was twenty-one. They had a daughter two years later and lived a happy life together. Jodi worked as an accountant part time from home while her husband was a lawyer in the city. Two years ago, her husband was on his way home from Pacific Park with their five-year-old daughter when their car was hit by a drunk driver and neither of them survived. Jodi was left alone, with no support system to turn to. She has no family and what few friends she had growing up had all moved away to live their own lives away from the city.

The only thing Jodi has in common with the other women here, is that there is no one looking for her. She keeps a strong persona around the others, but I can see the desperation in her eyes when she looks at me. She knows her chances of getting out of this are slim, but she isn't fighting her fate. She has nothing left to live for and has struggled with that for the past two years. This is a means to an end for her and it breaks my heart.

"How are you doing?" She asks me as I sit next to her and place a hand on Monique's shoulder.

"I'm okay." Smiling to myself at the irony of my answer. "Well, as well as I can be." My free hand rests on my slightly protruding belly. Thankfully, the baby is obviously doing okay since I'm starting to show now. If my math is correct, I'm around eighteen weeks pregnant.

"You feel anything yet?" Jodi asks, her hand resting next to mine now on my belly.

"Not yet."

"You will soon. I loved those first months with my daughter. The fluttering in my belly was the best part of my day." She pulls her bottom lip between her teeth and studies my belly absently. "We have to get these ladies out of here, Cypress." She finally moves her gaze to my own, a look of determination in her eyes.

"I don't know how to do that," I admit reluctantly.

Jodi jerks her hand back and presses her back flat against the wall as we both hear a noise in the main room of the cottage. "Fuck!" I hear David yell as he bursts through the front door.

"What's wrong?" Jase asks. They're voices carry through the empty hall in the cottage, echoing off the dusty wooden walls.

"We need to relocate sooner than I thought." He continues speaking in a loud voice. "I've been trying to reach Willow and she isn't answering her phone. We don't have a buyer yet and I can't keep holding them here until one shows up. Willow was the one with the connections and she isn't answering her fucking phone."

My brows lower in confusion as I replay what I'm hearing in my head. Buyer? Contacts? Gasping, I hold my hand to my chest as what he's saying sinks in. My mother is part of this? The trafficking ring that Chris has been trying to locate has David, Jase, and my mother wrapped up in it?

Oh, my God.

Footsteps move closer through the hallway, and I move my body to shield Monique and Ashley from view. They haven't moved since I entered the room and I fear they won't be waking any time soon. There's no telling what David will do when he sees their condition.

The door bursts open and David stands in the doorway, his bulky frame filling the space in, his presence both intimidating and angry. "What's wrong with them?" He points to the corner over my shoulder.

"They're tired," I answer, my voice trembling with fear. I've never seen David look so evil before and I'm not sure what he's capable of at this point.

"Bull shit." David reaches me in three strides and grabs my arm, yanking me off the floor and shoving me behind him hard enough that I nearly fall. Jodi is there in a hurry to help stabilize me and keep me on my feet.

I watch silently, my mouth hanging open, as David touches Monique's cheek first, getting a good look at her face. He reaches for Ashley and does the same before pushing up from the floor with his hands on his knees. I wait for him to start yelling again while he blows out his cheeks and releases a long breath. Placing his hands on his hips, he doesn't say anything more. He just stands there staring down at both of the women still passed out on the floor. He turns slowly, his gaze falling on me for several seconds, then walks out of the room and closes the door behind him.

No one in the room speaks. We're barely even breathing as we listen to the sounds coming from the other end of the cottage. We're waiting for something, anything to happen after what David just saw in this room. I know he wasn't happy when he walked out of here. But nothing happens. We continue to listen as David's footsteps stop in the main room of the cottage. Then we listen as the door opens and closes, remaining silent.

"Cypress," Jodi is lying on the floor next to me. Everyone else in the room has already fallen asleep for the night. Monique and Ashley still haven't woken up and it scares me. "You need to get out of this place. For the baby, you need to get out of here."

"I know." Rolling to my side, I face her silhouette which is the only thing I can see in the dark room. "I'm trying to figure that out. But I'm not leaving anyone here."

"I think you're going to have to. I know you want to save all of us, but you can't do that. Ashley and Monique haven't woken up yet and I don't know if they'll be able to move fast enough even if they did. I'll stay with them, you get everyone else out."

"Jodi." Raising my hand, I place it on her shoulder. "I'm not going to leave anyone here. Do you have any idea what kind of a fate is waiting for you if you stay here?" There are too many similarities to what's going on here and the case that Chris told me about a few months ago. I'm not so naïve to think that this isn't connected in some way. It's too convenient for the women that disappeared before to have coincided to when Jase showed up at my shop. And after hearing what David said last night about buyers, I'm not willing to stick around long enough to be sold to anyone. But I don't want that to happen to Jodi either. To anyone here for that matter.

"I do. I've been around long enough to understand what's going on here. I know what human trafficking is, Cypress."

"We're all getting out of here, Jodi. We're all going home."

"I don't have anything to go home to, Cypress. And if I can help you and the other women here to get away, I will. There's nothing left for me to fight for. But I can at least fight for you."

"We're not having this discussion, Jodi. Get some sleep." I admonish her and refuse to have this conversation. I am not going to leave her to sacrifice herself. She will not become a martyr for me or any of the other ladies here. She may not think she has anything to live for, but she does. She's young. She's beautiful. I know she feels like her life ended when her husband and daughter died, but she has so much more life left in her. I'm sure her husband wouldn't want her to give up, but I'm not stupid enough to say that to her just yet.

I wait until Jodi's breathing evens out and I know she's asleep. Rolling to my back, I stare up into the dark and wait for the darkness to pull me into a deep sleep. But it doesn't come. My skin is crawling, my blood buzzing through my veins, as I think over the possibilities of how to get all these woman out of this place.

My hand rests against my small baby bump, massaging softly, when I'm pulled from my thoughts. Sitting up, I listen for whatever noise I heard. It wasn't loud, but I swore I heard the creak of a board.

Holding my breath, I strain to listen for the sound to come again. My lungs burn with the desire to draw in more air when I finally hear it again. It isn't coming from the main room in the cottage. It sounds like it's coming from outside, by the only window in this room. A soft squeak like a nail being pulled from a board, followed by a sound of scraping metal.

I hear something hit the floor and the sound echoes through the quiet room. Throwing myself back to the floor, I curl up on my side and throw my arms over my head while squeezing my eyes shut tight. I wait for a blast or loud bang to come but it never does. The only sound I hear now is a long hiss. And then I smell the ozone and sulfur as if I have been standing too close to someone shooting off fireworks.

Then all hell breaks loose, and everyone starts to scream.

Chapter 27

Chris

Eight weeks. It's been eight long, grueling, weeks of not being able to eat or sleep. It's been agony knowing that Cypress was out here somewhere probably fighting for her life.

Willow was no help in locating David or Jase. She didn't know where he was holding his victims. She did confess to being the instigator and the main contact with the buyers. The only thing we've had going for us has been Pete.

For whatever reason, David and Jase have never switched to burner phones. I guess they didn't think they'd get caught. Or they didn't believe that Willow would be caught since she's stayed behind the scenes over the years. But once Pete was able to figure out which numbers belonged to them, he was able to do what he does best.

Pinpointing their locations.

They were smart enough to leave their phones turned off, untraceable until they were powered on and used to place a call. But they obviously weren't staying together in the same place.

According to trace reports, David has been on the move every day for the last eight weeks, rarely staying in one place for long. Jase, however, has been in the same location for the entire two weeks that Pete has been watching his number. He turns the phone on at the same time every day and reaches out to David. Pete has been there waiting for him every day when he pings the tower and his location hasn't changed.

Tonight is the night, though. I'm bringing my family home with me tonight. The whole team is with me from my precinct. Jackson, Noah, Ethan, and Lucas are all here as well, the detectives from the surrounding areas that collaborated with me on the trafficking case in Mexico City. We were successful then with bringing all of the victims home. We'll be successful this time too.

The cottage that we're preparing to infiltrate is out in the middle of the desert. There are no hiding places nearby, so we were forced to leave our vehicles a mile back and walk the rest of the way. We're practically going in blind, not knowing how many victims are inside this little cottage. We know that Jase is here, but we don't know if he has any reinforcement with him.

We don't even know if he's armed.

David was picked up earlier today just outside of Vegas and hasn't given us any additional information. He was transported back to San Bernadino by Ethan's team where he's being held and charged with abduction and human trafficking. We have thirteen counts against him so far, including Cypress. There's no telling how many more victims are going to add to his charges by the time we're completely done with everything.

The entire team is wired up for easy communication. I texted Matt before turning off my cell phone to let him know we found the cottage. He's at Devan's house, the four of them waiting to hear back from me when we get Cypress out. The guys wanted to come along and help but I told them they would be more help by staying there and staying safe. I'll call them when we're on our way out of here and they can meet us at the hospital.

As we step closer to the cottage, I realize the windows are boarded shut. Under normal circumstances, we would break windows by launching in smoke grenades before entering. There are no lights coming from inside that we can see. There are gaps in the boards on all the windows, easy access for smoke bombs if we can get close enough without being detected.

We stop moving while several members from our tactical unit spread out around the cottage. Once they've found openings, or created enough space for their grenades to enter they'll release the smoke, and we'll go in. My heartrate picks up, thumping a hard rhythm against my ribs, as I wait for the signal.

Bodyless voices come over the radio one by one indicating they are ready to engage. I listen as the commander of the tactical unit gives the go-ahead and wait. My breathing stops, a lump forming in my throat as I wait for the first tactical wave to enter. I brace myself for gunfire, waiting to see if Jase puts up any resistance, but the shots don't come and slowly my breath releases from my lungs.

"Clear!" I hear called over the radio and everyone outside begins to move. I have a singular focus on this mission, find Cypress and carry her out. The entire team is equipped with gas masks to make easy entry into the smoke-filled cottage. As I step closer to the threshold, I hear the screaming coming from the far side of the cottage and I recognize it as multiple women, obviously terrified. I feel the blood drain from my face as my stomach lurches at the sound of their fear.

I'd give anything to make sure Cypress doesn't have to face anything so terrifying again in her life.

A stream of women begins running through the hallway, an attempt to escape the smoke grenades still blowing out smoke in the back rooms. I press my body against the wall in order to avoid the stampede of frightened women and watch in the corner of my eye as each one is grabbed by one of the officers accompanying us.

Still no sign of Cypress and my heart skips a beat as I wonder if she's even here with these other women. I don't know what I'll do if she was already sold, or worse, before I was able to find her. I count nine women as they are pulled out of the cottage, the arms of the other officers wrapped around their waists and pinning their arms against their bodies to stop them from fighting.

"Chris," I hear Ethan call from the last room at the end of the hall. Pushing away from the wall, I make my way through the smoke and stop in the doorway.

There are four women still hiding in the far corner of the room. Two are laying on their backs, the other two kneeling next to them with their arms waving in the air. It takes me a minute to realize they are fanning the smoke away from the other two women's faces.

"We have four more back here," I announce through the radio while stepping into the room. I walk slowly toward the far corner, trying to keep my steps soft enough as to not scare the women kneeling on the floor. It's hard to make out their features through all the smoke and there is no light in the room aside from the flashlight in mine and Ethan's hands. He steps with me as more men enter the room from behind and we all approach the women in the corner.

One of them looks up, finally noticing our approach and she winces slightly at our appearance. We're all dressed in tactical gear with gas masks covering our faces. I'm sure we look a fright to someone that's been locked in this cottage for several weeks if not months. "Please," she pleads with us. "We couldn't leave them. They won't wake up."

Ethan and I being the first ones in the room, go to the ladies kneeling and help them stand in order for the other men entering to gather the ones off the floor. Ethan grabs the lady that pleaded with us a minute ago and begins to walk back the way we came. I reach for the other and my lungs seize in my chest as I realize that my Butterfly is alive. Alive and using her time not to escape with the other nine women that ran out of here, but to stay with the weakest, possibly wounded, women that couldn't help themselves.

Reaching for her arms, I help her to her feet and watch as she keeps her eyes on the women on the floor. She pushes against my chest until she sees the other men enter the room to assist them. Only then does she turn to me cooperatively and begins to step around me, ready to leave. I don't let her get very far before I'm scooping her up in my arms and holding her tight against my chest. I carry her out bridal style, her head laying against my shoulder while the rest of her body relaxes against me.

"I got you," I say softly. "I got you. I got you." I continue to repeat those three words like a mantra as we exit the room, walk slowly down the hallway, and out the front door of the cottage. It isn't until we're several feet away from the building, knowing that we're clear of what little smoke is still seeping out through the cracks in the walls and gaps in the windows, that I finally remove the mask from my face.

My first thought when I look down upon the relaxed features of Cypress is that she's passed out from shock. I immediately worry about the baby and wonder if these eight weeks have caused any damage to either of them.

Lights and sirens fill the void as the awaiting paramedics and local PD make their way closer to the cottage. Several that had walked here with us earlier are already triaging the victims as they emerge from the cottage into the clear night air.

"You good, Chris?" I hear Ethan's disembodied voice through my headset.

"Yep."

"That her?"

"Yes," I breathe out my answer, relief finally beginning to wash over me as the adrenaline subsides. I won't be completely relieved yet until I get her checked out though.

"Go. We got it here."

"Thank you, Ethan." Walking past the mayhem around me, I go straight for one of the ambulances and step inside. Laying Cypress down on the stretcher inside, I brush her loose hair away from her face and kiss her forehead softly.

"Alright," I'm greeted seconds later as one of the paramedics enters the ambulance and grabs and clean pair of gloves. "What do we have?"

"Her name's Cypress. She's one of the victims. She passed out as soon as I picked her up." I watch as he silently puts a blood pressure cuff on her upper arm, and I clench my jaw at the layers of dirt and filth caked to her flesh. Her hair is stringy and dry and has lost its usual shine. She's wearing the same clothes she was in the morning I dropped her off at her shop. "Be careful," I stop the paramedic as he grabs her arm to look for a vein to start an IV. "She's pregnant."

"She with you?" He asks as he eyes my hand still smoothing her hair back away from her face.

"She is."

"Don't worry Detective." He starts before turning his attention back to the vein in her arm. Surprisingly, he gets her vein on the first stick and hooks up the IV. "We'll take good care of her."

I don't respond as someone comes up to the back of the Ambulance and closes the doors. I feel the vehicle begin moving a few minutes later and finally begin to feel the tension leaving my shoulders. "What hospital are we going to?" I ask as I pull my phone out of my vest pocket and power it back on.

"Valley View is the closest. It's in Fort Mohave."

"Thank you." I pull up Matt's number in my contacts and call him while we continue to travel down the road.

"Chris," he answers almost immediately.

"We found them. I'm with Cypress in the Ambulance. We're on our way to the Valley View Hospital in Fort Mohave."

"Thank, God!" He exclaims and I listen as his voice becomes muffled as if he put the phone against his chest. He announces to the others with him where we're headed before coming back to the phone. "We'll see you there."

"It's got to be at least five hours from you, Matt. You don't have to do that."

"We'll see you there." He repeats and I sigh in defeat. "You're not going through this alone, Chris. I don't know how many times we have to explain that to you."

"Okay." I swallow down my emotions before responding again. "I'll see you in about five hours." He doesn't say anything else before disconnecting the call.

"I don't know anything yet," I tell Matt and Devan. We're sitting in the hallway outside of Cypress' room. She still hasn't woken up, but she's been admitted for close monitoring on both her and the baby. Julie and Marie are inside with her now, sitting by her bedside. I didn't think either of them needed to hear about the condition that I found Cypress and the twelve other women in when we got inside that cottage. "She's severely dehydrated and malnourished. The doctor says the baby is fine. Strong heartbeat. Measuring right on track for being between seventeen and eighteen weeks pregnant. Marie says she should be right at that eighteen-week mark if her math is right."

"Good. I was worried." Devan blows out a slow breath.

"Me too. According to the doctor, she's mostly malnourished because her body has been taking such good care of that baby. She was eating, just not enough. The other women we rescued from that cottage – well, all but two of them that we found unconscious – were also malnourished and dehydrated but didn't suffer as much because they didn't have a baby soaking everything up."

"How are the other women?" Matt asks, his hands fisted together on his knees.

"Battered. Bruised. Neglected. A few of them were violated. Two of them were beaten pretty badly and were unconscious when we got there. Cypress and one of the other women were protecting them from the smoke while the other nine women ran out screaming."

"That sounds about right." Devan chuckles, trying to find humor in the grave situation. "Was she…" He stops and audibly swallows several times. "Did they…" I see him struggling to phrase his question, but I know what he wants to know.

"No." I watch as both Matt and Devan relax, both their bodies visibly sagging with relief. "The doctor didn't see any evidence of that. Of course, I'll still want to ask Cypress when she wakes up. Just to be sure."

Matt places a hand on my shoulder as I slump forward, my elbows resting on my knees. "How are you holding up?"

I look up at him and force a smile on my face. "I got to hear my baby's heartbeat," I whisper.

"Yeah," he smiles and squeezes my shoulder tight. "That's pretty crazy, huh?"

"You have no idea." I huff out a quiet laugh. "It's fucked up though because I don't even think that Cypress has gotten to hear it yet. They keep asking if I want to see an ultrasound and I keep telling them no. I want Cypress to be awake for that part."

"Good call." Matt finally releases my shoulder and sits back in his chair. "How long do you think she'll be out?"

"There's no telling. She wasn't injured. There's nothing wrong besides being dehydrated and malnourished. She's probably exhausted though. One of the other women said that if it weren't for Cypress, they would have been a lot worse off. I know she was taking care of all those women."

"She's gonna be a really great mom." Devan states matter-of-factly from my other side.

Placing my hands against my knees, I push myself to standing and turn to face both of the guys. "Yeah. I know she is."

Turning back to the door, I place my hand on the handle and pause. Closing my eyes, I steel myself for what I need to do. It's something that I've learned to do over the years, so I don't allow my emotions to take over during an investigation or cloud my judgement. I just never thought it would be someone close to me that I'd have to witness lying unconscious in a hospital bed. I don't think anything could have ever prepared me for that.

"Thanks for coming guys." I turn back to both Matt and Devan before pushing the door open and walking inside. "It really means a lot to me that you're here."

"You know there's nowhere else we'd rather be." Matt states through his half smile.

Julie and Marie stand up from their seated positions next to the bed when I enter the room. Both of their eyes glistening with unshed tears. "We should get out of here and let you have your girl back." Marie smiles as she wraps her arm around Julie's shoulders.

"Let us know when she wakes up," Julie pats my arm as she walks past me toward the door.

"I will." Walking closer to the bed, I take the seat on her left side and thread my fingers through hers. "Are you all going back home tonight?" I ask before the ladies leave the room.

"No," Julie answers. She has the door held open and I can see Devan and Matt both standing, waiting for them to exit. "We'll be staying in town tonight. Maybe the next one too. Just depends on what happens here."

"Thank you," I whisper, my voice low enough that I'm not sure she even heard me.

"Anytime," Julie responds before walking out the door and pulling it closed. I guess she has better hearing than I thought.

Holding Cypress' hand, I trace my thumb over her knuckles lightly. The nurses were able to give her a bed bath, thankfully since she was covered with so much muck and dust that I could barely make out the color of her skin. She was unconscious when they did it and they didn't want to disturb her too much, so they didn't do a very thorough job of it. There's an attached bathroom in this hospital room with a nice walk-in shower that I'm sure she'll be ready to take advantage of the minute she wakes up.

My thumb stops running over her knuckles, and I focus on her empty fourth finger. I know I had been thinking of asking Cypress to move in with me before she disappeared. But I wonder to myself what she would think about getting married. And not just because of the baby. Never because of the baby. I mean, the baby has a lot to do with my decision obviously, but I think I wanted this even before I knew there was a baby.

I've had a taste of what it was like to be without my Butterfly. When I thought she had broken up with me, I thought my world had ended. I literally felt like I was dying and there was nothing I could about it. Then I found her gone and realized the truth and it slayed me. I don't want to go another day with that kind of doubt in my heart again. I love this woman so much that I would be willing to lay down my own life for her. She's given me everything I never thought I would have. Not only her love, but a future with a family. I would be stupid to let that get away from me a second time.

Looking at my smartwatch, I realize it's really late. I don't want to wake Wendy up, but I need her to do me a favor. I step over to the windowsill where I left my phone charging earlier and send a quick message to Wendy, letting her know what I need. Worst case scenario, this backfires on me and I end up co-parenting this baby with my girlfriend. Best case, we're married before we ever go back home to LA.

Chapter 28

Cypress

I know where I am before I even open my eyes. The overwhelming smell of antiseptic is a dead giveaway. But I still hesitate to open my eyes because there's another fragrance in the room. A familiar fragrance that I never thought I'd smell again. Leather and musk. The smell of love and adoration.

Chris.

I'm afraid if I open my eyes right now, I'll realize that I'm only dreaming. Imagining the one person that I want more than anything to be here with me is only a figment of my imagination.

How did I get here? I don't remember coming to the hospital. I don't remember anything after someone carried me through the back room, away from my fellow captives who were still lying on the floor in the back corner of that dark room. I remember the smoke filling the space and thinking that someone needed to make sure those women didn't suffocate on it.

Jodi and I had crawled over to the corner at the same time, obviously both equally worried about our friends. The smoke smelled strongly of sulfur and ozone, and I remember it turning my stomach as I continued to breathe it in through my nose while my eyes were tightly squeezed shut. There was nothing I could do other than suffer through it until someone came in and helped us move Ashley and Monique from their supine positions on the floor. I just knew that I couldn't leave them there alone. I didn't know what was happening around us, but I wasn't leaving them when they couldn't defend themselves.

I remember hearing someone entering the room behind us, and I thought it was perhaps Jase or David coming back to punish me for whatever was happening. At first, I thought that was stupid. How could they possibly think I had anything to do with smoke filling the empty space unless I had somehow started a fire. I heard the shuffling footsteps of people getting closer to us and I had held my breath waiting for a strong slap against my head, or a pulling of my hair. But it didn't come.

When I had turned away from Ashley and Monique, I noticed the two men with flashlights pointed directly at us. Jodi had said something to them in a quiet voice, I don't remember what she said exactly, but I know she was pleading with them. Not for herself, but for the women laying on the floor that couldn't help themselves out like so many of the other women had. Then I heard his voice. It was muffled behind a mask, and I could barely make out what he was saying, but I would remember that voice anywhere. I'd listened to that voice every night in my dreams for the last eight weeks.

Chris was there. I don't know how he found me, but he was there. It wasn't until he picked me up and cradled me against his chest that I knew it wasn't a dream, but he had really come for me.

Not a dream then.

He's really here.

Opening my eyes slowly against the harsh daylight coming in through the window, I scan the room. There he is, slouched back in a chair with his neck cocked at an unnatural angle, dressed in black pants, black long sleeves, and black boots. It's a look that I've come to love on him. No matter how hot it is in the Southern California sunshine, he's always completely covered. No one sees what lies beneath all that fabric but me.

He looks amazing, even in his exhausted state, and I wonder if he's been spending as many sleepless nights as I have over the last eight weeks. I wonder how long it took him to realize that I hadn't broken up with him or that I was being held against my will. Tears rush down my cheeks faster than I can blink them away as I think about what he had to have been going through or how his heart had been shattered when he thought I didn't want him anymore.

Everything I thought over the last eight weeks about wanting him to move on with his life comes back to me in a rush and I regret it all.

I don't want him to move on without me.

I don't want him to have found someone else. I never did.

I want him to pick me, to pick us.

A sob escapes my lips and I watch as Chris is instantly awake, his eyes meeting mine as if he knows exactly where to find me in the room even after a peaceful slumber. A smile instantly spreads across his handsome face. Just a quickly, his smile disappears and his brows lower. He pushes up from the chair and is across the room in two strides, scooping me up into his arms in a gentle caress.

"Don't cry, Butterfly. I got you." He presses a kiss against the top of my head before resting his cheek against it. "I got you." Those last three words spark something in my memory from the cottage and I remember him saying those exact words as he carried me through the cottage. Over and over again, he repeated those words like a mantra while he carried me to safety.

My hands fist in his shirt as I continue to cry. Tears that I've held in for the last eight weeks, all the feelings of loneliness and despair that I've kept hidden from the other women in an attempt to remain strong for them. It all comes out in a stream of incoherent mumblings against Chris' chest, my tears soaking into the fabric of his black shirt. "I'm so sorry." I cry out between sobs. "I'm so sorry. I'm sorry. I'm sorry." I continue saying it over and over again despite his calming pleas.

"Shh, Butterfly. You're okay. You're safe. It's over. I got you." He continues attempting to soothe me, but nothing is stopping this constant need to release the emotions that I've kept hidden for so long.

It feels like an eternity before I can finally put a coherent voice to the thoughts in my head. "Y-you c-came for m-me." I stutter out between sobs.

"Of course, I did, Butterfly. I'll always come for you. You're mine." He holds me tighter against his chest and kisses the top of my head. "I love you," he whispers into my hair.

Hearing those three words soothes my blood, my soul. I know them to be true. If they weren't then he would have never spent the last eight weeks trying to find me. I wouldn't be sitting here, on this hospital bed, with him right now if he didn't love me. "Oh, God," I whisper against his chest. "I love you too," I tell him honestly. "I'm so sorry. For all of it."

"No, Butterfly." Leaning back far enough to look at my face, he puts his index finger against my lips. "You have nothing to be sorry for."

"David told me that he broke up with you. Or I did. But he sent the text message, not me. I would never do that to you. I love you. I love you so much."

"I know."

"You do?" I look up at him confused. "Wait. You know what? That I didn't break up with you. But how?"

"Do you really think I'd believe you would break up with me by text message? Or that you wouldn't have acted differently that morning if you had wanted to break up? Come on, Butterfly. I think I know you better than that." He winks and my heart melts a little bit more. How can he joke at a time like this? That he is able to is just more reason for me to love him more than anything.

"Chris, there's something that I need to tell you." Tensing, I push him away enough for me to sit up straight on the bed. He leans over me and adjusts the pillows behind my back to give me more support. "I was going to tell you that day, but then everything happened. I swear I wasn't trying to keep anything from you." Swallowing several times, I try to clear the lump that's forming in my throat. "Chris…" He interrupts me again by leaning down and touching my lips with his. It's not a deep kiss. It's sweet, reaffirming, loving.

He pulls away from me and softly places his hand on my swollen belly. "I already know."

I look into his eyes, and I don't see any anger or resentment there. I just see love. "You do?" My brows furrow as a thought comes to me. "Oh. That makes sense. I guess the doctors would have told you when we got here."

"No, Butterfly. I've known for a while. We went to the boutique. I saw the project you were working on the day you were taken from me. Marie told me about the pregnancy tests you took with her and Julie. I'm not angry that you didn't tell me before. I love that you were trying to make something special for me in order to announce it."

"You're not upset?"

"Upset? About what?"

"About the baby. It wasn't planned. I was on birth control. I swear to you I didn't miss any pills. I wouldn't do that to you."

"Hey." He quiets me again with his finger on my lips. "I never thought that. I won't say I wasn't surprised. But I was never angry. Never. I want to show you something."

I watch silently as he backs away from me and reaches for the hem of his shirt. He gently pulls the shirt over his head, and I trace his tattoos with my eyes. Tattoos that I've looked at so many times, seeing a different design in all the black ink every time I see him. I've traced those tattoos with my fingertips and tongue so many times over the months that we were together.

He doesn't speak, doesn't move, as I take my time looking over the ink on his torso. When my eyes get to his chest, my breath freezes in my lungs and my hand lifts to cover my mouth. There, over his heart, is the only bit of color in the midst of all the blacks and greys. Three beautiful butterflies. Two larger ones, one in the brightest shade of blue, the other in various purples and pinks. A smaller one placed beneath them in different shades of green. They stand out so vibrant against all the other dark ink on his chest.

My hand reaches out toward him, and he steps closer. I place the tips of my fingers on one of the blue wings and gasp as my fingers brush over smooth skin. "These are not new."

"No." He closes his eyes as if my touch is the only thing anchoring him to the present. His head tilts to the side and he pulls his bottom lip between his teeth.

"It's us. Isn't it?" My fingers move to the purple and pink butterfly before lowering to the smaller green one.

"Yes." His hands are now fisted at his sides, his knuckles turning white with the force of his restraint.

"When?" Laying my palm flat against his chest, covering most of the butterfly wings, I close my eyes and relish in the feel of his heart pounding against my hand. "When did you do this?"

"Little over a month ago. Not long after you disappeared, and I found out you were pregnant."

"You really weren't upset." It's not a question. I'm overwhelmed by emotion when my fears are instantly dissolved. It was stupid to have ever worried about what his reaction would have been.

"I told you I wasn't." He places his hand over mine, his thumb caressing my wrist back and forth. "You've given me everything I never knew I wanted, Cypress. You've given me a future. A family. You are my family. You and the baby. I could never be upset about that."

Opening my eyes, I look up at his handsome face and see a single tear trailing down his cheek. "I did everything they wanted me to do while I was in that cottage. Everything they asked of me. I took care of the other women as they were brought in. All so they wouldn't get angry at me and hurt me. Hurt the baby. They were upset about it, but I wouldn't let them hurt our baby. I was just biding my time until I could find a way out. A way to get back to you and tell you it wasn't true. So, you'd know that I'd never leave you willingly. I would never take your child away from you."

"I know, Butterfly. I know." He steps closer and wraps his arms around me again.

"Is the baby okay?" I ask breathlessly against his chest.

"Yes. The baby is fine. You did everything right and took good care of it. I got to hear the heartbeat."

"Oh, my God." I pull back and look up at him. "Was it amazing?"

"It was so amazing, Butterfly." His lips curl up at the edges and I can see the happiness coming off of him in waves. "It was so amazing. I've never heard anything like it."

"Did you get to see it?"

"No. I wanted to wait until you were awake for that." He places his palm against my cheek. "I didn't want you to miss it. I wasn't sure if you'd gotten to do that before you were taken from me."

"I did when I first found out I was pregnant, but it was just a little peanut at that time." Placing my hand on my belly, I look down as if I can see inside myself, see what features the baby might have now to distinguish it from a peanut.

"I'll tell you what." Chris' hands lower to mine and he grasps them tightly. "How about we get you into the shower, get some clean clothes on you, then call the doctor in for that ultrasound."

"That sounds…" Sighing, I think about the last time it was that I had a decent shower. We didn't have any running water at the cottage, no way to clean ourselves. We didn't even have proper plumbing and had to resort to using buckets which I was made to carry behind the house and dump into a ditch every day. "That sounds amazing." Looking at my arm, I realize I'm still connected to the IV. "Can I get in with this thing in my arm?"

"Yeah." Chris pulls me to the edge of the bed and helps me stand. He braces one hand around my waist and grabs the IV pole from the side of the bed to trail along beside us. "I already asked the nurse and she said it would be fine. Matt and Devan brought us both some clothes when they came last night."

"They're here?"

"Yeah, Butterfly. They were worried about you too. Julie and Marie are here too. I'm sure they'll be stopping by at some point hoping to find you awake. Come on, let's get in that shower."

Blushing, I walk with Chris to the attached bathroom. He comes in with me and closes the door behind him. I see a bag on the counter which probably contains clothing for the both of us, but I don't ask. I allow him to untie my hospital gown and slip it off, standing in place as it falls to the floor at my feet. Keeping his hand on the small of my back, he reaches in and turns the shower on so it can begin to warm up. When I turn to face him, he unbuttons his pants and kicks off his boots.

Seeing him again, like this – naked in all his glory – I revel in the dark ink covering his left side to his ankles. It's amazing and beautiful to see the bright colors standing out on his chest. As if the butterflies are the most important piece of art on his body. We don't say anything as we step into the hot spray, and he helps me wash my hair and my body. I keep my eyes closed the entire time, soaking up the heat from the water and the refreshing feeling of the soap cleansing away the last eight weeks of my life.

Chapter 29

Chris

Reaching around Cypress, I turn off the shower then reach behind her to grab a towel to wrap around my waist. Then I grab another towel and wrap around her body before taking a third one to run over her head softly to soak some of the moisture from her hair.

Holding her hands, I walk her out of the shower stall into the main bathroom. There isn't much room in these hospital bathrooms, and I don't want her to be standing for long, I know how exhausted she still is after everything she's been through.

I grab the duffel bag off the bathroom counter and loop it over my forearm, grab the IV pole with the same hand, and wrap my free arm around Cypress' waist before pushing open the bathroom door. Peaking my head out to make sure we're still alone in the room, I lead her out to a chair and nod toward it, indicating that she should sit.

"I can do this myself. You know?" She giggles as I set the bag on the bed an begin to pull everything out.

"I know. But you won't be doing anything on your own for a bit." She stops giggling and glares at me. It's almost comical the way she's looking at me. Like she wants to appear angry but is struggling to contain her amusement at the same time. I narrow my eyes at her in return, a mock agitated look on my own face. She chews on her cheeks to keep from breaking and I lift a single brow up in my own show of defiance.

Throwing her head back, Cypress guffaws loudly and it's honestly the best sound I've heard in eight weeks. "You win." She continues to giggle as I hold up a bra and study the IV bag still hanging on the pole next to her.

"I didn't think this through very well." Chuckling, I grab the bag from the pole in one hand, the bra in my other, then feed the bag through the right strap. Hanging the bag back on the pole, I hold the bra up and smile at my achievement. Cypress lowers the towel and holds her arms out for me to help her put it on. "T-shirt or tank top?" I ask, turning back to the bed. "You have options."

"Tank top."

Grabbing the purple tank top that Marie packed in the duffel bag, I reach over and grab the IV bag again and repeat my previous steps. "Leggings or skirt?"

"Skirt please." Cypress giggles again and it makes my heart skip. I love seeing her this happy. I've missed our easy back and forth banter. Holding Cypress' hands, I help her stand and kneel for her to lift her feet one at a time for her panties. Then do the same for the skirt. I have both pulled up to her waist while still kneeling.

Wrapping my hands around her waist, I press a soft kiss to her slightly rounded baby bump before standing back up and kissing her on the mouth.

Directing her to sit back on the chair, I turn back to the bed and grab a pair of boxer briefs from the duffel. I just get them pulled up to my waist when there's a knock on the door. Thinking it's the doctor or nurse I call out, "Yeah." Returning my attention to the duffel bag, I'm shocked at the voice, or voices rather, I hear entering the room.

"Holy black ink covered hotness!" I hear Marie's voice exclaim from the doorway. Turning toward the door I see all four of our friends frozen in place. Their eyes and mouths are all open wide, clearly surprised at my appearance, as they look at me.

Cypress busts out laughing again, and I stand in shock as my friends continue to stare at me from the open doorway. They've never seen me without long sleeves and long pants on, so they didn't know that I was covered in so much ink.

"Damn, man." Matt saunters over, his eyes traveling down my arm and leg on the left side. "I'm suddenly feeling really inadequate." He has a bit of ink himself, at least from what I've been able to see. He has at least one arm almost completely covered to his shoulder. Same with Devan. Neither of them is a stranger to a tattoo gun, that's for sure.

"And I'm feeling really underdressed. Sorry about that. I thought you were the doctor."

"No worries." Marie walks closer and Matt sticks his arm out to stop her. "Really?" She looks up at him and pushes his arm out of the way.

"No wonder you've been keeping him to yourself, Cypress." Julie walks into the room next, Devan keeping an arm around her waist. "Damn, Chris. You are fucking hot!" She exclaims and Cypress giggles wildly again. I almost laugh myself when I hear Devan growl and see him pull her tighter into his side.

I'd be happy to keep this up all day if it continues to fuel my Butterfly's laughter, but I can feel the heat already rushing to my face. I'm not one for so much direct attention. Even if it is from my friends.

I grab a pair of black sweatpants from the duffel and step into them, my back turned to our unexpected visitors. Grabbing a long-sleeved t-shirt from the bag next, I slip it over my head. My feet are still bare, but at least I'm not quite so exposed.

I watch as Julie walks over and grabs the hairbrush from the bed, then walks behind Cypress and begins gently detangling her hair.

Marie pushes away from Matt and walks to Cypress, reaching down to grab both of her hands. "I've missed you. I'm so happy you're okay."

"I've missed you too. Both of you. Thank you for being here." Cypress, Julie, and Marie begin talking about everything that's happened over the last eight weeks and I turn to Devan and Matt and nod my head toward the door.

"How about we let these ladies catch up." I step toward Cypress, bending to place a kiss on her cheek. "I'll be right outside the door, Butterfly."

"Okay," she whispers back to me, and I reluctantly walk away from her.

The three of us sit in the hallway, our chairs on the opposite wall as the door to Cypress' room. No one brings up the scene they walked into a few minutes ago, for which I'm grateful.

"When did she wake up?" Matt asks in an attempt to begin small talk.

"This morning. Probably around seven."

"She's okay?" Devan asks.

"She's perfect. It's like nothing happened to her, she's her normal self."

"Keep an eye on her, man." Devan tells me. "She might seem okay on the outside, but she may be battling some demons on the inside. That was a shitty thing for her family to do to her."

"She doesn't know yet." I admit. "I haven't told her everything yet."

"Fuck," Matt breathes out.

"Yeah." Leaning forward in my chair, I rest my elbows on my knees. "We just haven't had a chance to have that conversation yet. She wanted a shower and I just finished getting her dressed before you guys got here."

"Hey." I look up at Matt and see him looking down the hall. He lifts his chin in the direction of the hallway entrance and I turn to follow his gaze.

Standing, I walk toward where Wendy and Braiden are walking down the hall. "Hey guys." I meet them and Wendy throws her arms around me instantly.

"Chris. How is she?" She asks before releasing her hold on me.

"She's good. She's awake." Wendy places a hand on her chest and sighs in relief before I continue. "Julie and Marie are in with her now."

"Well, that's wonderful." Wendy smiles a watery smile and I wonder if she's remembering her own rescue so many years ago. "I'm glad you were able to get her back, Chris."

"Me too."

Wendy grabs her purse and begins to dig through it, not saying anything until she removes her hand with a small black box held tightly between her fingers. "I brought you this."

Holding my hand out, she places the box in my palm. "Thank you." I wrap my fingers around the box and close my eyes. Wendy has been kind enough to hold this in one of her safes for me for the last few years. My grandmother's wedding rings. My father used them to propose to my mom. And now I plan to use them to propose to Cypress.

"Good luck." Wendy places her hands on my chest and looks up at me. "Not that you'll need it." She winks before placing her hand on Braiden's forearm. He nods his head in my direction before turning them both away and walking back down the hall from where they came.

Walking back over to the chair, I take my seat between Devan and Matt. Matt notices the box in my hand and nods his head toward it silently. Opening the box, I show both of the guys what is nestled inside, surrounded by a pillow of black velvet. A platinum band with diamonds embedded all the way around. Eternity band they call it, symbolizing eternal love.

"What kind of stone is that?" Matt asks as he lowers his head closer to the rings.

"Garnet." The engagement ring is a single quarter carat round garnet stone set in the center, a halo of diamonds surrounding it. "It's perfect actually because it's Cypress' birth stone."

"Holy shit." Devan speaks up from my left side. "Are you going to propose to her?"

"If I have my way, we'll be making a trip to Vegas to get married before we go back to LA."

"Hell yes!" Matt exclaims. Placing his hand on my shoulder, he pushes against me enough to rock me a few times to the side.

The doctor came in for the ultrasound not long after our friends left. They're going back home today, and Cypress and I are planning to stop by and see them when we get back. If all goes well, I hope to walk into Devan's house and introduce Cypress to them again as Mrs. O'Neil. Damn, just the thought of her having my last name sends a chill down my spine, a shot of arousal pooling in my groin.

"Can you believe it?" Cypress asks whimsically. She's sitting on the edge of the bed curled into my side, my arm draped around her shoulders. She has the ultrasound picture in one hand, her other pressed against her chest. "Our baby is okay. Isn't it amazing?"

"It is." Pulling her tighter into my side, I kiss the top of her head. "Thank you, Butterfly."

"For what?" She leans in and rests her head against my shoulder. Wrapping my fingers around one of the braids that Julie put in her hair, I trail the long strands to the end.

"For giving me everything I never thought I wanted. A future that I never thought I would have." Placing the index finger of my free hand beneath her chin, I lift her gaze to mine. "I love you, Cypress. You and this baby are everything to me." She smiles a watery smile, her eyes glistening with unshed tears, and I kiss the corner of her mouth softly.

"I love you too, Chris." She whispers. "I never thought I would have this life either. I've spent so much of my life hiding, feeling eyes on me so often I never felt safe. But with you, I know that I have someplace that I belong. I have a future."

"You always had a future, Cypress. You're a butterfly. You dance through life, flittering among the flowers. You float on the breeze, the power of the air in your wings. You are the manifestation of hope and life. The very thing that a butterfly truly represents. I'm just the lucky bastard that gets to experience it all with you. If you'll let me."

"That's the sweetest thing anyone has ever said to me," she tells me. Her brows are furrowed, and I can see the truth of her remark.

"That's a damned travesty." I wink as one corner of my mouth curls up in a crooked smile. Cypress giggles in response. "I spent eight weeks without you, and I thought all the color and joy in the world had disappeared forever. I didn't think I'd ever see another day as bright and hopeful as any day that I've spent with you over the last several months."

"I'm so sorry." She interrupts me.

"No." I pinch her chin between my thumb and forefinger and turn her gaze back to mine. "I'm sorry. I'm sorry that I didn't find you sooner. I'm sorry that you had to deal with your stepfather and stepbrother for so long. I'm sorry that I didn't protect you better from them. I don't ever want to spend another day without you, Butterfly. Ever."

"You won't." She places her palm against my cheek, and I lean into it slightly. "You don't have to. I'm here now. You found me."

"I want you in my life, Cypress. Forever. I want to fall asleep with my arms around you every night. I want to wake up to the beautiful mess of your hair every morning. I want to cook you breakfast and share it with you while we look out over our secret oasis. I want to help you create rainbow colored happiness every day in your shop and teach our child how to do the same and express their thoughts and feelings freely like their mother. I want us to be a family, Butterfly. A real family. I want you to take my last name and promise me that you'll be mine forever."

"W-what?"

Removing my arms from around her, I stand and face her. Kneeling to the floor in front of her, I pull the black velvet box from my sweatpants pocket and open it. I watch as a tear falls down Cypress' cheek and she covers her mouth with both hands. "Marry me, Butterfly. Promise me you'll always be mine. You and the baby."

I watch, my heart pounding against my ribs as I wait for her to give me an answer. For a brief moment, I fear that the answer she gives is not the one that I hope for. I resolve to deal with whatever answer she gives me, no matter the decision she makes, and try harder to convince her that she belongs with me. That we can be the family that I see us being in our future together. My smile spreads over my face wide enough that my cheeks start to hurt as I watch her head nodding quickly up and down.

"Is that a yes?" I ask, anxious to hear her tell me what I want so badly to hear. She continues to nod her head, tears falling freely down her face. "Tell me, baby. Let me hear it."

"Y-yes." She hiccups between sobs. She practically throws herself off the edge of the bed, my arms immediately wrapping around her and pulling her into my chest.

"Thank you, Butterfly. Thank you." I kiss her mouth hard. She immediately opens for me, letting me deepen the kiss. I claim her like I've wanted to do since I got her back, relearning every crease of her mouth, every ridge of her teeth. She clings to the front of my shirt, pulling me as if I can't get close enough to her. I keep one arm around her waist, pulling her tighter to my lap, my other hand wrapping around the back of her neck as I tilt her head how I want it in order to deepen the kiss even more.

Moaning, she pulls away from me, the most beautiful smile on her face and rosy blush coloring her cheeks. "I love you so much, Chris. I'll be happy to take your last name. I want to be with you forever, too."

"You've made me the happiest man in the world, Butterfly. "Are you ready to get out of here?" I ask her seriously. The doctor gave us her discharge papers after the ultrasound. Cypress is perfectly healthy considering everything she endured over the last eight weeks. Aside from needing to increase her calorie intake over the next few months to compensate for what she's gone without, there are no other discharge orders. Of course, we'll get her back to her OB/GYN as soon as we get back to LA. We should be able to get the sex of the baby in the next week or so if she wants to know what we're having. I don't care either way as long as the baby is born healthy.

I ordered a car from the closest rental place and it's already sitting out in the parking lot. I told Matt and Devan they didn't have to stick around since I had a ride back to the city. Now I just need to talk Cypress into marrying me immediately. I haven't gotten to that part of our conversation yet. First, I want to get her out of this hospital.

"I'd love to get out of here." She begins to stand, and I put my hands on her waist to help stabilize her. Still kneeling in front of her, I place my hands on either side of her small baby bump and lift the hem of her shirt up with my thumbs, enough to expose the skin just below her belly button. Closing my eyes, I press my lips to the exposed skin. Cypress runs her fingers through my hair, her nails scraping against my scalp. I hold my lips to her skin for longer than is probably necessary, but I don't care. I missed out on the last eighteen weeks of being able to share in this journey with Cypress. I won't waste any more opportunities to express my love to both her and my child.

Standing, I grab the duffel bag off the bed and sling it over my shoulder. Wrapping my arm around Cypress' waist, I walk with her toward the door. "Come on, Butterfly. I have a surprise for you."

"Oh, I love surprises." She smiles and presses her body into my side as we walk out of the room together.

We walk down the hall, tossing a quick wave over my shoulder to the nurse's standing at the desk in the middle of the hall, and enter the elevator. Once we're in the parking garage, I walk us over to the rental that was delivered this morning and hold the passenger door open for Cypress to get in. Pressing a chaste kiss to her lips, I help her lower into the seat and fasten her seatbelt before closing the door and jogging around to the other side. Tossing the duffel into the backseat, I sit behind the wheel and press the button on the dash to start the engine.

Pulling out of the garage and onto the busy street, I follow the GPS on the dash and head toward our destination. I'll wait until we're on the highway to give her any information on where we're going. I have other things that I need to discuss with her first and I would rather get the hard conversation out of the way now rather than wait until later.

Chapter 30

Cypress

I realize as we drive through town that I have no idea where we are, nothing looks familiar to me. "Where are we?" I ask curiously as I watch the scenery pass by the passenger window.

"Fort Mohave, Arizona." Chris answers. Reaching over, he places his hand on my leg and squeezes reassuringly. I turn my head toward him and smile, placing my hand on top of his. He turns his hand, placing his palm against mine, and twines our fingers together. Leaving them resting on my thigh, he turns briefly toward me and winks before turning his attention back to the traffic ahead of us.

Keeping my gaze out the passenger window, I watch as the tall buildings disappear and the landscape changes to a vast desert landscape with scattered houses. We turn onto the highway, but not in the direction of home. Instead, we continue heading away from home, the opposite direction. "Where are we going?"

"Figured you could use a little time away." I watch as the corner of his mouth curls up in a grin, but he doesn't look at me.

"Oh, really? As if I haven't already spent enough time away from home?" I realize when he winces that my attempt at humor was a huge failure. "Sorry."

"No, Butterfly. Don't apologize." He squeezes my hand in reassurance. "You're right. You have been away for long enough.

But you deserve to do something fun." He turns his gaze my way and smiles his full, happy, only-for-me smile. My heart melts and I fall just a little bit more in love with him.

"Okay." I relent, returning the squeeze to his hand. Still watching him when he turns back to the road ahead, I watch the expression fall from his face and he gets a serious gleam in his eye. He pulls his bottom lip between his teeth, and I know there's something that he isn't telling me. "What's going on?"

Shaking his head slowly side to side, he continues to chew his lip for several more seconds before answering. "There's something I need to talk to you about. I'm not sure how to do it."

"Just spit it out. There's one thing that we will never keep between us going forward. Secrets. This is a fresh start for us, and we should be able to tell each other everything. No matter how hard. If we can't do that, we have nothing."

"You're right." He chews his lip again and I watch as he checks the rear-view mirrors. "Maybe I should pull over for this conversation."

"Is it that bad?" I ask, concerned at how he's suddenly acting and attempting to brace myself for more bad news.

"Yeah, baby. It's bad. Give me just a second." He turns the hazard lights on and moves over to the side of the road. I turn in my seat, pulling my left leg up so I can face him fully. He still has a strong hold on my hand, and I realize that he isn't going to let me go. I don't know that I want him to. "Cypress, your mother was involved in everything." He watches me, waiting for a reaction.

Pressing my lips into a tight line, I think about what he told me about my mother. "What?"

"The trafficking. The women that disappeared. Your mother was involved in all of it."

I think about what he's saying, and it sparks something in my memory. Closing my eyes, I try to recall the conversation that Jodi and I overheard when David came crashing into the cottage a few days ago.

"Cypress?" Chris moves a hand up to cup my cheek and I lean against his touch, tilting my head to the side. My eyes squeeze shut tighter, trying to recall what was said about my mother the other day.

"David came to the cottage the other night. He was upset. He made so much noise when he came crashing into the cottage that he woke up all the women in the back room with the noise. He was yelling at Jase about something."

"Baby, you don't have to think about that. I know how hard it was for you being there, you don't have to go through that right now."

"No, I do. He said something about my mother not answering her phone. He said that she was in contact with the buyers and because he couldn't get hold of her, he didn't have any buyers." My eyes fly open in a rush, and I stare straight into Chris' concerned gaze. "The buyers. That's what all those women were there for? And me? We were being sold into slavery as walking sex toys to some buyers?"

"Baby, don't. You don't have to go there."

"Is it?" I demand an answer from Chris. I knew it was bad, whatever David and Jase were keeping us all caged up in that cottage for. I knew it wasn't going to be for anything other than nefarious reasons. But this is worse that I could have imagined. We were meant to be sold. Trafficked. Oh, my God. When I think about how close I was to never being rescued, my head begins to spin and I'm suddenly grateful that I'm already sitting down.

"Yes." He answers on a sigh. "It wasn't just David and Jase working the trafficking collection. Your mother was involved, probably always has been. She admitted to it when we picked her up on accessory charges. She admitted that she's been vetting victims for years at festivals and picking the ones for Jase to hit on in order to get close to them. Then David would pick them up. She would contact the potential buyers and set up an exchange. They've been doing it for years."

"Oh, my God." I breathe out, letting my head lay back against the door. I don't have the strength to hold it up anymore.

"There's more."

Sitting back up and facing Chris fully, I swallow audibly, my hands clenching into fists. "How could there possibly be more? You're telling me that my family has been trafficking women for years. There's no telling how many women that were involved. Or how many of them are still out there somewhere waiting to be found. But there's more?"

"I'm sorry baby, but you need to know" Chris unbuckles his seatbelt and turns in his seat to better face me. He grabs both of my hands in his before continuing. "Baby, they were going to sell you."

"Well, yeah. I kind of figured that out when you told me that's why we were all being held in that cottage."

"No, Cypress. Before."

"Before?"

"Before you went away to school. Before you became independent of them and left your life on the road to move to LA. They wanted to sell you."

"W-what?" I can't believe what he's telling me. "That can't be true."

I watch as he nods his head slowly, his eyes never leaving mine. "Do you really want to hear all this now?"

"I need to know. What are you talking about?" My hands tighten around his, bracing myself for more news. He swipes his thumbs over my knuckles on both of my hands.

"You told me that you knew Jase was watching you. He spied on you sometimes."

"Yeah."

"He wanted you for himself. Your mom and David convinced him not to touch you. They were supposed to be able to get more for you if you were a virgin." Tears that I have been trying to contain break free and spill down my cheeks. "Don't cry, Butterfly." Reaching across the seats, Chris unbuckles my seatbelt and pulls me into his chest. "You're safe now. I got you."

"D-does she k-know about t-the b-baby?" I stutter between sobs.

"I don't know. But I'll tell you I didn't even bother asking. I don't give a fuck if she knows or not. She will never be a part of our baby's life. Never. I'll protect you both to my dying breath, even from your family."

I fist my hands into Chris' shirt and sniffle a few times, willing the tears to stop. "You don't have to protect me anymore Chris. They are nothing to me. You are our family now. They can all rot under a jail cell as far as I'm concerned. Not just for what they did to me, but for all the women they've ever victimized. The ones you saved in Mexico, the ones you got out of that cottage a few days ago, and however many more are still out there waiting to be found."

"I'm sorry, baby. I didn't want to make you cry. But you deserve to know the entire truth."

"Thank you for telling me." I rest my forehead against his chest as he brushes his hand over my back several times. "You saved me, Chris. You put an end to the evil that I've spent most of my life trying to hide from. You're my redemption."

"You saved me too, Cypress."

"We saved each other." Sitting up enough to see Chris' handsome face, I place a palm against his cheek and run my thumb along the stubble on his jawline. It's obvious to me that he's had a hard time while he's been looking for me. My normally clean shaved man has several days growth going. "I kind of like this." I feel my cheeks heat as I think about all the places I wouldn't mind him rubbing this scruff.

"Hmm." He closes his eyes and presses his cheek into my hand. "Maybe I'll keep it for a while longer."

"Hmm," I mimic him in return. "So where are you taking me for the fun that you speak of?"

"Have you ever been to Vegas?" He kisses the tip of my nose then rests his forehead against mine.

My eyes open wide as I pull away from Chris and look up at his smiling face. "Seriously?"

"Yeah, Butterfly."

"I've been there once, but it was a long time ago. I wasn't old enough to appreciate it for what it was." Smiling, I sit back in my seat, turning back to face the front, and reach for my seatbelt. "What are we waiting for? Let's go to Vegas!" I exclaim, suddenly excited to see the lights again."

Chuckling, Chris turns back in his seat and puts the car into gear. Pulling back onto the practically deserted highway, he drives us to Sin City. A place I never thought I'd have a chance to see again. Even living just over four hours away from it, I didn't think I'd have time to go. Between my boutique and yoga classes, not to mention I don't have a car and the fare alone would break me, I never have the time to break away for anything as exciting as all the lights and casinos.

Chris holds my hand the entire time, our fingers twined together and resting on the center console. As we get closer to the city, the traffic becomes more congested. "It isn't much to look at during the day," he states plainly as we can see the taller buildings in the distance. "But once it gets dark, the city lights up brighter than the sun."

"I can't wait." I bounce excitedly in my seat, my hand tightening in his grip.

"I thought we could do a bit of shopping once we get there." I watch as the corner of Chris' mouth curls up slightly. I wonder what he has in mind. "Then maybe walk around a bit and take in the sites."

"Okay."

The rest of the drive goes by quickly, the excitement buzzing through my veins increasing as we get close enough to see the buildings shimmering against the sun. Its rays reflecting of the billions of lights that won't shine on their own until the sun goes down. The effect of the day light bouncing off the shiny bulbs is beautiful and reminds me of my crafting days when I was younger and experimenting with glitter. There wasn't a day in my youth that I didn't have the reflective metallic shards stuck to me somewhere – in my hair, on my clothes, stuck to my face. It's like someone stood over the city and shook a container of vehicle sized glitter all over the buildings.

Pulling into a parking garage, the light disappears so fast that I can still see the remnants burned into my eyes. Blinking several times to acclimate to the difference, I wait for Chris to find a spot to park in. I watch, silently, as he exits the driver's side of the car and walks around the back to my side. Opening my door, he reaches his hand out for me to grasp, and he helps me to my feet. As soon as I'm standing, he places a sweet kiss against my mouth, his palm cradling my face on one side. He holds my hand as we turn to walk to the exit of the garage onto the city sidewalk.

We visit several shops while walking through the city, hand in hand. Chris buys himself a new outfit, including shoes, and replaces his long-sleeved t-shirt and sweatpants with a broken suit. This is more the Chris that I'm used to seeing in his semi-professional appearance – all business on the outside with the bad-boy, tattooed persona kept hidden on the inside, waiting to make an appearance just for me.

We stop in a boutique and Chris sits on an oversized wing-back chair while I try on different wrap dresses. He smiles at each one as I step out from behind the dressing room curtain and model them for him. When I walk out in a bright purple dress, the hem hitting me just above the knee, he stands and walks over to me and places his hands on my waist. "This is the one." He brushes a stray hair behind my hear before leaning in for a chaste kiss on the mouth. "Keep this one on."

I watch as the dressing room attendant steps into the dressing room and gathers the remaining dresses, and my own clothes, and carries them to the counter at the front of the shop. She bags everything quietly and nods to Chris as we walk out of the shop, his hand now resting possessively against the small of my back.

It dawns on me as we continue walking, the buildings becoming more spaced out and father between, that we don't have anything with us. I don't know how I missed it before. We walked into each shop, and I watched as our things were bagged up with our selections, but we left each store empty-handed. "Where are all of our things?" I ask, curious as to what they are doing with each of the bags they put together for us.

"It's all being taken care of." He doesn't elaborate and I wonder what he's planning secretly in that head of his. Chewing on my lip,

I keep my focus toward where we continue to walk, not paying attention to the buildings we're passing by.

Chris grabs my hand and stops me from moving. I turn toward him in question, and he wraps his arms around my waist, pulling me against his body. His mouth angles over mine and I open for him immediately. Allowing him to deepen and control our kiss, I moan against him and feel his grip on me tighten.

Breaking our kiss slowly, Chris pulls back and gazes into my eyes. His eyes are dark with desire, a smile spreading across his handsome face. "I love you," he tells me. The truth of his words glimmering in his eyes, and I feel my heart swell as a lump forms in my throat. I'll never tire of hearing those three words come out of his mouth.

"I love you, too." I've never said those words to any other man in my life. To my mother, yes. But even that wasn't enough. I realize now, after everything that I've learned recently, that she didn't love me in return. Not really. This man though. He loves me. He genuinely loves me. I can feel it in every fiber of my being.

"So, what do you say?" Tilting my head to the side, I gaze at him questioningly. He tips his chin toward the building behind my back, and I look over my shoulder.

When I notice the sign over the door, I turn fully toward the chapel. "Are you serious?" I ask him without looking away from the wedding chapel sign hanging loosely over the door.

"Very." He pulls me back against him, his arms wrapping around me as his hands flatten against my baby bump. His thumbs trace gentle circles along my belly, and I realize he isn't just caressing me. He's caressing his baby. The love pouring out of this man for the both of us washes over me in waves and my eyes begin to blur as they fill with tears.

I realize in this moment, that I really do want to marry this man. I knew it before, when he asked me in the hospital room. Without a doubt, I knew I was ready to become his wife. His everything. But now, standing in front of this chapel, I realize that I'm ready now. "Okay," I answer honestly. "Let's do it." I turn in his arms, he loosens his hold on me but doesn't remove his arms from around me.

"Okay," Chris mimics back to me, tracing the slope of my nose with the tip of his own softly. He grabs my hand and pushes the chapel door open. We walk in together, single for the last time.

When we leave here, I will be Mrs. O'Neil.

Epilogue

Chris

"After you, Butterfly." Standing at the end of a row of folding chairs, I hold my arm out for Cypress to sit. Taking my seat next to her, I place my hand against my daughter's back, keeping her nestled against my chest. We've come a long way in the time since I rescued Cypress from her crazy family and made her my wife.

We purchased our house and moved out of the apartment building less than two months after we got married. Matt was a huge help when it came to looking for a house and, of course, we bought one of his recent flips. I refused to let him cut us a deal on the price and paid exactly what he was asking for it. The house is perfect with three bedrooms and two bathrooms on a private lot just outside of Echo Park.

I let Cypress have creative freedom with decorating our home and have been pleasantly surprised at the outcome. Gone forever are the dark curtains covering the windows and blocking out all outside light. She no longer feels the need to look in dark corners for peeping eyes or hidden spaces. Instead, our windows are covered with sheer fabrics in a variety of colors. Light shines in every window freely and livens up the entire space.

And my Butterfly flies freely, living brightly with a smile on her face every day. I like to think I have something to do with that, with her never ending happiness.

Our daughter, Meadow Blossom, was born exactly four weeks ago today in a whirlwind of events leading up to her birth. Cypress was miserable and already past her due date by four days. She had been nesting, desperately trying to make sure everything was ready for the baby to arrive. We had opted not to find out what we were having until the delivery and had decorated the nursery in a variety of pastel colors. It was exactly as I had imagined it would be coming from Cypress' imagination.

Cypress was in the middle of folding the baby blankets to place on top of the armoire for the millionth time when she stopped dead in her tracks, her hand going to her rounded belly. She didn't say anything as she looked at me standing in the doorway, her eyes open wide in surprise. Looking down her body, I could see the wetness soaking her lounge pants, and I knew it was time to go.

I went through the motions, helping Cypress to clean up enough to sit in the car, helping her change her clothes into something loose fitting and dry. The go-bag was already in the back of the SUV waiting for us to go to the hospital.

Cypress was amazing throughout the entire experience. She had read every book available on the subject of childbirth, and we had taken several classes together.

My anxiety burned through my veins as I walked into the hospital with Cypress in my arms, but I kept it maintained. She didn't need to know that I was a wreck beneath the surface. She needed me to be strong, to carry her through this to the other side.

She was a warrior, one like I had never witnessed, and I couldn't be prouder of her than I was in the moment that she pushed our five-pound eight-ounce daughter into this world. Meadow shrieked proudly, announcing her arrival, and it was the greatest sound I'd ever heard.

When they placed that tiny purple baby on Cypress' chest, my heart nearly skipped right out of my chest. I thought the day I married Cypress in that chapel in Vegas was the best day of my life, but I was wrong. Seeing that little human, the tiny creature that we had created together, was the best day of my life. I couldn't have stopped the tears from flowing if I had tried, and I didn't want to. I wanted the world to know how happy I was in that moment.

Cypress no longer teaches at the yoga studio, Celestial Beings, but she does still run her boutique. Though, now she works only part time. She hired a friend to help during the week, one of the ladies that was rescued with her from the cottage in the desert. Jodi was there with Cypress, the one helping to protect the unconscious ladies in the corner of the back room. She and Cypress continued a friendship that grew in the time they were together.

Cypress told me about Jodi a few days after we got back home from Vegas. She told me her history, about having lost her family to a drunk driver, and how she was toeing the line of being suicidal. Cypress had helped to keep that woman alive – the strong, caring person that she is always putting the well-being of everyone else over herself. She forged a friendship with Jodi that I believe aided in her fight to survive and continue living after her rescue.

Jodi has continued to be an asset to Cypress' shop and is a marketing genius on social media. Because of her marketing campaign, the shop has constant visitors and is continuously needing to increase its inventory. Cypress and Jodi have also started a weekly seminar in the back room that invites people of all ages to come and learn the art of tie dying fabrics. Needless to say, our daughter has some of the most colorful baby clothes of any baby on the Southern California coastline.

Meadow stirs against my chest, and I tighten my hold on her, swaying slightly side to side. This is my favorite place for my daughter to sleep, against my chest or curled up in my arms. There have been several nights in the past four weeks that Cypress has wandered into the nursery and caught me lounging in the glider rocker with Meadow curled up on me. I've opened my eyes and found her leaning against the doorway wiping tears from her cheeks as she watches the two of us together.

I've been told that I'm spoiling my little Flower. But I don't care. My daughter will never go a day without knowing that she is loved. Neither will her mother.

Cypress places a hand on my thigh, and we watch together as our friends begin to walk through the yard. We're back at Devan's house, in his back yard, on this beautiful winter afternoon. The weather is a comfortable sixty-seven degrees, and the sun is shining brightly. The familiar deck has been replaced over the pool and the entire yard decorated with bright yellow flowers and sparkling fabrics draped over every surface.

Devan and Matt walk out of the house together, side by side, and saunter between the rows of chairs. Matt has his hair pulled back in a low ponytail and a yellow daisy pinned to his lapel. I watch as both men stand in front of the arbor, on the deck that Matt built to cover the pool. The music changes soon after and everyone stands, me included with Meadow still sleeping peacefully against my chest. We turn just as Julie walks out of the house, her dress a cotton candy pink that reminds me of Marie's hair. She's carrying a small bouquet of yellow daisies. I watch as she smiles at us as she walks by.

Continuing to stand, we watch as Marie emerges from the house. She looks like a princess in her sleeveless dress, the skirt long enough to hide her feet. There's a single yellow ribbon wrapped around her waist, matching the yellow daisies in her bouquet. The stem of her flowers wrapped in a bright blue ribbon.

The ceremony is short, followed by dancing and cake. Meadow makes her rounds as Matt, Devan, Julie, and even Marie take turns cuddling her. She doesn't mind in the least, being the mild tempered baby that she is. She is every bit her mother in that regard.

Cypress and I watch, my arm wrapped around her waist and pulling her into my side, as everyone oohs and awes over Meadow's outfit. It's amazing to me how small her dresses are, she just did top out over seven pounds at her checkup this week. Her dress is a swirl of colors, courtesy of her mother of course, and she has a purple flower banded around her full head of baby-fine dark blond hair. Her hair is just a shade darker than mine, a perfect mix of both of us. But she did get my bright green eyes, which I am grateful for. I'm the only one in my family to have inherited my great-grandfather's green eyes and I can't think of a single person that I would want to have shared them with then my beautiful Flower.

Keeping one eye on my Flower, I place a hand on Matt's shoulder, my other hand grasping his in a firm shake. "Congratulations, man."

"Thank you," he answers in return. The smile on his face is quickly becoming a permanent feature and I realize how nice it is to see my friends so happy. We've all come so far in the last year. "Congratulations to you, too." He surprises me.

Cocking my head to the side, I turn my full attention to him. "For?"

"Everything. You have a beautiful family, man. That baby of yours is the sweetest little thing I've ever seen."

"Thank you." Grinning from ear to ear, I agree with him fully. That beautiful family he's speaking of is mine. Sometimes I have to fight not to pinch myself for fear that if I wake up it'll all disappear. If all of this is just a dream, then let me slumber peacefully for the rest of time.

It's late by the time we get back to the house. We stayed for most of the reception after the wedding ceremony. Cypress was having a wonderful time being able to laugh freely with her friends. It had been so long since she'd felt free enough to do so, there was no way I could pull her away from that.

Just before it started to get dark, Meadow began to get fussy. Cypress carried her off inside Devan's house and fed her before changing her diaper. She fell back asleep shortly after with a full tummy.

Walking into the house, I carry my Flower to her nursery to lay her down in her crib. She'll probably be awake again in a few hours for another feeding, but for now, I have Cypress to myself. Even though she hasn't been cleared yet by the doctor, I look forward to being able to cuddle up with her on the sofa and wrap my arms around her. We don't need the intimacy of sex to show each other how in love we are.

I sit on the couch, my shoes laying in the corner by the front door and wait for Cypress to get back from changing her clothes. She returns a few minutes later, her hair pulled up in a messy bun on top of her head, wearing a loose-fitting t-shirt and yoga pants. The outfit that has slowly become her normal daily wear since coming home from the hospital with Meadow. Smiling, she walks across the room and sits next to me, close enough that our thighs are touching. I reach up to pinch her chin between my fingers when we're interrupted by a knock on the door.

"I'll get it." Leaning over, I kiss Cypress on the temple before standing to wander to the front door. "Ethan." I greet as I open the door and find the detective from San Bernadino standing on my front porch, his arms crossed over his chest in an intimidating stance. "What brings you all the way out here?"

"I wanted to stop by and offer my congratulations. I haven't seen you in a while."

"Great timing. We just got home from a wedding not long ago. Come on in." Standing back, I swing my arm out inviting Ethan into our home. "How'd you know where I live?"

"Seriously? You think you're the only one good at your job?" He winks at me as he walks past, into the living room. He stops when he sees Cypress sitting on the couch, her knees pulled up to her chest with her crochet Afghan laying over them. She is flipping channels on the tv mindlessly looking for something to keep her attention until Meadow wakes up for her last feeding for the night.

Cypress looks up as we walk into the room and freezes, dropping her feet to the floor. "You," she gasps as she stands, the remote control slipping from her fingers and bouncing off the surface of the coffee table before landing on the floor.

My gaze shifts from Ethan to Cypress and I watch as she starts to sway. I'm to her in two strides, wrapping my arms around her waist and pulling her against me. "Butterfly? Are you okay?"

"Yeah," she answers weakly. "I know you."

I furrow my brows in confusion and look from Cypress to Ethan and back again. Turning back to Ethan, I watch as he struggles to control his movements.

"I'm sorry," he says to Cypress as he begins winking repeatedly, his hands fisting and unfisting at his sides. "I didn't know who you were at the time." He winks again and I feel Cypress relax against me.

"Wait," I loosen my hold on Cypress but don't move away from her. "How do you two know each other?"

"Would you like a drink?" She offers Ethan, always the perfect hostess.

"I'll get it." Stepping back, I watch as Cypress sits back on the couch and gestures for Ethan to sit across from her in the armchair. "Iced tea, okay?" I wait and both Cypress and Ethan nod in agreement but neither of them says anything to each other. Ethan is still winking uncomfortably as he sits across from Cypress. I watch as he fists his hands together in his lap before I turn to walk to the kitchen.

When I return with three glasses of tea, Cypress already has coasters on the coffee table. I place each glass down on a coaster before sitting next to her and pulling her into my side.

"So," I say as I reach for my glass to take a sip. "You want to tell me what you're really doing here, Ethan?"

"I came to apologize." He takes a sip of his own tea before setting it back down on the table. "To you." He nods his head in Cypress' direction before winking a few more times. "I really didn't know it was you when I came into your shop with Tammy."

"I'm confused. You know Chris?" She asks him. She places a hand on my leg, and I wrap my arm around her shoulder and pull her tighter into my side.

"Butterfly. Ethan is a detective in San Bernadino. He's been working with me on the trafficking case, and he was there when we found you and other ladies in Nevada."

"Yep." Ethan agrees. "Tammy is my partner. She and I were in Echo Park the day we came into your shop following a lead on your stepfather's truck."

"It's my mother's truck." Cypress interrupts.

"Right. Well, we had a witness from Nevada that had reported seeing the truck and we had tracked it to Echo Park. We were there following that lead and Tammy saw your shop and wanted to stop in to look around. I didn't know who you were at the time." He winks once more before sitting back in his seat.

"Well, to be honest, Chris and I had just met the day before you came into the shop. We weren't even dating yet at that point." She giggles softly and I watch as Ethan finally starts to relax, his ticks subsiding. "You kind of freaked me out that day."

"I know." Ethan chuckles and Cypress giggles again. "I have that effect on people."

"He really does." I finally relax into my seat and chuckle softly. "You should have seen it when I first met him."

"Oh, my God." Cypress throws her head back and laughs this time. "I can only imagine."

The monitor on the coffee table begins to light up and we hear Meadow beginning to squeak out from the nursery. "I'll get her." I stop Cypress from standing by placing my hand on her leg. "You stay here and relax a little bit longer." Leaning over, I kiss her again on the temple before whispering in her ear. "I'll go pick you a Flower."

Cypress laughs heartily as I stand and walk up the stairs toward the nursery. The squeaking cry gets louder the closer I get, and I walk in to find Meadow in full bloom, her arms and legs swinging wildly in her crib. "Oh, look at you!" I coo as I stand over her crib. "What kind of Flower are you tonight?" I reach in, a smile on my face, and pick Meadow up to cuddle her against my chest. "You're as bright as a poppy tonight." I pat her back and bounce while shift from one foot to another as I make my way to the changing table. "Let's get you cleaned up and then you can see mommy."

I make quick work of changing her diaper and getting her in a clean and dry nighty. It's like wrangling an octopus with as wildly she continues to swing her limbs, but I manage while keeping a smile on my face the entire time. She finally calms down when I pull her back up to my chest, one hand behind her head and the other on her butt. I walk with her back down the stairs and into the living room and pause at the foot of the stairs as both Ethan and Cypress are staring at me.

Shit. I realize to myself that they heard my entire exchange with Meadow through the monitor that I forgot to turn off. "That's eavesdropping." I laugh as I walk across the room and sit back on the couch.

"I didn't mind in the least." Ethan chuckles from his chair.

"Is she hungry?" Cypress asks, her hand held lightly against Meadow's back.

"She was dirty." I wrinkle my nose as I look at Cypress and she giggles again. Meadow shifts against my chest, and I know she's ready for her mommy, so I loosen my hold on her and hand her to Cypress' waiting hands. She already has the blanket tossed over her shoulder and a pillow in her lap. As always, I watch in awe as she effortlessly positions our Flower in her arms, her forearm resting against the pillow.

"Well, that's my que. I'll leave you three for your family time. I just wanted to stop by and meet you officially Cypress. And to apologize of course."

"You don't have to go." Cypress tells him as he stands.

"It's late." He steps over and places a hand on Cypress' shoulder. "You have a beautiful daughter. I'm happy to see that everything worked out for you."

"Thank you." Cypress looks up at him, her eyes glistening with emotion. "For everything."

"Of course." He steps away from her and walks around the couch toward the entryway.

"Thanks for stopping by." I stand and walk with him to the door. "Don't be a stranger. Okay?" I reach out and shake the hand he offers as we reach the door.

"Congratulations, man. You have a beautiful family. Take care of them."

"I certainly will." I watch as Ethan walks out to his car without saying another word. When he backs out of the driveway, I close the door and go back to the living room to sit next to my girls.

"Ya know," Cypress begins as I pull the blanket away from her shoulder and watch as she feeds my daughter. "For California being the third largest state in the union, it sure is a small world."

"You think so?"

"Well, yeah. Think about it. You know Marie and Julie from work. I met them at Celestial Beings when they took one of my yoga classes. You became friends with their husbands after helping them on their case. You know Wendy from work, and she happens to be one of Marie's best friends. I met Ethan when he came into my shop with his partner back when you and I first met, and he ends up being a detective that you've worked with. So many coincidences. Small world."

"Yeah." I run my hand over Meadow's hair. "I guess it is." When I look up, I see Cypress smiling at me.

"I love you, Chris."

"I love you too, Butterfly." Meadow wraps her fingers around my index finger and tightens her hold, not willing to let me go. "I love you too, my little Flower."

Everything that I've gone through over the years, everything that I've learned in my work. It all brought me to this moment in my life. A moment that I wouldn't change for anything. My friends, my family.

I'm the happiest man in the world.

Dear reader

As many of you know, I made my maiden voyage into the life of an author just over a year ago when I wrote and published my first book, The Story of Her Life. It wasn't the book I had originally wanted to publish, but life being what it was at the time, it ended up being the book that I needed to publish first.

There is so much of me in each of these books and I'm grateful that you have taken the time to read them all. I look forward to our future as I continue my journey into the life of an author. It's such a great adventure, and there's so much more for us to explore together.

This has been one hell of a ride, a rollercoaster if you will. There have been good days, and of course with every good day there is also a bad day. But, thankfully, the good days triumph, and we come through the other side of it with one hell of a tale to tell.

Acknowledgements

I have such a great support system, even though I seem sometimes like I'm losing my mind. I spend so much time carrying on conversations with myself, or in my head, just working out the scenes for each of these books. People have started to look at me like I've got lobsters crawling out of my ears. But I'm getting used to those looks. If it weren't for each of your looks, questions, and sometimes odd remarks, I wouldn't be sitting here today trying to find a way to thank you all.

First on my list is my wonderful and supporting husband, Danny. Thank you so much for putting up with my craziness for the last several months. Without you constantly pushing me to do just a little bit more, I would never reach my writing goals.

Tina, thank you for your continued support. You have been such a great help when I get stuck in my own head. You've always been there, even from a distance, to talk me off a ledge and convince me to keep going. I appreciate you for everything. This is a journey that you and I have been able to take together, and I love you so so much for taking this leap with me.

To all my friends and co-workers, thank you for putting up with me. You all have listened to me through all of the bragging, begging, crying. All my writer's nonsense that I'm sure you were tired of hearing about, I appreciate you all more than I could ever express.

My social media followers, thank you for sharing my posts and commenting on my rantings. You help me more than you could ever know just by showing up and expressing your interest. I wouldn't be here at all without all of you.

Finally, to you. My readers. Thank you for believing in me enough to read my books. I appreciate you and your time. I hope that one of my characters will reach out and touch you as deeply as they have touched me in the last year. I only hope to be able to introduce you to many more in the future. I look forward to hearing from each of you as you send me your comments and ratings and let me know what you think of my book.

About The Author

J.A. Smith lives in Virginia with her husband, son, and two overactive Pomeranians. She has found a balance of working a full-time job with reading an obsessive amount of romance novels while writing her heart shattering stories to share with the masses. Granted, this balance includes copious amounts of caffeine and aspirin.

www.ingramcontent.com/pod-product-compliance
Lightning Source LLC
LaVergne TN
LVHW021232080526
838199LV00088B/4316